T0312352

Sophie Jordan grew up in the Texas Hill Country, where she wove fantasies of dragons, warriors, and princesses. A former high school English teacher, she's the *New York Times*, *USA Today*, and international bestselling author of more than fifty novels. She now lives in Houston with her family. When she's not writing, she spends her time overloading on caffeine (lattes preferred), talking plotlines with anyone who will listen (including her kids), and streaming anything that has a happily ever after.

ALSO BY SOPHIE JORDAN

The Firelight Series
Hidden
Vanish
Firelight

**The Scandalous Ladies
of London Series**
The Duchess
The Countess

The Duke Hunt Series
The Scoundrel Falls Hard
The Rake Gets Ravished
The Duke Goes Down

The Rogue Files Series
The Duke Effect
The Virgin and the Rogue
The Duke's Stolen Bride
This Scot of Mine
The Duke Buys a Bride
The Scandal of It All
While the Duke Was Sleeping

The Devil's Rock Series
Beautiful Sinner
Beautiful Lawman
Fury on Fire
Hell Breaks Loose
All Chained Up

The Ivy Chronicles Series
Foreplay
Tease
Wild

Historical Romances
All the Ways to Ruin a Rogue
A Good Debutante's Guide to Ruin
How to Lose a Bride in One Night
Lessons from a Scandalous Bride
Wicked in Your Arms
Wicked Nights with a Lover
In Scandal They Wed
Sins of a Wicked Duke
Surrender to Me
One Night with You
Too Wicked to Tame
Once Upon a Wedding Night

A
FIRE
IN THE
SKY

SOPHIE JORDAN

ONE PLACE. MANY STORIES

HQ
An imprint of HarperCollins*Publishers* Ltd
1 London Bridge Street
London SE1 9GF

www.harpercollins.co.uk

HarperCollins*Publishers*
Macken House, 39/40 Mayor Street Upper,
Dublin 1, D01 C9W8, Ireland

This edition 2024

4
First published in Great Britain by
HQ, an imprint of HarperCollins*Publishers* Ltd 2024

Interior text design by Diahann Sturge-Campbell
Prologue and part opener illustrations © ratpack223;
Alexander Potapov; Olga; Phakamas; Victoria/Stock.Adobe.com
Chapter opener illustrations by Alexis Seabrook

Copyright © Sharie Kohler 2024

ISBN HB: 978-0-00-871234-1
TPB: 978-0-00-871235-8

MIX
Paper | Supporting
responsible forestry
FSC
www.fsc.org
FSC™ C007454

This book contains FSC™ certified paper and other controlled sources to ensure responsible forest management.

For more information visit: www.harpercollins.co.uk/green

This book is set in 9.5/15.5 pt. Brother 1816

Printed and Bound in the UK using 100% Renewable Electricity at CPI Group (UK) Ltd, Croydon, CR0 4YY

For Diana Quincy: thank you for being my person

Round about the fire winds go.
In the sky these words take hold.
Follow the beat of wings and gold,
Through tunnels and dens hidden deep and cold.
Dragon foe, hear my spell:
May the reign of dragon be gone,
May your mothers never spawn.
No more hatchlings,
No more hatchlings,
No more hatchlings shall see the dawn.

—CURSE OF THE SHADOW WITCH VALA,
YEAR 400 OF THE THRESHING

DRAGONS LIVE.

Everyone believes they are gone, the last of them annihilated in the Threshing. Lost to the annals of time, to the fade of memory, to be recalled only by the bards. It is the arrogance of man that holds to this—the wish for it to be so.

Wishing does not make it true, though.

Years ago, the kingdoms of man came together and ventured into the Crags. Legions of soldiers joined forces for the greater good, to see an end to the pestilent dragons. With their scale-tipped arrows and swords of dragon bone and droves of wolves, nursed since they were pups on the blood of dragons, humankind hunted dragons through the mists, deep into the ancient caves and winding tunnels of the mountains. For years, for decades, for centuries, they hunted, ridding the sky of dragon fire and claiming their caches of treasure for themselves.

No corner of the Crags was overlooked. Not a hollow or gully or wood left unexplored. No resource untapped. Soldiers ferreted out and slew every pride until the last winged creature was erased from land and sky. Until their fire was snuffed out for good. Until none remained.

Except one.

PART I

THE WHIPPING GIRL

1
TAMSYN

IT WAS A GOOD DAY FOR A WHIPPING.

I'd had my share. Too many to count. But today was special. Today the border lords arrived.

Word had reached the City and found its way to the palace. The party was spotted outside our walls, a meandering snake of warriors en route to us. They would be here soon, once they finished the ascent through the winding, labyrinthine streets.

The lord chamberlain was much too distracted to give me a proper flogging. Under normal circumstances, Kelby liked to linger over his work, panting in delight as he delivered each blow to the exposed flesh of my back. He would wait as I recoiled and tensed in pain. Wait until I relaxed. Wait until my body eased. And then he would strike again. He was an expert at meting out abuse. Just as I was an expert at taking it.

His dry fingers often trailed down my spine, a disturbing caress between the flays of the whip. Today there were no such caresses as I clutched my gown to my chest for modesty's sake. I leaned over the desk where he had directed me to take my position. He'd interrupted our harp lesson. Mistress Gytha, the resident harpist, had fled the room when he arrived and announced that he had come to administer my punishment.

Residents of the palace fell into two categories: those who could stomach my whippings and those who could not. Kindhearted Gytha was in the latter group. Members of that set never stuck around to witness the uncomfortable occurrences. No one ever objected, though. No one intervened. It was simply not done.

Kelby hurried about his task, lacking his usual vigor and thoroughness today, clearly resentful that I was keeping him from other diversions. No doubt he wished to be among the courtiers, hanging from the ramparts, marveling at the procession of battle-hardened warriors riding into the palace.

My sisters watched as my lashing was imposed. That was the protocol. Always. Perfect ladies all in a row, princesses bred to be queens, their hands demurely clasped in front of them, suffering the sight. And suffer it they did, for as the royal whipping girl, I was raised alongside them, brought up as their kin, called *sister* . . . even if I was not.

They would have to be heartless little monsters to feel nothing. Spoiled and shallow they may be, but heartless? No. And that was the point. That was the way in which a royal whipping girl served. My punishment became theirs. Something they felt. Something they regretted.

Ever since we were little girls, we had done everything together. Played together. Ate together. Took lessons together. There was no distinction between us. We were sisters. No difference except one. A very important distinction. I was the only one to bear any punishment.

Feena and Sybilia shifted restlessly where they stood. They, too, longed to join the revelry and feast their eyes upon the infamous warriors from the Borderlands. More animal than man, they were rumored to be, and the reason our kingdom prospered and remained intact. For decades they had successfully kept the enemies to the north at bay. The dragon threat was gone—ended a hundred years ago following the Hormung, that brutal final battle of the Threshing, which had driven dragons to the edge of extinction. But there were plenty of other dangers out there to fill the vacancy. Bandits within our borders. Raiders from the Crags. Pirates from the coast. Invading armies from Veturland and across the channel.

The whip cracked against my skin, and I flinched at the sting.

Alise closed her eyes tightly, an expression of contrition tightening her features. At sixteen, she was the youngest, and most affected by my whippings. Oh, Feena and Sybilia felt remorse, but Alise was the only sister ever reduced to tears when I was disciplined for their misdeeds. She belonged in the category of "those who could not stomach my whippings." Had she not been required to watch, she would have fled with Mistress Gytha.

The moment the fifth and final lash—the number that Kelby had decided upon as the punishment for Sybilia's and Feena's quarrelling this morning, over a hair ribbon of all things—struck my back, he tossed the whip to a nearby maid.

"See that puts an end to your unseemly bickering. We have important guests. Conduct yourselves as the Penterran princesses you are and do your parents proud." He took a moment to nod sternly at Feena and Sybilia before he exited the room. The girls didn't linger either, following fast on his heels to join the revels of the court.

Only Alise remained, helping ease my garments back into place, mindful of my tender back. "I am so sorry. No broken skin, though," she assured me, shooing away the maid who had stepped forward to help, but then, I knew that.

Over the years, I'd endured very few whippings that actually broke the skin. Those incidents stood out for that very reason.

"Not your fault," I said, wincing slightly as the full weight of my kirtle settled against my sore back.

"This time," she muttered as she laced up my gown.

I sent her a fond look. "It's hardly ever *your* fault."

Flogging by proxy achieved the desired results with Alise. She hated for me to be hurt so much that she hardly ever misbehaved. She was as close to perfection as humanly possible.

"Those two," she grumbled, sending a glare to where her older sisters had stood. "I'll be glad to see them married and gone."

I winced at that, because *I* would not be glad.

When Feena and Sybilia married and left—a situation that would no doubt happen soon, because the king was already in betrothal talks with the country of Acton across the Dark Channel as well as with the far-off Isle of Meru—Alise would quickly follow suit, and I was in no hurry to lose my favorite sister.

I did not know what her parents had planned for her, if they even had a plan yet . . . but they would. Eventually. They would not permit the loveliest and sweetest of the princesses to remain unwed. Not with the growing threat from the north. That would be a wasted opportunity. I'd gathered enough from snatches of conversations at court and between the king and the lord regent to know that Penterra was desperate to shore up its allies.

I swallowed thickly. When the princesses were married and gone, I would be alone. We may not be sisters by birth, but they were the only family I had ever known. What would become of me when I was no longer needed? What would I be then? The discomfort in my back paled in comparison to the heavy pang in my chest.

I might be trapped between worlds—royal and not royal, belonging and not belonging—but at least I knew my place, my purpose.

Once they are gone, this all ends. I will have to find a new place, a new purpose.

I pushed aside that insidious little whisper, which fed into my fears more and more of late. I sighed. No sense worrying about what I could not control. It wasn't as though the king and queen would cast me aside, after all. They cared for me and would undoubtedly see me well situated.

"They don't mean to get into trouble," I said.

It went deep, this instinct to defend them, even to each other. I knew nothing else. I'd been doing it ever since I was five years old and it was decided I was old enough to start paying the price for my sisters' misdeeds.

Alise rolled her eyes. "They don't *mean* to, but they do. They need to be mindful of how their actions affect you." A little late for that. I resisted pointing out that if they hadn't learned that lesson by now, they never would.

She seized my hand and tugged me from the chamber. "Come, Tam. Let us see what all the fuss is about." Her gaze searched my face, pausing. "If you feel up to it, that is . . ."

"Of course I do. Let us go." The border lords' visit had been greatly anticipated. I was as curious as everyone else and eager for a glimpse of them.

We made haste to the Great Hall, where the king and queen would welcome the arrivals as they did all esteemed dignitaries. Feena and Sybilia were already there, seated in their chairs to the right of the queen, their shining faces rapt as they leaned forward anxiously.

We pushed through the crowd. Everyone in the palace was here to witness the spectacle. The lords and ladies of the court pressed in thickly around me, the odors of sweat and perfume on unwashed bodies rising up to fill my nose. A feeble breeze passed through the arrow slits in the walls, but not nearly enough to circulate air among the mob of onlookers.

My gaze shot to the double doors of the Great Hall, the pulse at my throat leaping. I could hear them coming—the heavy footfalls of the approaching warriors. My skin turned to gooseflesh, vibrating and humming as they drew closer. It was a strange sensation. At once thrilling and foreboding.

My mouth dried in anticipation. They would be here soon, standing before the dais, where the royal family was seated in an impressive tableau—where I, too, normally sat, in the chair next to Alise.

My gaze fixed on the two vacant chairs beside Feena. One for Alise and the other for me. I could not move forward. My slippered feet were planted, stuck to the floor for some reason. The instinct to cling to the perimeter of the room pinned me in place.

I nudged my sister. "Go on. Take your spot with them, Alise."

She squeezed my hand and studied me curiously, replying lightly, "Let us both take our seats." She always did her best to make me feel like I was one of them.

I slid my hand free from hers and placed it over my suddenly churning stomach. I didn't want to sit in that chair up there in front of the outsiders. Not as uneasy as I felt. The very notion of it made me feel itchy all over . . . as if my skin were too tight.

"You know, I don't feel that well," I hedged. "I will retire to my chamber."

She searched my face, nodding slowly. "Very well. You should ring for some mint tea."

"I will do that." Turning, I moved away, losing myself deeper in the crowd, but I did not leave the hall. I could not make myself do that. I was still curious. It just felt . . . *safer* to watch from a distance. Unseen.

Convinced that Alise believed me gone, I tucked myself against a far wall, behind a lady in a voluminous gown. I peered over the woman's shoulder, hoping my red hair benefited me for once and helped me blend in with the bright scarlet of her headdress. If I was spotted, I could be compelled to take my usual place on the dais.

Suddenly a figure pressed close beside me. "What are you doing out here gawking with the rest of the court?" I jumped at the sound of the deep voice in my ear.

My hand flew to my chest, pressing against my suddenly galloping heart. "Stig." I released a breathy little laugh. "You gave me a fright."

A smile played about my friend's mouth. He nodded to where my family sat. "You belong up there."

I flushed beneath his shrewd gaze. Stig would not be as easy to deflect as Alise. For one, he was no naive girl of sixteen. He was confident and perceptive. At twenty-three, he was the lord regent's son and served as captain of the guard. There were plenty of petty whispers that he had been given the role simply because of his father's position, but I knew better. His father's cunning and ambition might have secured him the appointment as the lord regent, winning out over several other candidates and making him the second most powerful man in the realm, but Stig was more than competent in his own right. He was an exceptional swordsman and astute in the machinations of the court. His loyalty ran deep. He would not hesitate to offer his life for king and country. He also possessed something his father didn't: a heart.

"I would rather watch from here."

His half smile disappeared, and his expression clouded. "Tamsyn," he said in that softly chiding voice I knew well.

He had used it so often over the years, always making certain that I knew I was every bit as important as my sisters and due all the same honors. I could not count the times he had come to my rescue: strong, noble Stig chasing away the bullies who thought to put me in my *proper* place. Most people respected my role in the palace, but there were always a few. A few then and a few now. Bullies who thought it important to remind me that I was not a true blue-blooded princess.

I shrugged and gave him what I hoped was a reassuring look. "I'm fine," I insisted. "I merely prefer the view from here." I gestured lamely around me at the gaping spectators.

He looked at none of them. His gaze remained intently on me. "You are a princess of Penterra. You belong up there." His head inclined toward the dais. After a long moment, when I did not make a move to take my place, he leaned in closer, his eyes glinting as he taunted me in a deliberately small voice: "Are you scared?"

I flushed.

Those warm brown eyes traveled over my face as he continued to tease. "Scared of the big bad men coming through the doors? Don't tell me you believe all the wild stories about them."

I rolled my eyes and scoffed.

Scared? Of strangers? I had no reason to fear them. And yet . . . there was something I felt. I swallowed. Something that kept me from putting myself in their line of sight.

The teasing glint faded from Stig's eyes as he considered me. As though he saw something in me then, saw whatever mysterious and uneasy thing gnawed at me. His expression turned somber as a tomb. "Tamsyn?" His throat worked as he paused. "You know I'll always protect you."

I didn't have a chance to respond—to agree or disagree—even though of course I knew that about him.

The doors were flung wide, striking the walls, the sound reverberating through the vast space and echoing in my ears. The lord chamberlain led the way, his perpetually flushed face even brighter than usual as he bowed and scraped low before the king and queen. Kelby was enjoying this. The way his eyes gleamed reminded me of when he was whipping me—or devouring a roasted leg of mutton. Both favorite pastimes. "Your Majesties, they've arrived!"

A dozen border soldiers, eight men and four women, entered the hall, warriors all, thick-necked and brawny, attired in armored leather tunics, swords tucked away in scabbards at their backs, their heavy boots thudding in time with my hammering heart. They shamelessly bore the grime of the long journey as they strode in front of the silk-and-brocade-draped members of the court.

The women were tall and wiry. I looked them over with awe. I had never seen women such as these, dressed in armor and breeches, trained to defend and fight alongside the men. My gaze narrowed on one of the warriors, my nose twitching. Was that *blood* on her armguard?

"Maybe you should wait here, after all," Stig said gruffly.

I glanced sharply at him. His lip curled in a faint grimace as he assessed our visitors.

"Really?" It was my turn to tease. "Now who is scared?"

He didn't rise to the taunt, his attention fixed steadily on these outsiders filing into the hall. "Best steer clear of them."

"They're . . ." I searched for the word and then arrived at it. "Heroes." The reminder was just as much for me as it was for him. "We owe much to them."

He sneered. "What? We should thank them for what is in their nature to do? They're killers." He shook his head. "Don't be gulled by all the stories, Tamsyn. They take pleasure in bloodshed. Brutes, the lot of them."

"A little harsh," I murmured. "You're captain of the guard. A soldier. Not so very different from—"

"No. I am nothing like them," he cut in, his voice flat, lacking its usual warmth. "I serve the throne of Penterra. Your family." He smiled then, looking at me again. "You."

I smiled back. How could I not? My family was good to me . . .

but there were court nobles who treated me with disdain or indifference. Not Stig, though. He was always good to me. Always my friend.

He left my side then, striding ahead, taking his place beside the dais, flanking the royal family, a row of his most senior guardsmen beside him, resplendently outfitted in their red tunics with shiny buttons, their expressions stoic as they faced forward.

The border lord and his entourage took a knee before the king and queen. They each crossed an arm over their chest, hand knotted into a fist over their heart. The contrast of their appearance with all the elegant lords and ladies of the court was marked. Embarrassment would have been an appropriate reaction, but no such sentiment was evident on their dirt-encrusted faces.

My nostrils flared. Their scent reached me. Wind and earth and horseflesh. And something else. Something more. Something I had never smelled before. A ripple of heat passed over me, prickling my skin. On a deep level, I recognized it even if I could not name it.

Bewildered, I watched them in awe. These warriors were big and fierce and unkempt. Nothing like the polished guards of the palace, and Stig was the most polished of them all, his rich brown hair swept back from his forehead very precisely, his beard short and perfectly trimmed as he fixed alert and wary eyes on the party of warriors. One hand rested on the hilt of his sheathed rapier. I recognized what he did. Saw what he saw. They were violent. Dangerous. Scarred and battered for a reason. I felt only more certain that I was right to observe from the perimeter of the hall.

They wore their hair longer than was fashionable. Some with braids. Some with the sides of their skulls shaved. Inked designs crawled over their skin. The Borderlands clearly had their own fashion. I would not know. No one ventured there. It was an uncivilized place.

"It is him," the lady in front of me breathed in awe, shifting so that she partially blocked my view. "The Beast." I slid over a step and rose on tiptoes to better eye the man standing at the helm of the group. "Lord Beast," she added to no one in particular, as though clarification was needed.

Lord Beast.

He was bigger and taller than the others, and I was no slight woman. Only a few men could stand eye to eye with me, but him? He would tower over me. Not that there would ever be cause for him to stand near me.

His fellow warriors stood a pace behind in clear deference. I swallowed. Despite the stories painting him in mythical proportions, he was merely a man, and a young one at that, likely only a handful of years older than my twenty-one years.

His profile was sharp, his nose a slashing blade, his mouth an unsmiling line, his square jaw hard. Strange inked designs crept down his tan throat and disappeared beneath his leathered armor, and a thought slid unbidden across my mind: How far did those markings spread over his body?

My chest tightened, a pull starting at the center. I rubbed at the spot, willing the perplexing sensation away even as I felt a scowl forming on my features because my breasts weren't dormant either. They felt heavier . . . achy and prickly.

"Is that him?" Someone whispered what we were all thinking. Not just thinking. *Feeling.* The sight of him produced a visceral reaction. "The Border King?"

The Border King. Another one of his many monikers. Border Lord. The Beast. Border King. Lord Beast. He was all of those things.

Legions of warriors followed this man. He was the stuff of legends and nightmares. The strongest. The most vicious. The man who held this realm together.

The Threshing had scarcely ended, victory still warm on the lips, when the squabbles and infighting began. They continued to this day, as unremitting as waves in the ocean.

With the dragons finally gone, humans had turned on each other. Humankind couldn't hunt dragons anymore, but they could hunt each other. And witches. And they did.

Alliances broke. Attacks on Penterra flared. Ravaging invaders crossed mountain ranges and expanses of boglands, through deserts and over seas, to pillage my homeland for all its worth.

And that wasn't to say that threats did not still exist within our borders, too.

Little fires had always been there, strewn about the place, flickering conflagrations waiting to turn into full-fledged bonfires. Now, these days, those bonfires roared to life.

Bandits abounded. The roads were perilous. No palace retinue traveled anywhere without a full escort. Armed guards accompanied my sisters and me wherever we went—be it a quick foray into the village or a longer trip to the summer villa on the coast.

As bad as the bandits were, the raiders were worse.

Reports frequently came in about raiders holed up in the Crags, in the long-abandoned tunnels and cave systems that once served as home to the dragons. They struck the villages in the north hard, growing increasingly bold in recent years, venturing farther and farther south to raze vulnerable communities. The Threshing may have been over—no sighting of a dragon in nigh on a hundred years—but the country was hardly at peace.

Without the border lords, specifically *these* border lords, the ones currently standing in the Great Hall, our northern border would have fallen by now. *Penterra* would have fallen. Who knew where any of us would be?

"It *is* he," another voice confirmed.

I didn't look to see who was speaking. I looked nowhere except to *him*. The man who went by many names and yet whose true name I had never once heard uttered. Perhaps possessing an ordinary name like the rest of us would make him less remarkable.

I rubbed harder at the ever-worsening tension in my chest, beginning to wonder if I was suffering from some manner of apoplexy. And yet I remained, drinking in the sight of the new arrivals . . . of him.

His face was set as if stone. Eyes like the night frost, wintry cold and void of emotion as he swept his gaze over the royal family. He lingered over my sisters. Alise shrank back, not keen on his notice. Feena and Sybilia were less indifferent, squaring their shoulders so the thrust of their breasts was more apparent beneath their kirtles. They liked the attention of men. Apparently the Border King was no exception.

"Lord Dryhten, welcome, welcome." King Hamlin stood and moved forward. He appeared slight and diminutive standing so near the warrior. With his dove-soft hands and average frame, he was no warrior. He had never once fought in battle. He ruled from inside the security of these walls. Fortunately, he had men like the Beast to keep Penterra safe for him. With no male heir, the preservation of his realm would be secured in the advantageous marriages of his daughters to the princes of neighboring kingdoms.

He clapped Lord Dryhten on his thickly muscled shoulder. "Your visit is long overdue. We've feasting and entertainment planned for all of you."

The Beast inclined his head slightly, and one of his warriors stepped forward, carrying something covered in a swathe of linen. The warrior lord took it from him and flicked the fabric back to reveal a beautiful necklace laden with gemstones.

Everyone gasped. Even from where I stood I could see the glow . . . feel its draw. The jewelry was like nothing else. Not even the queen possessed anything so fine.

The Beast offered it to the king with a deep incline of his head. "Your Majesty, a gift uncovered by my father in the Crags during his final expedition."

I started at the sound of his deep voice, feeling it physically . . . as tangible as a rough-palmed slap on my skin.

The king clapped in delight and then accepted the necklace, measuring its weight. "Oh! Heavier than it looks." He carried it to his wife, and she admired it, caressing what I could now see were rubies and tourmaline with a loving hand. My sisters leaned in, admiring it, as well.

"So kind of you, Lord Dryhten. We are most grateful to you and all your compatriots. It is we who should be bestowing gifts." The queen's smile was so lovely, it felt like a gift itself. "We must make certain you are well rewarded for all you do for the good of the realm."

The king murmured in agreement with his wife, nodding. "Yes, we have been thinking carefully on how we can properly show you our gratitude."

"I can think of one way, Your Majesty." Despite his use of the honorific, his deep voice exuded a decided lack of deference.

Murmurs swelled through the hall at his boldness. Did he already think to make a demand mere moments after his arrival?

"Well, speak then, my good man." The king nodded in encouragement. "What is it?"

A pause followed. A hush fell over the hall as everyone waited for his answer. "I shall have one of your daughters to wife."

The hall fell silent.

No one breathed.

The pull in my chest deepened into a pulsing, persistent throb. The Beast did not move or speak again. He did not need to. His voice reverberated through the Great Hall, those words permanently carved into the air.

I shall have one of your daughters to wife.

I swallowed back a choking sound. Ridiculous. The king would not give one of his daughters to this uncivilized brute of a man. The gall of him. The absolute temerity.

I respected the hierarchy of the society that I inhabited. It was everything I knew. Everything I had been taught. Order. A strike in the face of chaos. Everyone had their place—their position, title, rank, and role. The Beast dared to think he could break free from that.

The offensive man held the gaze of the king for one long, interminable moment. If it were a test of wills, the king broke first. Rather ignominious for a monarch. And yet look away he did, seeking the lord regent. Stig's father counseled the king in all things.

Although this did not strike me as a matter that required counseling. The king should reply emphatically and definitively with a hearty refusal.

Such resounding rejection never came.

Instead, the lord regent looked at my sisters, assessing them as though he had never considered them before—which was patently untrue. They were at all times evaluated as if they were chattel. Everyone knew the future of the kingdom rested on the alliances made through them. The lord regent would not wish to lose any of the princesses to a fellow countryman—even if it was someone as vital to the well-being of the realm as the Border King.

The stalemate finally came to an end when the lord regent dipped his chin in the barest of nods. Acknowledgment. *Acquiescence?*

The motion had not been missed. Everyone erupted then. Movement and unquiet whispers rolled through the hall like a tide. Stig stepped out from the line of guardsmen, staring incredulously at his father, the hand on his hilt tightening as though he was tempted to use it.

The lord regent shook his head once in rebuke, scolding his son to remain silent. Stig mutinously compressed his mouth and stepped back in line. He might not like it, but he was a loyal servant to the throne and an obedient son. Perhaps when alone with his father, he could sway him, but he would not do so here.

I shall have one of your daughters to wife.

I could not get those awful words out of my ears. The lord regent could not consider something so outrageous.

I shook my head. It was not even a request. Not even a proposition. It was a statement of fact. A forgone conclusion.

The man who had raised and loved me as a father would never agree. *He could not.*

My gaze swept over Lord Dryhten in contempt, willing him back from whence he had come. A barbarian from the Borderlands who did not know enough to wipe his boots clean before entering the palace was not fit to marry one of my sisters.

And yet the king sat casually upon his throne, considering the Beast thoughtfully. The lord regent's gaze was steady and assessing and calculating. Dismay fluttered in my belly. Neither the king nor the lord regent laughed or scoffed or appeared offended—all reactions I deemed suitable to the situation.

Princesses belonged in palaces wearing the finest silks and jewels. And brutal warlords belonged on the dangerous borders of the kingdom. The two did not mix. They did not mingle, and they most definitely did not marry.

Feena and Sybilia no longer looked quite so intrigued. They swapped nervous glances. Fear gleamed in Alise's eyes. Even across the distance I could detect the delicate lines of her pale throat working as she struggled to swallow.

Not Alise. Please, no.

All three of them were the very image of innocence. I supposed that was why it made more sense for me to be the one to take their whippings. *I* did not look innocent. *I* did not look frail. I was a natural choice with my looming height and much too direct gaze and wanton hair. I looked like someone prone to wickedness. At least that was what the lord chamberlain always told me—hissing beneath his breath as he flogged my back: *You're a wicked, wicked creature. A lowborn wench, good only for the rod, bred to take the brunt of my whip.*

"Lady Tamsyn?" The voice pulled my attention away from the unfolding drama. Lady Dagny looked back at me with blinking eyes. "What are you doing out here?" She motioned around the crowd of onlookers with her plump, beringed fingers. "Should you not be sitting up there?" She nodded toward my vacant seat.

"I arrived late, and did not wish to cause undue distraction."

She shook her head and pursed her lips. I read her disapproval, her thoughts. Standing here seemed to proclaim my inadequacy. A true princess would be up there where she belonged.

With a properly repentant smile for the lady who was a close friend of the queen, I returned my attention to the front of the hall to see the king and his advisers departing with Lord Dryhten and two members of his party of warriors. My stomach sank and twisted.

"Oh, they're leaving with the Beast." Lady Dagny gave a disgruntled sigh. "I suppose we won't be permitted to hear how King Hamlin responds to that bit of nonsense." She flapped open her fan and began furiously stirring the air around her face.

It was encouraging to see I was not the only one who objected to the notion. Who felt as I did. Unfortunately, Lady Dagny was not the final arbiter. I feared the king and the lord regent were having a private audience with Lord Dryhten because they were not as opposed to the warrior's demand as they ought to be. What if the Beast persuaded them to accept him as a husband for one of my sisters? Nausea curled through me and settled in the pit of my stomach.

No. No. *No*. I could not let that happen. I had to protect them.

As though I could do something to stop such a terrible thing from coming to pass, I pushed through the crowd, reasonably certain where they would be continuing their conversation. There was not a corner of this palace hidden to me. The benefit of being less important, a less valued princess, was that I was not monitored as closely as the others. I had explored every nook and cranny of this palace at my leisure. The hidden passages were not hidden to me.

I knew precisely where to go.

2
FELL

I WAS MY FATHER'S SON.

He had taught me to fight. He had taught me the meaning of honor. That you bled for the things that mattered. Your homeland. Your people. A worthless and feeble king. I inhaled. The king whose lavish palace I now stood inside—who reaped the benefit of my protection in exchange for . . . nothing.

My father had been satisfied with the arrangement. Balor the Butcher did not question the act of fighting, bleeding, *dying* for a distant king. The honor of it all had been enough for him.

No more.

It was not enough for me.

There was no honor in being someone's whipping dog.

I was my father's son. I had learned everything from him, including from his mistakes, and I refused to accept *nothing* as payment for blood anymore. It was time the Borderlands were viewed as something more than the edge of nowhere, uncivilized country fit for only the dregs of humanity.

"Are you sure you want to do this? Any *wife* you get from this place will be dead by winter's end," Arkin muttered for my ears alone as we entered the chamber, his keen gaze flitting about the opulent space.

"You don't know that," I countered.

"That she will be weak and soft as pudding? Aye, I do know that. She's from here." He motioned around us with a disgusted flick of his fingers. "If she doesn't perish on the crossing from saddle fatigue or when we ford the river or in the first snow squall, I'll eat my shield." Arkin looked at me incredulously. "Come now, Dryhten. I saw those *princesses* sitting up there and so did you. You need a sword maiden for a wife. A strong woman to give you sons. Someone who can ride your cock all night and then ride a mount all day." The older man smirked. He lacked delicacy, but he had served alongside my father as his vassal and was now, in turn, mine. A border lord in his own right, of a smaller holding west of my keep, he was bred in savagery, making him precisely the manner of warrior you wanted with you in battle. I sighed. Perhaps, though, he was not the best man at my side in ventures of diplomacy.

"Enough," I quietly commanded.

The king and his retinue were only a few feet away, and I had no wish for them to overhear us speaking of cocks. Now was not the time for further debate. Arkin had aired his misgivings plenty on the ride south, but I had already decided. The princesses might not appear the heartiest of women, but this was the way it had to be. Penterra was under threat on multiple fronts. Yes, we had enemies, but that was not the only threat. Our people were starving. Famine and disease were rampant in the north, south— everywhere. Circumstances were dire and not improving under King Hamlin. I required a seat at the table to stop these toad-faced bastards from fucking things up even more—and marriage to a Penterran princess would grant me that.

A footman gestured for us to take a seat on any of the flimsy-looking furniture. Every surface was littered with tasseled pillows of silk and velvet and brocade. Fine paintings covered the walls. A fire crackled in a hearth large enough for multiple persons to fit inside. Did it even get cold enough in the south to necessitate such a thing? My top lip curled faintly as I lowered myself onto a bench. My stronghold was comfortable but nowhere near this opulent.

Wine was offered. It wasn't ale, but I took a long, savoring sip, watching over the rim of my jeweled goblet as the king took a seat. The lord regent had more influence than expected. I noted at once the king's gaze continually sought him out *before* speaking, *after* speaking, and even when not speaking at all.

"Your proposition is of interest, Lord Dryhten," King Hamlin said carefully, the purple of his tunic so brilliant and pristine it made the eyes water.

The lord regent remained standing, his lean form positioned to the right of the king, one hand gripping the back of his chair. I wondered if the king realized how controlling the posture appeared, as though he were merely a puppet with the man behind him pulling the strings.

I directed my gaze at the lord regent. "I believe I have earned significant recompense."

"A princess of the Penterran throne, though?" The lord regent smiled as though I were a child asking for the impossible and was yet too naive to know it. "You overreach yourself, my lord."

The king nodded almost regretfully.

"Do I?" I leaned back against pillows so soft and luxurious that my body did not know quite how to react to such comfort. I'd spent nearly a month riding hard and bedding down on the unforgiving ground to arrive here so that we would be back home before the first snow. There was nothing worse than being caught in a snow squall out in the open.

I'd meant to come sooner, but a fierce contingent of invaders from the north had occupied me for the past many months, and I was not the kind of man to send an envoy to collect a bride for me. Arkin had offered to go in my stead, but it seemed the kind of thing I should do myself, no matter the inconvenience. I had no desire to put it off another year. This business needed getting done.

A servant refilled the goblets all around and offered fruit. Such fruit was a luxury in the cold climate of the north. I selected a cluster of fresh grapes. Arkin followed suit, helping himself to a pear and biting down noisily on the juicy fruit, looking around at all the people gathered with blinking eyes as juice dribbled onto his graying beard.

"No one discounts that you have served the kingdom most

admirably." The lord regent's tone turned ingratiating, and it took everything in me not to cut him down. My fingers curled into a fist that itched to lash out and connect with his smug face. It wasn't the way, though. Not here. In my life, in my world, violence was the answer to most problems. Here the answer was talk. Lies. Currying favor.

I'd just arrived and I couldn't wait to get back home.

The lord regent feigned politeness, said the right words, but the sincerity was not there. His smile did not meet his eyes. I was not accustomed to anything less than deference, and this man's smug face needled my skin.

As did that of the young bastard watching me from where he stood across the room, his brown eyes bright and alive with loathing, his mouth an unforgiving slash of lips within his beard.

We had not been introduced, but he wore the regalia of an officer . . . and a scowl. He did nothing to disguise his aversion toward me, and I could almost respect that. I would take that any day over the fake smiles and empty praise the lord regent was sending my way. I supposed I should appreciate his lack of artifice. I lifted a mocking eyebrow at him, enjoying the ruddy flush of his features.

"Most admirably?" I echoed mildly, wondering if I was the only one who heard the patronizing ring to that.

The king's smile wobbled a bit. He'd heard it.

The lord regent's gaze narrowed slightly. "We do appreciate all your efforts," he answered rather forcefully, willing me to . . . what? Believe him? Feel flattered?

"Oh? Well. That is a relief," I replied with exaggerated enthusiasm, popping a grape into my mouth and chewing with casual slowness. "I shudder to think how you would view me if I did anything less than hold the northern border time and time again."

I let my words hang in the air. Not a threat. Precisely. But something they could turn over in their minds . . . as I was certain they would.

Arkin was the first to finally speak, unsurprisingly. He led with his sword into every fray, even when the battle was one waged with words. "Indeed. If not for our defenses, three thousand warriors from Veturland would have successfully invaded last spring. Another king would be sitting where you are right now." My vassal gestured—his thick fingers shining with the juice from his pear—to where King Hamlin sat. Trust Arkin to cut to the heart of it.

The lord regent's smile vanished, the lines of his narrow face drawing tighter. His eyes glittered, but he could not deny the charge, because it was true.

"And if that weren't enough," Arkin went on to say, "there are the raiders in the Crags. Those bastards can fight." This he said with a heavy exhale, shaking his head at the thought of them. He looked to me for confirmation.

"Good fighters," I confirmed with a single nod, sweeping a disgusted glance over the guardsmen in the room. They would not survive a confrontation with them.

The raiders occupying the Crags didn't number in the thousands, but they were a bloodthirsty lot. Highly skilled and ruthless and impossible to track. I knew. I had tried, and I was the best tracker in the Borderlands. My father had made sure of that. It was baffling. They were as elusive as smoke.

The king cleared his throat. "Our gratitude to you"—his gaze flicked to Arkin—"and all the border lords cannot be properly expressed."

"Perhaps it should be demonstrated, then," I suggested evenly with a lift of my eyebrow.

The king looked uneasily between his adviser and me, aware that he'd walked himself back into the matter at hand.

Silence fell.

I placed another grape in my mouth, rolling it over my tongue as I waited for the king to speak, taking pleasure in his obvious discomfort.

He knew why I was here. Everyone knew. I had not minced my words. One of his daughters would be mine. He could not afford to lose my fealty and still hold this realm together.

I crushed the grape between my tongue and the roof of my mouth. Chewing, I reached for another—and stopped.

My skin snapped with sudden awareness. The fine hairs on my arms vibrated. I scanned the chamber, quickly searching faces and reading nothing in those expressions, no hint of alertness, no hint of danger—and I was an expert at ferreting out threats. It was what I did. How I had survived for this long. My skin pulled and tugged with an awareness that I could not explain.

It was as though someone had entered the chamber and joined us, and yet no door had opened. No one had stepped inside. I stared at the same people as before. Except I felt a new gaze upon me. The scrutiny of someone I could not see. Could only sense. Feel. *Taste.*

Compelled by an invisible string, I stood from the bench and moved through the room. Walking the perimeter of the well-appointed chamber, I skirted furniture, my fingers grazing the back of a brocade-upholstered chair, the massive desk situated in front of a stained-glass window, a tapestry-covered wall, seeking, searching the space that suddenly crackled with heat and the energy of an impending storm.

The others exchanged glances, no doubt wondering at my strange behavior.

"My lord?" the lord regent asked, a hint of annoyance in his tone. "Is anything amiss?"

I ignored him. Angling my head, I listened, the whoosh of a heartbeat in my ears, thumping out a rhythm faster than my own.

I stopped before a painting of the final battle of the Threshing. The Hormung had taken place a century ago. My father's grandfather had been there. He had led our armies to victory that day, turning the tide in the war against dragons. The casualties in that battle were innumerable on both sides, but the dragons' losses were far greater. Devastating. After the Hormung, the end was just a matter of time. The few remaining dragons that had not been slain were hunted down. The stragglers were systematically rooted out, rounded up, and eliminated. No dragon to be seen again . . . except once. One time. An extraordinary, singular occurrence eighty years after the Hormung.

I continued to stare at the painting—into that night sky lit by dragon fire, countless winged creatures twisting and writhing in death spins over the armies of men, the dark, jagged outline of the Crags a looming shadow in the background. It was a remarkable work of art, in dark blues and fiery hues of red, gold, and orange.

I could not look away from the carnage. I had never seen a depiction of that day. I'd only heard the stories and accounts of the Hormung. On Sigur Day, the anniversary of that momentous occasion, we feasted and raised our glasses and celebrated. The old warriors shared the stories passed down to them from their forefathers: heroic tales of adventure, of good defeating evil, and we lapped it up. Including me. *Especially* me. I felt a part of that lore, connected to the distant past more than others because of my unlucky (or lucky?) beginnings.

I was three years old when my father rescued me. At least that was the best estimation of my age. I could never know for certain. What was certain? Twenty-three years ago, Balor the Butcher led a raiding party into the snow-swathed Crags, far into the cavernous deep. That was where he found me, underneath the mountain's thick skin, a hapless, naked toddler shrinking at the feet of a monstrous beast, waiting to be its next meal.

It had been eighty years then. Eight decades since a dragon was last sighted. Everyone thought them gone. Dead. Eradicated. Extinct. But there I was . . . in the den of a dragon. The last one. An anomaly. An outlier. Like a cockroach, the thing had holed up, buried deep in the bowels of a mountain, only surfacing under the cloak of night to hunt, to claim and devour what food it could find—in that instance, me.

Dragons lived for centuries, and that one, my captor, would likely have lived longer if not for Balor the Butcher. I owed the Border King my life. Not only had he saved me and killed the sole remaining dragon, but he had also taken me in and raised me as his son.

For others, this was merely a painting.

For me, it was more.

I understood what it represented. It breathed violence, pain, desperation. Loss and triumph. The triumph of humankind over the demon dragon, over those fiendish creatures who had taken so much and would have continued to take. Continued to destroy. Just as that one—my dragon—had taken my true parents and destroyed the family I would never know. *My dragon.* As fucked as that was, I would always think of that dragon as mine. The dragon that had stolen me and would have killed me.

And beyond all that, buried within the canvas's vibrant strokes of ochre and tempera, something else throbbed and breathed . . . and called to me. A . . . ghost of something. Something that prickled and tightened my skin to the point of anguish.

Something beyond the striking artwork and my fascination with the story it told.

I narrowed my eyes, peering harder, deeper into the scene, which was as visceral as a bleeding wound. Whatever I felt, whatever I sensed in this room originated here, in this painting.

I stared at it, illogically, impossibly convinced that it stared back at me.

My hands curled at my sides, fingers digging into the flesh of my palms. The chamber grew stifling. My breath steamed from my lips and nose.

"My lord?" The voice came from my left. The king stood beside me. I had not heard his approach, so intent was I on hunting whatever was affecting me.

I inhaled. Exhaled. It did no good. I was still too warm. My chest still too tight.

"Impressive," I murmured, unable to tear my gaze away from the scene, even though I knew I should have fully given my attention to the man beside me.

"I am told it is a remarkable depiction."

He was *told* through the annals. Not through the collective memory of his family.

No member of the royal family had been there a hundred years ago to pass down the tale of his exploits in that final, grisly battle. The armies from the south were not led by the king of Penterra. Not then. Not now.

The Hormung—the Threshing, for that matter—had largely been fought by the armies of the north. *In* the north. Dragons had crushed their bones to dust, burned their flesh to ash. The blood of warriors from the Borderlands had soaked the battlefields. Warriors like my great-grandfather. A hundred years ago, he led the armies of the north in the Hormung. No warrior had done more than he to eliminate the dragon plague from our land.

He had been a fourth son. Three brothers and countless cousins had fallen before him. Before he took up the mantle of Lord of the Borderlands. Before he formed an alliance with Fenrir, the sire of all wolves, and secured the allegiance of every wolf in the land to aid in the hunt for dragons.

That was the past, but it was not forgotten. Not in the north. And not now as I stared expectantly at the king, patience a thin, fraying thread in my hands. The Borderlands was done waiting for its due.

I was done.

He sighed, and there was resignation in the sound. "Well. I do have daughters."

The implication was very satisfying. *Daughters.* Plural. Multiple. The admission was a surrender. I had known he would eventually reach this decision. He had no other choice. He needed me too much not to capitulate. At least that was what I had been telling myself ever since I left home.

I smiled slightly, turning back to gaze straight into that painted hellscape, unable to tear my eyes away from it even with my goal so close at hand. "Indeed. You do."

"Your Majesty!" the lord regent blustered from somewhere behind us. "You cannot mean to say—"

"I have *several* daughters," King Hamlin clarified in a stern voice, no doubt meant to quell the lord regent's protests. It was the first time since my arrival that he had resembled a king. "Perhaps I can spare one for such a worthy man as Lord Dryhten."

Heat radiated from the painting. It was as though the fire flashing through the sky were real and had come to life to reach out and scald me.

I had won.

I'd accomplished exactly what I'd set out to do. Or very nearly.

I would have one of this man's daughters. A princess of the realm as my wife. In my bed. Maybe her belly would soon swell with my child. Which meant my voice would be heard in the decisions made in the ruling of this kingdom. At last. I felt my father then, reaching to me from the grave, proud, pleased. Finally, the Borderlands would get what they were owed.

The king's hand settled on my shoulder. "Come now, my lord. We have a great deal to discuss."

3

TAMSYN

I STOOD ON THE OTHER SIDE OF THE PAINTING, SHROUDED IN darkness, with only the thin spread of canvas stretched taut like skin between the men and me. Hidden in the secret passageway, invisible to those inside my father's chancery, I held my breath.

I was invisible to them, but they were not invisible to me. I saw and heard everything, and the fury pumped hard and fast inside me, battering within my veins like a storm. My father intended to give one of his precious daughters to the Beast of the Borderlands.

One of my sisters.

The man I called Papa—who doted on me alongside his natural-born daughters—would never do such a thing. He would not betray one of his own in this way. Or so I had believed.

I had never felt such rage, such helplessness. All my life it had been my duty to protect the princesses of Penterra. To be flogged in their place was a privilege. There had been a long line of parents offering their children up for the prestigious role. When the queen became pregnant, many had applied. Only I was chosen. It was an honor. At least that was what I had been taught.

My earliest memory was of Nurse sending me to bed without dinner. I was three or four and confused because I had not done anything amiss. Feena, months younger than me, adored playing hide-and-go-seek. She loved it so much she would play it long after Nurse called us in. It had taken over an hour to find Feena that day. Nurse had been in a panic, enlisting the entire palace staff to find the princess. Eventually she was discovered where she had fallen asleep, in the bottom of a wardrobe in one of the guest chambers.

That was my first lesson. My first punishment. I was sent to bed with an empty belly whilst Feena watched in wide-eyed incomprehension, too young to understand why Nurse, quivering with outrage at *her*, was sending *me* to bed hungry. I remember huddling in my bed, tears hot and salty on my face, choking on the injustice, my stomach growling with hunger as I stared into the dark, so hurt, so confused at what I could have possibly done to deserve such harsh treatment.

Eventually we would all come to understand, though.

Eventually my punishments would become physical in nature. First by Nurse's hand, then later by tutors, then by the lord chamberlain. Collectively, they all saw to it that the princesses faced consequences for their misdeeds. That *I* faced the consequences for their misdeeds. *Me.* For the things *they* did. All confusion and hurt ultimately faded as that became my accepted reality.

I was the whipping girl.

I had protected my sisters all my life. They needed to be safeguarded now more than ever—or at least one of them did. From *him.* The Beast had marched in here with his band of ruffians and his contemptible demand, and my father had conceded.

But I would not.

Outraged breaths fogged from my lips as I glared directly into the ice-pale eyes of the man who thought to claim Feena, Sybilia, or—God help her—Alise. My youngest sister was small and delicate. She would break under this warrior.

Scant inches separated us, the air hot and crackling between us. His dark hair reached his shoulders, the sides braided close to his scalp. I could practically feel his breath through the flimsy barrier. I studied his hazy face through the fibers of the canvas, taking comfort that he could not see me in the darkness of the damp corridor, and yet . . .

Why had he stopped directly in front of the painting?

Why was he staring at me like he *could* see me? As though he were on the verge of reaching through the canvas and touching me?

A fever rippled over my skin as I imagined those big hands closing around me.

It was impossible, of course. He could not know I was there.

My gaze flickered over his shadowy face, studying every line and hollow, the intense eyes, the hard set of his mouth. He looked . . . agitated. Perhaps I had given myself away with a sound. I had thought I was the height of stealth, but it was the only explanation for his fixation on the painting.

The king settled a hand on his shoulder and led him away so that they could discuss the particulars of his marriage to one of my sisters . . . but not before the king sent a disapproving glance toward the painting. I sucked in a breath.

My father *knew* I was in the hidden passageway.

Of course he did. Papa had lived in this palace all his life. He was the one who had first showed us the passageways when we were young children. I inched back, certain that he would not be pleased with me. For once, I may have earned a whipping all on my own.

I waited as the men continued their discussion, hoping to learn which one of my sisters was destined for such a vile fate, which one was to be bound forever to the infamous Lord Beast, bloodthirsty and vicious, purported to be more monster than man, the last human alive to survive a dragon.

And yet Papa never said a word. Never mentioned who he was promising to the Border King, and the dreadful barbarian never asked. It likely did not matter to the wretched man. The Beast doubtlessly viewed my sisters as being the same. They were all pleasing of face and daughters to the king. Interchangeable. That only increased my indignation. My sisters were more than that. They were individuals and vastly different.

Feena loved animals and was always smuggling one pet or another into her bed, whilst Sybilia would just as soon drink poison than let an animal anywhere near her for fear of them jumping on her and licking her. And then there was sweet Alise, who loved her watercolors and indulged in strawberries and cream every morning. She ate so many strawberries that she smelled of them.

I felt a chill when Dryhten insisted the marriage be performed at the earliest convenience. Papa agreed, assuring him it would be done. It was dizzying, how soon it was all happening. The queen had not even been informed . . . much less the *bride*. Everything inside me fumed that one of my sisters would be left at the mercy of a man known as the Beast. Did Papa not fear for his daughter?

They began to disperse, the lord regent reminding them that a grand feast awaited. Dryhten's warriors looked well pleased, and I wondered why he still appeared so sullen. He'd gotten his way. Should he not be smiling like the others? Tension feathered the skin of his jaw, and he sent one more glance over his shoulder to the painting—to *me*.

I stiffened and shook my head.

No, no, no. Keep walking, brute.

As though I'd uttered the words aloud, I pressed my fingers to my mouth to stifle any sound that might slip free.

He could not have heard my thought, and yet those flashing eyes of his narrowed. Across the distance, they were impossible to read, but I felt his suspicion as keenly as the edge of a blade pressing at my throat. His broad chest lifted on an inhalation I somehow heard—felt—and then he turned away, disappearing from the room.

I sagged back against the wall, bowing my head and dropping my hand from my mouth with a shudder of relief. Several minutes passed before I felt composed enough to move. I did not relish returning through the labyrinth of passages snaking through the palace, all manner of creepy-crawly things for company. It was a long, winding walk in the damp dark to the salon where my mother and her ladies liked to do their needlework. I lifted the latch, deciding to take the quickest exit.

With a push, the painting swung out like a door, and I stepped down into the room, my slippers sinking into the rug covering the stone floor.

The Great Hall would be crowded with revelers, eating, drinking, dancing in time to the troubadours assembled especially for this night. The Penterran court never needed a reason to celebrate, but the arrival of our special guests would result in long hours of carousing. No one would have noticed that I was missing yet. I had to find my sisters and warn them. I had to speak to Mama. Perhaps she could sway her husband. Perhaps I could approach Stig, and he could talk to his father. I knew he would be on my side.

Turning, I made certain the painting was back in place with no hint that it had been disturbed. Satisfied, I turned around and walked directly into a wall. A hard wall with arms and hands that came up around me. A wall that possessed a deep, growling voice. "I see this palace comes equipped with spies."

The Beast.

Instantly, I was assailed by the scent that I had noted earlier in the Great Hall. I was awash with it—with him. My nostrils flared. Wind and earth and horseflesh. And that indefinable something else.

Heat rippled over me, igniting my skin. I arched against the great slab of him, against pulsing, immovable muscle. I pushed my palms into his solid chest, desperate to break free.

I was fire. My entire body warmed at the contact, and fear clawed at my throat.

His eyes weren't narrow slits any longer. They blasted me, wide and alert, battle ready. This close, without a hazy barrier between us, I could see they were the color of frost, pale gray with a ring of darker blue. Gratification gleamed there. He'd sensed I was behind that painting, and now he'd caught me.

"I am not a spy," I said in a raspy voice I did not even recognize as my own.

"No? Who are you, then?" Those eyes roamed my face and my flame-red hair. His gaze lingered on my hair. The unusual color featured largely in the torments of my childhood, when children of the court would call attention to it as a visible reminder that I was truly not one of them—that I was not a *real* princess, just a stray taken in by a generous king and a queen with a soft heart. "*What are you?*"

What was *I?* What was *he?*

His eyes absorbed me in a way no one ever had before. I was largely overlooked in the palace. Except when a whipping was required or when someone felt like ridiculing me for my ungainly height or my unfortunate hair or my dubious parentage.

Then the brute lifted a hand.

I flinched.

He paused, his eyes communicating something to me. I could not say what, but I eased slightly. He waited a moment longer and then brought his big hand closer, touching a lock of my hair, rubbing it between his fingers gently, experimentally.

I felt a rumble then, and realized it was inexplicably coming from me, from my chest.

He released my hair. It fell back against my neck in a whisper, and the iron bands of his arms came back around me, circling tighter, bringing me closer. My fingers flexed against his leather tunic like a kitten kneading its paws, unable to resist, unable *not* to move and explore.

"The question is . . . do you spy for yourself or someone else?"

Moments passed before I could speak. "I am . . . no one."

He made a sound: part laugh, part growl. "Oh, sweetheart, you're someone . . . *something.*"

I shivered despite the heat engulfing me.

He was no longer a distant figure across a crowded room. No longer someone obscured by a veiled painting. He was here and real and pulsing against me. His hair wasn't just dark. It was tar black, flashing blue and purple as a raven's wing where the light from the nearby wall sconce struck it. I could distinguish the deep blue ring around his pale eyes. Admire the impossibly thick fan of lashes. And his mouth. By God . . . his mouth. His bottom lip was full and wide, deceptively lush for a man that was all hardness and brutality.

Blinking, I shook my head as though shaking myself free of a spell. This man was simply different. That was it. That was what entranced me so. With his big body and too-long hair and searing eyes, he was not like the men of the palace, and that fascinated me.

And terrified me.

"Unhand me," I ordered.

I was certain he was not a man who yielded to anyone. He was a warrior who took what he wanted. His existence was built on strength, on exerting force, on domination. For a moment, I did not think he would oblige.

Then he did.

"Of course." His arms loosened a fraction, allowing space between us. Even so, I paused, lost in the glory of that face and hair and eyes, bewildered at the tumult of sensations overwhelming me.

I finally broke free, staggering back a step. It did little to help. The air charged and sparked around us like an approaching storm. His eyes glowed, a beast stalking in the dark. Fitting.

He continued, "I'll let you get back to your . . . whatever it is you're doing that *isn't* spying."

I opened and closed my mouth, disliking his mocking tone and wanting to put him in his place and let him know . . . what? That he was *wrong*?

Because he was not. He was not wrong. I was spying. I didn't regret that either. I would do that and more to keep my girls safe.

The door to the chancery opened abruptly, and the lord regent stepped inside. "Ah, my lord, we thought you were—" The lord regent's gaze landed on me, and he startled, his lips thinning in displeasure.

I tensed. The pompous windbag tolerated me, but I knew he disapproved. Even though I provided a service as the royal whipping girl, he believed me too indulged, too embedded in the king's household. He especially did not like my friendship with his son. Sometimes I caught him watching me with Stig, and the look in his eyes frightened me. Made me feel as though I was doing something wrong. It was a sensation I despised. I tried so hard to behave properly. It was enough that I was punished for my sisters'

misbehavior. I did not need to be disciplined for my own missteps. *That* I could control.

"What are you doing in here, girl?" He stared down his long nose at me. "You shouldn't be here. Off with you, off!" He waved his hand at me, shooing me away, treating me as the nuisance he deemed me to be.

I hesitated only long enough to send Lord Dryhten one final, guarded look—as though expecting him to leap out at me and seize me, grab me and punish me for eavesdropping.

He didn't, of course. He let me go, and I fled the room, his gaze palpable, hot and feral, slithering over my back.

I didn't venture to the Great Hall as I'd originally planned. Lord Dryhten would be there, and one encounter with him was enough for the night. *For a lifetime.* There was also the possibility that he would call me out as a spy in front of the king and queen.

I shuddered at the prospect. The king and queen were good to me, but even they had their limits. I knew better than to shame or embarrass them in front of the court and our very important visitors.

I hastened to my bedchamber, where I paced its length, wondering if the lord regent would seek reprisal for finding me alone with Dryhten. Should I expect a visit from the lord chamberlain to deliver another whipping? It had been a long time since I'd had two whippings in a single day. I didn't relish it.

The distant sounds of merriment carried from the Great Hall below. I wanted to believe that the lord regent, deep in his cups, would forget all about me, but I knew that unlikely. The lord regent never lost his head to wine, and he would be extra vigilant with the border lords here.

One of the maids arrived to turn down the coverlet, but when she found me in the chamber she stayed and helped ready me for bed, brushing my hair until it crackled like fire and then securing it in one long braid.

"Did you have a nice time this evening, my lady?" she asked, assuming I'd been in the Great Hall with everyone else. With the palace brimming with people, it was a simple matter to lose track of one less-than-important princess.

"Yes," I lied, staring numbly at my reflection. There would be no explaining the truth—that I had not been to the Great Hall at all. "Have my sisters returned to their chambers yet?"

"I don't believe so. The celebration is still going strong."

Of course it was. Except the girls would not be downstairs much longer. Mama would not permit them to carouse late into the night. I would wait up for them. They deserved to know. They *needed* to know what was being planned for one of them. They needed to be warned. We could come up with a plan together.

A brief knock sounded on my bedchamber door. Without waiting for my summons, the king and queen entered, followed by the lord regent. My stomach dropped at the sight of Stig's father.

The queen nodded in dismissal at the maid. "That will be all. You may go."

The girl dipped a curtsey and left us. The door clicked shut behind her, and the sound reverberated through the space, which suddenly felt much too small. It was a wholly unique scenario—the king, queen, and lord regent alone with me in my private chamber, sucking all the air out of the room. I could only assume their presence here was because the lord regent had caught me alone with the border lord.

The Beast was a valuable individual to them. Clearly. They were giving him a princess as his bride simply because he asked. No doubt they were here to interrogate me about our encounter and make certain I had done nothing to offend Lord Dryhten.

I hurriedly got to my feet, wiping sweating palms down the front of my night-robe. I was not certain I hadn't offended the Beast. His narrowing eyes flashed across my mind, so frosty gray I felt their chill blow through me. I fought to control my expression and reveal none of my misgivings.

I curtsied in acknowledgment of my mother and father. I could muster only a stiff incline of my head for the lord regent. He stood stoically beside them, his expression as coldly cunning as ever.

My father studied me with a smile. "Tamsyn, I understand you found your way into the chancery when I was meeting with Lord Dryhten."

My cheeks went hot. Of course he had been informed. "Yes, Papa."

"Hidden passageway?"

"Yes, Papa," I confirmed.

He made a sound in his throat that was neither disapproval nor approval. "My fault, I suppose, for showing it to you and your sisters."

"Eavesdropping on matters that don't concern you." The lord regent tsked and looked to the king for agreement. "I've said it before, Your Majesty." His tone softened, lyrical but also wheedling. "You indulge her. She takes too much liberty."

"That is neither here nor there anymore," the queen said brightly.

The lord regent released a long-suffering sigh but gave the barest incline of his head in agreement.

And that felt ominous.

I looked wildly at the three of them, wondering *why* it was neither here nor there anymore.

The king turned to me. "I take it you know I've promised a daughter to Lord Dryhten."

"Yes, and I cannot understand why, Papa." This was my chance to talk him out of it. The perfect opportunity, here with the three people who made all the decisions. In my life. In my sisters' lives. In the lives of everyone who lived in the City . . . in all of Penterra. Until this moment, I'd thought they were the three most powerful people in all the realm. Now I knew better. Now I knew that there was a beast with a power that rivaled theirs. A beast that had come to our door, and my family was prepared to give him whatever he wanted.

"It is not for you to understand the reasoning of your betters," the lord regent snapped.

My mother approached, fondly stroking a hand down the thick braid of hair draped over my shoulder. "Oh, Tamsyn," she chided. "Always so staunch in your beliefs. It is commendable."

I relaxed a bit beneath the praise and sent a defiant look to the lord regent.

The king settled his hands upon my shoulders. "I know this is beyond you, my dear." He stared into my eyes. "But diplomacy is necessary in the ruling of a kingdom."

"I am sure it is challenging, but you cannot do this," I dared to beseech him, ignoring the lord regent's presence—knowing he was watching with displeasure at our familiarity, our closeness. Displeasure from him was nothing new, after all. "You cannot give one of my sisters to that man."

"He can do whatever he likes. He. Is. The. King." The lord regent punctuated each word with biting emphasis, and in his eyes was his usual contempt as he looked down his narrow nose. It gave him the appearance of being taller than me even though he was not.

I lowered my gaze. "Forgive me." The words were reflexive, but I was not sorry. Not sorry at all. Not when it came to protecting my sisters.

"Oh, tell her," my mother said with impatience.

My eyes snapped back up. Tell me . . . *what?* Which sister they were condemning to a bleak fate? Had they already decided? I swallowed against the giant lump forming in my throat.

"We are not giving him one of your sisters," the lord regent finally said, almost as though he savored the admission. And that did not feel right. Nor did the hint of a smile cracking his harsh features.

"Y-you're not?"

My father nodded. "That was never my intention."

I rubbed at the center of my forehead, relieved but confused. "I don't understand. I heard you agree to—"

"We had to agree. We could not refuse the dog of the Borderlands, unfortunately. We need his continued protection of our northern border." The lord regent's lips peeled back in a grimace of scorn. "Bloody barbarian. We will not taint the royal bloodlines with the likes of him."

"So what will be done?" Something had to be done. They had promised him a Penterran princess. I had not misheard that.

The king squeezed my shoulders encouragingly. "We will give him a princess of Penterra. As promised."

Frowning, I looked to each of their expectant faces and shook my head slowly. "But you said . . ."

"I know what I said," the king acknowledged.

Then . . .

"We are giving him," the lord regent finally clarified, "you."

4

STIG

I COULDN'T REMEMBER LIFE BEFORE TAMSYN. SHE WAS ALWAYS there. A part of me. Indelible on my memory. Ink forever stained on the canvas of my life, embedded in my skin.

My world had always been entwined with the royal family's. I had no memories of my mother. She never recovered from the rigors of childbirth and died before my first birthday. I was born into a life at court, born to an ambitious father who took notice of me only when I served a purpose. Excelling in my studies was expected, as was besting all the other boys on the practice field: outrunning them, outriding them, outdoing them in all things.

Everything done was done in the shadow of the king and queen, alongside the princesses . . . pesky little girls whom I endured. And I supposed that was family. Those you endured. The very definition of it. Somewhere along the way, though, over time, Tamsyn had become more (or less?) than a pesky girl. She became someone I no longer endured.

I was thirteen years old when I found her weeping in a corner of the palace, curled into a little ball, arms wrapped tightly around her knees as though she could make herself disappear.

I went to her even though I did not have much use for girls then. I especially did not have much time for *little* girls. If I was going to devote any time to a girl, she was going to be one of the pretty older ones who sent me and my friends flirty looks. But generally I didn't give much attention to them either.

Those days, all my time was spent training, honing my skills with a sword, and following my father's bidding in all ways. My boyhood was gone. The time for childish things was over. I had things to do. Important things. Adult things. And yet there was something about her. Something that had me lingering over her.

Leggy as a colt, knobby elbows, and flaming red hair perpetually untidy and falling from her pins to straggle into her face and down her back, she was a mess. I should have kept walking. Duty called. She hadn't even noticed me there. I could have moved right past her, but I stopped and stood over her, a mess that tugged at something inside me.

She looked so small and vulnerable and pathetic as I sank down beside her. I nudged her with my shoulder. "Why so sad?"

She startled, lifting her head with a gasp and swiping at her moist cheeks. Those drowning eyes scanned my face. "Why?" Her voice was brittle and dry as a leaf. "Why?" She sniffed back a soggy breath. "Maybe because no one will ever want me." She choked on the words as though they were too much, too big and unwieldy for her mouth.

I blinked, not sure what to do with them. I took a breath. "What are you talking about, Tam?"

Her words escaped in a torrent, so rushed that it took me a moment to decipher them, and even then I missed half. "Feena showed me . . . told me . . . I'll never wear Mother's wedding circlet . . ."

I shook my head, at a loss. I didn't understand. Was this some kind of sister squabble?

"Yesterday I was whipped for—" She stopped with a huffed breath, her fingers flexing around her knees. "I don't even know. Something Sybilia did."

The princesses were a handful. Everyone knew it. Princess Alise was the best behaved of the lot, but she was little more than a baby. She did not yet have the propensity for damage the way Sybilia and Feena did.

Tamsyn shook her head again. "I am no one. They *say* I'm one of them, but I can't even wear our mother's—"

I couldn't *hear* anymore. I couldn't *see* anymore. Not her bitterly choked words. Not her pained expression. I knew some people weren't kind to her in the palace. The whipping girl or whipping boy was a long-standing tradition, a position respected by most. But there were still a few people, petty and mean, who only felt better, only felt *above*, when putting others down. These were the same people who spoke to servants as though they were less than human. Who made Tamsyn sit here with tears on her face in the dark.

I stood abruptly and reached down for her hand. "Come."

She blinked up at me. Her gaze shot from my hand to my face. "Wh—"

"Come along. Let me show you something."

She placed her small hand in mine, and I pulled her to her feet, leading her down the corridor and through the palace until we reached the gallery. It was a narrow space that stretched forever, turning and branching out into other corridors and marble-floored antechambers. The gallery housed hundreds, thousands of framed paintings, sculptures, and ceramics.

I stopped very deliberately in front of one portrait.

Still holding her hand, I nodded at the image of the very dignified silver-haired man. "Do you know who this is?"

She studied the portrait with a petulant sigh. "Some . . . dignitary, I suppose? A relation to the king? Should I know him?"

Perhaps. The gallery was full of portraits of notable figures in Penterran history. You could spend a lifetime learning all their names and biographies. Was it any surprise the governess had not yet educated her on her legacy?

"He was the whipping boy to the king. Plucked as an infant from a yeoman's brood."

Historically, whipping boys and girls were chosen from lowborn families, burdened with a multitude of mouths to feed, to help alleviate their load. That youth was then raised in luxury, simultaneously lifting their birth family up out of poverty. The price of such an arrangement? An occasional whipping. It benefited all parties.

She stepped closer, peering intently at the likeness.

I went on. "Once he finished as the whipping boy, he served as an emissary to Acton. He married a noblewoman and settled there." Moving farther down, I pointed at another portrait of a woman dressed in garments from the past century. "This is Inger of Torsten, the famous poet." From her sharp glance, I could tell she'd heard of her. "She was a whipping girl, too. Did you know that?"

Tamsyn shook her head. "N-no. I've heard of her, of course. There isn't a bard who doesn't put her words to song, but I did not know that she was . . . like me."

"Your sisters' fates rest in marriage. They must form alliances. That is their duty but not yours. You will have a choice when it comes to your future."

"A choice," she murmured, as though tasting the words on her lips.

I motioned down the long wall of the gallery. "They're all here. Whipping girls and boys of the past. They went on to live important lives. Like you will. You aren't . . . no one. Not now. Not ever. You'll have a future beyond this, Tamsyn. You're important . . . and you always will be."

Her shoulders squared a little, her chin lifting. She suddenly looked taller as she gazed at the portrait of the woman who was once like her.

After a long moment, she moved along, stopping before another portrait. "And him? Was he a whipping boy, too?"

I nodded. "Yes. They all are here. On this wall."

She swept a glance down the row of portraits. "Tell me about them, please."

I'd obliged, going on to tell her everything I knew of them—the long line that preceded her and their prestigious legacy.

I never caught her crying in a corner again. She was different after that. *We* were different. I grew up with all the princesses, but my relationship with Tamsyn was special. Closer. Whenever we were in the same room together, my eyes always found her, followed her, stayed on her.

There weren't many days like that again, when I had to prop
her up. She didn't need that from me anymore. It was as though
a lever had been pulled. She never looked back, never descended
to those dark shallows again. Never questioned her role. She went
about her life, as did I. Both of us living. Both with our responsibilities.

I didn't think about her taking whippings. Didn't think about
a flog flaying her back. I knew something of a body being pushed
to its limits. Many a night I collapsed into bed aching and sore and
near the breaking point from the day's training. Like me, she was
strong. Our bodies would endure.

At twenty-one, she was nearing the end. It was never spoken of,
but I knew. I had thought about it often as the years fell away, as we
grew older, as she went from awkward to beautiful, as she inched
toward that vague end, the day when she would be free.

The princesses were of marriageable age, especially Feena and
Sybilia. They'd be gone soon, and when that happened, there would
be no more need for a whipping girl. Tamsyn would be allowed to
pursue her own life, to create her own legacy, like all those before
her. Just like I had promised her.

At least that was supposed to have happened. A heady anticipation regularly filled me at the prospect. She was going to be free.
Free to be. Free to choose.

I winced. My mistake. Now I realized she would never have a
choice. The king, queen, and *my father* would not allow that. They
had other plans for her, and they had made a liar out of me.

Never had I conceived of this scenario. I'd told her she would
have an illustrious future all those years ago, and I'd meant it. I
could not have anticipated them betrothing her to anyone—much
less to Dryhten.

It wouldn't happen. I vowed this. The bastard would not have her.

With this conviction burning through me, I endured the feast
in the Great Hall, my body humming with tension, my hands opening and closing at my sides as I observed the carousing nobles. With
a dozen warriors from the Borderlands in attendance, my presence

was expected—even if the only thing I wished to do was to leave and find Tamsyn.

It was my duty to remain, to wait until it was over, and everyone knew I, the lord regent's son, the captain of the guard, never ignored my duty.

So I waited until the Great Hall emptied. Until the last reveler went to bed. Until silence pervaded, thick and viscous as blood pooling and settling into every crack and fissure of the palace's stone walls.

When I was certain all were finally asleep, I moved quietly, silent as a ghost passing through the tomblike corridors. I had never dared to enter Tamsyn's bedchamber before. It was highly inappropriate. Highly irregular. But these were desperate times, and there was nothing I would not do to save her. Nothing. Nothing at all. I would sacrifice anything. Even my duty.

Even myself.

5

TAMSYN

WHEN I WAS TEN YEARS OLD, I LEARNED THAT THERE would be no grand state wedding for me. No multitude of guests. No weeklong festivities. No royal hunts for the wedding party. No lavish feast with all manner of entertainment. No bells tolling throughout the land. No marriage rites to a faraway prince or prominent dignitary for the betterment of the kingdom. A future such as that, the kind that glittered like a prism caught in light, dazzling and full of wonder, was reserved for my sisters, but not for me.

Not that I had devoted a great deal of time to thoughts of the future. Especially not at ten. Not yet. I was a little girl. I didn't worry about such things. I lived in the moment.

I spent my mornings learning with tutors and our governess. In music lessons. Dance. Art. Comportment. Playing with the fat tabby cat that slept in the kitchen. Riding ponies through the vast gardens. Romping and exploring with my sisters. Sitting transfixed by the fire in the Great Hall as visiting bards regaled us with stories of days gone by: of fire-breathing dragons and spell-casting witches, of beguiling huldras and hideous harpies, of sea creatures and the monstrous Fenrir, the sire of all wolves, who devoured anyone who dared venture into his territory.

I did not let the occasional whipping affect me. That was just a thing that had to be endured, like a dose of bitter medicine or a hairbrush pulling through the tangles in my hair. Unpleasant but thankfully brief. I refused to dwell on those occurrences.

In my youth, the king or queen or governess usually delivered the hard truths, schooling me in my role, training me and overseeing my punishments. The lord chamberlain had yet to become interested in me. That unwelcome attention didn't happen until my fifteenth summer.

Sometimes I fell under the hard gaze of the lord regent, though, especially if he caught his son playing with me. He did not approve of me, and he would periodically remind me of my place in the order of things. To clarify, he believed my place was somewhere alongside the scullery maid, not throwing darts with Stig.

The king and queen were not around the day I started to seriously consider my future, however. That day's hard truth came from an unexpected source, amid a child's game.

We had finished in the schoolroom and had a small amount of time to ourselves before lunch. The princesses were being unruly, and I was little better as we played a lively game of shadow tag, running up and down corridors and through bedchambers with shrill shrieks and stomping feet.

At some point I had stopped breathlessly in the king and queen's lavish sitting room that adjoined their bedchambers, pulling up short on the lush rug to admire the wedding portrait of the queen, so bright-eyed and rosy-cheeked in her bridal finery.

I studied her likeness on the canvas. Her chin was tilted at a coy angle, highlighting the slender column of her neck. She was young, of course, barely more than a girl, and the similarity to her pretty daughters was strong. I self-consciously twisted a strand of my red hair around my finger, acutely aware of how little I resembled them.

A gauzy veil flowed past her slight shoulders, a glittering gold and ruby circlet holding it in place and stretching across her smooth forehead. Her frame was delicate, almost birdlike. Unlike now—with curves aplenty, she was a formidable presence.

Feena stomped gleefully on my shadow as she came to a gasping halt beside me. My admiration of the portrait must have been visible in my gaze. She pointed to the dazzling jeweled circlet on her mother's head. "*I* will wear that on *my* wedding day." She twirled in a clumsy circle. "*You* won't, though."

She had tossed the words out so casually. Not cruelly and not to be unkind. That wasn't Feena. Feena held my hand almost everywhere we went. Any time she did something she was proud of she would squeal my name first, eager to show off her accomplishment to me.

And yet I'd felt her words like the stinging prick of a knife, a sharp blade sinking into my tender heart.

You *won't, though.*

"I . . . won't," I'd agreed, trying to sound as though I'd known that. As though it were obvious to me, too . . . even though no one had told me that directly. Even if I had never thought about the notion of marriage before. Suddenly, I was. Then I could think of little else.

I might have been the eldest by seven months, but around Feena—and even Sybilia to some degree—I had always felt behind. Less clever. Less knowledgeable. Less worldly. Just *less*, I supposed. A crystal with a little less sparkle. Gold with a little less shine.

Not so shocking since I was . . . *less*.

Less than them in the way that counted the most. I needed only to ask anyone for confirmation of that fact. I could recognize this with no self-loathing or ill will. It was simply the natural order of things. My entire existence revolved around this fact.

Feena had bobbed her head. "It's been passed down through the women in my family for generations. Those rubies were claimed from a dragon's hoard way back when they still filled the skies. I'll wear it first at my wedding. Then Sybilia will. And then Alise."

But not me.

Never me.

Treating me as a royal princess went only so far. It did not extend to a future in which I would marry in the grand tradition of a Penterran princess. Feena had only been informing me of what everyone else knew. I understood that then. I accepted it—with help from Stig.

He had consoled me, introducing me to all the whipping boys and girls captured on canvas in the gallery. He'd reassured me, persuading me that I would have a purpose. It wouldn't be a marriage formed to secure an important alliance. That fate belonged to my sisters. But my fate would be *something*.

And yet here I was on the eve of my wedding. Against all odds. Against Stig's reassuring words, against everything I had been led to believe, I would be married to secure an important alliance, after all. I guess he had been wrong.

I couldn't fall asleep for thinking about it.

I would be married on the morrow. To a stranger. To a barbaric border lord with no gentle manners, more accustomed to killing than to life at court. Was there even court life to be had where he lived? Any civilization at all among these coarse and vulgar brutes who wore their bloodstained garments into the royal palace?

The hour was late and growing later with every slow, crawling tick of the clock on my bedside table. The revelry had come to an end. The air hummed with silence. By now everyone had quit the Great Hall and found their beds at last.

The lord regent's voice repeated over and over in my head.

We are giving him . . . you.

The world had gone hazy at those words. Giving me . . . to him. As though I were an object. Not a person.

My throat constricted. As though they were serving me up like roasted pheasant at Eldr feast.

When I had recovered the power of speech, I'd made a mild protest. At first. But it was not in me to disobey. All my life, for twenty-one years, I had served the throne of Penterra, sacrificing myself for my sisters, for my country. It was the only thing I had ever known. I was good at it. This would be a continuation of those duties. The only person I knew how to be.

My door eased open with the softest groan of its hinges, but in the silence the sound was jarring. A bedchamber door opening in the middle of the night might set off alarm bells for some, but not when you had three sisters fond of barging into your room at all hours without knocking or even calling out.

Many a morning I had found myself with one or more of them curled up in bed beside me, arms and legs tangled with mine—especially following a punishment for one of their transgressions. They always felt terrible and guilty and had to reassure themselves that I was not permanently maimed by spending the night cuddled up next to me.

I flung an arm over my eyes and did not even bother to look. This was precisely the type of extraordinarily eventful day that would send all three of them scurrying into my bed.

I'd had a whipping earlier, we'd been invaded by barbarian guests from the north, *and* I now found myself betrothed to one of them—to the scariest one of them all. I was surprised the girls had not appeared sooner. Although, there had been a raucous party going on downstairs. They loved a party, even though they would not have been allowed to stay long.

A lump formed in my throat considering how many nights I would have left to myself in this bed. Perhaps there would be no more than tonight. I was not certain when my husband-to-be would wish to depart for the Borderlands, but until then, where would I sleep? Here? Elsewhere? Alone? With him? I gulped. The uncertainty gnawed at me.

I flipped back the coverlet in invitation. "Very well. Come on. Get into bed."

The voice that spoke did not belong to any of my sisters. "That's more of a welcome than I was expecting."

I lurched into a sitting position, shoving the hair off my forehead, blinking and letting my eyes acclimate, grateful for the glow from the fire that saved me from complete darkness. Stig's outline stood at the foot of my bed, an invading shadow, his familiar features cast in gloom but unmistakable.

I launched from the bed, my bare feet landing on the rug-covered floor. "What are you doing in here?" I glanced around as though there might be other unexpected visitors with him.

As close as we were, he had never dared to enter my private quarters. There were lines not to be crossed, rocks not to be tossed.

Perhaps that was why we gravitated toward each other. We understood this. We were alike in that way. We did what was expected of us. We followed the rules. We performed our duties unfailingly.

Stig being here was not expected, and it was strange seeing him in these surroundings, in my domain.

I reached for my dressing gown where I had discarded it at the end of the bed and slipped it on, tightening the belt around my waist as he gazed at me with feverishly bright eyes.

"Should I not have come?" he demanded with a snort that conveyed his incredulity. He paced a short, hard line to the left, then the right. "Should I have stayed away? Is that what you think I would do?" His voice was biting in a way I had never heard from him. Especially when addressing me. He was always kind. Always gentle. Always listened when I spoke—and when I did not.

I shook my head in response, ignoring the bleak squeezing in my chest. "You should not be here." My world had been upended. The person I had been at the start of this day was not the same one standing before him now. There were many things I didn't know, but that much I knew to be true.

Stig surged forward then and closed his hands around my arms. "You cannot be *fine* with this." His gaze burned brightly into me, the rich brown molten, lit from an unseen fire. "This is not fair. Not right at all, Tamsyn."

"Stig," I said carefully. "It doesn't matter what I want." I didn't utter this with any disgruntlement or with a low opinion of myself. I knew my life held value. I served a purpose. It was only that my preferences were never a priority.

"It matters. *You* matter."

I gave him a look. "Really? It's never been about me. You know that." *He* had told me that all those years ago. The whipping girl did not belong to herself. She belonged to the royal family.

I was theirs, bound to them until they released me, free only when they declared it.

They would never declare it. I knew that now.

"You cannot do this—"

"How can I *not*? I do as I'm told." Always. And so did he. That was who we were. "Why are you acting this way?" He had never once challenged me to go against my parents, or the role that had been decided for me since infancy. Quite the opposite. I resented this from him. Resented *him*. It was as though the book I knew, with all its familiar words and characters, with its satisfying ending, had suddenly rearranged itself on the pages . . . the story rewritten into something else. Why would he fill my head with such thoughts? With thoughts of rebellion? Why was he making this harder than it had to be? "Why are you doing this to me?"

"*Me*? What am I doing to you? I'm only urging you to think about yourself, to put yourself first."

Now? Now he was advising that? He thought he was doing me a favor? I shook my head fiercely. "No. Don't. You're not being fair."

"I'm not fair? I'll tell you what is not fair. You marrying that barbarian. You giving yourself, giving the rest of your life to—"

"For my kingdom. For the people of Penterra," I cut in. "No less than what you would do." He was captain of the guard. A soldier. That was his duty. He had always taken great pride in that. He should understand. I shouldn't have to convince him.

"They demand too much of you this time." His fingers flexed where they held me. "They're asking for your life."

"As a soldier you risk no less."

"You're not a soldier!" he exploded, and then compressed his lips as though regretting the outburst. He sent a wary look to my bedchamber door as though expecting someone to barge inside.

"That is precisely what I am. What I have been doing all these years . . ."

His chest lifted on a rough breath. "This will be worse. Worse than anything you've endured before."

I bristled. What did he know of what I had endured over the years? We did not speak of my beatings. I never shared those details. Not with him. Not with anyone. He had never witnessed them either. Never even asked about them. The closest we had come to discussing that part of my life—that very *big* part of my life—was the day he introduced me to the portraits of the others in the gallery. The ones like me. The day he told me that it would all end eventually and I would become someone else, someone with a life that belonged to me and me alone. At least it was supposed to have gone that way.

I shrugged free from his hands and put space between us. What did he know of my pain and discomfort? What did he know of the lord chamberlain panting in my ear as he brought the whip down on my back?

I'd buried those feelings, and now he dared to poke and prod at them, to expose them and drag them kicking and screaming out into the open. He cast light on them here in the dead of night in my bedchamber . . . on the eve of my wedding to the Beast of the Borderlands.

He continued in a hoarse voice, "You do this . . . and you will belong to him."

Was that so different from now? I didn't belong to myself here either.

I lifted my chin, steeling my resolve. "You should go. Now."

A desperate look came over his face. "*We* can go. The two of us. *We* can leave before the rest of the palace wakes."

I smiled, and it felt pained on my face. "The one thing I know about you, Stig . . . is that you always do what is right. You would never abandon your responsibilities for me. For anyone."

"I would. For you. *I will.*"

"No," I whispered with a slow shake of my head. "I won't forsake my sisters. One of them will have to marry him if I don't. I can't let that happen."

"Let it happen! It has always been their fate to marry for an alliance, to take a stranger for a husband. That is *their* fate." He stabbed a finger through the air at me. "Not yours."

"And my fate has always been to protect them, to do whatever is asked of me in order to do that."

He shook his head. "Not this." Nodding to the armoire, he commanded, "Pack a bag. We will go."

"We?" *We.* He would go with me? Run away with me as if we were two wanderers in the wind, troubadours or bards, free to do and go wherever we pleased.

It was impossible to fathom.

"Yes. I'll take you away from here. Away from—"

"You can't leave here." I nodded at our surroundings. "You're in this just as deep as I am. We have our duty."

"Damn my duty and damn yours!"

I flinched. I'd never heard him like this. Never so angry. Not on my behalf. Not on behalf of anyone or anything. He was never this . . . intense.

"Running away together will destroy us both," I insisted.

In the end, that would be the result. Who would we be but two people who deserted those who loved and relied on us? My sisters. My parents. Our country.

Stig had position and respect here, a shiny future with some highborn bride. How could I take him from that? He would come to resent me if I took him away from this world. Here, he was someone important. I would not let him sacrifice that for me.

"This isn't you. You're the most honorable person I know. The most responsible. People follow you because you're *you.* Not because you're the captain of the guard. Not because you're the lord regent's son. You don't run away from what's important."

Stig had been my champion for so long. He had always been there to make everything better, taking me for a ride or playing draughts with me or exploring the hidden passageways of the palace, entering through one room and popping out in another much to my delight.

"You're right," he agreed. "I don't run away from what's important."

And he kissed me.

I didn't close my eyes, too shocked at the warm press of his mouth. Stig's mouth. On mine.

Stig. Me. Kissing.

I expelled a breath, and he swallowed it, taking it inside him. Stig, my closest friend, was kissing me.

His lips moved over mine. He kept space between us. His well-formed body was of similar height to mine. I didn't have to angle my head, and he did not have to dip his lips. I lifted a hand, touched his cheek, fingers grazing over the silken pelt of his beard. It was pleasant, as comfortable as wrapping myself up in the weight of a familiar blanket.

He pulled back, his gaze crawling over my face with a tenderness I had never seen from him before. "We're leaving."

I moistened my lips and gave my head a small shake. "Where would we go?" It was a mistake to ask. Relief flooded his eyes, and I knew I'd given him hope. Hope that could never be fulfilled.

There would be no safe place for us in Penterra. We would be hunted down and found. We could reach Acton or the Isle of Meru on a passenger ship. The voyage would not be easy. The Dark Channel was notorious for its perilous waters. The ships that crossed safely were those that tossed live bait overboard to appease the creatures lurking beneath the black waters. Goats and pigs usually did the trick . . . but sometimes other bait was necessary. Criminals sentenced to death were condemned to the holding cells of ships bound abroad as silage. I shuddered at the thought of their last moments, cast out into monster-ridden waters, even if they were guilty of terrible crimes. The cold rush of the sea, the sharp terror and even sharper tear of teeth . . .

Assuming we could safely reach one of those distant shores, we could not rely on refuge from our allies if our identities were ever discovered. We would be forced back home. There would never be a day lived without looking over our shoulders, without gauging whether what we said or did might give us away.

"There is no escape," I asserted. "This is my life. I won't hide from it. Or run away. Besides. They would find us. Your father . . ." My voice thinned, fading like a dying wind as I shook my head. His father would never let his only son go. He would put bounties on our heads and send the most seasoned trackers after us. "We would never be free."

"I don't care."

I smiled indulgently and lifted a hand, brushing my thumb against his bearded cheek. Now he was behaving like a child. "Yes, you do. You have to care. And so do I. I care about my sisters. I cannot abandon—"

"They're not even your real sisters!"

The words gouged into me like fangs. All my tenderness vanished in a flash. "I can't believe you just said that to me." He sounded like my bullies . . . like his father and those who never accepted me, who made certain I always felt like an outsider: the children who whispered loudly enough for me to hear their words, the housemaids who exchanged looks and rolled their eyes when I was formally announced alongside my sisters. I never thought he would stoop to uttering such words to me, to becoming one of the dark shadows in my life.

He gazed at me intently, imploringly. "Tamsyn, I'm not trying to be hurtful. But it's true. You're not one of them. Not really. You take the beatings. You take their abuse. You don't matter to—"

"Who even are you?" I shook my head. This was not the boy who had filled my head with stories of the other whipping girls who had come before me and gone on to do great things. He began to speak, but I held up a hand, not really interested in his response. "Stop. Enough. This is what I do, what I am. What have I been all these years except for *this*?" I demanded in a heated rush, lifting my arms wide at my sides. "You never objected before, but now, suddenly, it's so very wrong?" I dropped my arms, staring at him accusingly. "Take comfort. At least I won't be a whipping girl anymore. That's finally done."

His eyes went hard, the warm brown sinking to a dark granite. "You know that, do you?"

Anger flashed through me. "Well." The word twisted bitterly around my lips. "Whatever the case, it shouldn't bother you. It never has before."

This time, he flinched, and I felt both satisfied and awful. I didn't want it to be like this. We'd only ever been friends. I didn't want this ugliness between us.

A long moment passed before he pronounced grimly, "You will go through with this, then."

I nodded once, suffering the force of his deep brown eyes, so full of pity and disappointment that I reached inside myself and questioned whether rejecting him—*rejecting us*—was a mistake, after all. I had never disappointed Stig before, and my stomach sank and twisted at doing it now.

"You will marry him," he went on. "Go to his bed. Let him take you north, to those savage lands. Far away from here." He paused a beat. "Far away from me."

I peered into his face, read within the lines of his expression what I had never seen before, what I felt still in the numbing tingle of my lips. It took everything in me not to reach for my mouth, not to touch the echo of him there.

I pressed my hand deeply against my side. "Tomorrow I will do my duty and marry Lord Dryhten. And who knows? Perhaps he won't even want to take me with him."

Once he learns the truth, he might want to get as far away from me as possible.

Stig shook his head, a frustrated little sound breaking loose from him that I felt resonate inside me. "Oh, he'll take you with him." His breath sawed out of him, more animal than human. "He wouldn't leave you behind."

I studied him in the gloom, not sure what to make of that assertion. I was not nearly as confident.

Moistening my lips, I said in a shaky voice, "Life is full of hard choices, and this—"

Stig laughed then—a cruel sound that made me recoil. "Oh, Tamsyn. Is that what you think? That you've *ever* had a choice in anything? You speak of your duty, but what is it really but bondage? You will trade one captor for another tomorrow."

I took a step back, bewildered at why he was punishing me with such unkind words. He was supposed to be my friend, like always, but he might as well be calling me stupid. That was what I heard. My eyes stung, welling up with moisture.

"Arranged marriages happen all the time, Stig. You will likely—"

He cut in. "Who knows how he will treat you? What he will do to you? There will be no one to stop him. He could kill you and no one would do anything about it."

I suddenly felt cold all over, as though I was already a corpse, warm blood draining from me, and I hated him right then. I hated my friend for making this so hard . . . for putting this bitter fear into me.

As though he could read my thoughts, his voice lowered. "Tamsyn." He took my hand in his and gave it a squeeze. "I'm trying to free you . . . to save you."

My lungs ached, my breaths coming harder. It was like he was squeezing my chest and not just my hand. I felt a flicker of something akin to longing. Just as quickly, I crushed the impossible emotion, stomping it down like a bug beneath my shoe.

"Good night, Stig." I pulled my hand free and stepped several paces back from him, chafing my arms, suddenly chilled. My words rang with finality. "I'll see you tomorrow."

Tomorrow, on my wedding day.

Tomorrow, when Stig would be but a face in the crowd, a spectator, a distant shore left behind as I sailed into my new life.

His jaw hardened beneath the shadow of his close-cropped beard, and I knew he finally understood, finally accepted my fate for what it was. A life without him.

"Good night, Tamsyn," he said.

But what I heard was good-bye.

PART II
THE
WEDDING

6

TAMSYN

PREPARATIONS FOR MY WEDDING BEGAN AS SOON AS I awoke the following morning.

It had been a restless night. A long night.

A night of fractured dreams and wide-eyed moments of clawing panic when I gazed into the almost dark contemplating what I was doing, what I was *going* to do . . . what I *had* to do.

After Stig left my chamber, I'd sat in that firelit gloom, seeing *nothing*, seeing *everything* as the fire slowly died in the hearth, ebbing away until the embers turned to smoldering ash. Doubts plagued me as I replayed those moments with Stig, wondering if I had made a terrible mistake, one I would regret for the rest of my life, however much remained of it.

Stig had been it. He was my last chance. His wild offer to run away with me my only hope of escaping this fate. But then I assured myself that I had not made a mistake. I could not abandon my duty and creep away like a thief in the night without even saying farewell to my family, leaving my sisters, deserting them to face and endure what I could not. That was not in me.

I wished the oncoming day away, hoping it would never arrive, willing the dawn into nothingness, for the night to last forever, to hold fast, to hang on, fingers clinging to an edge. Futilely.

Eventually the night let go.

Day came as it always did.

The first glimpse of purpling light, soft and tender as a bruise stealing through the window shutters, was a thing of dread.

As the light grew, so did a rising drum in my chest, beating louder and louder, harder and harder, until I was rubbing between my breasts, urging the sensation to fade.

I did not break my fast in the Great Hall as usual. A tray was delivered, and I forced myself to eat the bread, cheese, and fruit provided. I chewed and ignored that the food tasted like sand on my tongue. I had to eat something. I would need sustenance for the day ahead. The life ahead.

For my wedding night.

The words were a blight, a bleak streak across my mind that brought forth a shudder. I never thought I would have one. A wedding night. A marriage. At least, it hadn't been a foregone conclusion.

My sisters were the ones destined for arranged marriages . . . groomed to be wives and queens. Powerful women married to powerful men. I was merely groomed to take punishment. I winced.

So this would not be so very different then.

The queen's ladies attended me. Beautifully coiffed and fragrant, they bustled around me like bees swarming a hive. I knew them all, of course. These elegant noblewomen were the mothers of the children who had tormented me throughout my youth. Naturally, my peers learned from their mothers that I was different from the rest of them . . . lesser.

And yet now those same women treated me with deference, plying *me* with mulled wine, the spiced sweetness rolling over my tongue and down my throat. I drank greedily, enjoying how relaxed and soft it made me feel inside, numb to what was coming. And perhaps that was their intention—a kindness they would do unto me by rendering me muddled on my wedding day.

My head lolled on the back lip of the tub, eyelids heavy as I enjoyed their gentle ministrations. They bathed me with fragrant soap and oils. Vanilla and bergamot wafted on the air, mingling with the tendrils of steam floating above the water. A low moan escaped me as Lady Frida, the queen's cousin and closest friend, scrubbed my shoulders and arms with a sponge. When prodded, I sat up and leaned forward so she could turn her attention to my back.

"You are fortunate your skin bears no evidence of your . . . er, vocation."

I tensed slightly, my eyes opening, at once understanding her meaning.

It was indeed a marvel that I bore no scars, a fact I did not like to call attention to, for it was something that had bewildered the lord chamberlain.

More than once he had accused me of being a witch—specifically a blood witch, notorious for their flame-red hair, possessing the darkest and most powerful magic. He had warned the king and queen that I had been planted in their midst to bring forth ruin.

Fortunately, thankfully, they'd never given the lord chamberlain's charge any real consideration. In my parents' eyes, my resilience was proof that I was destined to be their whipping girl. If they had been convinced otherwise, a burning pyre would have been my fate. I would have been tossed into the flames, fed to the fire—destroyed. As all magic was.

When the Threshing ended, attention had turned to witchkind, and the war on witches had commenced. Witches, like dragons, had to be hunted to the ground. They were outlawed. Bounties placed on their heads. Blood witch, shadow witch, wood witch, bone witch—all. There was no distinction. They were different. And different was always feared. They were creatures of magic, and that was something *more* than feared. It was reviled. It was not merely dragons or witches who were hunted . . . it was magic.

Magic was the enemy.

The witches who managed to escape fled to the far corners of the kingdom rather than face the same fate as the dragons. Those who did not escape suppressed their magic, buried it deep below the surface, and did their best to blend in with the human population. They became wives, mothers. They were the village seamstress. The local midwife. The cook's assistant. They killed their magic, crushed it to dust within them lest they end up dust them-selves, ashes lost to the wind.

I knew I wasn't supposed to root for them. They were wicked creatures. They used their magic for ill. I'd heard the stories. How they corrupted and twisted minds, stole away babies, seduced good men and women away from their spouses, robbed innocent people of their wealth with a simple spell. Except . . .

Except I had heard other stories, too.

I'd heard they allied with humankind in the war against the dragons. So why had we liked them one moment and not the next? Why had we turned on them?

When I had asked the governess for clarification, she told me to stop asking stupid questions and to let her finish the lesson. So I quit asking. But that did not stop me from thinking about witches and wondering. Envisioning them out there running, hiding, sur-viving. And, wrong or right, I was glad for them. Glad for them to be alive, however few of them remained.

Over the years, the lord chamberlain took my so-called resil-ience as a challenge and got carried away on numerous occasions, meting out my punishment with ferocity, determined to perma-nently score my flesh. I'd gone to bed on those nights bent over in pain, my back throbbing, the skin broken and bruised, lined with bloody and oozing welts, only to wake in the morning healed and recovered—something I did my best to hide lest others begin to believe the lord chamberlain's wild allegations against me. It was a constant battle. Hiding what my body could miraculously do.

With a swift shake of my head, I shoved those thoughts away. At least I no longer had to live with that fear. My days as the whipping girl were over.

You know that, do you?

Stig's words from last night haunted me, echoing in my ears.

My stomach bottomed out, and I closed my eyes, awash with dread. What did I know of Lord Dryhten except that he was a war-lord whose currency was violence and bloodshed? Stig was right. He could very well beat me every day.

"Such soft, lovely skin," Lady Frida murmured as she rinsed the soap from my back. "That barbarian of yours is in for a treat. He has likely never seen the likes in the Borderlands. They're a rough, unrefined people."

The others murmured in assent, and I could not suppress a shudder as I swallowed back the protest that he was not mine. Not yet. Likely not ever. Not even after we were married.

"You're brave," another lady said as she began rinsing my hair of soap. "So very brave."

I knew the words were meant to be complimentary, even encouraging, but I felt the overwhelming urge to cry—or to smack her. The more I was treated like I was headed to my execution, the more it felt like I was, and that was *not* beneficial.

I was helped to stand, everyone concerned that I did not slip in the tub.

I had never been pampered like this a day in my life. Oh, I was treated well—periodic whippings aside. I had been educated, well dressed, well fed, provided with my own chamber in the same quarters as the royal family. And yet no one had ever indulged and pampered me like this.

The queen entered the chamber, a pair of maids trailing behind her bearing my bridal gown, an ornate kirtle of silk-woven brocade in shades of cream, gold, and yellow. It was a glorious sight. I had never worn anything so fine. I did not think the princesses had ever worn anything so fine either.

Lady Frida exclaimed at the sight of it, clapping her hands. "It shall look stunning with your hair."

The queen cut her a glance. "Her hair will not be visible," she reminded her.

"Ah. Of course, yes, yes." She nodded deferentially.

I gulped nervously at that. My final act of hiding. Hopefully, Lord Dryhten would not react too badly when all was revealed.

When *I* was revealed.

The only mother I had ever known eyed my naked body from top to bottom, appraising me. I tried not to fidget, resisting the impulse to cover my breasts. I wasn't particularly modest, but I'd never been unclothed and on display before dozens of eyes.

She nodded, the glowing gemstones set within the circlet nestled in her gold hair catching the light. "I think your husband will be . . . pleased." She uttered this with such clear hope. Not precisely a ringing endorsement.

I swallowed against the thickness in my throat and forced a smile. "Thank you."

"Perhaps we could slip some sejd into his drink," one of the ladies suggested, her implication clear as she eyed me dubiously. *Because I might not be enough to tempt him.*

I took no offense. Honestly, not tempting him was rather reassuring. I feared the bedding. *Better me than my gentle sisters.* That was the only reminder I needed. I squared my shoulders beneath my mother's continued scrutiny. I could do this. He might be a warrior, but so was I. In my own way. Even if Stig disagreed.

"Too risky," my mother pronounced, and I exhaled with relief.

The potion was notoriously effective. Almost too effective. Some who ingested sejd were driven so mad with lust that they required numerous partners before the effects wore off. It was even purported that one man, so overcome, took to the sheep scattering the fields.

They wrapped me in a robe and led me to a bench situated before a dressing table and a mirror. Once I was seated, they set to work on my hair, brushing the wet snarls free.

My dressing robe was unceremoniously parted so that they could rub perfumed lotion on my legs. When hands reached for my belly and breasts, the queen stopped them, slicing a commanding hand through the air.

"No. We don't want her tasting of perfume."

My stomach lurched, and I struggled against the bilious rush in my throat.

Tasting?

My face burned. He would *taste* me? My skin? My breasts? With his mouth and tongue? Was that what husbands did to their wives?

The queen must have read some of my confusion in my face. She seized my hands in hers and chafed my suddenly cold fingers. "Now don't fret. It's only a possibility."

"Aye," Lady Frida agreed. "He will likely not even touch you above the waist. He'll have his way with you and be done in a flash, as most men do."

"If he's deep in his cups," another woman volunteered, "the ordeal will be over in two pumps." She snapped her fingers for emphasis.

The ladies all laughed, their eyes shining with a merriment I could not feel.

Dread sloshed in my stomach like poison. None of this felt real. I was accustomed to enduring, but this was something else entirely. Invasive in a whole new way. I would be taking him *inside* me. A warrior from the Borderlands. We would join. Mate. Become one. The only escape from each other would be death.

I couldn't breathe.

"Look at her! Her face has lost all color. None of you are helping with your talk of the bedding," the queen said, chastising her maids. "Leave us. All of you. Be gone."

With murmurs of apology, they all filed from the chamber. She sank down beside me on the cushioned bench, taking my hand again and giving it a comforting squeeze.

"You've been a gift to me, Tamsyn. From the moment you were found in the bailey in that basket, you were my daughter." She bent her head and pressed an affectionate kiss to the back of my hand.

I blinked away the sudden sting in my eyes. I knew the story well. My story.

The young, tenderhearted queen had been increasing with her first child when I was found. She'd always possessed a soft spot for children, wanting several of her own, but her sentimentality was especially acute then. The moment she lifted me from my blanketed basket and held me in her arms, she had insisted on keeping me.

She had been my champion from the start, claiming me as her

own despite those who called it unseemly for an orphan with no known origins to be raised among the future offspring of the Penterran throne.

The naysayers, led by the lord regent, had almost convinced the king to ignore his new queen's wishes and hand me over to a peasant family, to be brought up alongside their brood, another body to help them in the fields. But then the notion had been put into the king's head that *I* could serve as a royal whipping girl.

The conversation had already begun, after all. The search was in the works. It was a long-standing tradition among royals. With one child on the way—and there would certainly be more to come for the young couple—the burgeoning royal family would have need. Children, even royal ones, required discipline, and it was forbidden for anyone to lift a finger against the divine issue. It would be death for anyone who dared. It was customary for royal children to use a proxy, here and in other kingdoms, even across the sea in Acton. Presumably even north of the Crags, in Veturland, the land of our enemy.

Oh, there were concerns over the mystery of my parentage, to be sure, but the queen declared it fate that I'd materialized out of nowhere. No one saw anyone leave me in the middle of the courtyard, abandoned in a basket. My appearance was almost . . . magic. A sign. A cosmic gift. They would need a royal whipping child. And there I was.

I was brought into the fold then. A princess on the outside, attired in silks. A soldier on the inside, serving the Crown.

Today would be my final test. Once done, I would be Lady Dryhten . . . whipping girl no more.

Fortifying myself with the reminder that we all had our burdens to bear—even my sisters would one day wed as commanded—I studied the queen, my mother. Love softened her gaze as she looked at me. Love for me. It was bittersweet consolation. I would miss her. Miss all of them. This was more than marrying a stranger and subjecting myself to him. It was taking myself across the kingdom to where I knew no one. Where I would be alone, an outsider in the eyes of everyone.

She tucked a damp strand of hair behind my ear. "We all have our duties in life. Mine was to cross the sea and marry the young king of Penterra and strengthen the bonds between our countries." Her eyes had a faraway glimmer as she exhaled. "Now it is your turn. I know this Border King is not the man you envisioned for yourself, but—"

"I've never envisioned a man for myself," I interrupted, so very startled at the notion.

My life ran parallel to my sisters'. Once they were gone from the palace, once they walked their own individual paths, my course had always been vague in my mind. A fogged-over path that led into a dark and unknown wood.

Unbidden, the image of Stig flashed across my mind. Strong and noble Stig. His deep brown eyes. The pressure of his mouth on mine. The sensation of his short-cropped beard beneath my fingers. I shifted my weight uneasily on the bench. I should not be thinking of him now.

Mama looked at me in surprise. "No? Not even . . . Stig?"

I flinched. Had I said or done something to give away my thoughts?

"Stig?" I echoed. Not until last night had I ever considered him as anything more than a very dear friend. He had kissed me. I'd had no idea he harbored such intense feelings for me.

Now, looking at the queen, I marveled that she had seen what I had not.

"Yes, Stig," she confirmed.

"No. Never." At least not before he'd appeared in my bedchamber last night. "I never thought marriage even a consideration for me until the princesses were wed."

She gave a satisfactory nod. "Well, that's for the best. I'd hate for you to suffer a broken heart."

"I won't suffer," I declared . . . and wondered if that was true.

Indeed, something felt broken inside me as I headed into my future.

Her smile turned tender, encouraging. "Perhaps it will not be so very bad. You will be the wife of a powerful man. And," she added, "he's not an unattractive man." She wrinkled her nose. "If you like that sort."

That sort. The hard and menacing sort.

If he doesn't kill me when he learns he has been tricked.

As though she could read my mind, the queen warned, "Keep the wimple over your hair and the veil in place." Her grip on my hand tightened. "Do not let him see your face until the deed is done."

"He will eventually discover—"

"Not until after the bedding."

The bedding.

"And then," she added, still staring intently at me, willing me to accept what she was saying, "it will be too late."

It will be too late.

Too late to change that I was married to the Beast.

Too late to save me from my fate—to save me from him.

"Should we be worried how he might react? What if he—"

"Oh." She waved a hand dismissively. "He will come around. He's here to sow goodwill. He will accept you as his wife. You will see."

Hopefully that was true. I nodded dully, retreating inside myself.

I fought to swallow. To breathe. A difficult task when contemplating *that* portion of the evening, when he would climb into bed with me . . .

I gulped against a giant lump in my throat and shuddered at the idea of something so intimate happening between that brute and myself.

I recalled colliding into the hard wall of him when he caught me emerging from behind the painting. The thick arms and hard hands and that deep, rasping voice that felt like a tremor running through me as he growled: *I see this palace comes equipped with spies.*

I recalled it all distinctly. The sensation. His scent filling my nose. Wind and earth and horseflesh. The hot animal ripple of my skin. The way it felt to be caught up in his arms. The way my body had arched against the massive pulsing slab of him. The way he had towered over me and made me feel small for the first time in my life. And it had been only for a few moments. Stig's kiss lasted considerably longer and was much more intimate, and yet it left less of an impression.

Even now, the following day, I could recall little of it specifically. Meanwhile, the memory of the Beast flashed through me like a bolt of lightning across the sky. I supposed it made sense. I was nervous. Afraid of the unknown. My life loomed ahead, stretching out long and winding and hazy. He was the only certainty.

Shortly following the wedding, I would progress to the marriage bed, where he would join me. I moistened my suddenly dry lips. I was untried in the act of bedplay, but I knew how to handle physical discomfort. Pain was fleeting. I could take it. I would survive.

"You understand, Tamsyn?" Mama pressed. "I need to hear you say you will keep your face covered."

"I understand." Now that he had seen my face and believed me to be a servant, this was more critical than ever. "The wimple and veil stay in place until after the bedding." *After the bedding.* Then the hiding would end. And . . . everything else would begin. I swallowed reflexively.

A smile curved her lips. "That's a good girl." She was all efficiency again. "Now. Let us finish preparing you."

She summoned the ladies, and they resumed their work on me.

I was shrouded head to toe. My forearms and hands—pale, trembling appendages no matter how I tried to control their movements—were the only things visible beneath the loose sleeves of the kirtle.

The wimple covered my hair and revealed only the circle of my face, and then, for good measure, a gauzy veil was added that left just a vague outline of my features. I stood in front of the mirror, staring out through the sheer material that cast a miasma of gold over my reflection. I was unidentifiable. Only an indistinct countenance behind a veil.

"Fret not," the queen assured me, tugging on the fabric and checking the thin gold circlet around my head to make certain it was secure. "It has been explained that this is the custom. He won't expect to see your face."

I nodded, glad she could not see my expression either. Glad no one could. If even a fraction of my mounting panic was glimpsed, Lady Frida would be diving for the sejd to make certain I was properly agreeable to the impending bedding. *No, thank you.* I would do this without any potions or tonics. It would be *me* going into this fate and not some dazed and befuddled version of myself, so out of my head I would willingly couple with anyone.

We departed the chamber and wound our way down the castle steps and through the Great Hall. One of the queen's ladies waited there with a cloak. "Don't wish you to catch an ague, Your Majesty. A strange chill has taken the land. I blame it on the arrival of these barbarians." The woman sniffed as she settled the cloak over the queen's shoulders, pulling the fur-lined hood over her head.

"I'm sure it has nothing to do with our guests." A cloak was offered to me, but the queen waved it away. "We don't wish to ruin the efforts we have taken with her appearance." Before stepping outside, she turned to me. "You can do this, daughter."

I nodded.

She clasped my shoulders. "You must go the rest of the way alone."

I would take the long march to the chapel on my own, through the deepening day. I understood this. There were some walks you must go alone in life. This would be one of them.

I passed through the double doors, and a cheer went up that I absorbed like a physical blast. The din was deafening. Flowers were tossed. Colorful pennants waved. People filled the bailey, all come to watch a princess of Penterra make her momentous walk to the doors of the chapel, where the Beast of the Borderlands waited for her.

Waits for me.

We would enter the church together. The evening air was indeed cool, opaque, hinting prematurely at the winter to come. I counted my steps to ease my anxiety.

Sixty-seven, sixty-eight.

I recognized Lord Dryhten's form across the distance, taller and bigger than everyone else, even if I could not clearly make out his face.

Ninety-three, ninety-four.

With my vision impaired, I proceeded carefully past the onlookers, their faces featureless smudges against the darkening night.

One hundred and thirty-nine. One hundred and forty.

I was almost at his side when I stumbled, my slippers tripping over a bouquet of flowers someone had tossed. *Hell's teeth.* This veil was a nuisance. I longed to yank it off, but that would only result in a far greater nuisance—this warrior uncovering the perfidy being played upon him and running me through with his sword.

He stepped forward and caught me, one steel arm sliding around me.

Dread unfurled in my chest as I looked at him through the gossamer fabric. He was so near I could feel the hot puff of his breath.

This close, the most prominent features of his face stood out starkly through the sheer material brushing my nose. The dark slash of his eyebrows. The deep-set eyes. The nose that might have been large on someone else but fit his face perfectly. His precise expression eluded me, but he was definitely *not* smiling. Did this man even know how to smile?

His stare cut into me, and I feared how much he could see of me. Enough to know I was the girl from the chancery that he had caught spying?

I felt his scrutiny in my bones, in the very marrow of me. The intensity of his gaze drilled deep, attempting to see past my veil.

This is it. This is when he will recognize I am not Feena or Sybilia or Alise. He will know he holds a fraud in his arms.

"Shall we?" he asked in that deep voice, which I felt like a lick of heat on my skin.

I waited a heartbeat and then nodded.

He slid his arm from around me and picked up my hand, interlacing his warm fingers with mine.

Together, we entered the chapel.

7
FELL

THE HIGH PRIEST WAITED AT THE ALTAR.

I did not glance at the assembled guests as we strode down the center aisle. The king. The queen. The lord regent. Arkin and a handful of my warriors. A few nobles of the court. I did not look at any of them. My focus was on the woman at my side. A prize for the Borderlands.

My prize.

Not only was I marrying a stranger. I was marrying her sight unseen. She was covered from head to toe. Only her hand in mine was visible, and I gazed down at it curiously, the pads of my fingers rubbing against the soft skin, which was not the milk white that I had expected of one of the cosseted princesses of Penterra, whom I'd spied from a distance, but rather sun-kissed, almost . . . golden.

Her fingers were long and slender, the nails short, buffed to a healthy shine. Faint blue veins crisscrossed at her wrist and along the back of her hand. I tracked those veins, a strange awareness seizing me. My eyes began to ache as I scrutinized the meandering blue web . . . the faint rush of blood whispering beneath her skin. Not only could I hear it in my ears . . . I felt it, too.

Impossible. I blinked and swallowed thickly. I was not myself. Had not been since I'd arrived here. I was eager to take my bride and leave, return home, to a world of cool mists and fog-swathed hills, to the things I knew—starting with myself.

I stopped in front of the priest. Behind him loomed an altar, a great monstrosity constructed of overlapping iridescent discs in an assortment of colors. Dragon scales. Most were shades of purple-winking onyx, but there were several bronze discs, and occasionally blue, green, and a pale gray. A few were even red. The rarest kind, I knew, as they came from fire-breathing dragons.

The dragon graveyards to the north had been picked clean of the scales a century ago. They fetched a hefty price, as they were used to build shields, armor, weaponry, or, in this case . . . altar displays.

The sight evoked a deep satisfaction in me. A dragon had killed my parents. Incinerated them so that not even a proper burial could be performed. At least that was the assumption. There had been no remains found in that den. I was saved by Balor the Butcher before I could be finished off, too.

I felt only grim approval as I gazed at what amounted to relics of a species that had taken everything from me. So many had perished in the Threshing. I could have easily been another, not even a footnote in history.

I was one of the fortunate ones. A survivor. My father, a widower and without issue, believed finding me was destiny. His and mine. That I was fated to be his son, his successor. A child strong enough to survive a dragon had to be the future leader of the Borderlands.

The priest began to speak over us, and I pulled my attention away from the ornate altar. My bride and I stood shoulder to shoulder. I tried to focus, but she proved too distracting, and I continued to slide glances at her, as though I could see beneath her shroud.

I might tower over her, but she wasn't short. She stood taller than most men. I wish I had paid closer attention when I'd observed the princesses in the Great Hall yesterday so that I might guess at which one hid beneath the bothersome veil. I knew they were all fair-haired with fine features. They had seemed delicate, as Arkin pointed out, but this woman's hand in mine felt sturdy. Strong but with a definite tremble. I could not stop myself from stroking the back of it once in a reassuring swipe. I might be known throughout the realm as the Beast, but I would not devour her.

I had no shortage of women in my life. There was nothing like the blood-pumping exhilaration of surviving a battle, of emerging from the blood and fog and realizing you're not dead. There were plenty of sword maidens in my army eager to hit the furs following a fight. Of course, a gentle princess would know nothing of fucking like that. I would have to approach my wife with care.

True, this was no love match. It was not even a *like* match. It was an arrangement. An alliance to strengthen my position against the growing threats to Penterra. When war came—and it was coming—I wanted my voice heard. As son-in-law of the king, I was guaranteed that.

I realized that she was a pawn in all of this, and I would try to honor her as my wife and shield her from the harsh reality of life in the Borderlands, but if she ended up being as fragile as Arkin predicted . . . I winced. Well. War brought sacrifice. That was the nature of it.

The richly robed priest turned to accept a long rope of vines from one of his acolytes. He presented it to us. I stood uncertainly, and he indicated we should both present our arms to him.

My bride seemed to know the practice. Releasing my hand, she pushed back her loose sleeve to the elbow, stretching out her arm. Yet another custom I was not familiar with, and it only reinforced just how far apart and different the Borderlands were from this place . . . how far apart she and I were.

Our arms stretched out side by side. Hers slender and shorter. Mine thick, roped with sinew and pronounced veins and sprinkled with dark hair.

There was a flash of steel, and I tensed, ready to deflect, until I realized it was all part of the ceremony. The priest took a jeweled dagger from another one of his acolytes and positioned it over my palm, carving an X in the center. Instantly, blood swelled and puddled in the cup of my palm.

Turning, he did the same to the princess, cutting her tender skin. Blood sprang from the open wound, dark and viscous. My jaw clenched. I did not like anyone taking a blade to her, sanctioned ritual or no.

Not a movement or sound escaped her, though. Surprising. A pampered princess raised in the protection of this palace had likely never suffered a splinter.

Our hands were forced back together, slashed palms kissing, blooding us. Warmth centered there, pulsing hotly where we joined, mingling. Energy spread up my arm and throughout the rest of me like tinder catching fire.

Did she feel it, too? This revitalizing heat?

A pervasive cold clung to the chapel. It was unusual this far south. I was accustomed to it in the Borderlands, but down here, it was all sunshine and balmy winds.

The wedding guests burrowed within ermine-trimmed cloaks, their hands encased in fur-lined kid gloves. Stone walls kept out the worst of the frigid air, but there was no hearth in which to light a fire in the chapel. The guests shivered, except for my warriors, who were well accustomed to the bitter winters of the north. Even our summers held a hint of a chill. Our hearths burned year-round. The perpetual damp clenched cold and hard around the bones. Fog flowed and ebbed over the hills, never vanishing entirely.

And yet now, in this moment, with her hand locked in mine, our arms aligned, our blood mingling, I felt only blistering heat.

The vine rope came next, wrapping around us, starting above the elbows and winding down to our fingers. The greenery twisted like a snake, holding us captive, binding us together. A tenuous chain, but it felt as solid as iron as the priest proclaimed the final vows, marrying us. Two strangers bound together for the rest of our lives.

Life had never seemed so long.

8

ᴛAMSYN

IT FELT LIKE EVERYONE IN THE ENTIRE KINGDOM HAD crowded into the chamber with me. They observed me with a well-satisfied air, their eyes glassy and heavy-lidded from copious amounts of wine and revelry, their faces flushed from the gluttonous feast that had been provided following the wedding.

Thankfully, I had not attended the feast. Even if I could have kept food down, it would have been difficult to consume a meal with a veil covering my mouth.

My absence was explained away. Prior to the ceremony, the lord regent had explained to Lord Dryhten that it was not customary for the bride to attend the feast. Another deception. Now so very many of them. Not that I regretted missing the meal. Sitting beside *him*, worrying about my every move, my every word, that unforeseeable thing I would inadvertently do to give myself away. Yes. I could miss out on that.

My fingers curled, digging into the mattress beneath me. Rich drapes of thick, impenetrable brocade hung to my right and left and behind the tall headboard, effectively curtaining me. Only the drapes at the foot of the bed had not yet been pulled close. I peered out through that yawning opening. My husband would enter the bed there—*our marriage bed. My husband.* How could such words now be a normal part of my vocabulary?

I stared out at the wedding guests lined up along the walls, witnesses to this final rite. The marriage would not be official until it was consummated. It could still be overturned. Technically. I knew that. Traditionally, three witnesses were all that was required to legitimize a union, though, so this many observers was definitely overkill. Spectators come for the show, like wolves at the scent of blood.

I easily spotted the king and queen, resplendent in their full regalia. Also in attendance: the lord regent, the lord chamberlain, the high priest who had married us, high nobles of the king's council, and nobles of court, including several of the ladies who'd helped prepare me for the day. I would not be surprised if a stable lad hovered in a corner. A bitter laugh welled up in my throat, which I managed to suppress. No sight of the princesses. Naturally. Maidens were not allowed to witness a bedding ceremony, and even without that rule, they were being kept out of sight for obvious reasons.

My last glimpse of Lord Dryhten had been as I was swept away by the queen and Lady Frida following our vows. The king and the lord regent flanked him, speaking intently, deep in a conversation that he had not appeared to be following, though he was following *me*. His gaze tracked me over their heads.

That was hours ago. And now here I was, trying so very hard *not* to feel like a sacrificial lamb.

A couple of minstrels sat in the corner, playing the lyre and drumming on a tabor. I struggled to swallow against my constricting throat. It was a proper party to watch me get tupped by the Beast of the Borderlands.

My husband.

I scowled beneath my veil. At least I had that in my favor—a protective barrier concealing my expressions from gawking onlookers. And from him.

A lady laughed at something a gentleman murmured in her ear. She swatted him with her fan as she took a sip from her goblet. Her eyes found me in the center of the bed, and she lifted her goblet in salute, her lips glistening red from her drink.

A sour taste filled my mouth. My life, my sacrifice, was a diversion for others. A joke. Even if I served the realm. Even if I was equal to any warrior. I swept a glare over all of them. These people didn't see me that way. Only my family appreciated me.

I supposed that was the nature of sacrifice. Was it ever appreciated in the moment?

In this, doing *this*, I had not earned respect. Had I thought I would?

I exhaled, reminding myself that I was not doing this for appreciation or recognition. One did the right thing simply because it was the right thing. If I was expecting appreciation or recognition from the nobles of the Penterran court, I would be waiting forever.

The only other person who looked unhappy with the situation was the lord chamberlain, and I surmised that this was because he'd lost his whipping girl. The bitterness in my mouth faded a bit. Some good would come of this. I would no longer have to endure the man's hitched breath in my ear every time he flogged me.

Now you will only endure the Beast.

I pulled the coverlet up to my chin, feeling myself shrink into the mattress at the prospect. The moment was nigh. My gaze landed on the queen. She stared intently at me as though there was no veil between us at all. I heard her voice in my head: *Do not let him see your face until the deed is done.*

I wrapped that reminder around myself. Unclenching my fingers until they no longer felt numb, I lowered the coverlet to the top of my chest with an expelled breath, telling myself not to appear so skittish.

Countless judging eyes assessed me as I waited. Bloodlust hung in the air. They expected a show. And not just the spectacle of the bedding—although they would not hate that. They wanted to see what was to come *after* the bedding. The people in this room knew the truth. They knew who was—and wasn't—behind the veil, and they knew the fallout was going to be spectacular once the Beast knew, too.

They craved that inescapable unmasking. We had tricked him. All of us. They expected rage and violence and visual confirmation of every rumor and legend they had ever heard about him. They did not realize that they were to be excluded from that revelation, however.

The queen had already promised me that the chamber would be cleared of all witnesses immediately following the bedding. It made sense. Lord Dryhten's ego would already be smarting. No need to add to his inevitable humiliation by including dozens of witnesses to the uncomfortable situation. The king and the lord regent would do the unmasking and offer forth explanations.

The queen had smiled at me amid her reassurances. "We shall explain to him that you, too, are a daughter of the throne. As precious to us as any child born of our line."

Her words were meant to reassure me, and I wanted to believe her.

The door to the room opened, and he emerged, stepping inside with thudding steps. The sight was not comforting.

He was not alone. Two of his warriors accompanied him. The bearded older man from the chancery and a sword maiden who just might have stood eye to eye with me. The sides of her head were shaved, the top portion of her black hair braided and pulled back with a single band. Ink crawled over the brown skin of her exposed scalp. The details of the design were indistinct through the veil and across the distance, and I longed to examine them more closely.

Lord Dryhten turned in a small circle, surveying the chamber with slow, even steps. The evening air found its way inside through the half-dozen arrow slits in the walls. It felt cooler than it had moments before. Like this Northman had brought the chill with him.

"Quite a crowd," he observed. "And this is necessary? Another one of your customs?"

Did his voice sound irritated?

"Witnesses are required," the priest replied.

"And they must number in the dozens?"

The priest sent the king a swift look, because the answer, of course, was no. My father gave him a nearly imperceptible nod. The holy man broke rank to approach my husband. They stood close and spoke for a few moments, their words inaudible, especially over the building roar in my ears.

My husband. My thoughts tumbled over this new reality, my mind still floundering to grasp it.

I was married to him.

Lord Dryhten finished with the priest and stared hard at me, in the center of the vast bed. Never had I felt so small and vulnerable—not even with my back bared as I was flogged.

There were always witnesses in those moments. My sisters were forced to watch my punishments, of course. That was the whole point—for them to watch and feel remorse for their behavior. Often there were others around, too. Servants. Tutors. Other children. Anyone really. Just as I wasn't new to vulnerability, I wasn't new to being at the center of an audience, but this was a different kind of attention.

Dryhten could see nothing of my body buried under the coverlet, and yet it felt as though he peeled back all the layers and looked beneath, to the very core of me. Hair unbound. Body naked and shaking. My cheeks a revealing red. I didn't need to see my reflection to know that. When my face felt this hot, it burned as red as my hair.

The priest said something. Words I missed, because the only thing I could concentrate on was the man watching me from the foot of the bed.

My husband looked sharply at him. "What do you mean her veil remains on? Still?"

The priest lifted a hand in supplication. "It is our custom, my lord. Not until your vows have been consummated and you are truly one may you have the privilege of—"

With a grunt of laughter, Dryhten let his head fall back as he looked up at the ceiling beams. "Another fucking custom."

I flinched and glanced wildly around the room for the others' reactions. I'd never heard anyone speak so crassly among such elevated and important society.

But then, the Lord of the Borderlands was important, too. Just not important enough to marry one of my sisters.

My father stepped forward as though to grasp the end of a

fraying rope that threatened to break loose of its mooring. "Alas, it is our way. The bride remains veiled throughout the bedding to show her humility to her new husband. 'Tis a long-standing tradition we cannot break."

Until that moment, I had not realized just how adept a liar the king was. When he had said diplomacy was necessary in the ruling of a kingdom, I had not grasped his meaning. Now I understood. He meant lying. Subterfuge.

The Beast held my father's unwavering gaze for a long moment before sending a scowl around the chamber, as though he might find corroboration that this was truly a tradition in the faces of the onlookers.

Everyone merely stared, their expressions stoic. No one moved. Not a hint of the treachery at play was revealed. Too much was at stake.

Stig's glowering face leapt out at me from the crowd, and my heart jumped into my throat. *No. No. No.* He must have slipped inside the room after Dryhten. I would have noticed him before. Make that two displeased faces now. It was not just the lord chamberlain's. But Stig's was the only face I cared about.

He stood rigidly, a slat of wood among the rest of the bodies. I willed him away. Anywhere else. I did not want him here. Not for this. Apparently I did have a limit . . . and Stig being feet away as this warrior climbed into bed with me was it.

I tried to convey this to him, staring intently through the veil covering my face, willing him to leave. He did not look at me, though. He glowered only at my husband, and I swallowed down this new misery, telling myself I would survive this shame and embarrassment because surviving was what I did.

The sword maiden stepped forward and murmured something for Dryhten's ears alone. Whatever she said eased some of the harshness from his features. He gave a single nod, and I was vastly curious what the woman had said to calm the Beast. Perhaps she could give me some tips.

He stepped closer to the bed, stopping before the footboard and staring hard at me for a long moment. My bandaged palm tingled, and I pressed it into the mattress as though that might quell the sensation.

I wondered if this was it. Was this the moment when he would say "enough" and demand to see me—the princess he had been promised? The one whom—let's face it—I was not.

And then what?

He would reject me, of course. The marriage would not hold without consummation. I knew that. So did he. So did everyone. Would that not be for the best?

There could be no goodwill following a betrayal such as this. Had the king and queen and lord regent truly considered this? I told myself that they must have. The queen had seemed so confident that this was the right course. I was no mastermind on governing a kingdom. Certainly, they knew better than I did.

Lord Dryhten looked away from me then, glancing down to his hand where we had been blooded. He flexed his long, tapering fingers in the air, stretching and curling them inward as though he had never felt this part of himself before, as though they were new to him, foreign appendages.

My own palm throbbed in response. Little eddies of awareness swept through my body, pebbling over my skin, running through blood and muscle and bone.

Would it always be there? This strange, bewildering ache? This alertness? A bond between us even if our marriage did not stand?

I assumed this bedding would happen. We were on a path, propelled forward by a force greater than us. Like two lodestones drawn together. There was no going back. Our marriage would be consummated and legitimatized in the eyes of all, and he would take me north with him.

But what if he does not? the voice whispered in my ear. *What if he leaves without me?*

Would he return to his home far away, leaving me behind with this gaping wound? The echo of him in the palm of my hand . . . in *me?*

I held my breath, waiting for his next move, waiting to see the outcome, whether he would push the matter or accept that he would have to bed me without seeing my face.

Silence pervaded the chamber, the soft stringing of the lyre and the rhythmic beating of the tabor the only things audible over my rasping breath. The flames within the wall sconces cast patches of light and flickering shadows over everyone's faces.

At last, he gave an almost-imperceptible nod. "Very well."

Very well.

It was happening. I would remain hidden. Veil in place.

He moved then, undressing himself without a shred of modesty. Startled glances were exchanged all around.

His leather armor came off, followed by his under tunic. He passed them to his sword maiden. The bearded man who accompanied him maintained an expression of disapproval, arms crossed as though he wanted nothing to do with the situation.

I struggled to swallow against my tightening throat. My eyes drank in the impressive expanse of the Beast's bronze skin, replete with hard lines and tantalizing swells of muscle. He was big. Warrior big and seething with raw power. My hands could endlessly roam those shoulders and that broad chest for a long time and still not touch everything. Not that my hands would ever dare.

My belly squeezed and dipped the way it did when we went sledding behind the palace in the brief winter months, wind and earth whooshing past in a blur as we launched ourselves down hills. Except this was no fleeting sensation. My stomach twisted and turned and dove over and over again as my gaze ate him up.

His boots hit the floor, one after the other, and I jerked at each thud, releasing tiny gasps that sent the fabric hiccupping over my face. Even that simple action made him look tempting, his muscles undulating with his easy movements. And I wasn't the only one to think so.

Several ladies—and even men—watched him with wide-eyed yearning. He was beautiful. Intricate warrior ink traveled down his neck to creep over one shoulder and down his arm and chest. I couldn't see his back, but I suspected there was more of that there, too.

Not a scar marred the inked bronze skin. Unusual, perhaps, for a battle-hardened warlord who'd spent years defending our borders. His body was a honed weapon. A marvel. And yet his face held me prisoner. Captive. Those fathomless eyes and a mouth too tender for a man forged in war.

And he is about to be mine.

My heart stuttered and then jolted into a fierce hammer. No. *Not mine.*

He didn't voluntarily give himself to this—to *me*. He believed he was giving himself to one of my sisters.

I swallowed miserably, convinced this wouldn't end well. At least not for me. The king and queen would insist they had honored his request and given him a royal daughter. He would not be able to dispute it. He would be married to me (and bedded). There would be no severing that. His wrath could go nowhere.

Nowhere but toward me.

His hands settled on his breeches, and I could not think on the matter any longer. He was undressing completely? In front of everyone?

I strangled on a gasp.

The sound went undetected as other choked cries charged through the air.

"My lord!" the priest cried in affront. "You need not remove your clothes in their entirety—"

He gave a rebellious slant to his head. "Everyone here wants a show," he replied with shameless candor. "Then I shall give them one."

His leather breeches were shoved down and removed with surprising speed, leaving him *abundantly* naked and on display.

I had never seen a man fully unclothed, but I looked my fill now.

Shocked whispers rolled through the audience. Several gentlemen tried to cover the eyes of the ladies nearest them, but the

women evaded their efforts, determined to gawk unreservedly at
this man who was so different from every other man in our orbit.

He lacked all modesty as he placed his breeches in his sword
maiden's waiting hands. Not a stitch of clothing covered him. Only
a necklace touched his skin. A black opal, gleaming dark as the
night sky, threaded with green and red and blue. I had never seen
the like.

My mouth dried, then watered. Those legs, thickly muscled,
were even more impressive without the snug leather encasing
them. Tree trunks.

I was too curious not to look *there. And why not?*

No one could see *where* I was looking. The word *cock* floated on
the air.

My gaze dipped as though commanded. Oh. *Ohhh.*

The titillated whispers instantly made sense. He was big everywhere. Stirringly daunting. I wet my lips in trepidation . . . and
something else. Something that ignited a winding flame through
me, quickening in my belly.

I had spent enough time in the stables with the horses. I had
even spied on a stable lad and a kitchen maid in an empty stall once.
I hadn't planned to do it. It just happened. I heard them. Uncertain
of the noise, I investigated, peering through the cracks between
the slats of a neighboring stall. I watched the lad's bare buttocks
flex as he pumped between a pair of plump thighs. They'd both
uttered heated words that stung my cheeks, and I was left with the
impression that copulation, at least for some, was not an altogether
dreadful thing.

I understood how fornication worked. At least the mechanics of
it. The desire, however, the physical stirring, had eluded me. Perhaps not anymore, however, if the butterflies in my stomach served
any indication.

Although desire clearly did not afflict him now.

Well-endowed though he was, he was not in a state of arousal.
I grimaced. Evidently a shrouded, shapeless sack of a figure on a
bed and a roomful of voyeurs did nothing for his passions. It was

a grim realization. He did not want to be doing this. But he would. He would do his duty. Dark amusement twisted through me. It was the theme of my life, and I guessed we would have that in common.

He placed one knee on the bed, the mattress sinking slightly beneath his not-inconsiderable body. His hands followed, bearing his weight. First one, then the next, moving, climbing up the bed.

My chest squeezed tight. Too tight for my fluttering heart. That pull at the center was back again, tugging insistently, pulling me toward some unknown fate. I scampered to the side of the bed, avoiding contact with him. It was regrettable and silly. The moment I moved, I knew that. Self-preservation, however, was its own mistress.

He could not be avoided.

This could not be avoided. Lodestones, I thought again, feeling a little dizzy.

He turned around on the bed, reaching to close the curtains and grant us a semblance of privacy.

"My lord." The priest spoke up, a touch of urgency to his voice. "If you please, leave the drapes—"

"I do not please," he growled. "I've enjoyed enough of your customs for the day. Now it is my turn. *I* shall bed my wife without spectators. That is my custom."

I shifted uneasily, panicked at the thought of him bedding me in the privacy of this curtained bed. Would he remove my veil then, away from prying eyes and without anyone to object? I pushed up on the bed a fraction, craning my neck, searching desperately for the queen, hoping for a glimpse of her that might give me some direction. Her voice resounded through my mind: *Do not let him see your face until the deed is done.* And yet what if he insisted? What if he overpowered me?

"This is highly irregular, my lord," the king broke in, placing a reassuring hand on his lady queen's arm. "How can we be certain you will consummate the union? That you will not remove our daughter's veil?"

"You may be certain, Your Majesty. I shall do my duty and not

disturb the princess's veil in the process. It's not her face that matters here, after all. Is it?"

I flinched at that, but he was correct, of course. My face meant
nothing. *I* meant nothing. It was only my body that mattered.

A bubble of mirthless laughter welled up in my throat. If only
he could remember his words when I later revealed my face to him.

Lord Dryhten's words seemed to satisfy the king. He exchanged
looks with the queen and the lord regent and then nodded his blessing.

Without waiting for further comment, my husband yanked the
drapes closed, sealing us inside for the night.

9

TAMSYN

WITH THE CURTAINS DRAWN, MY WORLD WAS DARKER, but not without visibility. Not completely. The opening above the bed staved off total darkness.

I sat up and inched back until I bumped against the headboard and could go no farther. My heartbeat filled my ears in a whooshing pulse. One of my hands stretched above me. My fingers curled into the smooth-worn wood, hanging on as though I were caught up in a storm—or bracing for an impending one.

He crouched at the end of the bed, watching me, reminding me of the Beast he was purported to be. Not just in name, but in fact. A great, coiled animal on the verge of springing, attacking his prey.

I took a gulp of air, marveling at how I could feel so warm even in the uncommon chill of the chamber. Not a sound reached us from outside the bed. We were sealed inside our own little cocoon, tucked away from the rest of the world, and I was grateful for that. Dread gnawed at me as I thought about all the people out there. I absorbed that fact in a way I couldn't before, not until this moment, and a surge of bile rose in my throat thinking about them just beyond the drapes, listening to us, straining for a peep or a glimpse beyond the curtains, relishing in my suffering. Because that was what they wanted. They didn't want silence.

They wanted to see. They wanted to hear. They wanted drama.

The air inside the curtained bed was murky and soft. Of course it was less murky for him. A veil didn't cover his face.

We remained poised as we were for several moments, frozen in a standoff, not moving or speaking, and I wondered if he had in fact lied to the king. Perhaps he had no intention of consummating and making this marriage between us real at all.

I was sifting through that possibility in my mind when he finally spoke. "We best get to this, hmm?"

So not a possibility. A certainty.

We would do it, then.

Swallowing, I nodded. It was for the best. Not doing it presented a whole host of complications.

He pushed off and crawled on his hands and knees toward me. "Do you lack a voice along with a face, lass?" he asked, his voice a husky scrape on the air. Evidently he, too, preferred not to be overheard. At least we were in accord on that.

I commanded myself to relax and eased from my position huddled in front of the headboard. "I am ready."

As ready as I will ever be.

Apparently my agreement was all he needed to hear. One of his big hands circled my ankle and dragged me down the bed onto my back in a single smooth move. I gave a small yelp, aware that the motion swept the voluminous folds of my nightgown up to my knees.

His gaze rested on the prim laces tied at my throat. "They did not dress you for enticement."

I recalled his dormant manhood and wondered if he was finding it difficult to get up the nerve to bed me.

He braced a hand on either side of my head and leaned over me, all that nakedness radiating heat like a stove, flushing me with warmth, and I sucked in a lungful of air.

"Who is in there, hmm?" The words fanned directly over my lips, and I felt the scald of them through the gossamer fabric.

I trembled—partly from the effect of his proximity and partly because the question sent a bolt of panic through me. *No one he wants.*

Shoving that aside as a problem for later, I moistened my lips and replied, "I am your bride, my lord."

A faint cough from outside the bed curtains reminded me that dozens of people were just beyond. Listening. Waiting in anticipation. I sent the drapes a baleful glance.

He followed the turn of my head. "Ignore them."

I shuddered. "I will try."

The warm fall of his breath ruffled the thin veil against my cheek. Our faces were so close. His features were vague and obscured, but I recalled them distinctly. The deep-set eyes beneath slashing eyebrows. The square jaw. The wide, unsmiling mouth.

His hands went to the laces at the throat of my modest nightgown, and I tucked my hands under my hips, quelling the impulse to slap at his questing fingers.

He made short work of the ties, his deft ministrations pulling them loose, peeling my nightgown open, exposing me to his gaze.

He went still.

I tensed, forcing my reticence aside. This was the obligation of a wedding night, and I always fulfilled my obligations. Not that the open vee of my nightgown fully displayed my assets. The opening wasn't wide enough, and, at any rate, I had always thought my *assets* rather underwhelming. No bigger than peaches. My breasts would scarcely fill his big hands.

And yet the way he stared, holding himself very still, I felt utterly naked, stripped down to my bones, and my peaches grew heavy, tingling with sensation. I was laid bare to the center of my torso, only a hint of my breasts visible, the inner swells vibrating from my labored breaths.

"Your skin," he murmured almost thoughtfully. He put one finger on me . . . gliding the tip down the valley of flesh in a fiery trail. "Flawless."

I couldn't breathe. I wanted to reply that he was flawless, too. That all of his smooth skin was remarkably perfect. Not a single imperfection or scar from battle or childhood mishap.

A movement beyond him snared my attention, and my stomach pitched.

The pale smudge of a lady's gaping face filled a crack in the drapes where the fabric had not—*could not*—fully come together.

I stiffened as she ogled us, her eyes wide as she drank greedily from her wine goblet. How very *nice* she had refreshments whilst she enjoyed the spectacle. I wanted to upend the wine into her face. I wanted to hide under the coverlet. I had been fooling myself into thinking I could pretend others weren't in the room with us.

"What is it?" he asked, noticing me stiffen. He looked over his shoulder where the drapes hung an inch apart, seeing the woman watching us for himself. "Fucking jackals," he growled, leaving me and seizing the edges of the drapes in a violent yank. To no avail—they would not completely close.

I gazed at the magnificence of his great muscled back, skimming the inked designs snaking down his shoulder blade. I tracked the long indentation of his spine, and wondered how even a man's back could be so beautiful. He lingered at the foot of the bed, his shoulders lifting as he inhaled heavily, clearly angry.

The moments stretched until he finally turned and faced me, his body filling my vision. "Don't look there."

"How can I not?"

"Eyes on me." He pointed to his face. "Look only at me."

A strange little thrill fluttered through me at the deep command . . . at the glittering pale of his eyes detectable even through the veil. And more than that. There was a sudden kinship between us. We were allied in this.

Until it's over and he learns the truth.

I settled back with a shiver, fixing my gaze on him and trying not to think about the lady watching outside the curtains of the bed.

The solidness of his warrior body pressed down on me, sinking us deeper into the mattress. My hands fluttered uncertainly to his chest, palms resting there over inked flesh, appreciating the strong thud of his heart. That black opal, gleaming dark as night, threaded with vibrant colors, dangled between us, brushing my skin, and I hissed, startled at the shocking spark from it, the humming warmth.

Looking up, my eyes blinked and sharpened, questioning what I was seeing.

The damp cold had churned itself into fog. It floated mist-like above the bed. I snuck a glance around his shoulder at that dreaded crack in the drapes. The same fog had infiltrated the chamber. I could no longer see the lady's face through that narrow opening. I could not see anyone or anything anymore save a milky-gray vapor. The fog intensified, found us in the bed, curling around our limbs as softly as fingertips, enveloping us . . . protecting us.

Exclamations rose from outside the curtained bed, remarks about the sudden haze stealing inside the chamber through the arrow slits. Complaints of the growing cold. Distress at the lack of visibility. Feet shifted and scuffed along the floor, and I realized some of the witnesses to the bedding were departing the room.

A relieved smile curved my mouth as I gave thanks, at least in this case, for unforeseen acts of nature.

He touched my face, and my smile slipped, alarm skittering through me. Would he break his vow? Would he pull the veil off me and look his fill?

Braced, I waited for what was to come. He made no such attempt, and, after a few beats, I exhaled.

My heart stuttered at his hand on my face. The veil barred skin-to-skin contact, but I felt that caress through the fabric as intensely as a brand. I managed not to flinch or recoil as his thumb stroked side to side, rasping the fabric against my cheek. I felt dazed that he should care enough for me, his wife of a few hours, whose face he had yet to see, to so tenderly touch me.

He lowered his head, brought the side of his face against mine, and whispered against my ear, his warm breath sending a tremor through me: "Trust me?"

Trust him?

I didn't even know him. Only his reputation for savagery. For death. And yet he was asking for my trust when he didn't have to—

when he didn't need it to complete this bedding. He could go about this however he wished.

I pulled back and looked into those eyes staring so earnestly, even though he couldn't see me. I trusted him, I realized with a little astonishment. This stranger. My husband. I really did.

I nodded.

He smiled then, slow and beguiling, and I died a little inside.

This man was attractive when he was grim and unsmiling, but like this? He was viciously beautiful.

"Still not one for words?" he asked.

"I . . ." My voice came out as a croak, and I swallowed and tried again. "I trust you."

Commanding myself to relax, I melted back into the bed, accepting him.

And he wasted no more time.

He nudged my legs open with his body, settling his weight there, his hips between my splayed thighs.

My chest rose and fell, my breath coming quicker, sending the material draped over my face fluttering. My hands flew to his biceps, fingers burrowing deep into firm muscle, overcome with the impulse to hang on to something, to anchor myself. Hanging on to *him* seemed a fine notion. He could probably withstand a tempest.

He shifted, his member pulsing hot as it nestled against my sex, and I gasped. Only the linen of my nightgown impeded us. Hardly substantial.

"All will be well," he reassured, and then frowned. "I would kiss you . . ."

"But you can't," I finished, even as my belly came alive with butterflies at the notion of that mouth on mine, mating with my lips.

That mouth. Wide, well-shaped, and much too soft-looking for such a hard man. I couldn't resist.

I lifted my hand from where it clung to him and brushed my fingertips searchingly . . . curiously over his lips, wondering what it would be like to have his kiss. I had so little experience with kissing. Stig had been the only one.

He stilled above me, and I worried I had done something wrong. If I shouldn't have touched him. If I should have remained motionless, a limp fish beneath him. What did I know of these matters, after all?

He turned his face then and pressed a hot open-mouthed kiss onto my palm, his tongue slowly sneaking out to taste my skin, and I forgot all about what I should or should not have done. Sparks lit up my arm at the contact.

Hell's teeth. What is happening to me?

He reached for my other hand and pressed a fervent kiss over the bandage covering the fresh wound, still raw from the priest's blade—and yet that did not prevent the tingles from stirring beneath the dressing. The carved X throbbed and buzzed at his caress.

"Ohh." I sighed a breath that twisted into a gasp as he rocked his hips into me. I felt him . . . bigger. Harder. Alive for me. No longer indifferent to our coupling. Not as he had been when he first climbed into the bed.

He was aroused.

He finished devoting himself to my palm, pressing a last, lingering kiss to the inside of my wrist. Dropping my hand, he turned his mouth to my throat, feathering me with scalding-soft kisses that belied everything I had judged him to be: the Beast. Terrifyingly big. Ruthless. Unkind. Strong enough to break a person should he will it.

My neck arched, instinctively offering him more as I breathed in the cool moisture surrounding us like a frosted morning. And yet I was hot. So hot. Achingly hot.

He obliged, his teeth lightly scoring the taut skin before licking me, savoring me with his tongue as though I were some sweet confection.

I was possessed. My body was not mine. Something else. Burning. Scalding against him. Two fires coming together, merging into one inferno.

The heat in my chest snapped and expanded, catching ablaze,

popping and racing along every pore and nerve. It was a shared fever between us. A wildfire gone unchecked.

My hands ran down the great expanse of his back, seizing him and pulling him closer, hips lifting up, grinding his hardness against me. The black opal settled and nestled heavily between my breasts, a scorching stamp, branding me.

My sex clenched. Moisture rushed between my legs, dampening my nightgown where he slid slickly against me.

"Fuck." He grunted.

There was a flurry of wild movement. His hands. My hands. My nightgown gathered and shoved up forcefully, bunched at my hips.

A shudder racked him that vibrated into me. His lips burned at my throat.

Need pumped in me, primal, as vital as the blood swimming in my veins, as thick as the viscous air filling my lungs.

I reached between us, found him, circled his thickness with my hand, running my thumb over the plump head. He groaned.

Emboldened, I guided him to my entrance, where I most ached. "Please," I said, the word a needy catch on the air, my voice unrecognizable.

I didn't understand anything except this driving hunger to have him, to possess him . . . to be possessed.

It was wildness. A frenzy. His hard hands seized my hips, fingers digging—and at first I feared he was pushing me from him, forcing me away.

An anguished sob broke from me. "Don't go . . . don't stop—"

"Not if there was a sword to my throat," he growled, and then those digging fingers were angling my hips, lifting me up and guiding my thighs to wrap around him, his hardness right there at my slick opening.

He pushed inside me, burying himself deep, and the pleasure-pain of it shattered me. Overtook me. The fullness. A stretching, tingling burn that begged for pause. For a moment.

"Oh!"

His eyes locked on my hidden face, glowing icy gray, wide with his own shock. "You're tight," he grunted.

I panted, hanging on desperately to him, the joints of my fingers aching.

"My apologies. It will ease," he promised with a formality that felt absurd as he pushed into me again, lodging himself to the hilt with a moan. "Fuck, you feel good."

He held himself still then. I was aware of the hard length of him, the throb and pulse of the cock inside me. He waited.

I flexed around him, working through the burning fullness, contracting and yielding to his shape until I was trembling, huffing, until I started to move and wriggle restlessly beneath him.

"Oh . . . oh," I whimpered, my inner muscles experimentally squeezing. My desire for more intensified.

More movement. More friction. More of the Beast.

I couldn't wait. I wasn't able. I didn't like this stillness, this paralysis. I was too overcome. My body clamored for action.

I reached down and bit him on the shoulder through the veil, tasting his salty-clean skin through the thin material, my teeth sinking into hot flesh. I didn't know how I knew to do that, but it achieved the desired result.

He snarled and drove into me again, plunging hard. Again and again. One of his hands flew from my hip and seized the gaping bodice of my nightgown, tugging it down. There was a brief rip as my breasts spilled free. He cupped one, lifting it to his descending head. He didn't break pace, thrusting inside my pulsing sex as the hot suction of his mouth closed around one nipple, drawing me in deep.

I cried out, despising the wild sound, knowing everyone could hear me outside our cocoon.

As though he could read my thoughts, his head came up and he covered my mouth through the veil, swallowing the sound.

"Forget about them," he commanded against the fabric. Against my lips.

That mystifying fog was everywhere now. Flooding the chamber, creeping into our marriage bed to cover us, curling against our bodies like a lover, smothering my overheated skin with a cooling film.

I sobbed, feeling a great pressure rising up in me. Wild. Confusing. I didn't know what to do with it. To fight the mounting swell or to dive into it? I moaned against his mouth, my veil wet and clinging like a skin between us.

He wrapped an arm around my waist and pulled me up until we were sitting, facing each other, still joined, panting, chest to chest. I rocked against his rolling hips, riding him instinctively, desperate for the friction.

I clung wildly to his shoulders as the tension built and built, deliciously, excruciatingly good. Even as the cold mist shrouded us, the air between us crackled and sizzled like food on a spit.

His fingers dug like talons into my bottom, anchoring me for his pistoning hips. His cock pushed and pulled deep inside me, fast and wild and relentless.

We lost any kind of rhythm, our urgent actions frenzied and clumsy. My fingers curled over his nape, clinging to him as my sex tightened around him, squeezing, working hard toward some indefinable goal.

I found it then. That elusive rapture.

My body erupted into a violent bliss. Bright spots blinded my vision as I burst apart and then went pliant, sagging against him as tiny shudders of pleasure eddied through me long after I had stilled.

He pumped several more thrusts, seeking, claiming, grinding out his own satisfaction with a deep, purring groan until he jerked still inside me, flooding me with his seed.

I dropped my face into the crook of his neck, overcome with embarrassment now that it was over.

Now that *later* was here.

He twitched inside me. His hands left my bottom, roaming upward to rub my back. I tensed, unaccustomed to such tender ministrations on my back. My back was not a place for gentle hands.

I looked at him, and even through the fuzzy barrier I perceived his pleasure, his astonishment. In this. In me. *His wife.*

I released a ragged breath, feeling the same pleasure, the same astonishment, and not a little shattered, because I knew it would be short-lived.

He grabbed my waist and lifted me off him, pulling us apart. The euphoria left me. Went with him. As though a piece of me had just been cut away. I felt depleted. Hollow. Suddenly as cold on the inside as the room.

The pull in my chest reasserted itself, a demanding clench. I covered a shaking hand over the area, rubbing, willing it to go away, to stop. With space between us again, I used my other hand to hold together my gaping nightgown, attempting to reclaim my modesty, however pointless that might be now.

"'Tis done," he breathed, the sound ragged.

Reaching for my veil, he pulled it from my face.

10
FELL

I WAS A FOOL. THAT WAS INSTANTLY, PAINSTAKINGLY CLEAR.
She had seduced me with her sumptuous skin and soft cries
as I plowed between her thighs like it was just the two of us in that
bed, like I was an untried youth with his first woman, believing,
remarkably, that she was the princess I had been promised. The
wife I had been seeking.

She was not.

I knew this woman. I knew her face. The wide amber-gold eyes.
The trembling mouth. My gut tightened as I recalled how I had
tasted that mouth beneath a kiss-soaked veil, whilst the whole time
it had been the bold little spy I'd caught emerging from the painting in the chancery. The very same servant girl the lord regent had
sent scampering away with a stern admonition. I'd just wedded
and bedded her. *Her* lips. *Her* golden-skinned body. *Her* long legs
wrapped around me, quivering under my hands.

And she was *not* a princess of Penterra.

To further confirm this, I reached for the wimple covering her
hair and yanked the headdress off with unkind fingers, tossing it
aside. My anger twisted higher, tighter, a fist driving through me.

She gave a small cry as the mass of her flame-red hair was exposed, but I could not find it in myself to care. I seized the thick-as-
my-wrist braid hanging over her shoulder in a fierce grip.

"What is this?" I snarled, wrapping the rope of her hair once
around my hand and tugging her closer, seething as my inner beast

bristled. I usually kept that side of myself in check, unleashing it only in combat, and even then I kept it tightly contained, but this felt like war. The first assault had been made, and I had not even seen it coming. The next move would be mine.

Her eyes widened. She must have recognized the danger. Before I could guess her intent, she balled her hand into a fist and struck me solidly in the mouth.

My head snapped back, her punch splitting my lip, drawing blood.

I growled. *Fuck.* Attacked unaware. *Again.*

She yanked open the drapes and bounded from the bed with surprising speed and agility for someone who lived in the shelter of a palace.

Chest heaving, I followed, unconcerned with my nakedness, my cock streaked with her maiden blood for all to see. Faces swam before my eyes. The king and queen. The lord regent. The priest. Nobles of the court. That glaring face of the captain of the guard, flushed in anger. There were fewer people than when this farce started, but I could still see plenty of dumbfounded expressions through the fading fog.

The chamber went silent as a tomb as the mist melted away, everyone somber and wary of me: the Beast emerging from his marriage bed feral and glowering, bloody-lipped and intent on reprisal.

And they should have been wary.

I spit blood upon the floor and swiped savagely at my mouth. "Explain," I bit out.

Her wide-eyed gaze looked from the blood on the floor to me. She hummed and vibrated with an emotion I could not name. It could not possibly be outrage. I was the only one with rightful claim to that particular reaction. She was the deceiver. The liar. The fraud.

She stood out of arm's reach, a mutinous, ready-to-bolt look on her face. No doubt she would run—or quite possibly take another swing at me—if I made a move toward her. The warrior in me smoldered at my core, willing her to do it, to try again.

The lord regent was the first to speak. Clearing his throat, he said, "What is . . . amiss, my lord?"

I blinked. Was this asshole in earnest?

"What is amiss?" I echoed, stabbing a finger toward the woman I'd just divested of her maidenhead upon the bed behind me, putting the stamp of legitimacy on our marriage. "She is *not* a princess of Penterra." Not the bride I was promised. Not the bride my father always insisted I deserved.

"Ah, but she is, my lord. Tamsyn is recognized as a member of the royal family and she *is* your wife." The smug bastard flicked a glance down my body, his attention pointedly on my cock.

Well, that sounded like some very fine politicking if I'd ever heard it.

And complete horseshit.

One of the nearby nobles came alive to chirp, "Don't suppose it's necessary to hang the sheets from the ramparts as proof of consummation. We can all see the evidence for ourselves."

Titters met the snide remark, and I swung a murderous glare around the chamber. The laughter ceased, and gazes steered away from me uneasily.

Shaking my head, I advanced on *my wife* with hard steps. Everyone else faded away. I would have the truth from *her.*

She shivered, and I wondered if it was from the chill of the chamber or the threat of me. The fog may have abated, but the frigid air clung. Still, she held her ground. Her scent filled my nose as I closed the distance between us, and fuck if the blood didn't rush to my traitorous cock in primal recognition. It wasn't just her scent that hit me. It was the scent of *me* all over *her.* That satisfied me in a way it shouldn't. Only minutes ago, I had been buried inside her. Clearly I had yet to shake off the effects. I was ready for another go even now. Even though that was the last thing I should want.

"Who are you?" I growled. Her gaze flicked uncertainly to the lord regent. "Look at me." My voice cracked like thunder on the air. "Answer my question."

"I'm . . . Tamsyn."

"A daughter of the crown?" I pressed, even though I knew.

She started to look away again, doubtlessly seeking direction on how to answer me. I held up one finger, catching her attention and holding it. "I'll not ask again. Speak the truth."

"I am Tamsyn," she repeated, her throat working as she swallowed. "The royal whipping girl."

Arkin swore.

I did not look to my vassal; all my searing focus was fixed upon the woman I had just bound myself to for life.

The royal whipping girl?

I glanced at the faces of the Penterran court around me. The king and queen stared back in a way that said everything. All I needed to know. It was true, then. She was a whipping girl, which I understood to be someone who . . .

"You take beatings for the princesses?" I demanded.

Her chin lifted. "Yes." As though it was a point of pride for her. Her amber eyes glinted fire, daring me to demean the practice.

Spittle flew from Arkin's lips as he ground out, "She is but their dog, and they think it fitting to give her to you for a wife."

The queen spoke up in stout denial: "The royal whipping girl is an esteemed position in the palace. The tradition predates written record. Tamsyn is a daughter to us and given all the courtesy and regard due a royal princess."

"Except you whip her," I replied, feeling my lip curl in distaste. "Esteemed, indeed."

The room fell silent. It was a truth no one could deny. The truth, at last, finally, from these people.

I recalled my father's voice then. He'd always said King Hamlin could not be trusted—that the Penterran court was a nest of vipers.

They're different from us. They expect safety and nice things, but they won't bleed for it. They expect us to bleed for them.

King Hamlin spoke at last, his gaze fastened on me. "Do you intend to refuse her?"

"He cannot," the lord regent blustered, affronted at the question, hot color splashing his face. "The ceremony is done. The girl is bedded. They are wed!"

Do you intend to refuse her? It was a weighty question. Loaded with implications. What he meant was: *Do you renounce this sovereignty?*

I held the king's gaze and saw that he did not believe I had a choice. He and the lord regent were in accord on that.

I considered them all, my gaze in turn sliding to her—Tamsyn— and stopping there. Her white-knuckled hands gripped the front of her nightgown, precariously holding the fabric together over her breasts. I had ripped the material from her in a fit of unexpected desire. I grimaced. Nothing about any of this had been expected.

I had expected the bedding to be perfunctory. Purely transactional. I would get it done while hopefully bringing as little pain and embarrassment to her as possible. I wasn't a sadist, after all. That had been the plan. I liked fucking as well as anyone, but this night's bedding had not been about what I *liked*. It was not meant to be about pleasure, and yet pleasure was what I had found. With my wife. *The wrong wife.* This woman before me whom I had *not* agreed to marry, but whom they had tricked me into claiming.

Fury seethed through my veins.

I looked her over with a leer. Had they chosen her simply because of her position as a whipping girl?

Or had they suspected I would respond to her charms with fire. She could cling to her bodice and try to cover herself up, but I knew what was there. She could not hide that lush golden skin from me. I remembered everything.

"Bedded or not, this marriage cannot stand," Arkin charged. He was apoplectic, the pale skin above his beard breaking out in red splotches. I would be hearing his *I told you so* later.

"It cannot be undone," the lord regent insisted.

"Oh, there is one way it can be undone." Arkin dropped glittering eyes onto the girl, letting the threat hang. I understood his meaning perfectly, and my skin prickled and muscles tightened. He was a warrior, accustomed to solving problems with his sword.

I cut him a swift glance, shaking my head once in warning. More than brawn was needed here. They had already proven their crafty, devious natures. They were snakes in the grass, and I had to use cunning to outsmart them.

I could tell the others did not understand Arkin's threat. They looked at each other with blank stares and shrugs. None of the Penterran nobles would grasp his meaning. They did not solve problems by the sword. No, their choice of weapons were lies, courtly intrigue, and machinations.

One glance at her—Tamsyn—though, and I knew she understood. Perhaps a whipping girl knew to expect abuse, to look for the snakes in the grass . . . that her life was so very expendable.

Perhaps she had always known it would come to this when she was swept up in this charade. Had she expected gentleness from me once I learned the truth?

The lord regent continued, his voice smug. "You wanted a daughter of the king, Lord Dryhten. Now you have one."

My hand opened and flexed at my side, longing to pound that smugness off his face. "She is not what I asked for, and you damn well know it," I snapped.

A voice penetrated through my haze of fury and betrayal. "She's too good for the likes of you."

I searched and found the source. It was the captain of the guard. We'd been introduced yesterday, but his name eluded me. I had expected someone more intimidating as head of the guard. He was too young, too pretty, too clean. I'd wager his flawless red tunic with its gold buttons had never seen a battlefield. I could not envision him lasting through one skirmish in the Borderlands.

When my gaze locked on his face, the venom in his eyes blasted me. *If looks could kill.* He vibrated with a rage I could taste on the air.

My gaze shot to her with understanding. *Oh.*

This was about her. Tamsyn. My wife. My. *Mine.* The word welled up inside me like someone else, *something* else, was speaking within me, a beast growling from the shadows.

The captain looked from her to me, his hand ready at the hilt of the rapier attached to his belt, gripping it until his skin had turned a bloodless white. I cocked an eyebrow. He was dangerously close to using his weapon—or trying to, at any rate. I wished he would. I felt like hurting someone.

Did he fancy himself in love with her? What manner of man stood by and let another have his woman? Where were his objections an hour ago? I looked him up and down contemptuously. "Is that so? It is *I* who does not deserve her?"

I was the one deceived.

"Indeed. You don't." The pretty soldier took a belligerent step forward.

"Stig," the lord regent snapped, annoyance flashing across his face. "Stand down."

He looked like a sullen youth. "Father, I told you this was a bad—"

"Hold your tongue. You forget yourself!"

Father. His son, eh? I should have guessed. This Stig was just some spoiled court brat they stuck into a uniform and named captain of the guard. I doubted he even knew how to use his sword.

Stig fell silent but continued to glare at me. Something dark and primal surged inside me, and I once again found myself wishing he would reach for his rapier. Did she love him back? *My wife?* This boy playing at being a man?

I moved across the chamber with a casualness that belied my predatory nature. Stopping before him, I angled my head and looked him over in a deliberately insolent manner, hoping to incite him—this coward who thought it right to announce what my wife deserved after he had not lifted a finger to save her from sacrificing herself to the Beast of the Borderlands.

He tensed, ready for an attack, ready *to* attack. I heartily wished he would. Wished I could unleash my aggression on him.

Ugly emotion slithered through me. Leaning forward, I murmured for his ears alone, "Sorry it wasn't you?"

He snapped. Lunged at me with a curse. Just as I expected and exactly what I wanted.

What I *needed*.

I hated that Arkin had been right. I should have never come to this place. From the moment I arrived, I'd felt out of sorts. Almost feverish and not right within my skin. And the bedding had left me shaken. Had a spell been cast over me? Was there some witch lingering in the shadows of the palace fucking with my head?

Even now I wanted to drag Tamsyn back to the bed and have her again . . . and again, until I was satiated. The impulse baffled me. I was always in control. Never led by impulse or cock.

I ducked the oncoming fist and delivered a swift blow to the young man's ribs, unleashing my wrath, gratified at the crunch beneath my knuckles. He sucked in a breath and staggered back. I moved in to rain down more abuse, but bodies got between us, palace guards protecting their own.

The king and queen were swept from the chamber, their security a priority.

Arkin roared, unsheathing his sword and diving into the melee.

Rapiers were pulled. Women screamed. Decanters and goblets shattered on the floor. The priest started shouting prayers.

Suddenly my wife was there, pressing a hand on my chest, impeding me from inflicting more violence. "Enough!" And then softer, her eyes pleading: "Please."

One hand on my chest, one word from her, and I stopped. I resisted the impulse to fold my hand over hers and keep it there on my beating heart, imbuing me with her drugging warmth that I remembered only too well.

How was it she had this effect on me in so short a time? I had not met a more treacherous woman in all my days. I despised her and what she had done, and yet she held me in the palm of her hand.

It could not stand.

Everyone stilled. Arkin's head whipped around before landing on me. "Fell," he barked in bewilderment, clearly wondering why I had paused rather than bust heads alongside him.

Because she asked me to stop.

I would not dare admit it. I felt weak even thinking it.

The captain of the guard was looking at her now, his expression wounded as he stared at where she touched me with her hand. "Tamsyn," he croaked, his face crestfallen, as though she had somehow betrayed him. I wanted to strike him down for daring to speak her name aloud when I had not even done so yet. I might not want her for my wife, but she was mine. Mine and not his. I wanted to break him.

She glanced at him briefly and then settled her attention back on me. "Lady Dryhten," she corrected firmly, sending me a wary look, as though seeking my approval.

Stig's eyes bulged. "*Lady Dryhten?*" he choked out, shaking his head as though he could not fathom it. "Tamsyn, no . . ."

"Yes," she insisted, nodding slowly, still holding my stare. "Yes. I am Lady Dryhten. If his lordship agrees."

Agrees?

Now she wanted my agreement? I glared at her. After the fact. After her deceit. After it had become impossible to reject her without causing civil discord.

This little skirmish would be but a taste of it. If I refused her as my wife, the whole of the Borderlands would rally to my side. It would divide the entire kingdom. It would be war.

But maybe it was time.

Hamlin had had his chance, and this country was close to the breaking point. Without the Borderlands propping it up, Penterra would have already fallen. He should be ousted. Toppled from his gilded throne. I looked away from her, this whipping girl, and around the chamber at all the angry faces.

I did not have the whole of the Borderlands here with me now.

I had a dozen warriors. Highly skilled, willing to follow my every command, to fight to the death. And yet resisting, revolting here and now, would mean death for us all. We could not take on the palace guards. There were too many of them. Too few of us.

There was no choice. I had to fake a smile. Agree. And plan my revenge. Bide my time. Plot my next move.

This would not rest. The treachery, the disrespect. I would not forget. I would not forgive.

"Aye," I said slowly, my gaze skimming over her with a crude thoroughness she could not mistake. There was nothing else I could say at the moment. "I'll have you."

And God help her, for I would make her pay the price for it.

11

TAMSYN

I WASN'T DEAD.

I had thought I might be. Especially the moment Lord Dryhten ripped off my veil. I shuddered. The look in his eyes . . .

I'd reacted when I struck him. Unthinkingly. Automatically. Apparently I had some fight in me, after all. Some instinct for self-preservation. It was a revelation, and I did not regret striking out at him. My life was not only about forbearance. Just because I was a whipping girl did not mean I was *his* whipping girl.

I returned to my chamber, knowing full well that if Lord Dryhten wished me elsewhere, then he would let it be known. He was my husband now. I was his to command. Luckily for me, he had suffered enough of me for the day. Likely he could not stomach the sight of his betrayer.

I was not summoned that evening. It seemed I would have one final night for myself in the only home I had ever known. As night fell, a maid arrived to begin packing my things for the journey. I was leaving. Still. He had not put a stop to it. I would be departing tomorrow. With him. To his home in the north. I digested this slowly. In pieces.

The maid held up items, asking me what I wished to take with me. I responded numbly with nods and shakes of my head and monosyllabic answers.

There was little I could bring with me. No trunks or valises. We

would travel on horseback. No carriage or carts or retinue of atten-
dants. I would not even be bringing a lady's maid with me. There
would be no such courtesy extended, and I could not help wondering
if that would have been the case if I were Alise or Feena and Sybilia.
Pointless conjecture, for I was not any of the princesses. I was me.
And I would be tossed atop a horse and expected to keep up with a
party of warriors. At least I could ride—not that anyone had asked
that of me.

The maid rang for a bath. My second one in a day. A rarity, but
necessary. I scrubbed my skin raw with soap and a sponge—but to
no avail. I still felt him. Still smelled him on me. He filled my nose,
and a now familiar heat curled through me, at once softening and
tightening my muscles.

Shifting in the tub, the twinge of tenderness between my thighs
served only as a further reminder of my recent bedding. Had that
only been a short time ago? I felt as though I'd lived a lifetime since
then. Certainly my world had changed ten times over . . . and would
continue to do so.

Once out of the tub, I seated myself before the fire. With my hair
washed, brushed, and fanned out over my shoulders to dry, I gazed
into the flickering flames.

I felt numb and hollow inside, scarcely noticing as the maid silently went about the room, packing the whole of my life into a
single rucksack.

My head snapped up at the sudden arrival of the queen and
princesses, striding inside my chamber without announcement.
Except Alise. She was not with them.

"You're so very brave." Feena cupped my face and kissed both
of my cheeks.

Sybilia pushed her aside to embrace me so tightly she squeezed
the air right out of me. "We're going to miss you so much."

At mention of that, Feena snapped, "Mama! We cannot let our
Tamsyn go with that wretched Lord Dryhten. She married him . . .
and did her duty." Her nostrils quivered, as though the notion of

my sacrifice was most foul to her senses. "She can remain here where she belongs now."

"She must go with her husband," the queen countered evenly. "Being a wife goes beyond one night together."

I swallowed miserably. *Being a wife goes beyond one night together.*

After the way he had looked at me, I doubted his shadow would ever fall upon my bed again. His expression had been so full of contempt.

Sybilia rolled her eyes. "She is Lady Dryhten now, Feena. Of course she must go with him."

Lady Dryhten. I winced. I scarcely felt like a wife—vigorous bedding notwithstanding.

Feena leaned forward to hiss in my ear, "Was it so very terrible? Did it hurt?"

I doubted her mother would appreciate my answering that question. These girls had their own marital responsibilities ahead of them. The queen would not want me to fill their heads with alarming ideas.

"Where is Alise?" I asked instead, hoping to see her one more time before I departed on the morrow.

The three of them swapped looks that communicated something indecipherable. At least to me.

"She will be along shortly," the queen replied blithely.

"She was quite upset," Sybilia volunteered, darting a wary glance at her mother. "She blames Mama and Papa for—"

"Enough of that, Sybilia," the queen said, reprimanding her. Looking to me, she repeated firmly, "Don't worry yourself. She will be along shortly."

Alise was not along shortly. She was not along later.

The queen and the princesses said their farewells. The maid left me, and, with my hair mostly dry, I settled on my bed to wait for Alise. My hand went to my breastbone, to that area that felt so tight and warm and throbbing since the Beast's arrival—since he'd joined me in that bed. I rubbed my fingers in a gentle circle there, over the discomfort.

All of me was one giant, pulsing ache. Perhaps that was normal. The way every woman felt following her first time with a man, and it would fade.

I fell asleep like that. Hoping. Waiting. A hand resting on my chest.

I DREAMED OF FIRE.

Flames everywhere. The Beast was there, cutting through the crackling heat, coming for me through the fire. He reached me. Sparks popped and lifted off me when he touched me. And then he suddenly burst into flame.

I woke strangling on a scream. For several moments I sat upright, gasping, gulping back sobs. I looked to my window, and the faint purpling sky foreshadowing the emerging day.

With a shuddering breath, I flung back the coverlet and dressed myself. A maid soon arrived, carrying a tray. I ate a hasty breakfast of bread, cheese, and fruit. I forced the food down, not knowing when I would next eat, if they would even bother to feed me. None of the border warriors would be kindly disposed toward me. Perhaps in time I would gain their respect and trust. Of course, that would only happen if Lord Dryhten treated me with kindness and respect. They would take their cues from him. Not the most reassuring thought. His eyes had burned with such anger once my veil had been removed and he clapped eyes on me.

I sat before the dressing mirror, my feet tapping anxiously as my hair was separated into several braids and then wound around my head in a coronet. As soon as the maid was finished, I bounded from the bench, knowing I had little time.

"My lady," she cried, confirming this suspicion. "You're expected downstairs straight away."

"See that my bag is sent down. I will be there soon."

I couldn't leave without saying good-bye to Alise. I didn't know when I would see her again. If ever. My last moments with her would not be in front of an audience. I swallowed thickly. I would be in the Borderlands, and she would be elsewhere, married to some distant king or prince. Perhaps even across an ocean. This could be our last time together.

"But they insisted on leaving at first light!"

I sent a quick glance at the murky dawn floating through the window of my bedchamber.

"I will hurry," I promised. "Make my excuses."

She called out after me, but her exact words were lost. I was already out the door and hastening down the corridor.

I made a beeline for Alise's chamber. She was not an early riser, and I was confident I would catch her still in bed.

I was wrong. A maid was tidying the room.

"Princess Alise?" I demanded. "Where did she go?"

"I believe she went to the kennels, my lady."

The kennels.

I winced. My least favorite place. I hesitated only a moment before stiffening my spine and rushing through the mostly empty palace. For Alise, I could endure it.

Only a few servants were up and about, stirring the fire awake in the Great Hall's hearth. I emerged into the bracing air outside. For Alise, I would brave the kennels.

Down the winding path, past the outdoor kitchen and stables I went. The wolves were housed in the farthest building in the exterior courtyard, closest to the postern gate, away from the heaviest traffic. The capricious beasts were not placed in proximity of the horses.

They were restless this morning. I could hear them prowling in their cages. As I advanced, they grew more agitated, louder, yipping and whining, scratching and pawing at the walls. It was always that way. The wolves did not like me. I tried not to take it too personally. They didn't like many humans. Except for their keepers, of course, and the rare individual.

Once upon a time, wolves had been instrumental in the Threshing for their skill in hunting dragons. Wolves hunted much less threatening game now. Time had lifted the threat of dragons. These days, King Hamlin and his nobles kept the wolves for sport.

Wolves were still used in the distant outposts, helping in the waging of war in the outer regions of the kingdom. I could only assume the border lords kept them, too.

Taking a deep breath, I stepped inside the kennels, peering down the shadowed middle aisle for a glimpse of Alise. She was one of the rare individuals. The beasts adored her. She was as natural with them as any of the keepers tasked with their care.

They didn't attack humans. Not unless directed to do so. At least that was what their keepers always assured me when I ventured too close to the kennels and the wolves started foaming at the mouth. Only desperation to see Alise could bring me here. They were deadly, feral, brutal animals, and I had never been able to view them as pets, as Alise did.

"Alise?" I whispered loudly.

As soon as I spoke, the already charged air exploded. Every wolf came alive—barking, howling, snarling—jolted awake by the sound of my voice.

They wanted to tear me apart. This moment only confirmed the rightness of my instinct to stay away from them. And yet here I was now.

The wolves nearest me could actually see me through the bars of their kennels, and it sent them over the edge. They charged the bars, flinging their considerable weight against the iron with no thought to hurting themselves. They were relentless in their need to reach me, to tear me apart.

There was a sickening crack as a giant gray wolf to my right hurled himself against his cage. He yelped in pain, but that did not stop him. With his front leg dangling unnaturally, he kept coming, wild eyes crazed and rolling, fixed on me, mouth foaming, spittle flying. I jumped back, which only brought me closer to the kennel on my left. A she-wolf shoved her snapping muzzle between the bars at me.

"Tamsyn!" Alise appeared. She hurried down the aisle to me. "What are you doing here? You don't like the wolves."

I resisted pointing out that *they* did not like *me*.

Seizing her hands, I tugged her out of the kennels. That did little to quiet the wolves, however. The animals could no longer see me, but they could still hear me . . . smell me. That was all they needed to track their quarry. *Scent.* Historically, that was what guided them deep into the ancient caves and winding tunnels of the Crags to ferret out dragons for the scores of warriors following behind them.

Alise glanced over her shoulder in bewilderment. "They've gone mad."

I shook my head. She didn't recall that this was how they were when it came to me. It had been years since I'd ventured close to the kennels. For this very reason.

"You didn't come to tell me good-bye." My voice trembled with a faint accusation.

Tears welled in her eyes. "I just couldn't." She shook her head. "I couldn't bear seeing you, knowing what we forced you to do—"

I pulled her into a hug. "Don't say that. You didn't force me to do anything."

"Our parents did. The lord regent. And I know you did it for us. For me and Feena and Sybilia. You've always done everything for us."

Her hot tears dampened my neck. I pulled back to look at her, searching her face. "I'm not sorry. Life was going to change anyway. It was coming. This is . . . fine. *I* will be fine," I vowed, pushing a fair tendril back, off her moist cheek.

She nodded. "It's just that he is so . . . frightening. Aren't you scared of going with him?"

I had a flash of him as he had been last night inside our curtained bed—so very decent and tender. *All will be well.* He'd promised me that before he had proceeded to wring pleasure from me. Shattering, gasping pleasure as his body joined with mine. He didn't have to say those words of comfort . . . or to make me feel so alive, so good, so hungry for him. And yet he had.

There it was. The uncomfortable truth. My weakness. I would not mind doing yesterday with him all over again—this time without a veil between us. This time with no one else in the room.

Except now he hated me, and rightly so. I could not blame him.

The wolves were deafening now. I could hear the keepers within, arriving with buckets of food to appease them, tutting under their tongues and cooing to the agitated beasts, clearly perplexed at their distress.

"There you are!"

At the thundering voice, I turned to watch my husband—*still* strange, that—storming down the path toward me, his boots biting into the dirt-packed ground.

My body sprang to life at the sight of him, the familiar warmth pervading me, the mystifying tightness pulling at the center of my chest again.

He was dressed to ride, his leathered armor stretched across his wide chest. The dark hair framing his face did nothing to soften his expression. The hilt of his sword peeked out from behind him, and I could well imagine one of his thick arms reaching for it in one swift move, sliding it from its scabbard before cleaving me in half.

Alise shrank behind me, and I hated that she had to see him like this, glowering and intimidating, when she was already afraid for me. She would worry for me long after I left.

"I was saying good-bye," I snapped, annoyed at the impression he was making, at the unease within her that he did nothing to quell. Not that he owed her anything. Not that he owed me anything.

Alise sucked in a breath behind me at my tone.

He paused at my rebuttal, and then resumed his strides, his expression only more cross as he advanced. "Were you not informed we would be leaving at first light?"

"I was on my way."

Tension rippled across his taut jaw. "We will not pander to your whims. The crossing is long and grueling. Your leisure will not be a consideration."

My sister's hand tightened on my arm. If I had any doubt that he was still angry, it fled in an instant. I could expect no softness from him.

"I had assumed as much," I replied.

"Good." He grasped my elbow. "Then let us go. We should have already departed."

I twisted free to turn and face Alise. "I will write to you as soon as I can."

Alise nodded jerkily. "As will I." She sent a nervous glance to the big warrior. "Do not hurt her, my lord," she blurted with a thrust of her chin. It was the hardest and meanest I had ever seen her. "Or you shall have to contend with me."

Something flickered across his face, and I waited tensely for some nasty rejoinder from the man, but he gave a single nod. "Understood." It seemed enough to satisfy Alise. She surged forward and hugged me again.

Turning, I stepped around him and resolutely began marching back to the stables, my riding skirts swishing around my boots. He fell in beside me, a big heat-radiating wall next to me.

"Thank you for that," I grudgingly offered.

"For what?"

"Giving her that assurance. I know you did not mean it."

He sent me a sidelong look and grunted. Not precisely a denial, and that stung. I supposed I had been fishing. I wanted him to insist that he had meant it. Apparently I would get no more than that grunt from him.

We passed the stables.

"They're waiting for us in the bailey," he said.

Indeed they were waiting, staring crossly at me as I came into sight. The dozen warriors were assembled and already mounted atop their destriers, the horses so much larger than anything I had ever seen in the palace stables. The royal family and the lord regent and several other retainers stood on the steps of the Great Hall, come to see us off.

I ignored Lord Dryhten and his warriors. Their impatience was palpable in the morning air, and I ignored that, too, approaching the steps. I accepted kisses on my cheeks from the king and the queen.

The queen cupped my face, her fingers gentle on my skin. "The day you were brought to me, I knew you were special. Be well, daughter. Forge your path."

A lump formed in my throat at her reference to the day I was found abandoned in the palace bailey. The queen chose me when no one else wanted me. She had saved me from an uncertain and precarious fate and served as a mother to me—the only mother I would ever know. I nodded. "Yes, Your Majesty."

Her gaze glided over my shoulder and then returned to my face. Leaning in close, she whispered, "You have more power than you know."

I glanced to where she had looked over my shoulder. My husband stood there, muscled legs braced apart, his expression impassive, enigmatic eyes hooded beneath slashing dark eyebrows.

Did she mean to imply I held power over him? I grimaced, thinking of the way he had looked and his angry words when he found me with Alise. That was wishful thinking on her part.

The lord regent spoke to me in exasperation, gesturing for me to move away. "Off with you, girl. Be a good wife. Do not make them wait on you." His gaze flickered beyond me apprehensively, as though he feared they might leave without me or still yet denounce this entire affair.

Turning, I started down the steps, stopping at the sound of my name.

Stig stepped forward from where he stood among stoic-faced members of the guard, his gaze fixed intently on me, his boots tapping softly on the stone steps.

His father glared at him. "Stig, get back in—"

"I will come for you," he said, addressing me, ignoring his father, ignoring everyone. His soft brown eyes were fastened on me with a single-minded focus, and I could not help the flutter in my chest at his obvious concern. I would never have another friend like him. I didn't even know if I would have a friend at all where I was going. I would miss him. "If you ever have need, send word and I will come for you."

I opened and closed my mouth, uncertain how to reply to that, when I felt a sudden presence beside me. A hand fell upon my shoulder and I felt the weight of it, the radiating warmth traveling bone-deep, a brand penetrating me through my garments.

A quick look at my husband revealed he was not, however, staring at me. All his searing attention was trained on Stig. "And know that if you ever step foot in the Borderlands, you will not take what is mine. If you even try, I will end you."

I gasped, marveling at the ring of possession in his voice. *For me.* As though I were some sort of commodity and not a wife he had been saddled with against his will through duplicitous means.

Stig's lips flattened into a mutinous line, but he said nothing. His eyes clashed with the Beast's in silent battle before sliding to me, the promise of his words still glowing there despite my husband's threat, and I knew—he would come if I needed him.

The big hand on my shoulder slid down to clasp my elbow. He guided me to the horses. "We've delayed long enough."

My feet worked to keep up with his long strides. Even as tall as I was, he was taller. Two of my steps matched every one of his.

He stopped beside a docile mare I recognized from the palace stables, and I released a sigh of relief, reaching up to fondly stroke the white star on her forehead. I had feared I would be forced to mount one of the hulking destriers.

"Can you ride?" he asked tersely.

Without waiting for my reply, Lord Dryhten's hands suddenly seized me by the waist, and I was airborne.

I squeaked, my hands flying to his shoulders as he settled me atop my mount.

I'd been taught to ride alongside the princesses. Even though I'd excelled in those lessons, outshining my younger sisters, I feared my instruction had only been rudimentary. Anytime I traveled a significant distance, I was in the comforts of a carriage.

"I hope you do," he added with a grim set to that lush mouth of his.

"Yes. I ride," I replied with far more bravado than I felt, telling myself to reveal none of my doubt among these hard-faced warriors. *We will not pander to your whims.* I most definitely would *not* be offered a carriage at any point in this journey. There would be no velvet seat cushion. No blanket for my lap with hot bricks to warm me. Then and there, I vowed I would become an expert horsewoman . . . and if I didn't, I would not dare complain.

"Aye, we heard just how well you like to ride," one of Dryhten's men, whom I recognized from the bedding ceremony last night, taunted.

Laughter broke out among the warriors.

Mortification stung my cheeks. Like most of the warriors, he was brawny and thick-necked. His flinty gaze collided with mine, and I felt a shiver of apprehension at the animosity reflected there. I quickly looked away, moistening my lips, preferring my husband's apathy to this.

Lord Dryhten sent a warning look to his warriors. They all quieted under his sharp gaze. There was no humor in his expression. For a long moment nothing could be heard over the clinking of harnesses and stomping hooves and wind whistling through the bailey. At last my husband signaled with a whirl of his fingers that we should all move out. Riders turned their horses and started toward the gates at a swift clip, eager to be on their way.

My husband lingered, hovering close to my mare and looking up at me. "Where are your gloves?"

I dipped a hand into the pocket of my riding skirts and dutifully pulled them out. He waited as I slid them on, the supple leather smoothly encasing my fingers.

He took up my reins and passed them to me. Accepting them, I looked at him questioningly. He glanced after his warriors, who had filed out of the courtyard. From them he looked to the king and queen and their retinue, then back to me again.

Was he having second thoughts? Contemplating leaving me here, after all?

His expression was unreadable, and I held my breath, not certain what to hope for in this instance. Whatever he decided did not change that I was bound to him for the rest of my life. Here or in the Borderlands, I was his wife.

"The crossing isn't for the weak," he warned me. "You need to keep up and do as bade, understand?"

He was decided then.

I nodded and moistened my lips. "What shall I call you?" Should I forever address him as *my lord* or *Lord Dryhten* or *you there*? He was my husband, after all. If he was going to be bossing me about, I'd like to know what to call him.

He considered me thoughtfully and sent a glance after his party. They were well ahead of us, through the portcullis now. His eyes locked with mine again. "You may call me Fell," he said, but there was a strange note to his voice. Resentment, maybe.

Fell.

Something jumped inside my chest then. A flicker of reaction that I could not decipher.

He left me and swung up into his saddle without even touching the reins or seat horn. I whispered his name soundlessly, trying it out, tasting it on my tongue, and that spot in my chest flared like an ember catching to life.

Shaking my head, I tightened my grip around the reins and braced myself to follow him. My mare seemed to know, falling in immediately behind him.

We formed a line out of the palace, plodding down into the City, mindful of bodies in our path. People stepped aside in the streets, their expressions wary as they paused to watch us pass. Several mamas tucked their children behind their skirts, pushing down the cheerfully waving hands of their youths as though such friendliness to the barbarians from the north would draw undue attention to them.

Once we cleared the outer walls of the City, the road widened, and we spread out a little more. My mare dutifully trailed Fell's horse. The warrior lord moved as one with his destrier, his big body rolling and fluid atop the giant beast, and I knew he had probably never once been a passenger inside a carriage. He looked born to the saddle.

I admired the impressive breadth of his shoulders and back, my cheeks heating as I recalled the sensation of Fell's muscled back beneath my palms. I wrenched myself away from such lusty thinking. I'd never had such thoughts before. It was astounding how much could change in so short a time.

The older warrior from earlier rode back to us from the front of the group. "I'll take the rear," he volunteered, easily managing his spirited mount.

Fell gave a single nod.

The grizzly warrior passed my husband and then wheeled around, riding abreast of me. I glanced at him uncertainly and gave a perfunctory incline of my head. "Good day."

He ran his pale white fingers through his thick beard as he considered me bitterly, the barest hint of his lips visible through the coarse hair. He smirked as he assessed me bobbing atop my saddle. I knew *I* didn't look one with my horse. I couldn't even pretend otherwise.

"It's a long and dangerous journey, lass. Anything can happen on the crossing." He glanced ahead to my husband, who was unaware of or indifferent to the conversation happening behind him. The morning sun emerged, breaking through the clouds and striking my husband's tar-black hair, the strands flashing purple as a raven's wing in the sunlight. "Even the most veteran warrior can perish. And you"—the older man savored the words—"are no warrior." The pronouncement sent a chill through me, and that was when I knew.

If this man had anything to do with it, I would never reach the Borderlands alive.

12

STIG

I STOOD AT THE RAMPARTS, MY HANDS DIGGING INTO THE ancient rock, grit sliding beneath my shorn nails as wind buffeted me. The joints of my fingers ached as I watched her go, stone crumbling in my palms.

My gaze strained, peering through the morning air at the winding tail of warriors, a snake slithering away, fading into the distance.

This couldn't be real.

Nothing about this felt real.

And yet it was. Permanent. Terrifying. All too real. I felt off-balance. Dizzy. Sick. As sick as I'd felt during the bedding ceremony. It was the stuff of nightmares. I'd tried to flee, to step out from the room, unable to bear it, unable to stomach the sounds, the knowledge of what was transpiring behind the curtains . . .

But my father had stopped me, his hard hand pressing into my chest as he hissed in my ear that I would not leave, that I would not run away like a coward. *It's your duty as captain of the guard to stay and maintain security. Now act like a man.*

I'd stiffened my spine and remained, but not for the reason my father believed.

I agreed with him on one point. It was my duty to maintain palace security, and that extended to Tamsyn. So I had stayed put in that room just in case. For her. In case she needed me. In case she changed her mind and called out for help. Nothing would have held me back then. I'd stayed and endured, biting the inside of my cheek until blood filled my mouth.

I inhaled through my nose, trying to supply my shrinking lungs with air as I struggled to make sense of it all. One moment Tamsyn was here, with me. Now she was gone. And not just gone . . . but gone with him. The Beast. The thought of her out there alongside him . . .

Bile surged in my throat. She wasn't safe.

It wouldn't be permanent. I vowed that. My fingers clenched, tightening around the rampart. I leaned forward as though I could reach across the distance and pluck her from their midst.

It wouldn't be forever. I wouldn't abandon her. Somehow. I didn't care what my father said. I didn't care what the king decreed. I didn't care that she had married another man. It was all a lie—something forced upon her. It would not stand.

I would see her again.

I would save her.

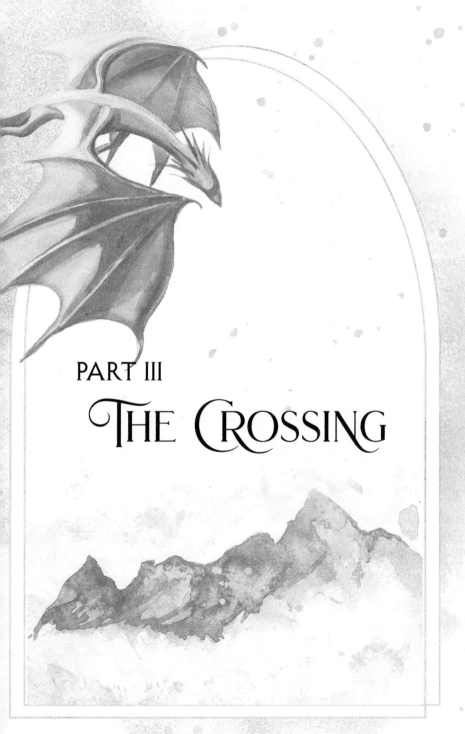

PART III
THE CROSSING

13

TAMSYN

THEY THOUGHT THE JOURNEY WOULD BREAK ME.

It was the hope. At least it was Lord Arkin's hope. I had since learned his name after his not-so-vague threat. It seemed wise to know all you could about your enemies, and it was clear to me that Arkin was determined to be my enemy.

It was not yet clear, however, what I would be to Fell. Or he to me.

The other warriors cast looks of disdain in my direction as we made our way north. I was an outsider, a proven deceiver, and they did not hide their contempt. They viewed me as a bumbling, inept addition to their party. Little did they know, I was made of sterner stuff. Life had conditioned me for this. I was not glass. I did not break. I was bred to survive.

As arduous as the hours in the saddle proved to be, I ignored the discomfort and clung to my composure, studying the changing landscape. I'd never ventured this far from home. The coastline to the south of the City, where our summer villa was located, was smooth and flat with tall willow grass that curled like fingers in the sun-kissed breeze. It took only a couple of hours by carriage to reach there. This was decidedly more vigorous an excursion, and the sun kissed nothing here.

The farther north we progressed, the more untamed our surroundings became. The trees grew bigger, taller, greener; the brushwood wild and overgrown in a tangle of land. The terrain, laden with fog, undulated in soft hills and valleys, in readiness of the mountains to come.

I'd never before felt the throb of the world in my bones, the whisper of grass in my ears. Never heard the birds or animals shifting and chittering in the unrelenting press of the countryside. Even the rocks possessed a heartbeat. A flow. Blood whooshed through the veins of the earth beneath me.

It felt as though we were leaving civilization behind. There were no towns and few villages, and those villages we passed through were humble, meager affairs full of decrepit thatched-roof cottages. Dogs with jutting rib cages gave our party a wide berth. Children with dirt-stained faces peered out from shutterless windows into the misty air. Their hollow eyes made them appear far older than their tender years. Slump-shouldered, bone-thin women pumped water at the wells. Men were scarce, ostensibly breaking their backs somewhere in the mines or in the distant fields. It was scarcely the prosperity of the City.

"Not what you're accustomed to, is it?" the dark-haired sword maiden beside me asked, her wiry body rolling easily with the motion of her mount as we followed the winding road into higher country. Her name was Mari, and she was the only one who deigned to speak to me, and for that she was my favorite person.

I cleared my throat. "No, it is not."

"Deprivation isn't pretty."

"How . . . ? Why—?" I started, at a loss in the face of so much suffering.

"Penterra pours all its wealth into keeping its ruling class and allies abroad happy. Can't lose their support." Her voice twisted bitterly. "They don't give much attention to those in need here at home." She nodded to Fell ahead of us. "That's why he was determined to marry you. Well. A princess of Penterra, anyway." She continued talking as though she had not just delivered a blow. "He wanted a seat at the table, so his voice could be heard, so he could make a difference."

Oh. *Oh.*

So he had failed in his quest. Because he was stuck with me.

At least *he* thought he had failed. As did the rest of them. Their cold attitude toward me made even more sense now. I swallowed miserably. I thought Fell just wanted to marry one of my sisters, because what man didn't want the great prize of a princess? I had thought it was ego and greed and status-seeking. I had not felt much remorse over tricking him, considering all of that. But now that I understood his motives, I saw myself the way they all did. Not only as a deceiver, but as a poison, tainting and spoiling their great hope.

A baby started wailing from inside one of the cottages. The muffled sound ricocheted in the murky air. I'd heard babies cry before, but this sounded different. There was pain and need in it. Hopelessness in the disembodied sound that lifted up like a wraith on the air. A ghost child trapped in misery.

Cold shivered down my neck and spine. I felt sick as my gaze swept over the dying village. I knew this was none of my fault, but I had not stopped it. I had not prevented it from continuing. I had not helped these people. Marrying Fell, stopping him from gaining the power he needed to make a difference in their lives, had only made things worse, only pushed innocents deeper into the abyss.

I blinked my stinging eyes, lifting them to Fell ahead of me, but he wasn't there anymore. He had fallen out of line. He moved toward a well, where several women stood, warily clutching their buckets at his approach. I watched, my breath catching in my chest as he reached inside the satchel draped over his saddle. He said something. His lips moved as he tossed several coins down to them.

The women grasped the coins gratefully, calling out their thanks as he turned back around, nudging his destrier into a trot. His gaze met mine, but I could not bring myself to hold his stare for very long. Not with this sudden knowledge that I had foiled his plans—that these plans were even necessary, that my father was such a terrible ruler. My throat closed. *A terrible ruler.* But what else would you call a king who let his people starve?

Shaking my head, I got out tightly, "I thought things were supposed to be better after the Threshing."

That was the whole point behind the war against dragonkind. It was the doctrine espoused by the throne. Not to mention the dogma spoon-fed to me in the schoolroom. The Threshing may have lasted for centuries and cost innumerable lives, but it was supposed to have fixed everything. It had been necessary and, ultimately, successful. And . . . it was over.

Finished. Done. Ended a hundred years ago with the Hormung.

So why was Penterra like this now? Why was there still such misery?

Humans had blamed dragons for all ills: drought, famine, disease. To say nothing of the destruction of the occasional village or town that fell prey to their fiery wrath. Dragons had sat on great caches of treasure, prospering whilst man wallowed, eking out the barest existence. The Threshing was humanity's way of turning the tables and ridding dragons from the pecking order forever. It had solved all our problems. At least that was the belief.

Mari shrugged in response and murmured, "Makes you wonder."

"Wonder?" I echoed.

"Whether dragons were the real problem," she finished.

A slap could have no more astonished me. I glanced around sharply. Such talk felt almost . . . sacrilegious. I'd never heard anyone say such a thing. She was a sword maiden. She lived in the Borderlands, the place where the bloodiest, most fearsome fighting had taken place against dragons. Now, however, instead of dragons, the fighting was against bandits who had taken up residence in the dragon-free Crags and against invading soldiers from Veturland who dared to cross the border.

I didn't reply. I couldn't. But Mari's observation sat with me as we rode on, a heavy stone grinding against my chest.

Whether dragons were the real problem.

Certainly all the wealth that had been uncovered from the dragon troves had since been dispensed. And famine and disease were still here. Destroying the dragons had not destroyed those things. Indeed

not. And this, coupled with the other revelation of the day—that Penterra was not as prosperous as I had been led to believe, that my
father was no great king—was something of an adjustment for me.

I glanced at the broad expanse of Fell's back ahead of me, wondering if he shared the opinion of this sword maiden. Did he think
the Threshing had been pointless, too?

As the son of Balor the Butcher, and the great-grandson of the
border king responsible for the victory of the Hormung, he couldn't
possibly. The Lord of the Borderlands had to be bloodthirsty and
single-minded in everything, just like his forefathers.

Dryhten was a killer without regret. Not someone who looked
back at his father's legacy and thought any part of it was a mistake.

Not someone who would happily accept being married to the
wrong woman.

I WAS NOT prepared for this new world.

The crossing offered no comfortable quarters. No warm bed. No
generous meals. No freshly laundered clothes. No maids helping me
with my toilette. *No casual beatings.* I gave my head a small, fierce
shake. I had never minded that before. That had been my duty. An
honor bestowed upon me. My service to the throne.

Just as this was my duty, too.

It wasn't as though my former life had been free of threats. It
was only that the crack of the whip against my skin had been familiar. At least at home, I knew what to expect. Here, everything
was unpredictable. I felt as though I was balancing on a rope—one
misstep and I would topple over.

Home. The palace was not my home. Not anymore. I would have
to stop thinking of it as such. I had no home at all. No hearth to
warm my feet by, with loved ones surrounding me. And yet I could
not think of my home as the Borderlands either, a place I had never
even been. The mist-shrouded foothills of lore. With him, the Beast,
who did not want me as his bride. It was impossible to comprehend.

The Beast. *My husband—*

I could not finish the thought. When would thinking of him as *my husband* not feel strange? Not untrue? When would it not result in this unremitting squeeze in my chest?

When would I no longer feel an intruder among these border warriors? Beside *him?*

Despite his flash of anger on the night of our bedding, Fell was less transparent than his warriors. They treated me to cutting glares, but he never even looked at me as we rode. Just that brief meeting of our gazes in the village, in which I thought I'd read accusation in the gray frost of his eyes before I looked away.

There was no conversation between us. He was stoic, cold, and indifferent.

And that was perhaps worse. His anger would have been preferable to the icy silence.

He withheld his company, and I wondered if this was how it would be between us. Would we never get beyond our shaky start? Would we live as strangers forever? Would I live at all? I shuddered. That was Stig talking. The memory of his voice pushing through, angry and bitter. *He could kill you and no one would do anything about it.*

I swallowed against a lump in my throat. I could not help it. The doubt. The fear. They sank deep. Clamping teeth that would not release me.

Whenever we stopped, Fell disappeared, and Mari stepped forward, tasked with my care. I was grateful for her. She guided me into the woods to relieve myself and bedded down beside me each night. There were no tents erected. Indeed, they did not worry about such things as comfort. She saw that I ate and instructed me on rolling out my bedding at night and packing it away each morning. I took her grunts as approval that I was doing everything correctly.

A weary sort of monotony fell into place. A rhythm of waking, riding through air that felt like cold soup, eating food tasteless on my tongue, bedding down on hard earth. Repeat.

I would often look up and catch Arkin staring at me. His gaze was more than malevolent. His eyes felt faintly scheming and made the tiny hairs at my nape vibrate.

Whenever I searched out Fell to see if he noticed his man's fixation on me, I found my husband elsewhere, paces away or with the horses or nowhere to be seen at all. Avoiding me. He had told Stig I was his, but he didn't seem to care about me. Perhaps he had changed his mind and decided I was too much trouble and not worth keeping around.

He could kill you and no one would do anything about it.

No matter how I tried, in these dark moments—riding, plodding along—I could not get Stig's words out of my head where they had burrowed deeply.

Fell's indifference stung more than I would have liked to admit, and I began to consider something I had never dared.

I thought about it carefully in the silent hours, and there were plenty of those—hours during which I never spoke, hours during which no one spoke to me.

I toyed with the idea, testing it out cautiously, like it was a new pair of shoes that had not yet been broken in, experimenting with the notion that maybe, just perhaps, I should take my chances and run away.

14
FELL

MY FATHER WAS THE ONLY FAMILY I HAD EVER KNOWN. I never had a mother. No brothers or sisters. No uncles or aunts. No cousins to love or hate, to wreak havoc with like wild things during periodic visits.

Balor the Butcher was well past middle age when he found me in that dragon's lair and saved me, when he brought me out of that dark den and into the light. Me and the black opal—two prizes wrested that day from the clutches of an onyx dragon.

Onyx dragons were the foot soldiers of dragonkind. The most common dragon, black as winking charcoal. The biggest, the fiercest, the fastest, the strongest. Great slabs of muscle that served on the front lines. And Balor had defeated her, this outlier clinging to life eighty years after the Hormung. A she-dragon who shouldn't have been alive, who held me captive, who had stolen me from my true family and likely killed them. *That* I would never know with any certainty. I only knew that when my father found me, I was lost. An orphan destined for the jaws and belly of a monster.

She had put up a valiant fight. She had survived a long time, when all the rest of her kind had perished, after all. But Balor had triumphed, hacking off her head with his axe . . . a piece of bone hewn from a dragon's pelvic wing. That axe now hung on display in the hall of my keep, staring down at every meal and feast like a watchful eye, a symbol of the war waged and won.

Balor was not an easy man, but he took me into his hearth and heart—what he possessed of a heart, anyway. He was not sentimental. Not a scrap of tenderness or softness within him. I had few lessons from him that had not ended with a bloodied lip or nose. *Blood is weakness*, he was fond of telling me. *Be strong and you won't bleed.*

A widower with no children of his own, he had sworn off marrying again, insisting that he was too old to pander to a wife. He claimed me as his son and heir in so bold and resolute a manner that no one dared challenge the decision.

Who would challenge him anyway? He was the warrior who beheaded the last dragon, an onyx dragon. Stern as he was, he had loved me. As well as he could love anyone. And I loved him as well as I could love anyone, which wasn't to say I had loved him very well or fully or wholly. Not, perhaps, as well as I should have. I grimaced. That part of myself was lacking, as small and shriveled up as a plant left too long without water.

I respected my father. I owed him my life. He saw strength in me from the very start, something worth saving, and for that I would always honor his memory.

But what did I know of love and marriage and family? Those things had certainly never been included in my lessons of swordplay and hand-to-hand combat. All my life had been about battle and death—or rather beating death.

Oh, I had friends. Comrades. Lovers. Many times, with the battle sweat still beading hot on my skin, blood simmering through me like a stew, I had found release and comfort in another. There was nothing like a quick fuck to affirm your existence—that you still lived, while others did not.

But that was just fucking. It wasn't meaningful. It wasn't lasting. It was relief. A balm. Sweet wine to a parched throat. Temporary. In the end, I always returned to my bed alone. Slept alone. Woke alone.

I lived as an island, focused on protecting my people, so that they did not become like the other villages surrounding my lands, continually crushed and razed by those who reveled in lawlessness, in destruction, who terrorized the weak and the vulnerable like hungry wolves.

Still. In those fleeting moments of calm, resting in my bed at night, the breath easing from me as soft and warm as wool, I stared into the darkness and considered my future and whether there would be a woman next to me in the bed at the end of day. A wife.

I'd always assumed I would marry someday. It was my responsibility to do so. My father had been clear on that.

I had wondered if maybe I would form a bond with her. Then, she had been a faceless, nameless, formless figure. Someone soft to pull to my hardness. A gentle hand to find in the dark.

Would there be that closeness between us that some husbands had with their wives? I'd seen those alliances. The shared, knowing glances. The lips that would lift at private jokes. The little intimate touches. The couples who seemed to exist for each other as much as they existed for themselves. Not a frequent sight, but frequent enough to know they were real. It was perhaps attainable.

Now I had a face to consider. A form. A name. *Tamsyn.* A wife. My wife.

Perhaps, if I kept her, there would be children. Those of my own blood. I'd never had that before. I'd existed without seeing myself in anyone else. I had no blood. No kin. No one to look at and say: *family.*

When I studied my reflection—that frosted gaze, the hair dark as a raven's wing—I could not point to someone else and think: *There, too.* There was no shadow of me in anyone else.

A dragon had stolen that from me—the ability to see myself anywhere else, in someone else. Tamsyn could change that. If I accepted this. If I accepted *her.* Yes, I would make Hamlin pay for his trickery. I would bring down the throne. Especially that sour-faced lord regent. But that did not mean I couldn't keep her.

I tried to envision it, to feel it, to see it in her unearthly gaze, in eyes like sunlit amber. I tried to see the future if I kept her. Our future. Perhaps a family. That did something to me. Made my chest warm and snap like a fire crackling in a pit. I definitely didn't mind the idea of creating those children with her. At least the begetting part would not be a chore. The push and pull of our bodies together had been a sweet, blissful thing. The blood rushed to my cock, remembering it now.

It was something. A start. Even if she was a liar.

She was a peculiar thing. A puzzle I could not quite piece together. A non-princess. I didn't care what they called her. No royal took a beating with a smile and called it duty.

I glanced at Tamsyn, and my palm instantly reacted, the marked skin jumping, the X humming as though longing to press against her, craving contact—a return to her.

She rode along silently, her lips like ash, her face pale, the healthy golden glow to her skin that I'd first admired when I met her now gone. Clearly she was not accustomed to the rigors of the crossing, but there was little I could do about that. We still had the river to ford. And winter was coming. We needed to make haste lest we find ourselves caught out in the open in a snow squall. People became disoriented in squalls, riding right off a cliff or freezing in a snowdrift.

This was not the time to indulge her. *And why should I look after her comfort?* That stubborn voice inserted itself, an aching bruise, raw and sore and slow to heal.

She was my wife, true, but only through foul means. Only because I had been robbed of choice. She was no innocent. She was a cog in the wheel turning to make a fool of me. And now I was stuck with her. For all our days together, however long or brief they were, we would have this ignominious start, something never shaken. Like spilled wine, it would forever stain the fabric of us.

As we rode along the winding and rutted road, the forest a tangle encroaching on either side, she stood out like a flag flapping in the wind, calling attention to herself in her elegant riding habit, marking herself as different. Not one of us. As though she was out for a country ride and not a cross-country passage.

I dragged my gaze away, at war with myself. Part of me wanted to keep on ignoring her, but the other part of me, the pitiless, merciless part—*the Beast*—wanted to stop and camp early for the night, to erect a tent and climb inside with her, to strip that ridiculous riding habit off her and punish her with pleasure until she wept.

For my hands, lips, and tongue to explore and map every inch of her until she was no longer such an unknowable thing, no longer a mysterious, uncharted realm waiting to be discovered, waiting to be made mine in a way that a duplicitous bedding had not achieved.

Until there were no more veils between us, and I marked her as well and truly mine.

I nudged my destrier ahead to the front of the party, increasing our pace and vowing that we would not stop until nightfall.

And I would set up no tent.

15

TAMSYN

THE WOODS WERE ALIVE. I KNEW IT. FELT IT.

In the ensuing days, this knowledge took hold of me, deep as teeth sinking into my skin, through the meat of me, clinging tightly.

We moved along at a swift pace that was far from comfortable, especially in the increasingly opaque air. The limited visibility worried my nerves, but the others carried on as though the fog were an ordinary thing. I could see directly in front of my horse to the rider before me, but beyond that, the world turned hazy, draped in a fine wool. Shapes, vague shadows. Trees towering, amorphous giants. There could be anything out there, ahead of us, beside us . . . waiting.

I would have preferred to travel slower, to see better, to take more breaks, to stretch my screaming muscles and unkink my back, to rest—even if that meant adding more time to what already felt like an endless journey. We had been at this for over a week, and we were not yet halfway there.

But my preferences didn't matter. I told myself I would become accustomed to the relentless pace, to my grinding weight, to the exhaustion and the soreness and the aches, to the ill-humored company I kept.

All of it.

We would reach our destination eventually. I just had to hang on until then. Endure. I could do that. I knew *how* to do that.

Except . . .

I felt the eyes on us. Always. Tracking us, marking our progress as we journeyed, observing us even at night when we bedded down, and in the mornings when we woke, unfolding our bodies into the cold gray.

Every sound felt suspect. A birdcall. A snapping branch. A whispering wind. A chattering creature. I seemed to be the only one nervous, adjusting my grip over and over on the reins as we rode, my hands sweating inside my gloves.

Sleep was hard won. I could blame it on my growing discomfort, my hurting body. The hard ground. The unfamiliarity of sleeping outdoors. The strangers all around me, husband included. Husband *especially*.

Or it could be my gnawing conviction that others lurked in the impenetrable woods, watching . . . waiting for the right moment to pounce. It certainly put to rest my thoughts of running away. At least for now. I would not flee from one untenable situation into another, into something worse . . . into what felt like certain danger.

The border warriors were vigilant but undaunted as we rode. They knew themselves, confident in their strength as they sat atop their warhorses, moving fluidly with their beasts. They were formidable. Even I could see that. My gaze flicked to the thick press of trees. Anyone watching us could see it, too. And they were out there. I knew it in the marrow of my bones.

And I was not wrong.

I forgot all about what the grueling pace was doing to my body when we rounded a bend, and they were there, blocking the road, poised atop their mounts, completely at ease, arms and hands relaxed, reins loose between their fingers. Clearly they had been expecting us.

At the front of this motley band, dead center, was a handsome young man with a trim beard who reminded me a bit of Stig, even if he was dressed shabbily, the scarf around his neck tatty and worn.

He smiled widely. His easy manner felt contrary to the tension swimming on the vaporous air. He lifted a hand, flicking it mildly.

Instantly his men moved in, unfurling across the road, fanning around us.

"They're flanking us," Mari growled in warning.

Fell lifted his fingers in a circular motion, signaling his warriors to action. Our warriors closed in tighter, hands drifting to the weapons at their sides and attached to their saddles—all movements done with an ease and idleness that belied the edge upon which we all precariously balanced.

I might never have traveled this far from the City before, but I knew enough to know that the situation was fraught. Danger thickened the air as Fell's warriors dropped into multiple rows in a defensive tactic. I was maneuvered behind Fell. They squeezed in on both sides of me, clearly trying to make me less . . . *less*.

It was as though by attempting to hide me they only shone a light upon me. The leader sat a little higher in his saddle, craning his head, peering over and around bodies to settle his gaze on me. I knew I looked different from the rest of them. I lacked the bearing and appearance of a warrior from the Borderlands. I was dressed as a Penterran noble, in my riding skirts and cobalt-blue cloak lined and trimmed in pale fur.

"If you wish to pass, you need to pay the road tax," one of the bandits announced.

Fell pulled his sword free, the steel singing in the air. "I will pay no tax." His words rumbled loose from him in an almost bored manner. Perhaps he was not surprised. Had he sensed them watching us, tracking us, too?

"We are no defenseless travelers," Arkin cut in. "You've picked the wrong people to fuck with. Now stand aside, dogs."

The leader snapped his gaze to Arkin, his nostrils flaring, and I wondered if it was the wisest course to insult him.

Fell muttered Arkin's name under his breath while training his gaze steadily on the leader. "Penterran roads are free to all travelers," he inserted in an unruffled voice, smooth as churned butter.

"*Penterran* roads?" The leader grinned a toothy smile, although his words held no lightness, and his eyes were cold as night as they scanned us. "You've been misinformed. This road is mine. All who wish to use it must pay a toll." He scratched his bearded jaw with long fingers. His speech and manner were quite refined. Not what I would expect from an outlaw here along the edge of nowhere.

"Should have taken another route north," one of the bandits suggested with a mocking twist of a smile, revealing his rotting teeth.

"What other route? Through the boglands? Or the skog?" Arkin's expression revealed how intolerable he found either.

I'd heard of boglands, treacherous swamps where no one traveled, much less lived. The marshy ground was unstable. One wrong step plunged man and beast into sinkholes, never to emerge again. I'd never heard of the skog, and I filed that word away to ask about later.

The leader nodded, feigning a look of contemplation. "Those are options."

"Go ahead. Take your chances in the skog," Rotting Teeth encouraged with enough relish to let me know this would be the worst choice.

"Or," the leader suggested with an air of magnanimity, gesturing to the road ahead, "you can pay the toll and be on your way."

"We traveled south this very route weeks ago without you jackals harassing us," Arkin complained.

The leader shrugged. "Well. We must have been occupied elsewhere. Now we are not. Now we are here, and you need to pay us."

"How much do you want?" Arkin snapped.

Fell held up a hand. "The amount does not matter. I won't pay it. I don't give in to thieves."

I looked at Fell with some annoyance. Was this even worth the fight? He had the coin to spare. He could pay, and we could avoid any trouble.

The leader's eyes found me again. "Coin isn't the only payment we accept. We can barter . . . other things."

I didn't miss the direction of his gaze. Neither did Fell. His expression unreadable, he looked to me and back to the brigand.

I held my breath, my fingers clenching my reins tightly.

Still grinning, the leader nodded to me, adding, "We can take the girl there as our due."

No one moved.

I waited, wondering if Fell would agree. He didn't want me, after all. If they wanted to be rid of me, this would be the opportunity to do so without being directly responsible. He would have an explanation to give my parents and the lord regent. *Sorry, bandits took her.*

Rotting Teeth frowned at me. Shaking his head, he muttered, "Bad luck, that."

His leader sent him an annoyed glance. "What are you on about?"

"The hair." He shook his head. "She's . . . wicked."

I resisted rolling my eyes. It would not be the first time I'd heard that allegation.

The leader gave his insufferable grin again. "I like them wicked." Then he shrugged as though he were not talking about something as significant as my life. "What can I say? I like redheads. See so few these days."

"For good reason," Rotting Teeth muttered, referring to the war on witches. Not that there was much of a war anymore. They had all been run to ground in the past few decades. Eradicated. Or they hid themselves so well that they avoided detection.

Arkin leaned to the side, the leather of his saddle creaking as he whispered something to Fell. I couldn't hear the words, but I could guess.

Let him have her.

"She's not for the taking," Fell declared after a long moment, ignoring Arkin.

The bandits' leader tsked. "Come now. She's not one of you. Anyone can see that. She looks ready to topple off her saddle. She must be slowing you down."

I bristled. Did I look *that* feeble and pathetic? I pulled my shoulders back as though I could suddenly appear more stalwart, as strong and sturdy as the rest of them. I hadn't uttered a complaint in the days since we'd started this hellish ride. I bit back a retort insisting that I was not slowing them down. They merely moved at a fast clip. At least, I didn't think they had slowed their pace because of me. I now eyed Fell suspiciously. Would they be moving faster if I wasn't with them? That did not sit well with me. I did not want to be a burden and give him another reason to resent me.

"Oh, now you're doing me a favor by taking her off my hands, is that it? So considerate of you." Fell laughed darkly. "Which is it, friend?" The way he stressed *friend* was decidedly unfriendly. "Is she a burden? Or valuable enough to barter?"

The brigand's smile slipped. Clearly he did not appreciate being laughed at. He leaned forward over his mount as though ready to impart something significant. "Either give me the girl or I'll litter the road with pieces of you." He gestured to our full party with a mild flick of his fingers. "All of you."

Suddenly my skin snapped and pulled tight as warmth rose up inside me. A sense of foreboding rushed over me. Air tremored from my lips . . . from my mouth, which suddenly tasted of copper.

Compelled for some mystifying reason, I lifted my gaze from the menacing man and peered into the dense walls of foliage to the right and left of us along the road. It was impossible to see within the thick press of towering trees, but I looked anyway. I tried to see whatever it was I felt staring back at me . . . at us. I couldn't see them, but I felt them. Felt their hot gusts of breath, the rush of blood through their veins, their humming excitement ready to be unleashed upon us.

There were more. More brigands lying in wait, ready to cut us down like a scythe to grass if the order was given. It was not just the manageable dozen or so in front of us.

A panicked gasp left me. My gaze flew to Fell. His attention was also on the trees. He knew, too. Perhaps he had always known, from the moment we rounded the bend. And, looking at me, he saw that *I* knew. He read that knowledge on my face as easily as one scanned a map, and I felt his surprise. It was the same curious way he had looked at me in the chancery, when I'd emerged from my hiding spot behind the painting. The same way he had looked at me in our marriage bed—his eyes full of wonder and curiosity.

He'd been unable to see my face through the veil, but still he had looked at me, surprise flickering across his shadowed face as his body took mine. I'd felt his shock . . . his bewilderment as we joined, me taking from him as much as he took from me. My face burned fire.

"Give us the girl."

The words jarred me back to reality. I had forgotten everyone else, lost in the memory of that bedding and the pleasure I had found. At the voice, Fell and I dragged our gazes back to the brigand.

"She's my wife," Fell said. Just like that. A statement of fact.

The admission affected me, though. The pulse spiked at my throat. It was the first time I had ever heard him acknowledge me as that. It made our marriage feel all the more real—equal parts terrifying and exciting. His voice, those words . . . My belly dipped.

I blew out an exasperated breath. This was what came of thinking about that night, about our bedding, and why I had become so careful to avoid thinking about it. It was too confusing, too . . . stimulating. I would think about it later and attempt to sift through my feelings then. There were more important matters at hand.

"Ah." The leader chuckled and looked to his cohorts. "I didn't have that sense. Wouldn't have guessed that at all. Did any of you?"

My face burned now for different reasons. Of course he did not have that sense. Fell wasn't even riding close to me. He hardly appeared to be a husband enamored of his wife.

There were chuckles and murmurs of agreement among the bandits.

"Well, she is mine," Fell affirmed in a hard voice. "And I will keep her." The last bit rang with a challenge, which was only emphasized as he lifted his sword and pointed it directly at the brigand. Fell stared down the length of the blade and gave a slight squint, as though bringing the man into better focus. "Now. Let us pass."

All levity vanished from the leader's face. He wasn't going to move. He wasn't going to relent, I realized, and gulped. And neither was Fell.

The coppery taste in my mouth intensified. It was dreadful. I'd only tasted it once before. I was barely five years old then. I'd knocked out one of my front teeth prematurely. I'd been running, and I tripped on a toy and landed face-first on a wooden block in the nursery. Blood, hot and thick, had filled my mouth. I remembered that I bled forever, and it had tasted like copper coins.

Nurse had exclaimed over the blood spurting from my mouth and declared that my adult tooth would likely never grow in. A real shame, she'd insisted. *You're already frightfully unattractive with that unfortunate hair, and now you will be gap-toothed.* No surprise I remembered that insult so keenly. She had been wrong, though. My adult tooth eventually made an appearance, breaking through the gums like the arrival of a long-anticipated guest.

This was like that. Copper coins in my mouth again. Except I wasn't bleeding.

That was when I knew. Somehow.

Blood would soon soak the ground. I smelled it like impending rain.

"Or," Fell said in the hushed pause.

"Or?"

"I have another proposition that won't result in anyone getting hurt. Well, anyone other than you."

The man snorted. "Cocky bastard, aren't you?"

"I'll fight you. Just us. You and me. If I win, we continue on our way unmolested. *With* my wife."

The leader laughed lightly, and I braced myself for his rejection of the proposal. Why would he accept such terms? He and his band outnumbered us. He needn't risk injury to himself to get his way. *To get me.*

"You and I can settle this," Fell said, baiting him. "Come. Show us your prowess. You can tell everyone you beat the Beast of the Borderlands." From the gleam in Fell's eyes, it was clear he did not think he could be defeated.

The leader's eyes widened as he looked him over. "Is that right? You're the Beast?"

"That's right," Fell agreed with a slight incline of his head. "Even if I win . . . it will make a damn fine story for you. Admit it."

The leader almost looked tempted to smile at Fell's cajoling. Then he gave a single shake of his head and replied soberly, "I'm not in this for stories. I have people to feed."

Fell nodded at me. "And how will she feed your people?"

At that, the leader's smile returned. "There is more than one appetite to be fed."

I sucked in a breath.

Fell's frosty eyes iced over. His hand tightened on the grip of his sword, knuckles clenching white.

The taste in my mouth became unbearable, telling me everything I needed to know. *No.* I could not let this play out. Lives would be lost. I might survive only to become a captive of these brigands. If Fell was too stubborn to see that, so be it. *I* was not, though. I was not, and I would not let that happen. I had to stop these idiots before they killed each other.

Enough was enough.

Seized with purpose, I squeezed my travel-sore thighs and nudged my mount forward with my heels. My mare reacted to my prodding quicker than I'd expected, lurching forward with a jangle of the bridle.

Mari noticed my movement and grabbed for my reins, but she was too late. She made a muffled sound as I passed Fell and the rest of his warriors. They seemed frozen, darting puzzled looks at me. Clearly no one had expected me to do anything. They'd expected me to sit in silence like a great lump, letting life happen to me without a whimper.

Perhaps I surprised even myself. I was accustomed to taking abuse. Never resisting. Never fighting back.

I was not one of them. I wasn't a warrior. At least not like they were. I wasn't even, as far as they were concerned, a real princess. I was nothing.

Sitting atop my horse between the two groups, I felt all eyes on me.

"Tamsyn." Fell finally found his voice. "Get back behind me."

"No."

He blinked in astonishment. He had not expected that. His destrier must have sensed some of his sudden tension, because he pranced in place and tossed his head with an agitated neigh.

The leader laughed, enjoying my show of rebellion. "Ohhh, I like her."

Ignoring him, I lifted my arms to the clasp of the necklace I wore. It was a gift from my last birthday. Well, on the day we celebrated my birthday. No one knew my actual birthday. Not with any certainty. I couldn't have been but a day or two old when I was found in the castle bailey.

I owned a few pieces of jewelry. All gifts from my family. Nothing too extravagant. All sentimental, now more than ever that I was gone from them.

But I would give it up. To save lives, it was a small sacrifice.

The clasp unhooked, and I lifted it away from me, fastening the clasp again so that the four charms did not slip loose.

"Here." I stretched out my arm, the chain dangling from my fingers. "Take it. I'll pay the tax."

All my life I had been paying the tax. What was one more time?

"Tamsyn." Fell growled my name.

I sent him a hard stare and declared, "There will be no fighting." I looked back to the brigand. "Here. It is quite valuable, I assure you. Take it."

He studied me thoughtfully before dragging his attention to the necklace in my hand. He inched his mount forward, crossing that remaining bit of space between us. He reached for the necklace, letting his fingers stroke my glove-encased hand as he did so.

Fell pushed up beside me, his destrier bumping into my mare. His warhorse flashed its teeth before nipping at my horse. Fell looked ready to flash his own teeth and take a bite out of something, too. Me, presumably.

The brigand tested the weight of my necklace in his palm, assessing the gold chain, examining the four hearts, each studded with a different gemstone, each one representing the four princesses of Penterra. Yes. One was even for me.

My heart had swelled that day when I opened the pretty ribboned box that contained the necklace. I had felt so touched, so included, so *seen*. The gift had been an affirmation, proof of the royal family's commitment to me, their embrace of me into their family.

I experienced a little pang at the loss, to see it in the hands of this thief, to know I'd never see it or wear it again. Just as everything else I had left behind, I would be leaving this behind, too. Another thing lost, given up, tossed into the wind like dust.

I blinked my suddenly heavy eyes. *It's just a necklace.* A material thing. It amounted to nothing.

Lives were more important. What was one more sacrifice? This one hardly felt as substantial as my body, my life, my freedom . . . all things I had already given over to Fell.

It was worth it. I knew this. Which was why I didn't understand the fire in Fell's gaze as he looked at me. Fire enough to reduce me to ash. I shifted uneasily upon my horse.

My mouth dried, but the coppery taste was gone. There was that. I scarcely registered the brigand announcing that he was satisfied with the barter. "We will take our leave of you. Safe travels."

I didn't spare him or his followers a glance as they turned and filed down the road. I couldn't look away from Fell. Not while he looked at me with such fury and betrayal . . . as he had when he pulled off my veil to reveal my face.

I had done a good thing, but no one would know it from his expression.

He was only inches from me. The rest of his warriors stayed put, several yards away. "What were you thinking?" he demanded.

"I was thinking that we should just pay the toll and move on." Simple. Logical.

He inhaled, dragging a hand over his face as though I'd just said the most ridiculous thing. Lifting the hand off his face, he blasted me with his icy gaze. "We don't surrender to the demands of an enemy."

"Never?"

He nodded once. "It is not a thing *I* do."

I pressed my fingertips to my temple, feeling the throb of a headache. "So you would rather engage in a skirmish and endanger lives? Possibly lose your very own warriors?"

His head whipped around, assessing the avid stares of those same warriors. "We're not doing this here."

He dismounted and moved to my side, holding up a hand for me. I accepted it and was instantly cognizant, even through my gloves, of the carved X in the center of his palm. Of the carved X in the center of *my* palm. All these days later, even though it had healed, I still felt the throbbing mark there where we had been blooded, alive and sparking at the contact with him. Awareness swept up my arm and throughout the rest of my body. He glanced at where our hands were joined, and I had to think he felt it, too.

I dismounted, my legs managing not to give out—just barely. He pulled me after him, his hand still tight around mine, still burning like a brand into me. His long strides carried him off the road, into the trees. I tripped after him, trying to keep up on legs that felt as unsteady as jam.

"Let me explain something to you," he tossed over his shoulder. "I am the Lord of the Borderlands." He wove us between the thick trees, the lush grass squelching beneath our steps. There was no sight of anyone else. I supposed they had moved on with the rest of the brigands. "I keep the peace in the Borderlands. I know it mustn't seem like much to someone who grew up in the comfortable and hallowed walls of the palace, but the Borderlands are my home. My responsibility." He stopped then, dropped my hand, and turned to face me. "To care for my home, to keep it safe, I require respect, and, when need be . . . fear." His face inched closer, his mouth emphasizing that last word as though extra force was necessary for me to comprehend him. "Can't you see? The moment I am no longer feared, I lose control . . . and the Borderlands are lost."

Eyes sparking, jaw tense and clenched, he was mesmerizing, magnetic, even spitting fury like this. Not a proper reaction. I knew that. Men like him should repel. Not compel.

"I know a thing about responsibility," I attempted to argue. "That's why I—"

"What happens if I let some lowly brigands take from me? What happens to my reputation then? What does it look like when my own woman takes the necklace off her neck and gives it to some outlaws just so we can use the road every citizen in this country has the right to use?"

I blinked and tried not to consider the way "my own woman" sounded hanging in the air between us.

Just as I tried not to hear his fair point.

He answered his own question: "I would look weak. Like a man who could not protect or defend his lands. I would be inviting invasion. Every brigand in Penterra and every enemy from Veturland would try to take what I have."

I had not thought of that.

"Oh." It was a single word. A puff of sound, small and insignificant as a fluff of dandelion floating on the air.

"Oh," he echoed, nodding firmly.

Some of the fight returned to me then. Should I have let them go at each other over a bit of coin? It seemed so senseless. "I doubt this one occasion has ruined your reputation."

He shook his head and growled in disgust. "You don't know this world out here. Every day is a fight. It is imperative that you listen to me and do as I say. Because this won't be the last situation to arise. I warned you that the crossing is dangerous."

"I understand." Everything was dangerous. That's what he kept saying. I understood that, and yet I couldn't keep the bite out of my voice.

He dragged a hand through the long locks of his hair. "Even when we reach home . . . In the Borg, there will be perils, too."

Home. That didn't ring right. How could a place unknown to me and full of assorted perils ever be my home?

"I understand," I repeated, tossing my hair over my shoulder in a move that was pure defiance and at odds with my words.

"You understand, but do you agree?" He stared at me, waiting.

I struggled to get the words out, like they were something foul-tasting on my tongue. "As it is your world out here, I will defer to you."

"It is my world, but it's yours now, too, and you would do well to learn how to live in it."

"I will learn," I promised.

He leaned back on his heels, appearing mollified. He glanced back in the direction of the road where our party waited. "Let us continue, then."

Taking my elbow, he led me back to my mare. I kept my expression neutral as he helped me mount, hiding my discomfort as my most tender parts once again made contact with the saddle. What I would do for a soft cushion.

The other warriors watched impatiently, all of them wearing vaguely recriminating glares. Even Mari. My favorite person did not seem such a favorite anymore as she stared at me with disappointment. As though giving my necklace to that bandit had been some kind of failure on my part.

Never had I felt so alone. My throat was bare; the comforting weight of my necklace warm and humming on my skin was gone. Mari's expression, Fell's lecture, this unkind world I did not seem able to fit within—all of it pressed on me.

I really was not one of them. It was as though they all knew some fundamental thing that had been handed out at birth, but this trait had skipped me. I'd told Fell I would learn how to live in this world, but what if I couldn't?

What if I never belonged?

16

TAMSYN

IMPOSSIBLE AS IT SEEMED, OUR PACE QUICKENED AFTER THE confrontation with the brigands. Fell set a grueling speed, driving us like a relentless wind. Well, driving *me*. The others did not seem pushed beyond their limits. It was just me who felt as though I were a sapling battered in a storm, ready to snap. Just me. Different. Solitary. Lonely. Not yet broken in to the ways of this life.

It felt like a punishment for my actions, for my boldness with the brigands. The border warriors looked at me and saw stupidity. Weakness. As though I were a wayward child lacking all sense. My jaw locked. They were wrong. I would show them. Somehow. I would prove myself not useless.

This land had teeth. Sharp little points ready to sink into you and bleed you dry. I clung to my reins, leaning forward as my mare carried me faithfully. The air felt thinner as we moved through the hills into higher country, and I breathed deeper, harder, stretching to fill my lungs.

The new pace was shattering the last of my strength. I could not imagine my sisters bearing it. I'd always been the hardy one, the one built to withstand the rigors of life. Obviously. But then I wondered if they would have had to. Would Fell have made other arrangements for them? Would he have cosseted Alise? Sheltered Feena? Pampered Sybilia?

Would he have tucked the princess, the wife he sought, into a carriage and traveled at a slower pace? I glared at the back of Fell, hating him.

I hated all of them and their ability to weather this crossing with such obvious ease.

Fell was still angry. It radiated off him in waves. He wanted to be home already. He wanted to deposit me inside his stone walls and forget about me. Forget that I was his wife. I felt certain of this.

I told myself it couldn't get any worse. Short of forcing the horses into a gallop—and he wouldn't overtax the poor beasts that way—it couldn't worsen.

Then the sky opened.

IT RAINED FOR two days.

Intermittent rain that fell like needles on the skin. Still we pushed on. It was as though nothing ever affected these warriors. They were inhuman. My clothes never had time to fully dry out between downpours, so my discomfort never abated. My garments stuck to me like a clammy hand, wet and heavy. There was no part of me dry.

"Will we stop anytime soon?" I asked Mari in one of the rain-free spells when we could actually hear our voices. It was a question. Not a complaint. Complain I would not do.

Mari shook her head, her expression worried. "We need to reach the river before the water gets too high. It might already be too high to ford."

"What do we do then? If we can't cross?"

"We go west." She didn't look happy. "It will add days to our journey. And it also puts us close to the skog." She looked even unhappier at that, and I could tell this potential threat was a bigger concern.

"What's wrong with the skog?" I asked, recalling the brigands' taunts about it.

"Oh." She grimaced. "You don't want to travel through the skog if you don't have to."

"Why is that?"

She opened her mouth and closed it before saying, "Let's just say, not every traveler who goes into the skog comes out."

That sounded ominous.

Mari continued, "Have you ever heard of a huldra?"

"As in a . . . forest nymph? A seductress? I've heard the bards speak of such a creature, but I assumed that was just a myth."

Her lips twisted. "That is what they'll probably say in the future about dragons and witches. In some distant era when the world is a place we can't even imagine."

The rain started again and talking proved pointless beneath the pattering. I leaned low and forward over my mare's neck. It seemed to help, relieving the worst of the grinding pressure on my nether parts. It also reduced the risk of me toppling over the side.

Several hours later, we reached the Vinda River. It was the widest river in Penterra, crisscrossing the continent north to south and dumping into the Dark Channel.

It was alive. A writhing serpent. Swollen and wild and churning with death.

We stood along the bank, watching the tossing waters, and I recalled something I'd heard from one of the palace's visiting bards, that the swords of the dead churned beneath the waters of the Vinda River, ready for those who fell in—fodder for the stab of their immortal blades.

Suddenly I tasted blood in my mouth again. Copper coins sitting on my tongue. I worked my mouth, trying to get rid of the taste as I stared hard at the bubbling white foam and knew there had to be some truth to the stories. Those who fell into the rushing current would never resurface. The river carried death.

Fell finally reacted. The first to move, he maneuvered his horse about, declaring with a grim set to his mouth, as though he, too, knew death lurked in that water: "We go west."

There was a ripple of discontent, a surge of cold air.

Fell's destrier broke into a trot, his flank muscles undulating beneath his shiny coat as he took the muddy slope that led up from the bank. We all followed him. I hung on to the saddle pommel, the rough jostling assaulting my body and bringing a wet sob to my throat. I bit my lip, swallowing the sound, determined not to reveal my agony.

Fell never bothered to ask after my well-being. Perhaps if he did, I would tell him. I would say: *I am not well. My well-being is not . . . well.*

But I had promised to learn this new life, and learning meant . . . enduring.

A quick glance around at my traveling companions revealed mild and unaffected faces. No one else seemed the least bit uncomfortable or pained from the grueling pace, so I would pretend the same.

I would die before uttering a complaint.

I WAS DYING.

I clenched my teeth to keep from crying out when my mare hit a rut in the path that bounced me in the saddle. My eyes stung. It was worse than any thrashing I'd ever suffered at the hands of the lord chamberlain. Those abuses were always fleeting and easy to get past, but this was unremitting. Ceaseless. A burning, unrelenting torment. Pain layering upon pain upon pain so that there was never any relief, never any time for my skin to properly heal. Fortunately the rain had stopped, and I was finally dry. That was one misery no longer plaguing me.

Each night I fell asleep the moment I hit my bedroll. I could scarcely be bothered to eat anymore. Just a few mouthfuls to appease Mari, and then I was falling like a boneless rag doll onto my bedroll. The demand for rest won out over food.

Unfortunately, it felt as though I was nudged awake as soon as my eyes closed. All those afflicted areas screamed in protest during my stiff movements, but I dutifully dragged myself back on top of my mare each morning.

Three days after we left the river behind, we stopped near a stream to water the horses and take a small repast. When we dismounted, I slid down onto the ground and my legs betrayed me, crumpling like brittle leaves.

I collapsed in an undignified heap, unable to move. I blinked up at the puffy white clouds drifting across the bright blue sky, grimly accepting that this would be where I died. A good enough place. I couldn't stand, and I didn't care anymore. I could no longer pretend.

My view of the sky was suddenly blocked by a great shadow. Fell peered down at me, asking in a gravelly voice, "Are you hurt?"

I snorted. "*All* of me is hurt."

At this point it seemed fair to complain. I was dead . . . or very well on my way to death. Certainly, I was unable to get to my feet, and there was no way I could get back on that mare. Fell and the others might as well know the truth of the situation.

Fell reached down and grasped my arms, hauling me to my feet in one move, as though I weighed nothing at all. A cry escaped me at the sudden motion before I swallowed it back with a whimper. My head lolled on my shoulders as pain lanced through me so intensely I saw spots.

His hands flexed upon my arms, giving me a slight shake so that my gaze snapped to his. "What ails you?"

"My . . . uh . . . lower half is not quite accustomed to this." I didn't know a more delicate way to phrase it.

"I thought you said you ride," he said accusingly.

"I know *how* to ride. An outing here and there. An hour at the most." Trips longer than that called for a carriage.

He closed his eyes in one long-suffering blink. "Fuck." Opening them, his cool gray eyes swept over me. "Can you walk at all?"

"Of course." I took a staggering step forward as though I could prove it. My knees gave out. I was on my way down when he caught me. One of his arms went under my knees and another around my back. "Ah!" My hands flew to his shoulders, my palm with the carved X at once sparking and tingling when it made contact with him. It was a strange contradiction—that enlivening heat there while the rest of me throbbed like one great wound. "What are you—"

"Make camp," he commanded in a biting voice to his warriors, ignoring me.

It was then I observed that we had gathered quite the audience. They hesitated, swapping glances.

Arkin stepped forward with a belligerent swagger. "We've half a day of good riding left—"

"You heard me. Set up camp." Fell nodded at the closest two warriors. "Vidar, Magnus, put up a tent."

The two warriors scurried off to do his bidding.

Arkin aimed a scowl at me. "For *her*," he sneered, and I flinched. "We're stopping for her. She's weak and slowing us down. We might as well have let the brigands keep her, for all the trouble—"

Fell held up a single finger. "I'll not hear another word about her from your lips." His voice rumbled up from his chest and vibrated against me.

Arkin jerked as though he'd taken a blow. He compressed his mouth into an outraged line. Clearly he had not expected my husband to come to my defense. Truthfully, neither had I.

Fell continued, sweeping another glare over his warriors, "Or from anyone else. Is that understood? She is mine to deal with."

Several nods answered. A few "ayes" resounded in the afternoon air.

Mine to deal with. Not exactly the stuff of romantic dreams.

Arkin pursed his lips in silent accord, but agreement did not light his eyes.

"I want a tent waiting when we get back," Fell added, and then he was moving with me in his arms, covering the ground in long strides.

"Where are we going?" I asked.

"To the stream." He paused and whirled back around as though something had occurred to him. "Mari," he barked over his shoulder to the sword maiden. She appeared instantly. "Will you please see that there is food ready for us when we return?" He sent me a considering glance. "Something hot and nourishing."

Her dark gaze shot to me, then quickly back to him . . . but not before I read her thoughts. She pitied me. It was humiliating. She thought me weak and broken. I would have preferred her condemnation. "Of course, Fell."

I wondered at the hint of intimacy I detected in her voice. Were they something to each other? She was beautiful. Was she more than a sword maiden to him? He more than her liege lord? The notion did not sit well. Not that I could do anything about it except feel this awkward sense of inadequacy, this sense that I was an intruder in his life, a wife gained through duplicitous means. I had no claim to him and could not expect to be treated as a true partner deserving of his loyalty.

He carried me through the trees. I looked up at the canopy of whispering leaves. Sunlight streamed in thin ribbons through gaps. I was no dainty woman, but he did not grow the least bit winded. I opened my mouth, wanting to protest that I could walk, but that would not have been true, so I stayed silent, pressing my pulsing palm into his shoulder as if I could burrow my way past garments, to the flesh of him.

I heard the stream before we reached it—the burbling of water over eons-smooth stones. The trees thinned out and cleared enough to reveal a rocky shore. He chose a moss-covered slab that jutted out from the brook, lowering me down onto its verdant, yielding surface.

"Let me see," he demanded, reaching for my hem.

I slapped at his hand. "Don't. You. Dare."

His gaze down there—on me—would be my final shame. It would finish me.

"Come now." He continued reaching for my hem. "Don't be embarrassed. I've seen beneath your skirts before."

My face heated all the way to the tips of my ears. "This is not the same."

"No. It's not," he agreed succinctly. "We are alone. And I'm trying to help you. This isn't the kind of thing you can do for yourself." His expression darkened. "If you had told me sooner, I could have offered you relief."

I slapped at his hand again. "Indeed? It's not as though you have been the most approachable," I snapped. "And you warned me that weakness would not be tolerated, that I must learn this way of life. Why should I have said anything to you at all?"

We stared at each other, both breathing hard, gazes locked, and more than my hand was humming now. My chest fairly purred, buzzing and pulling and tightening in that way that made me long to apply pressure there.

Finally he gave a nod and spoke. "Allow me to help you. Please, Tamsyn."

I blinked slowly at the softening of his voice. It was not a command but a politely worded request. I felt my resolve crack as I gazed at his striking face. He was my husband. It was an incontrovertible fact. I was in pain. Another incontrovertible fact. If he could help me, I should permit him.

I relaxed my grip on the hem of my riding skirt and dragged the fabric up my legs, the breath seething out of me slowly, expanding my nostrils. I leaned back rigidly, exposing my limbs inch by inch to the day . . . to his sharp eyes.

We were far enough north now to really feel the nip of impending winter, and yet presently I felt flushed, the warmth in my chest spiraling throughout my body, heating up the blood in my veins. My face burned hot, and still I kept tugging the fabric past my hips.

He lowered his eyes and reached for the bottom of my shift, the final barrier to my modesty. His fingertips brushed the insides of my knees, and I flinched. His hands settled there, his palms covering the rounded bends, and I whimpered at the throb of his palm where we'd been blooded together. It was *not* my imagination. That X pulsed hotly against my skin.

He felt it, too.

Frowning, he pulled his hand back momentarily. He flexed that big hand and gave it a little wiggle, working his fingers in the air as if that could rid him of the sensation. Shaking his head, his hand returned to my knees, parting my thighs wide for him. Another moan escaped me at the discomfort, at the pull on my desperately unhappy muscles, at the air on my ravaged thighs and vulnerable sex. I swallowed back a whimper, but then it was done.

He could view me now, splayed open as I had not even seen myself. As no one had. This was dispassionate. Of course there was no amorous intent in this. I was certain nothing about this inspired his lust. Only his pity. Perhaps it even inspired his disgust. My fingers dug into the moss-covered rock, fighting for my dignity in such a very undignified position.

He ducked his dark head between my knees and hissed a breath before muttering a curse. The foul word was a steaming puff on my vulnerable skin. "Ah, what have you done to yourself?" *What have I done?* "Why did you not say anything?"

"I already explained that you were not the most approachable."

He grunted and lifted his gaze to mine. "Come here," he growled.

Before I realized what he was about to do, he had me in his arms again. Keeping my skirts hiked around my waist, he carried me into the water.

"It's going to be cold," he warned without giving me time to prepare. I screeched as he submerged me in the icy stream. "It will help bring down the swelling and redness," he advised, holding on to me, mindful not to let my riding skirts become soaked.

I clung to his arms, panting against him in protest of the cold. Gradually I realized he was correct. The cold water did soothe my inflamed skin. The shock eventually ebbed, and I sighed in relief at the icy rush over my abused flesh.

"We will rest today and resume tomorrow," he said, still holding me, hugging me really, and I tried not to think about the bewildering way my chest pulled and constricted at the center. My heart beat faster, almost like it longed to break free. "In the future, speak up if you're hurt or sick."

"All right," I agreed, cautiously hopeful that he would now acknowledge my existence and not leave me to Mari all the time. Perhaps we could get beyond our rough start and forge something together. What was the alternative? Remain as strangers? Enemies?

A crunch of pebbles alerted us that we were no longer alone.

Fell stiffened against me but managed not to drop me into the water as he swiftly twisted around. I searched the bank and found the interloper.

A woman stood across the stream. I didn't know what I expected to find—Mari or one of his warriors or more brigands. This hooded figure was not any of those, though.

Her cloak covered all of her except for the oval of her pretty face. A strong wind stirred, buffeting her garments against her shape. The breeze cracked branches and rustled leaves. A fine mist emerged from within its fold, curling over the ground, coming toward us in a swelling gust. Her expression was mildly curious as she eyed the strange sight we must have made.

"Hello," she said evenly. Her eyes, far older and wiser than the smooth brown skin of her face would suggest, flitted back and forth between us.

Fell's voice rumbled against me, although there was no warmth or welcome in the sound. "Hello."

"Is she ill?" she inquired with a nod at me, and I shivered, uncertain if it was from her dark eyes or the sudden swathe of chilling fog.

"Saddle sore," he replied casually, although I detected the tension in him. His gaze scanned the fogged bank and tree line, clearly searching for anyone else who might be accompanying her.

She bent her head slightly to fumble with a satchel at her side, beneath her cloak. The action slipped the hood back on her head, and her red hair came into full, glorious view. It was not a fiery red, though, shot through with various shades of red and gold like mine. Her hair was a deep scarlet, all one hue, almost unnatural in color. She wore the straight crimson curtain pulled back at her temples with a pair of simple combs. "I have something to help with that."

She produced a small cork-topped jar from her bag. Without waiting for an invitation, she crossed the stream, dragging her hem through the water indifferently. Fell tensed as she reached us and motioned me onto the mossy rock I'd earlier occupied. "Come now," she chided. "I'll not bite. Sit yourself there and let me attend to you."

I glanced at Fell, but he did not move. His attention remained fixed on her, and I was seized with the conviction that should he wish it, we would be gone, vanished into the rising mist. *If* he deemed her a threat.

She sighed and propped one hand on her hip, clearly aware of his reticence. "Come now. I'll not harm her." She glanced at me and waved her little jar. "I'm guessing you would appreciate this."

I considered her for a moment before giving his shoulder an encouraging squeeze. "I would appreciate that," I replied, then assured Fell, "It's all right. Set me down."

After a few moments, he gave a curt nod and carried me back to the slab of rock. Once I was settled upon it, she gestured for me to lift my skirts, and I obliged, marveling that I would permit two strangers to assess me so intimately on the same day. Or, well, ever.

Fell hovered close, clearly still wary of her intentions. Upon examination of me, she clucked her tongue and sent Fell a reproving look. "You should have better care for your woman."

My face burned hot at those words. She could not know he was forced to have me, and I would not dare explain our unusual situation to her. One embarrassment at a time was enough.

She uncorked the jar. The pleasant scent of juniper and rosemary and other fragrant herbs reached my nose. "This salve will make you feel better and help hasten the healing," she kindly explained. I sucked in a breath and tried not to recoil when she dabbed the mixture against a particularly tender area.

"Apologies," she murmured. "You have a few spots rubbed quite raw." Another accusing glare was sent Fell's way, and he actually looked a little shame-faced.

Finished, she pulled my skirts back down. I shifted experimentally and exhaled. "That is . . . incredible. It already feels so much better."

"Of course it does." Her beautiful face broke into a smile then. "Here." She offered me the jar.

"Oh no. I couldn't—"

"Yes, you can," Fell broke in, proffering a coin he had produced from somewhere on his person. "Take it," he said to the woman.

Her smile slipped. "I don't need your money, border lord." She flung out the designation like it was something foul on her tongue.

She knew he was a border lord? I acknowledged that he had a certain look to him, a certain air of authority and command, and he dressed as a Northman. He could never be mistaken for a soldier of the City.

His expression went hard.

She looked at me again and winked, patting my hand like one would stroke a pet. "We must stick together." *We?* I stopped short from asking what she meant by that. Likely she meant *we* as in women collectively. How else could we be alike? "My name is Thora."

"I'm Tamsyn."

"Lady Dryhten," Fell supplied. "My wife."

"I would wager she is new to the title and position." Sniffing as though she smelled something offensive, she pushed to her feet, her smooth and unlined features the height of judgment as she considered him. "Might I suggest, my lord, that if you want your lady in riding shape, you attend to her with more care." She looked at him archly, and I suspected she was not speaking of horseback riding. At least not only of that.

It was all rather perplexing . . . and humiliating.

I wanted to proclaim that I was not his wife—not in truth. Not of his choice, at any rate. Whether it was my choice was up for debate, too.

It had been nearly two weeks, and he had not placed a finger on me. Not looked at me. Only spoke to me when I'd pushed him to the edge and he wanted to vent his ire. Cleary he was not interested in intimacy between us.

Fell's expression did not crack. He nodded grimly. "I will have more care."

Thora extended a hand and helped me to my feet. Suddenly standing close, she leaned in and whispered into my ear. I heard the words . . . but failed to understand them. What did she mean?

There was no time for clarification, though. She moved away as abruptly as the utterance passed into my ear.

Wading through the stream, Thora tossed over her shoulder, "Safe crossing, Lord and Lady Dryhten."

We watched her disappear through the murky haze and into the trees. After a moment, I glanced down at the small jar in my hands. If not for its solid weight in my palm, I would wonder if she had even been real and the entire encounter not some bit of whimsy I had imagined.

"Well. That was lucky," I murmured.

"Was it?" he asked vaguely, his strong profile pensive as he stared at where she had disappeared.

I turned to study him curiously. "How could meeting her have been anything other than chance?"

"Indeed. How could it?"

We made our way back to camp and the large tent waiting for us. Someone had prepared a stew, and we ate in silence. I wolfed down my steaming bowl with embarrassing speed. When I was finished, Fell took my bowl and pointed to the bed, his gruff command to sleep so at odds with his previous solicitousness.

The bed of furs was the most luxurious thing I'd ever felt beneath me, and that was saying something. My accommodations in the palace had always been quite agreeable. I snuggled in with a sigh, marveling that such comfort had been provided—that it had been available to me all along. I tried not to let that annoy me and reminded myself that I would have the remainder of this day and all night to rest and recover. It would be heavenly. I might not feel as though I wanted to die when I took to the saddle in the morning.

My heavy eyelids drifted shut. As I floated off to sleep, Thora's low voice wove through my mind as if she was still before me, her words a soft rasp in my ear: *Take heed. He will not tolerate the likes of you. He would sooner see you dead.*

17

TAMSYN

I WOKE SEVERAL HOURS LATER TO FIND MARI OVER ME, prompting me to eat and drink. Fell was nowhere to be seen, and I felt a bit deflated. Perhaps he was back to avoiding me. The fading light of dusk greeted me when I emerged from the tent to relieve myself in the nearby woods. The rest had served me well. Already I moved with more ease, my limbs looser. The earlier fog was long gone now, so there was no fear of losing myself within the trees. Everyone was settling down for the night, and no one even seemed to notice me slipping back inside the tent.

I climbed into the bed, stretching languorously within the furs and marveling at how much better I felt. Only a faint twinge of soreness lingered. That salve was truly miraculous. Or perhaps the long nap had given me time to begin healing.

"How are you?"

I jolted upright at the deep voice.

Fell ducked inside, setting a lamp down. The flickering flame cast writhing shadows over his face. Standing over me, he removed the scabbard at his back, lifting it over his head. The leather loop caught at his ink-dark strands. He shook his head slightly, freeing his hair. His arm bracer came off next. I watched avidly as he went through the motions of undressing, reflecting that this was what he did every night. Watching him perform this routine felt intimate, reinforcing that I was now a part of his world—and he was a part of mine.

He sank down onto the edge of my bed of furs and pulled off his boots. His hands moved to his leather armor. Off that went, followed by his under tunic. Each item hit the ground with a heavy thump.

His attention slid to me, and I realized I had yet to answer his question.

"Much better," I replied, shaking my head slightly.

He grunted in acknowledgment, which I took for approval.

He stripped himself to the waist. With a trip of my heart, I wondered if he would be staying the night in the tent with me. Glancing around the space, I verified no other bedding awaited him.

"It's unbelievable, really," I added, seeking words to fill the crackling air between us. "But the salve seems to be working."

"Not so unbelievable," he replied tersely, not looking at me.

"What do you mean?"

"A blood witch knows a thing or two about the healing arts."

"A blood witch?" I stared intently at his back. "You mean . . . that woman? Thora? She's a witch?" A bona fide witch or just someone unfairly suspect because of her red hair?

He sent me a wry look over his shoulder. "More than likely."

I shook my head. "No one has seen a blood witch in years. Decades. Not since—"

"Since they took to living in isolation? Those who weren't hunted and put to fire at least." He gestured around us. "We're in the middle of nowhere. Miles from the closest village. And way too close to the much-avoided skog for my liking. A perfect location for someone wishing to live undetected."

I fell silent, my mouth closing with a snap, thinking about that, thinking about witches running for their lives to the far corners of the realm when men started hunting them after the Threshing, eager to collect the bounties offered for them. Yes. What Fell said made sense. She could be a blood witch, one of a dying breed, living in seclusion rather than be tossed onto the pyre.

One of my earliest memories was looking out from the palace and seeing bonfires dotting the hills in the distance, a burning row of five pyres outside the City. I'd asked Nurse what they were. Her

answer had been immediate and without inflection, her eyes gleaming with savage delight. *That is peace coming to the land at last.*

And I had believed her. Only later had I learned that her version
of peace meant death for others.

Unlike dragons, witches were harder to identify. They looked
human, after all. I wondered how many put to death had not even
been witches. Mistakes happened. Paranoia was a real thing. The
lord chamberlain was proof of that. If he'd had his way, I would have
been kindling for the pyres because of my red hair and my keen
ability to heal . . . and there was always the mystery of my parentage.
He insisted that was a mark against me.

Thora's whispered words echoed in my mind. *He will not tolerate
the likes of you.*

What had she meant? Had she recognized something in me?
The same thing that existed within her?

A chill chased down my spine like a rush of icy fingertips.

I had an unwelcome flash of memory then. The taste of blood
in my mouth. Copper coins rolling along my tongue and teeth.
My conviction that blood was about to be spilled. Perhaps it was a
reasonable hunch, though, given the dangerous circumstances of
coming face-to-face with brigands. I inhaled a shuddery breath and
shook my head. I would know something like that about myself.
Wouldn't I? It was not possible. Magic did not course through me.

"In any case," he continued. "I'm glad the salve is working. We
need to press on in the morning."

"I'll be ready."

I gazed at the great expanse of his back, at all that sprawling
inked flesh. My fingers tingled, recalling the texture of his skin.
Smooth and firm and warm. The X buzzed in the center of my
palm, vibrating with energy and heat. The light from the nearby
lamp painted his body in dancing red and orange, breathing life
into his tattoos, twisting the strange symbols that I could now detect formed the shape of a screaming dragon.

He turned to look at me, asking almost grudgingly, clearly re-
senting that he should care about my welfare, "Are you cold?"

I realized I was clutching a fur up to my chin. "No. I am fine."

He stared at me for a long moment, and I fidgeted, reading his distaste for me in that cool gaze.

What did he read in mine?

The silence stretched between us. We were alone. This was no chamber full of prying eyes and ears. There was no contingent of warriors flanking us. The evening pulsed around us like a beating heart, and we existed alone inside our impromptu shelter for the night, a sanctuary from the rough country surrounding us.

"What am I going to do with you?" he murmured, in a way that made me think he was truly mystified and open to suggestions.

I moistened my lips. "I know I'm not what you wanted."

"No," he agreed. "You're not."

That did not even sting. Not after our ignominious beginning. It was the truth. I knew it and so did he.

Nodding as though coming to a decision, he reached for the edge of the fur and tugged it down my body, his voice low and deep. "But we can try to get on."

I released a ragged breath of relief, hoping that was true, giddy at the prospect of what that might mean for us.

We can try to get on.

Maybe we could manage a proper marriage despite our rough start. Maybe.

"Now," he added gruffly, sliding down the length of my body to the end of the bed. "Let me see if the witch's salve is really the miracle you claim."

"Oh," I said breathlessly. "You don't need to—"

"Don't be nervous. We've already been through this."

An irrational little laugh bubbled up inside me, but I stifled it. *We've already been through this.*

Had we, though? Been through *this*? It had been different before. I'd been out of my head beside that stream and hurting and desperate for help. I would have lifted my skirts and let anyone examine me if they promised to ease my pain. I thought of Thora and winced. Case in point.

Pain was the last thing I felt, though, as I settled back onto the furs. I gulped as his hands went to my hem, flipping it up. Despite my lack of conviction, I told myself this was like before. A dispassionate inspection. It should be far less embarrassing the second time around.

I told myself that, but still felt my face catch fire as he parted my knees. Air hit my exposed body. The breath hissed past my lips, and too late I realized that this was *not* like before. I was feeling too many things and none of them pain.

His fingers trailed over my knees, skimming the tops of my thighs, and I bit my lip, fighting to stay silent even when I felt the press of his big hands, the warmth of his palms, the singeing X where my blood had joined with his. That brand swept a burning path up my leg.

My arms stretched above my head, hands clenching into fists to stop myself from touching the endless breadth of shoulders below me. That would make this something more than an impersonal examination, and I needed to keep matters as detached as possible.

He's just checking on me to see if I'm fit to ride.

"Your skin . . ." His fingers brushed the inside of one thigh, and I trembled from head to toe in a full-body shudder.

I peered down at him. "Am I . . . better?"

"Perfect," he replied, looking up at me, and my chest constricted at the hot, angry flash in his eyes . . . at the husky scratch of his voice. Why should he look so angry? So . . . accusatory?

I waited, expecting him to lower my hem now that he'd looked his fill.

But that didn't happen.

He wasn't done.

His fingers grazed me, inching up and up . . .

"The redness is gone . . . and the blisters, too," he marveled, staring fixedly between my legs.

I murmured something unintelligible that swung into a gasp when I felt the slow swipe of his fingers down my sex.

His gaze shot to my face. "Does that hurt?"

"N-no. You just startled me."

His breathing reached my ears, a rough, erratic rhythm. "Your poor little quim. It was so abused earlier. Red and chafed raw. Now it's a pretty pink."

My head dropped back, and I flung my arm over my eyes, feeling those words as though they were something visceral. As potent as his touch. I shifted, rotating my hips in an embarrassing way, seeking another stroke of his fingers against my suddenly aching core.

The flat of his hand on my thigh opened me wider, and I obliged, offering myself to his questing touch, gasping as he traced my cleft and eased one finger inside me.

"Does this hurt?" he asked, and his voice sounded strange to my ears. Lower. Deeper. Almost like *he* was in pain.

"N-no," I panted.

I shook my head and moaned as he pumped into my sex then, his finger moving slow and steady in deep thrusts. Not too hard. Clearly he feared being too rough, but the pace was agonizing, intensifying my torment, fueling my desire. I wanted it harder. My hands opened above me, grabbing fistfuls of the fur, hanging on as his hand worked between my legs.

He added a second finger and curled it inward, rubbing at some hidden patch of nerves I never knew existed. I started to shake. Tears seeped from the corners of my eyes.

"This is . . . comfortable?" he asked, turning his face to kiss the inside of my thigh.

Comfortable? Was he joking?

"Oh," I cried out brokenly, my chest rising and falling. "It's good." My body moved against his hand, wild with need, eager and hungry, desperate for more pressure, more friction. "So . . . good."

His thumb landed on a spot at the top of my sex, a little button tucked away that I had never known existed. He found it and pressed down, rubbing and rolling the swollen flesh.

"You like that?" he growled.

I arched my spine off the bed in response, bursting, coming

apart into a thousand pieces. Moisture rushed from me, coating the fingers wedged inside me.

"Tamsyn," he breathed against my skin, his mouth opening, teeth scoring gently, tongue laving my goose-pebbled skin. "My little lying wife."

I fell back, overcome, dizzy and gasping for breath, not even caring that he'd called me a liar. It was true. Maybe I had been without a choice. Or maybe not. I didn't know anymore. Either way, I had done it. I'd married him. Bedded him. Fooled him. And now I was here, stuck with the consequences . . . whatever he decided those to be.

He lowered my hem back down to my ankles and crawled up the bed, dropping down beside me with a grunt.

I sighed. Ripples of pleasure eddied through me, turning my body the consistency of pudding. His bare arm aligned with mine, radiating heat.

We didn't have this the last time, this lingering in the bed, this closeness. The aftermath was shattered when my veil was yanked away, leaving only betrayal and fury in its place. I shivered at the memory.

"Cold?" he inquired, rolling to his side and draping an arm around my waist, pulling me close, spooning me flush against him.

On the contrary. Wrapped cozily in his arms, I felt warm and soothed.

And I felt his black opal necklace between us, a great buzzing current connecting us in a way something lifeless should not, burrowing past skin and muscle and bone.

My hand settled lightly on his corded forearm. His face nuzzled into the crook of my neck.

I swallowed, struggling to even my labored breathing and slow my violently pounding heart, trying to reclaim my composure and not get carried away with the hope that he was starting to care for me. I felt him, rock-hard against me, and I knew at least he desired me.

"Are you . . . ?" I didn't know how to ask what I was thinking. How to inquire if he wanted me. If he was interested in finding his own release.

"Go to sleep," he instructed, his voice gruff.

"What about you?" Could I have been wrong? Perhaps he didn't want me.

"I'll sleep, too."

"That's not what I meant, and you know it." I told myself it was my sense of duty as his wife that made me push the subject. But that wasn't it. It was a lie I told myself. The pulsing throb between my legs was the truth. Maybe the most honest thing I had ever felt. As much as he'd satisfied me with his touch, I wanted more.

I wanted him inside me again.

"You've been through enough. I know they call me Beast, but I'm not such an animal that I will fall upon you in your condition. Rest now."

So he was holding himself back out of concern for me? It seemed more likely that he held himself back because he couldn't bring himself to bed me. The first time he had been compelled, required. No one was forcing him now.

"I've already slept," I argued, wanting to add that I wasn't saddle sore any longer. My earlier rest and Thora's miracle remedy had done the trick.

"Stop talking and sleep again," he responded firmly, his tone reminding me that this man was a warrior lord. He might be holding me in his arms, but he was not about niceties. I was his lying wife. He would never forget that. Never forget the ugliness of our beginning. It was chilly, and the ground was hard, so we were sharing a bed. This was about practicality. Nothing more. This was not a romantic honeymoon. He was not a tenderhearted lover. He was about giving orders and being obeyed.

I sighed, thinking sleep would never come while I was wrapped up in his arms like this, feeling his heartbeat through the carved X in his palm, the opal sparking and humming between us . . . my wanting him and enduring his nearness, his warmth while my chest pulled and tightened the way it did whenever he was close.

It was my last thought before I closed my eyes.

18

FELL

I WOKE CURLED AROUND HER.

I didn't move. Her hand rested on my arm so trustingly in her sleep, the only movement from her that pulsing X against my skin. I peered over her shoulder at her slim fingers, limp and relaxed, the nails shorn to the quick, jagged and uneven, like she had used her teeth on them rather than scissors. This whipping girl was without frills and airs. She was strong and quiet with quick, watchful eyes, like a deer in the brush. Fiery amber eyes, so like her hair.

And she was mine.

Whether I liked it or not.

This woman, who was not the princess I had set out to claim . . . who was something else I could not yet decipher.

She'd suffered beatings all her life. Willingly. As though there was nothing wrong with it. It galled me. I rebelled at the idea of any-one putting hands on her. I wanted to go back and turn the whip on every one of those bastards for raising a whip to her—on the king and queen for allowing it, for supporting it, for condemning a child to take beatings for their daughters' transgressions.

I felt feral. A growl swelled in the back of my throat. I'd been brought up to fight, to protect my people and lands, to do what needed to be done to survive, to win. The impulse to protect her burned within me.

I stared down at her hand. It was the one where we were blooded, the carved X on her skin still palpable, a heartbeat on my arm. My flesh hummed and vibrated, rising up to meet the mark like a plant seeking light.

I was a warrior. I knew wounds. This, however, I did not know. I did not understand it.

Slow, soft breaths lifted her chest. When she was asleep like this, there was none of the guardedness staring back at me from her eyes. Her body was boneless, sinking into the furs, leaning back against me. That fiery hair had unraveled from her braid, and it fluttered against my lips as I breathed. I had the urge to sink my fingers into those locks, to grab a fistful and wind it around my hand. To roll her onto her back and come over her, push inside her . . .

I inhaled a ragged breath. Time enough for that later, when she was well mended and restored from travel. Later, when she was comfortably installed within the walls of my keep.

I grimaced. While I had been avoiding her, leaving her to Mari's care, she had very nearly broken herself. If not for that witch and her magic salve, she'd be ruined for riding.

I'd warned her that the crossing was not for the weak and that she needed to keep up, but that didn't change the fact that I felt like a right bastard when I saw her pretty skin chafed raw. She had said nothing. Nary a complaint for days. Which was what a whipping girl did, I realized. She sacrificed herself. Her wants and needs. Her body. Her necklace to a gang of bandits. I stifled a curse. A necklace. Such a trivial thing, but it should never have happened.

Something told me it would not be the last time she put herself at risk. Deciphering the truth behind her eyes and her silent lips would require close attention. She may have rid herself of the veil, but she still shielded her true self from me.

That damn veil. I blew out an angry breath. It might as well still exist between us.

I still saw red, seething over what could not be undone. She was forever mine, but I recoiled at the idea. I clung to the fury I'd felt the night of our bedding, wrapping my sense of betrayal around me like impenetrable armor—but looking at her, *being* with her, pushed it right out of me, dispelling it like motes of dust through the air.

I was so fucked.

My gaze traveled the length of her body. I'd already accepted her in one very significant way. I didn't find *that* a chore at all. She had her . . . charms. And why not enjoy them? I should get something out of this mess. And it was messy. War always was. Nothing short of war would come to those bastards who'd played me the fool.

Accepting her did not mean I accepted what had been done to me. There would be a reckoning, in due time.

I slipped from the bed, careful not to disturb her. Silently, I dressed, one eye on her face, so soft and peaceful in slumber. Something stirred in my chest. Lifting my scabbard over my head, I stood over her in the quiet.

Shaking my head, I exited the tent. The sky was a deep purple. Dawn had not yet arrived. No one else roused as I made my way to the horses.

I felt him before I heard him, well familiar with his heavy gait.

"Sleep well?"

I didn't bother turning to face Arkin. "Well enough." The bridles clinked in the hush of predawn as I collected my destrier and then Tamsyn's mare and started to lead them to the stream.

"You've gone soft for her."

Soft was the last thing I felt around her—but I wouldn't admit that to Arkin.

I didn't react immediately, considering my response.

I peered around at the sleeping camp and the dark shape of the tent backlit by the rising dawn. "She's my wife."

"She's not one of us."

"I was always going to take an outsider to wife."

"Aye, but she's not a daughter of the crown. She is beneath you and weakens your position."

"She serves a purpose."

"And what purpose is that? Wetting your cock? Your father must be rolling over in his grave. What did that girl do to you, lad? Geld you?" Arkin sneered. "Two weeks ago you wanted an indisputable claim to the crown. Now you will accept this? They've insulted you. All of us. We fight their battles, bleed for them, and they laugh at us. They think we're their dogs."

I shook my head and started leading the horses again, turning my back on him. "Have no fear. It is I who shall have the last laugh."

Arkin crowed with approval, "You have a plan!" His heavy steps crunched over leaves, hurrying to catch up with me.

Of course I had a plan. It involved assembling my army and laying siege to the City in the spring after the snow melted—showing King Hamlin and the lord regent that no one fucked with me.

"I'll not forget the insult," I calmly asserted. "They will pay." In addition to being immensely satisfying, routing the incompetents from power would be a kindness to every man, woman, and child of Penterra.

"That's right!" Arkin crowed gleefully. "And we should leave her here! That will show them what we think of their *royal princess*. If the animals don't finish her, brigands will, or maybe a huldra will find her and make a soup of her. We're close enough to the skog, after all." This last bit he flung out accusingly, a stab of censure. He didn't like that we had stopped and set up camp. He thought we should be pushing on.

I dropped the reins, swung around, and shoved him to the ground. "I grow weary of your insolence. You serve me, Arkin, and I already warned you to leave off. She is mine to deal with."

He glared up at me. "You protect *her*? What would your father think?"

"He's dead. Has been for some time. I'm Lord of the Borderlands now . . . and she—" I stopped. Shrugged. I didn't owe Arkin an explanation. I didn't owe anyone an explanation. Not even the king. As far as I was concerned, he had forfeited my allegiance when he lied and trapped me in marriage to the wrong woman.

Tamsyn was a pawn. She didn't deserve the fate Arkin would have her suffer. I didn't know what she deserved or what we would be to each other—if anything—but I wouldn't hurt her.

"This is it, then? I served your father. I serve *you*. And you treat me like . . ." His words faded, and he shook his head in disgust, latching on to what offended him the most. "You choose her."

I gathered up the reins in my hand again, giving him a curt nod. "You understand my meaning."

Turning, I left him in the dirt.

19
TAMSYN

THERE WAS SOMETHING DIFFERENT IN THE AIR WHEN I woke. A quality that had not been there before. A crisp newness. Except that was wrong. This world, this wild country teeming with life and magic had been here long before I was born, long before my parents—whoever they were—drew breath. There was nothing new about any of it. It was ancient, primeval, still humming with the echo of dragon wings and spells cast into the ether.

I was the *new*. A stranger entering the cool, mist-shrouded morning with eyes blinking like an infant against an unfamiliar world.

I was alone in the furs, my body warm, muscles relaxed. A boneless, sinking weight.

I had slept hard. A dreamless slumber. Fell was gone, but he had stayed most of the night with me. I knew that without owning the memory. His scent remained, clinging, wrapped up in the bedding, in me. I felt him still, that big body folded around mine, his warmth lingering, the echo of his black opal a nourishing stamp on my skin.

I gazed up at the canvas of the tent, the sifting shadows. The faint stirrings of the world outside alerted me to the fact that I was not the only one awake and that I needed to rejoin the land of the living—the party of warriors who thought me weak and in need of coddling, who looked at me as though I were a ghost among them, someone already gone. They did not expect me to endure.

Shaking my head, I moved briskly, reapplying the salve to my skin, although I hardly felt a need for it anymore. Thora had instructed me to do so, and I felt compelled to oblige her. Dressed, hair braided once again, I emerged from the tent, revitalized, to face the day.

Warriors were packing up in the predawn. As soon as I stepped outside, they moved in and started working to disassemble the tent.

Mari appeared, waving me to one of the few remaining fires with her usual efficient manner. "Come. Eat."

I motioned to the tree line. "I need a moment first."

She nodded. "Don't stray far." Rotating back around, she returned to the fire and tea brewing there.

Another quick scan failed to reveal Fell. He must be with the horses, watering them for the day's ride.

I felt eyes on me, smug and knowing, and was glad to escape them as I slipped inside the cover of the woods. Embarrassment slithered through me. While everyone slept out here on their bedrolls on the hard ground, we'd enjoyed the comfort and privacy of our tent.

I moved into the crush of soaring trees. My head fell back, looking up, searching for where they finished. The branches came together in the sky, tangling into a high canopy that blocked out the rising sun. Only patches of soft gray reached the forest floor.

The only time I'd departed the palace was in the company of a full retinue, and only then was it to travel to the most civilized of places, taking the smoothest, most well-traveled paths. This was a strange and mysterious place. Ageless. Magic hummed and throbbed in its bones. The dragons were long gone, but the land had not forgotten them.

I felt my solitude keenly as I walked through knee-high ferns and grass, dragging fingertips over the scratchy bark of a tree five times the width of me. I thought of Mari's warning not to stray far, but I could not stop my legs from carrying me into the lush morning, through the dewy air, which pulsed and enveloped me like a second skin.

All of this had been kept from me while I had been cloistered away in lifeless stone walls. While I had lived overlooking a crowded city, miles away from land this wild, this free, where magic hid from those who sought to destroy it.

I felt alive.

I lifted my face to the mist, my faithful companion of late, inhaling the clean sweetness of it, tasting the new day in its fold. Birds shrilled, and I peered into the high branches, discerning a white bird, stark against so much green. I wondered how it survived, standing out so dramatically against its surroundings.

It cocked its head, turning an inquisitive pale blue eye on me, studying me unblinkingly for a long time. I wondered what it saw in me.

At last it turned, presenting a profusion of tail feathers. There, amid the abundant plumage, a needlelike stinger vibrated a warning. I blinked at that danger swathed in so much beauty.

The wild creature pushed off the branch into flight. I admired the span of its stretched wings gliding on the wind . . . envying such freedom as it disappeared from sight. The display reinforced how little I knew of this world beyond the safe, tidy corner of Penterra I'd left behind.

An eerie trill sounded from the distant woods. It was something different, unknown. Vaguely . . . human. I turned in that direction. Who knew what manner of beasts lurked in this forest? I thought of the huldras and jerked to a stop, listening for it again.

I knew I should return to camp, but when the cry did not come again, I threaded my way between the towering trees as the gray morning slid into a soft pink. Muted ribbons of light filtered down, dappling my skin as I went deeper into the forest.

Long drapes of moss sagged from lofty branches. It was a wondrous thing. Otherworldly. I passed in and out of the curtains of green, smiling to myself, imagining *I* was as free as that bird.

My fingers closed around one skein of moss, pulling the gossamer-soft length aside so that I could step ahead—only to reveal the man waiting there for me.

"Oh! You startled me." I staggered back and flattened a hand over my suddenly pounding heart. I willed it to slow and steady.

He was no brigand. No foe. Arkin was one of my husband's most trusted men. And yet I could not feel at ease before him, this warrior whose eyes looked upon me with such coldness. Such hate.

"Oh," he echoed, the word full of mockery.

"I was just heading back to camp." I motioned vaguely behind me.

"You're going in the wrong direction."

I nodded nervously and turned in the correct direction, suddenly eager for the protection of Fell and Mari and the other warriors, but then he was there again, moving to block me, not letting me pass.

He angled his head sharply. "I warned you. The crossing isn't for the weak." He swept his gaze around us then, at the dense green pressing in so thickly. "You should not have strayed this far."

I met his mean little eyes with a lift of my chin. "I am not weak."

"So brave, eh?" he mused, scratching the pale skin above his beard in long, curling strokes. "But I know what you really are."

"And what is that?"

"There is nothing brave about you." His gaze flicked over me in contempt. "Once a whipping girl . . . always. You're not fit to be Lady of the Borderlands."

Holding his stare, my stomach soured. A telling nerve twitched at my temple, and I resisted rubbing it into submission. I knew when a blow was coming. The lord chamberlain had trained me well. It was my gift. My curse. I could read the hunger for violence in a man's expression.

My wide eyes ached in my face, unblinking, anticipating. "You think Lord Dryhten will approve if you harm me?" It was a gamble. I didn't know my husband that well yet. He was cold and stoic, but I felt safe with him. I didn't think he would want this. I didn't think he would *do* this.

"Who says he will ever know?" He smiled then, a chilling, humorless grin that cut through his grizzly beard and filled me with dread. "There are many dangerous things in these woods."

I clung to bravado. It was all I had. "Fell does not strike me as a man easily fooled."

"Oh, I don't know about that. You seem to have made quite the fool of him."

I shook my head, insisting, "He will know. And he will make you pay." I wanted to believe this was true, but more important, I needed for *this* man to believe it true.

"This is what is best. For him. For all of us. Now." He clapped his hands together jarringly, and his smile faded. "I will give you a head start."

I gulped, panic swelling, rising up in my throat to choke me.

"Go on," he prompted. "Run."

That look in his eyes. I knew it. Knew his foul intent.

Arkin had followed me into the woods to do more than harm me. He was here to make certain I never came back out.

"I'm a sporting man," he continued. "I'll count to three. One—"

With a swift breath, I spun and fled, darting through the trees. Blood rushed to every limb as my fingers clawed, ripping through sheets of moss.

He gave chase, his breath crashing on the air after me. Not from exertion. It was the thrill of the hunt taking him. He was older, twice my age, but strong, his warrior body well honed and accustomed to this kind of sport.

He was the predator and I his quarry.

Fear flooded me as my legs pumped, carrying me deeper into the woods. I was too loud, panting, tearing through the brush like a wild animal. Desperate. There was no hope of losing him. I knew it. Knew how this game would end.

My chest tightened, the pressure building there, coiling, hurting. I gasped at the pain of it, but there was no time for pain. My head whipped from side to side, trying to decide where to go. What to do.

Fire blazed through my veins. My skin snapped, heated. A fever rushed to my face, reaching the tops of my ears. Tears blurred my vision. I had no idea which direction to turn, which way to the camp. I was lost.

Fell.

The thought of him burned through me. I willed him to appear, to help me. Perhaps Arkin was right. Maybe Fell would be glad to be rid of the wife forced on him through lies and trickery. Just as soon as the thought entered my mind, I rejected it with a fresh sob. *No.* If Fell wished to be rid of me, it wouldn't be like this. It wouldn't be through my execution. He wouldn't have sicced his man on me.

It didn't matter, though. He was not coming. No one was.

The only person who could help me . . . was me.

Arkin tackled me. I screamed as I was flipped over onto my back. He pinned me beneath his suffocating weight, glaring down at me, triumph gleaming in his eyes. My chest pulled and clenched. I fought through the pain of it, slapping and clawing and punching at the hateful face above me. I fought as I never had. As the whipping girl never could. And still it was not enough. I could not break free. Could not escape him.

He overpowered my efforts, forcing my arms to my sides, jamming them down and trapping them with his knees. His hands went for my neck, hard fingers circling, squeezing. My throat ached for air beneath his crushing grip. Awful sputtering sounds spit from my lips. Spots filled my vision, distorting his terrible face.

No. No. No. No. I was not ready to die. Not yet. Not like this.

The heat continued to course through me. My head throbbed, and a buzzing pealed in my ears. Deep vibrations started in my chest. Tears filled my eyes, rolling freely down my hot face, hissing on my suddenly sizzling cheeks. Steam rose from me . . . and I didn't understand it. Somehow there was smoke coming off me.

My once muddled vision cleared. Focused.

I could see as I never had before. Colors were brighter. Sharper. Every nuance improved, refined. I could count his pores, the fine hairs on his bulbous nose, minuscule crumbs from his breakfast in his coarse beard.

My core purred, simmered, flared through me in a wave of wildfire impossible to contain.

Arkin swore and yanked back his hands, gaping at his bubbling, blistered palms. "What did you do to me, you little bitch?" He fell off me and staggered to his feet, looking from his scalded hands to me in fury.

I shook my head, bewildered, as a seething vapor ate up my throat . . . as my bones pulled, my muscles stretched, my back tingled.

I continued to burn, to smoke.

Arkin unsheathed his sword. "What the fuck are you?"

I held up a hand as though to ward him off and gasped at the sight of my skin. My hand rippled and winked red-gold.

His eyes widened, and he lifted the sword higher with a battle cry.

"No!" I shouted, but it wasn't my voice anymore. The word was thick, garbled by smolder and ash in my mouth. I shook my head, watching in horror as he charged me, his blade glinting.

My body burst. Ripped free of my clothes in a blinding flash of light.

Shock crossed his face as he brought his sword down, descending toward me for a deathblow.

I inhaled deep from within my contracting lungs and blew out a river of flame.

Arkin was right. There were many dangerous things in these woods.

I just never realized that I could be one of them.

20

FELL

TAMSYN HAD BEEN GONE FOR A WHILE. TOO LONG. I didn't like her being out of my sight. I told myself it was about being in control, about safety, about knowing where everyone was at all times: my warriors and now . . . Tamsyn. She was no warrior. Obviously, she should be monitored for her own protection.

Of course, it was more than that. More than I was willing to admit to myself. The feeling was different and unfamiliar, like the fit of a new sword, the grip strange in my hand.

When I returned from watering the horses, Mari pointed in the direction Tamsyn had gone, and I set off, following her meandering tracks, easy enough to find in ground still moist from the recent rain. I shook my head as they went deeper and deeper into the dense forest. She should not have strayed this far. My frustration with her was tempered by my own sense of responsibility for not keeping a more vigilant eye on her.

I crouched low, assessing, touching the freshly broken ground as another set of tracks joined hers. They belonged to a man. Blood rushed to my head. I unsheathed my sword as I stood and wildly glanced around. Heart pounding, I increased my pace, jogging lightly on booted feet, stealthily, circling and following tracks that suddenly became wild and abundant on the forest floor. Were they . . . running?

I resisted the urge to call out for her. I didn't know who else was out here with her, but I didn't need to alert them that I was on their trail.

That goal fled at her first scream.

Squawking birds bolted from their branches.

I started in one direction, my ears straining, detecting distant cries. The sounds of struggle. Thuds. Grunts. Flesh striking flesh.

Bitter saliva coated my tongue, flooding my mouth. I paused, swinging around, sword poised, roaring her name.

She did not respond. Instead, there was a man's bellow, followed by an eruption of light from the trees to my right. An explosion. I lunged that way, smelling smoke as my sword cut through moss and foliage until I pulled up at the sight of a charred and smoldering body motionless on the ground.

I gagged at the overwhelming stench of scorched flesh. I was accustomed to the trappings of battle in all its forms. I knew the odor, but it did not make it any less offensive. I surged forward, examining the body. My chest deflated with a breath of relief. *Not her.* Not Tamsyn. The words reverberated through me in a comforting mantra.

I peered intently at the smoking corpse. The bulk of the damage was to the face and upper body. Hair and skin were gone, revealing only widespread patches of white and blackened tissue, but it was a man. My gaze trailed down the rest of the body.

His legs and boots were still identifiable. *Recognizable.* I knew those boots. My gaze went to his sword beside him. I knew the sword as well.

Arkin.

My chest sank. What was he doing out here? *Dead?* Had he followed her? What happened to him? And where was Tamsyn? Had the bandits followed us and decided to claim her anyway? Or was this the work of something else?

I circled sharply, muscles taut and ready to spring as I searched for her, for an attacker who had done this . . .

My heart seized in my chest when I spotted scraps of Tamsyn's clothing littering the ground. The familiar fabric of her riding skirt. The blue shredded bits of her cloak.

"Tamsyn!" I roared, acrid panic eating its way up my throat.

A branch creaked and groaned. Leaves rustled, several falling, raining over me.

My gaze shot up, searching the tree, colliding with a pair of eyes. I went cold beneath their searing regard. Dark vertical pupils flickered and shifted, snakelike, following my movements warily as I withdrew my bow and pulled an arrow from my quiver.

The beast moved, and the branch splintered under its weight. It emerged from the tree, the color of flame, and dropped, all twenty feet of it catching itself on the air, its great shuddering wings unfurling with a snap around its lithe form, creating a gust of current that lifted the hair off my shoulders.

Dragon.

The word filled my mind. Exploded into harsh reality as I stared up at the terrible beauty of it.

My focus sharpened on its talon-like fingers, at the shreds of Tamsyn's cloak tangled there, and my stomach rebelled. Bile rose in my throat, and it was all I could do to stop from being sick.

Its face shimmered like firelight as it watched me with an intensity I took for hunger. I braced myself for a torrent of flame. The firestorm did not come.

Shaking with rage, I nocked my arrow and aimed, ready to let loose on this monster, this merciless killer. It had incinerated Arkin and taken Tamsyn, leaving only remnants of her clothing.

Those golden eyes blinked once, and then it vanished, soaring off into the sky.

My arrow fired after the creature, missing—not that it would have done much good. My arrow was simply an arrow. Long had been the day since we'd needed scale-tipped arrows.

It was gone.

Chest heaving, legs braced apart, I watched it, a bright point in the sky, until it faded from sight.

Fury and shock and a whole host of emotions seethed over my crawling skin.

The dragon was back. Or rather, it had never left.

First my parents. Then Arkin. And now Tamsyn.

My wife.

It felt as though a limb had been severed from my body. The distress I felt over that . . . over losing her, was knee-buckling. Astonishing in its fierceness. I'd only just found the girl, only begun to contemplate that she might be someone I wanted to keep . . . that she might not be the princess I set out to obtain for myself, but she was more, better than anything I had imagined . . . the hand in the dark that I could reach for.

Staring where the dragon had once filled the sky, I vowed vengeance.

I would find it. Hunt it to the ends of the earth. Nowhere would it be at peace. Nowhere would it be safe from me.

I would kill it dead.

PART IV
THE DRAGON

21

YRSA

The Crags
Twenty-one years ago . . .

THEY WERE DYING. NOT TODAY. NOT TOMORROW. BUT eventually.

Eventually.

That made the end sound as distant and elusive as the fog circling above them. And yet death would be sooner than eventually for some. *For most.*

So many were already gone. Too many.

If she were honest with herself . . . the days were numbered for her pride. And yet being honest with herself was not something Yrsa was very good at doing. Not anymore. Not in a very long time. Not since the Threshing had begun all those years ago.

She preferred to hope and dream of a future. A future where she did more than cling to existence like it was the last leaf of fall on the branch. A future where she thrived. She still hoped they could go back to the times depicted on the walls of their dens and chronicled in their histories. A time when dragonkind flourished, when they teemed in the sky like banners in the wind, when their troves were overflowing with gemstones.

She had been a young dragon when the Threshing began. Little more than a hatchling. Just a dragonling when her life had become a haze of war. Blood and fire. Death and smoke. Dragons falling from the sky like rain. Entire prides wiped out in a single day.

She was over five hundred years old. She'd spent centuries committed to the fight, devoting herself to surviving the Threshing. Always on the move. Hiding. Striking like a serpent in the grass. Doing her best to use her talents and protect members of her pride from those hunting them. It was exhausting work. Ceaseless struggle. But it was the only thing to be done. Do or die. Die or do.

There was time for nothing else.

And yet amid it all she had taken a mate. Not just any mate. Asger, the heir apparent of their pride, son of the alpha. When his father had fallen in the Hormung, Asger had risen to the role.

They were already mated by then. She had not looked for it. Had not wanted it. And yet it had found her . . . And when love found a dragon, it could not be denied. Before she knew it, they were bonded. There was no severing them. For as long as she lived, there would be no other for her. Like a seed to the pod, they were a set, a duo, a pair.

Not that there were a great many options for mates these days.

Their population had declined dramatically, dwindling down to sixty, maybe seventy, since the Hormung. She couldn't know every pride in existence. Hopefully there were others out there, more prides with more dragons. But they might be it. The only pride left. The only dragons left. It was grim to contemplate. Especially considering they had once filled the sky with their vibrant colors and the clapping beat of wings. No more.

Now the skies were silent.

The labyrinthine tunnels and caves they called home were still, too. Hallowed and hushed as graveyards, their tread and voices no more than whispers for fear of giving away their location to those still hunting them.

Survival depended upon how well they hid. They came out only at night and only when necessary. They were safe as long as the world thought them gone. Dead. Extinct. They had once ruled this world, but now they were reduced to this, scurrying about like rats on a sinking ship. The Butcher of the Borderlands was determined to pick off the last of them. Most humans believed them all long dead, but the Butcher was ever cautious even these many years later. He had eyes on the skies, giant catapults capable of slinging enormous scale-tipped arrows of dragon bone into the air aimed and ready. Ironic. The only thing that could break through dragon hide was . . . dragon.

Which was why this day was all the more significant. Hatchlings were rare. A gift. A blessing to a dwindling species, to a dying pride. A gift when so many of their kind had been slain, struck down from the heavens, torn apart by wolves, cursed by witches.

With their numbers on the decline, each new birth was cause for celebration. Yrsa had longed for a hatchling for years, ever since she had bonded with Asger. Even in their war-torn world, she had wanted that.

A dragon could only expect one, perhaps two hatchlings in a lifetime, but in the chaos of the Threshing, few hatchlings had been born. Not nearly enough to replace the dragons lost. They were well on their way to extinction, just as humankind had wanted.

Yrsa functioned, fought side by side with Asger, using her talent as a shader to muddle the minds of many a hunter who discovered dragons deep in the caves of the Crags. Her efforts, combined with the skills of other dragons in her pride, had saved them on more than one occasion.

So busy surviving, she almost didn't realize she was spawning until Eyfura looked her over and proclaimed it. As a verga and one of the oldest dragons in the pride, she would know. A verga dragon knew all about healing and herbs . . . and spawning.

It was a miracle. Yrsa was bringing new life into the pride.

For months, Asger hovered and fussed over her, plying her with food, covering her with furs, stopping her from leaving their moss-shrouded den, insisting it was safer within and that others could perform her duties, patrolling the tunnels and hunting for food aboveground when darkness fell. To be fair, Asger wasn't the only overprotective one. She had no shortage of visitors. Everyone checked on her, sat with her, brought her meals. Yrsa didn't mind, though. There had been little happiness for them. A dark cloud had dimmed their days and nights long enough. They needed this, and she would gladly share her joy.

Even when she began to labor, she was still in high spirits. With pain ripping across her distended abdomen, she felt only anticipation. As Asger's great form paced their den, she panted. The pressure tightened, radiating through her.

"Is this normal?" she asked Eyfura after several hours. "It's . . . taking . . . so long," she gritted out as another clenching wave rolled over her.

She was not weak. The Threshing had killed all that were weak. War had taught her what pain was in all its names and forms. This was a good kind of pain, a pain that you didn't mind, because it brought reward. She told herself that, reminding herself that she would have a hatchling of her own at the end of this.

The excruciating tightness released with a snap. Relief came in a rush. She fell back, her muscles immediately loosening.

There was a gasp—Eyfura's—followed by several beats of silence.

Asger's great muscled form crouched beside Eyfura, his fire-gold eyes gleaming anxiously.

"Well?" Yrsa attempted to peer down her body. It was the lack of response that bothered her. There were no exclamations of delight, no congratulations, no reassurances given. In fact, Eyfura looked . . . worried, which was not something one wanted to see at a moment such as this.

And then . . .

A high-pitched wail. Decidedly un-dragon-like. Never had such a sound echoed through the deep caverns of the Crags. Hatchlings sounded different than this.

This sounded like . . .

No. She couldn't even think it.

Everyone outside her den had to have heard it, too. Even beyond that. It would serve as a beacon for any humans within range—a fact that should have alarmed her, but she could not even summon concern. She could only gaze in bewilderment at . . .

It.

"Impossible," Eyfura breathed, lifting the bundle in her arms and setting it on the waiting bed. Leaning forward, Yrsa looked down into the basket she had so carefully and lovingly readied for this moment.

"What in all that burns is that?" Asger asked, baring his teeth with a snarl.

"A . . . baby," Eyfura supplied, her bright green eyes wide and unblinking in her face. "A human baby."

His snarl turned into a growl. "It's a monster."

The declaration struck her like a blow. *A monster.* She shook her head. "No."

Asger didn't hear her. Or at least he didn't acknowledge her. His sleek skin flickered like firelight through stained glass, amber struck by the sun.

"Destroy the thing." He lifted his great taloned hand toward the baby, his talons glinting and ready to slice the little body to shreds.

"No!" Yrsa moved quickly, unthinking. Purely reacting. She flung herself before the fur-draped basket that held the naked child wiggling its plump little legs.

Asger's narrow pupils vibrated and throbbed within his red-gold eyes. She knew what that meant. He only ever looked that way before battle.

"Yrsa," he chided firmly. "I know you're feeling things right now, but this is not right. It is a human child."

A human. The enemy. Responsible for the ruin of dragonkind.

"It came from me. From *us.*"

He shook his head, his fiery skin catching the light cast from a wall torch, making him look feral and dangerous. "It's not natural. It must be a curse . . ."

Eyfura nodded. "Aye. A witch's work, no doubt."

"We cannot keep it. Cannot allow it to exist." Asger sent a wary glance toward the opening of their den, his voice falling to a hush. "We shouldn't let the others see it either. It will not help morale." He shuddered as though the shame of that terrified him.

She swept her gaze over the rosy-cheeked newborn, confirming what she suspected. From the beginning she had thought she carried a daughter. She'd felt it deep within her, as certain as she was that the sun would rise on the morrow. She had known it. So why had she not known *this*?

Why had she not known there would be no hatchling? Why hadn't she known that she would give birth to a human?

"Stop calling *her* an *it*. She is ours. Our daughter." Yrsa didn't know where her fierce determination came from, but it throbbed within her like a heartbeat that wouldn't quit. Short of death, she would not be stopped from saving this child.

Asger growled. "Don't say that." He flicked his hand out at his side, his talons snapping wide and flashing in the air like sun striking steel. "Now stand aside, Yrsa."

A growl awoke and stirred in her chest. It was instinctive. This need to defend, to protect what was hers. Be it dragon or human, this baby was hers. As essential as air, as necessary as bones to a body. She could not hand the child over for death. To kill this baby would be to end her.

"I'll make it quick," he added, as though that would be a comfort to her.

Yrsa loved Asger. They belonged to each other. There had never been a moment of strife between them. They had worked together to build a life, to survive, to protect their fading pride. A hatchling had been their dream. Their hope for the future.

It was her dream still, even if no longer his.

Swallowing, Yrsa carefully modulated her voice to reveal none of the desperation trembling inside her, bubbling magma deep beneath the surface. "I will do it." She placed a hand on his sinewy arm, his sleek scaled skin tensing under her touch. His fiery gaze locked on her, but he permitted her to ease his arm down.

He studied her doubtfully. "Are you certain?"

"She came from me." Yrsa paused at the sight of the ridges along the bridge of his nose contracting. "I will be the one to end her," she insisted. "It should be me."

He nodded. "Very well."

Turning, she gathered the basket up into her arms.

"Where are you taking—"

"I will do it," she cut him off. "My way."

The firelit skin of his face glinted, the strong lines of his cheekbones appearing more pronounced, sharp enough to cut stone and as unyielding as the mountains shrouding them.

Either he was worried for her . . . or he did not trust her. "Yrsa—"

"I will not spill blood in our den." She had to convince him. He had to let her go.

He nodded again. "Very well. Then I will accompany—"

"No. I will do it alone. I will see to this . . . business myself."

Eyfura held her tongue, but the way she looked at Yrsa made her wonder if she believed her. Perhaps it was female intuition. Eyfura was a mother. She knew what it was like to spawn a hatchling, to bring life into the world and love that life, nurturing it as carefully as one did a garden, feeding and tending and watching with anxious eyes, always searching the horizon, wary of the storms. For there were storms aplenty in this life, ready to break loose and take all you love. Eyfura knew that firsthand. She'd lost her son in the Hormung.

With her babe bundled close, Yrsa swept from the den. Asger didn't stop her. He trusted her. Through generations, they had never been anything but honest with each other.

Until now.

She avoided the gazes of her brethren as she passed through caves, angling her basket away from their view, slipping into tunnels that dripped with water, winding her way up to the surface, and bursting from the mountain like a geyser erupting from the earth.

She lifted up, leaving behind the Crags like they were a great slumbering giant in the night. She took to the dark sky with her daughter in her arms, turning south.

She flew through the night. When morning dawned, she went higher into the clouds for cover, the thick vapor matching the silvery gray of her skin. She clasped the basket to her chest, using her body heat to keep the baby warm and dry as she navigated through the dense air.

By the time night rolled around again, she was close. What would take a horse and rider weeks, she could accomplish in two days, flying fast and hard in a direct line, like a dart through air.

She knew where she was going. The safest place for a human, where no one would ever see her child as a monster. A place where her daughter could be accepted and loved. The enemy's lair.

The hour was late. The palace asleep. Her wings worked effortlessly, thoughtlessly, holding her aloft. Hovering over the City, she peeled the basket away from her chest to look down at her daughter for the last time, memorizing her face: the sweet curve of her cheek, the big eyes, the barely there thatch of red hair. *Be well, little one.*

Yrsa landed within the palace grounds and set her precious cargo down on the cobblestones. A quick glance around confirmed that no one was about. The baby shook her fists wrathfully in the air as though to announce herself to the world. Yrsa knew she needed to go, but she could not stop herself from standing over the child, *her* child, gazing down at her with a heart that felt like bursting.

The baby opened her little mouth full of pink gums and let loose a howl.

Silent and swift as a phantom, Yrsa launched herself up into the sky, losing herself in the dark.

22

TAMSYN

I WAS CHAOS. A MONSTER. THE KIND THAT HAUNTED CHILD-hood dreams. The kind recounted to small children to terrify them into obedience. Char and ash filled my mouth. I could taste only that as I careened through the damp sky, writhing, twisting on the rushing wind, trying to rid myself of this body, cast it from me like a fisherman's net.

It didn't work. Nothing worked. It stuck.

My body was not my own. The great slapping beat of wings on the air matched the hammering of my heart. *Wings.* I possessed wings. Or they possessed me. Those appendages worked with no thought or deliberation, but through instinct. Why? Why I should have this instinct and never know of it . . . never suspect . . . ?

There was a deafening roar beneath the howling air. The sound came from me. The noise climbed up my simmering throat. Blasted from my fanged mouth. My ceaseless scream.

I was the monster.

And this was no dream.

I DIDN'T KNOW how long I flew. *Flew.* I was flying. *I am a dragon.* That legendary pestilence that had plagued civilization since the earliest record of time. Until humankind rose up in a great swell, a tsunami determined to engulf them all, no longer willing to be the victim of winged demons.

Now you're one of them. A winged demon.

For nearly five hundred years the Threshing had raged, burned over the land like a bushfire, destroying all in its path. Armies fought, soldiers fell, villages were razed to rubble . . . so that dragons would no longer exist.

For a hundred years the skies had been free of them. There had been no sightings save the singular time Balor the Butcher found the outlier who had taken Fell. The Crags had been plundered. Pillagers mined the tunnels and caves, searching for the dragons' treasure troves. Never had a dragon been spotted in all that time. Not a glimpse. Not a roar. Not a whisper.

Humankind had succeeded. This was believed. Accepted as truth. Dragons were gone. Reduced to a chapter in history. Ultimately, they would become a page . . . and then a footnote. Someday not even that. That was the fate of all magical things that ceased to exist. They faded from fact to rumor to myth.

So why was I here? Like this? How?

How how how how how how how how?

The answer took shape, formed into something solid, into rock. Grew into words that hardened into a single irrefutable truth. *History was wrong.*

Everything we knew. Everything we had been taught. All. Wrong.

I was wrong, trapped in this body, a cage from which I could not break, could not escape.

I vibrated, denial bubbling through me, pushing at the bars. I could not be that thing of lore and nightmare—ghost stories told to children so that they would behave and be home before dark.

Dragon. My horror mounted, the word a poison spreading, overtaking everything.

Dragon. Me. *Killer.* All one and the same.

I was a killer. I'd taken a life. Granted, Arkin had been on the verge of taking *my* life, but I'd been the one to do the killing in the end. And with such terrifying and brutal ease. I'd smote him like I was blowing out a candle.

I didn't know how long I spiraled through the air with these agonizing thoughts.

My hands were not hands. They were weapons: amber-hued fingers tipped with sharp talons, which clawed the wind as though seeking purchase. Talons. Not my only weapon, though. I worked my smoke-steeped mouth, tongue lifting, testing the roof, the sides of my cheeks, running over the tips of incisors sharp enough to nick my tongue. More deadly gifts at my disposal.

My lungs pulsed and crackled with embers as I looked up and out, as though the answer was there, salvation in the clouds. I tore through the drifting vapor, catching glimpses of mountain peaks far away, just the summits, rising like jagged pyramids of marbled black and white. *The Crags.* More awesome and terrifying than the bards ever conveyed. So big—even just these crests—that they could be seen from miles and miles away. My heart reacted, jumping, banging against my rib cage like an overexcited puppy, eager to reach its favorite person.

And that was its own brand of terror. The Crags should mean nothing to me. I should feel nothing at this sight of them.

I wrenched my gaze away and dropped down below the clouds, determined to look upon them no more.

I assessed the ground so very far below. Trees like dots. Lakes like mirrors. The swollen Vinda River a curling ribbon. Streams like blue veins in the earth. So much vibrant green. Panic swelled in me. How was I even doing this? How was I not crashing to the ground? Falling and slamming to earth and breaking into a million pieces?

Fell. He had been there. He had seen what I'd done to his man. I'd looked back and glimpsed him standing over Arkin's body, those frost eyes blazing ice, looking up after me. He saw me. Well, he saw the dragon. He could not know *I* was the dragon. He would not leap to such a conclusion. Perhaps he would think me dead, killed by the dragon? Whatever the case, he was rid of me.

A sob worked its way up from my contracting and expanding lungs. They burned. Smoldered in my chest. The heat brought me no pain. Fire did not hurt me.

My gift. My curse.

I tore through the air without grace or direction or purpose. I'd fled in fear. The impulse to go, to run—*no*. To fly. It was an immediate response, reflexive, but there was nowhere to go. No place to flee, no refuge on the entirety of this planet safe for the likes of me. And yet I could not stay airborne forever. I gazed around wildly, looking for a place to land below.

Somehow I descended. I willed it and my body obeyed, muscles reacting and working, so that was something. I could command my movements. Perhaps there was hope that I could command myself to turn into a human again.

I lowered down, my legs lifting and tucking in close. My wings beat and churned the air into wind, generating great gusts. My body snagged on leaves, popped and cracked thick branches like they were twigs. I came down clumsily, the soles of my feet making contact a split second before my bent knees crashed to the ground. Grass and leaves crunched beneath my weight. I crumpled and folded in on myself, tail curving around my body as though seeking to shelter me.

A familiar sting pricked my eyes. It was the only thing familiar about any of this. A sob pushed up from inside my chest, but only more chuffing sounds escaped my mouth. Nothing intelligible. No words. Nothing human.

I leaned forward on my bent knees and stretched my arms before me, choking out wild, desperate sounds, clawing the ground, dirt and grit sliding beneath my talons. I looked down at those arms. At my skin . . . my scaled skin winking fire. Proof of what I was.

I dragged trembling fingers down my cheeks, my nails—talons— scoring my skin as though I could tear the flesh from my bones and find myself buried somewhere beneath, like a person trapped inside a cocoon.

The pressure I exerted should have done that. It should have drawn blood, but this skin was tough as armor. I would have to go deeper to inflict damage. Deeper to find me.

Turn. Go back.

I concentrated on the wish, willing it to happen, for me to change.

Nothing. No transformation. I was still this creature with the taste of hellfire in my mouth and smoke in my nose.

Lifting my gaze, I looked around and marveled at the world. Everything was brighter. The greens greener. The browns lush and sparkling in a way I had never thought possible. Colors I had never seen before, never knew existed, seared my vision.

My ears perked up at the sound of burbling water running over smooth rock. I grabbed fistfuls of earth and crawled, dragging myself over ground toward the body of water, smelling it as much as I heard it. Muskiness and loam and sulfur filled my nostrils as I followed the scent.

The grass thinned away to rough rocks and pebbles that didn't hurt at all even as my weight crunched against the sharpness. My long amber-hued fingers worked sinuously, seizing and pulling me along to the water's edge. At the first cold lap, my skin contracted, greedily tasting the wetness.

My hands sank into the shallow depths, into sludge and shale. I leaned over the water, smooth as glass, and peered down, taking my first solid look at my reflection. The wide ridged nose. The teeth big and deadly like daggers in my mouth. My eyes had changed, too. Were more feline . . . the pupils dark, elongated slits along the sides of my face now.

Not my face. A dragon's face.

I lashed out and swiped the water with an angry snarl, spraying droplets, ending my reflection. I only wished it was as simple to end *this* . . . what I'd become, this impossible thing I could not be. I inched back, away from the water, as the ripples settled and the surface returned to glass. Collapsing on my side, I curled into a tight ball full of ragged, animal breaths. Smolder baked in my chest. I wrapped my arms around my knees, willing myself smaller, willing myself to return to me again.

I turned and rolled my face into the ground, tasting grit on my lips. Closing my eyes, I tried to form words, to speak my thoughts. Instead I could only mouth my pain and fear and longing voicelessly into the ether. Unintelligible sounds chuffed from my mouth.

This isn't real. This isn't happening. This is a bad dream. Wake up. Wake up. Wake up.

For a moment, my mind went gray, thoughts unspooling, rolling out and away. I forgot everything. Forgot where I was. Forgot what I was, which was a relief. A great gust of breath eased from my body. If I could, I would never remember again. I would stay in the gray.

I was back home in the City, in the palace, in the comfort of my bed, cozily ensconced in plump pillows, swallowed up by deep bedding, the coverlet tucked up to my chin. Soft sounds stirred on the air around me. The trill of birds outside my window. Voices. Footsteps. A maid's distant song as she moved down the corridor. All of this as familiar to me as a well-trod path.

Safe. Comfortable. Again the royal whipping girl, secure in my role, content in my place . . . any secret longings for more, for something else, no longer a faint whisper in my heart, no longer an itch beneath my skin.

The gray was peace. Dappled light on grass. A morning breeze on the downy feathers of a bird. The clean wash of rain through a garden. If I breathed slowly and deeply enough, I could almost believe I was there. I could almost believe it was real.

It lasted only a moment. Then I remembered.

I was back in the present, in the sharp fangs of the woods.

And I remembered everything.

I WANTED TO hide and fold myself away like flower petals closing at the end of a day, preparing for the night. I wanted to stay stuck in night, hidden from the world, rather than remaining this creature. Rather than living in this monstrous form, capable of such damage and destruction. Only feared. Never loved. Alone.

I contemplated how I might do that.

How could I put an end to this wretched existence?

According to the bards, dragons lived a long time. They were not immortal, exactly, but close. They lived for centuries. It was impossible to wrap my head around that. *Centuries.* Close enough to immortality for a mortal, and I was still thinking very much like one of those. Like a human. Frail. Brittle as a winter's branch. Someone who had expected—hoped—to count birthdays well into the double digits. *Never* the triple digits.

Very little could kill them. Them? Us. *Me.*

That would never feel normal or right. Never slide off my mind and tongue with ease.

Typical weapons didn't destroy a dragon. Obviously not fire. At least it would not harm me. That particular element was at the core of me now. It bubbled through my veins like oil beneath the earth's skin.

My anguish was all edges and angles, sharp and pointed and digging. I lowered my head, panting, crying without tears for the girl I was, the girl lost. A dry sponge trying to wring out water. Not a drop fell. Dragons didn't cry. A fact I never expected to know. Now I did. Now I knew.

"Oh. Hello there."

My head snapped up at the voice, in this place where there should not be a voice. My gaze sharpened on the woman who stood a few feet away. *Thora.*

She blinked mildly, not appearing the slightest bit surprised or frightened, or any of the reactions one might show when coming face-to-face with a dragon.

She angled her head. "You look like you're having a bad day."

She spoke casually, unconcerned, like the sight of me was as normal and familiar as the shape of the back of her hand.

I opened my mouth, but her name did not emerge. Speech, human speech, eluded me still. I couldn't manage it. The words lodged themselves in my throat like great rocks that could not be budged, rolling marbles in my mouth that could not escape.

I hung my head, burying my face in my strange hands—hands that felt like they belonged to something else. Some *thing.*

Why was Thora not afraid and running away?

Fell had said she was a witch. Perhaps that was why she was not afraid of dragons. Had she known what I was when she first saw me? Was that what her puzzling words signified?

Witches and dragons. Both magical creatures. They existed on the same plane. *We.* We existed on the same plane. A magical plane.

Thora stepped closer, unafraid. Then, incredibly, she squatted down so that her face was close to mine. "It's you in there, isn't it?" Her words whispered over my skin, as comforting as a balm. She peered at me, seeing me. I didn't understand how, but she did.

I nodded.

"I thought so." She looked me over. "Do you know how to change back?"

Change back? *Could I?* Was that even a possibility?

I wanted to ask her about that, but, of course, I couldn't. I would have to change back to do that, in order to speak the question, and that was not happening. A twisted, mirthless bubble of laughter lodged in my chest alongside those inescapable words.

"Well." She stood back up, dusting her hands off on her skirts. "Come along, then. Can't stay here in the mud forever. Let's get you sorted out."

Sorted out.

I didn't know if that was possible. It seemed an insurmountable task. But with so few choices, I would follow her anywhere.

23
FELL

SHE WAS GONE.
  Gone.
Gone.

Gone.

Gone gone gone gone gone gone gone gone gone gone gone gone gone.

I had failed her. Assumed, arrogantly, that Tamsyn would always be there, just like time: days, hours, moments winding into forever. Something as solid and lasting as an old oak that would stand years from now, well into old age. That *she* would always be there, the *wrong* wife, the wife I had never set out to claim.

I should have nourished the seed I felt growing between us, strengthened the roots. Instead, I had left her alone, vulnerable, easy prey for a monster that was not supposed to exist. And for Arkin . . . another monster.

I was not blind to the fact that he had been with her. He had been alone in the woods with Tamsyn when he ought not to have been, after expressing his fucked-up desire to get rid of her. I shouldn't have trusted him. Clearly, he had ignored my command and taken matters into his own hands. Pigheaded bastard. All things considered, I didn't feel a great amount of grief over his loss. The world had a way of setting things to rights, balancing the weights. Evening scores. Arkin had tried to hurt Tamsyn, and he'd got what was coming to him.

I'd owed her safety. My protection. It was the most fundamental thing I could do for her. Perhaps the only thing anyone believed I *could* adequately provide given who I was. No one would believe anything soft or tender pulsed within me. I was the Beast of the Borderlands. An expert killer. A ruthless warrior. Feared. Revered. Unbreakable. A liege lord who could be counted upon to protect all those around him . . . especially his wife.

She was mine, and I had not held on to her tightly enough. Not closely enough. Not enough.

The loss of her burrowed deep inside me, teeth clamping down and sinking, clanging against bone. The guilt and misery of it vibrated through me, smarting, stinging, fueling my hate. My desperate thirst for revenge.

Dragon.

It was out there. Still taking from me. Stealing away the things that made up my life. My parents. Tamsyn. Its existence blew open the doors to the old hatred I'd thought long buried. Buried with the dragons—as they were supposed to be. Dust littering the earth.

"Fell." Mari emphasized my name in such a way that I suspected she had been saying it for quite some time.

Blinking, I focused on her face.

"We need to stop and rest the horses." She glanced behind her to where our party was working hard to catch up.

We'd been riding since yesterday. Without stopping. Without rest. Without sleep. The cold cut deep, like knives on skin. Our breaths clouded in front of our lips. And yet the horses were lathered with sweat, muscles quivering beneath their gleaming coats as we made our way through the skog.

There were only four of us. My three best warriors: Mari, Magnus, and Vidar. The rest I had tasked with finding the nearest falconer and sending a message both north and south. North, to the Borg. My people there needed to be warned. Needed to prepare and brace themselves. And south, to the City, to Hamlin. He deserved to know, too. Or rather the people did. He had citizens to protect.

An alarm needed to be raised. A warning. A single word heavy enough to strike terror into the heart of every man, woman, and child. *Dragon.*

Only the one word was necessary, but I had included more. I'd sent additional information. To the south, I instructed my warriors to enclose a message informing them that Tamsyn was missing. Lost. *Taken.*

They were her family, even if they were a wretched lot who had used her as their whipping girl. She was devoted to them, and they seemed fond of her. That had not been pretense. Their eyes had softened whenever they looked at her, when they bid her farewell.

And there was the captain of the guard. That bastard wanted her for himself. I could see it in the way his eyes tracked her, his pupils dilating, his mouth parting as though he was preparing to take a bite out of a juicy bit of fruit.

Even now my hands tightened inside my gloves into bloodless fists at the memory . . . that he would look at her as his when we were just wed, when she was mine.

Fuck. This was not the time to feel jealous, an emotion I had assuredly never once felt in my life. It was beneath me. Right now she was out there all alone, belonging to no one and needing help in the most desperate way. If not from me, then from someone else. Anyone else. Even those I did not like. If her shit family could help get her back and keep her safe, I wasn't too proud to call on them to do so.

A flash of tattered clothing filled my mind. Shards of blue fabric scattered on the ground and in bone-thick talons. I rubbed hard knuckles against my eyes as though that might erase the memory swirling thick and viscous through my head, unrelenting since yesterday.

I didn't want to believe the worst. I couldn't accept she was dead. Devoured before I got there. Not yet. No. After all, a dragon had stolen me away and I'd survived. Tamsyn was far sturdier than a child. And cleverer. As much as I had scolded her, she had resolved our encounter with the brigands in an efficient manner, taking her necklace right off her own neck to pay them.

Maybe she was alive in a dragon's lair somewhere, just as I had been as a child. I only needed to find her.

Desperate thinking. Grasping. Hopeful. Pleading. But it was not impossible.

I could not bring myself to think her dead. Even though everything pointed to it, I could not. Could not imagine it.

Those moments had been a blur. I'd been so fixated on the danger. On her shredded clothes. On Arkin's smoking corpse. The stink of charred flesh. The twenty-foot dragon that wasn't supposed to exist hovering midair, wings churning great gusts of wind.

That didn't mean Tamsyn hadn't been there, though, in the fray. Tucked beneath a dragon arm, clutched where I couldn't see her.

Desperate thinking. Grasping. Hopeful. But it was not impossible.

If she was alive and something happened to me, if I failed to find her, if the dragon I hunted got the best of me, I needed to know someone would look for her. Someone else would save her.

I will come for you.

As much as I wanted to break him in that moment for speaking those words to my newly wedded (and bedded) wife, the captain of the guard—Stig, she had called him—had said that. He'd meant those words.

For Tamsyn's sake, I needed to make certain her people knew what had happened to her. *Her people.* That went down my throat in a bitter swallow. *I* was supposed to have been *her people.* Me. As much as I had resisted the notion.

I hated that I might need them, need *others.* That I might not be enough to save her. And yet I emptied my head of that thought, because the only thing that mattered was Tamsyn.

Tamsyn not dead.

Tamsyn whole and unharmed.

Mari stared at me with frustration creasing her usually smooth brow, and I realized she was waiting for me to respond. "We cannot keep this pace."

I swallowed back the burn of defeat. We had to keep going. A dragon flew faster than we could ever ride. We could not stop.

Given our quarry was airborne, there was no trail to track. Not as I was accustomed. I'd only marked the direction the creature flew. It could be anywhere by now, could have turned in any direction. It was impossible to know. And yet I had a sense. A knowing that I trusted. I couldn't explain it, so I didn't try.

But my warriors were less than trusting. I'd heard them muttering behind me over the last several hours. A first in my life. They gave me their allegiance and obedience and had always followed me unquestioningly, but they had their doubts now.

"Fell . . . the horses will drop if we don't rest."

I growled, "If they drop, then we get up and keep going."

Mari's eyes widened. It was something I would never have said before. I had now, though. And stubbornly, I kept on. Tamsyn had to be found. The dragon had to be put down like any feral, man-eating creature.

Ahead of us, the narrow path we traveled split into two even narrower paths, nothing more than game trails each, trampled down by the recurring tread of smaller animals.

Because people went no farther than this.

Mari sidled up beside me, the fine lines bracketing her mouth settling into deeper grooves. "Now what?"

I nudged my heels and advanced before stopping hard at the fork, as though I had struck a wall and could go no farther. My destrier neighed and pranced, not having it. He sensed it, too. He wasn't even willing to try. It was as though an invisible hand had reached up to block him.

Just as well. Our mounts would not fit down either path. We would have to leave them behind.

Mari expelled a breath as though it was too big to keep inside herself. "See. We can go no farther."

I motioned with my hand, quieting her . . . poking around and feeling inside myself for the voice that was not a voice, for the *feeling* that was more smoke and shadow than substance. Just an instinct. A persistent knowing.

And there it was. It came to me, brushing against my mind like a feather. As I knew it would. As it had ever since that dragon took flight. Ever since I gave pursuit, hunting the dragon, searching for Tamsyn.

It beckoned with gentle hands, a fine, fragile thread pulling me forward. My fingers curled inward, tracing the carved X that pumped like a bleeding wound, a guiding pulse that diminished if I went one way, the wrong way, and then intensified if I went another way, the right way. The way to her. I couldn't fathom it, but it was how I knew she was still alive out there, how I knew which way to go.

"This is the direction." I pointed west, into the densely packed wood. It was a living, breathing, pulsing wall of green. High above the treetops loomed steeper foothills. Beyond those hills, beyond the Borderlands, were hazy mountains, the distant Crags. Fog circled the peaks like gauzy rings of smoke.

The dragon had taken her that way. I wouldn't even try to explain my conviction to Mari. I couldn't. I didn't understand it myself.

The warrior shook her head, her dark braids slapping against the thick leathered armor covering her shoulders. "We can't know that. A dragon flies as the crow . . . and as fast as wind. We cannot know which way it turned once it left you. It could be across the sea by now."

I didn't think so. Not unless the creature had abandoned Tamsyn somewhere, and I doubted that. My experience echoed within me, a story I'd heard so many times that it felt like my own recollection, an imprint that went beyond memory, another tattoo etched on my skin, there until I was dead and rotting in the ground. I imagined the winged demon had the two of them holed up in a den somewhere.

But whatever the case, I felt *her* like my own heartbeat.

It was gut deep, this knowledge. A bone-penetrating awareness. I sensed which way to go, compelled forth as though we were connected. Even though I couldn't explain it, I trusted it.

"We go this way," I ordered.

Stopping, I swung down onto the ground. With an idle pat for my taxed destrier, I tied off his reins to a nearby shrub and stepped into the great maw of the forest.

24

STIG

I MISSED TAMSYN. TWO WEEKS WITHOUT HER AND EACH DAY the ache in my chest only intensified.

I could not stop wondering how I might have saved her. What could I have said in her room that might have persuaded her to run away with me? What could I have said to my father to change his mind? What could I have done to stop Dryhten from marrying her, from bedding her?

What? What? What?

The questions kept me up at night. Guilt niggled, pushing down between my shoulder blades, an endless pressure.

I'd failed. Tamsyn. Myself.

The day she left ran through my mind on repeat. Everything, every horrible moment a slow slide of memory I wished I could forget, but I couldn't, because it was carved, a deep scar on my heart. She'd left with him. She was out there alone with those barbarians, suffering indignities I could not fathom.

Footsteps sounded outside my chamber. Loud, discordant shouts, distant and near, alerted me that something had happened.

Someone pounded on my door. The palace was abuzz.

I dressed quickly and grabbed my rapier, attaching it to my belt as I walked in long strides down the corridor, my boots ringing out over the flooring as I followed the din.

I was stoic when I entered the king's chancery. I felt dead inside, and I knew I looked it, looked how I had felt for weeks now.

Nothing gave me joy anymore. Nothing filled me with purpose. I went about my duties and training because there was nothing else to be done. I carried on because there was the remote hope, a thin flame of chance, that I would hear from her again, that she would send for me.

The room was alive. People were everywhere. It was chaos. Voices loud and overlapping. The queen looked pale, and one of her ladies helped her down into a chair, rapidly fanning her. My father looked unusually flustered as he talked to the king and other members of the council.

The back of my neck tingled as I made my way to the front of the chamber. I stopped beside my father, and his gaze landed on me, his brown eyes so like my own, except now they were fever bright.

"Stig!" He snapped his fingers several times, and a palace guard appeared bearing a piece of parchment. "A falconer just delivered this."

I took the message. My gaze scanned the words. The unbelievable words. The couldn't-possibly-be-true words.

My body physically rebelled. My stomach dropped, and I feared that my earlier meal might return on me.

"It's not true," I announced in a hard voice, steeling myself against the storm of emotions flooding me. "He's lying. The bastard is lying." I crumpled the paper in my fist and tossed it to the floor, not caring who might still want to read it.

My father nodded grimly, his gaze fixed on me. Beyond him, the king lowered himself down beside his queen, pulling her into his arms, comforting her through her tears of grief.

A single word lifted over the crowd, rippling through the room again and again, on the tongue of everyone.

Dragon.

I didn't believe it. It was a lie. A trick.

My father stepped close. "What do you make of this?"

"He's killed her. There is no dragon. It was him, and he invented this ridiculous story to cover his actions."

My father nodded grimly. "I think you're right." He added in a sneer: "Dragon. He must think us fools. Well. We can't let this stand."

"No," I agreed. Tamsyn was lost. Gone. And I was lost, too.

I would not let it stand. She would be avenged.

25

TAMSYN

I WOKE SLOWLY, SWIMMING TO THE SURFACE, EMERGING from a deep, milky fog, so like the fog I perpetually found myself folded within these days.

I shifted, and a piece of hay jabbed me in the side. Grimacing, I readjusted, seeking escape from the needle prick, wondering where I was.

As much as the hay poked and prodded at me, it smelled sweet. Faintly herbal. Slightly tangy. It did not reek of mold or, worse, manure. There was that, at least. As far as beds went, it could be worse. So much worse.

And then I remembered just how much worse it actually was.

As my world came into focus, I lifted my hand, held it up in front of me, bracing myself with a sucked-in breath, needing to see what horror awaited me this day, needing to know, fearing, hoping . . .

The familiar fingers were there, the nails as short and jagged as ever, but I stared at them like they were something new, a marvel, slender digits flexing in front of my face, my movements experimental, shaky and juddery as a new colt gaining its legs.

I am me again.

My arm. My hand. My fingers. No clawlike appendages. No talons. No scaled flesh.

No dragon here.

My hands roamed over my body, assessing, reassuring. I was

myself again. In the truest sense. Naked in the hay with a wool blanket twisted around me, exposing far more than it shielded from the raw morning air.

I blew out a breath of relief that immediately steamed when it hit the cold.

"Yes. You're you."

Apparently I had spoken the words aloud, put the thought out into the world, let it materialize and take shape like something real, something I could touch and hold in my hand.

My gaze snapped to Thora. "You." Apparently I hadn't dreamed her up.

The events of yesterday flooded back over me. Arkin. Me . . . bursting from my skin. Fire like saliva in my mouth. Fell. His bellow of rage filling my ears, trailing me like smoke up into the sky. My wild, directionless flight before I landed, before Thora collected me—something broken and in need of repair. She'd led me back to her home with a casual manner, as though she came across dragons all the time in the course of her day.

When I didn't fit through the door to her house, she guided me to her barn, where I bedded down alongside the rest of the livestock. Two milking cows, a horse, and a mule. They all eyed me with understandable distrust. In the soft light of morning, their gazes still reflected that distrust, although the mule looked a little less wild-eyed as it munched on a bucket of feed.

Thora angled her head thoughtfully as she peered at me within the pile of hay. "But perhaps I should say it is the *other* you. Because the dragon is you, too," she said so absolutely, so matter-of-fact that it sparked the panic inside me. The panic not so very different from what I had felt while careening wildly thousands of feet above the ground.

No no no no no no no.

"I am not a dragon." Fear sharpened my tongue. "I would know!"

She gave me a pitying look.

"I am *not* a dragon." My fear slid into something softer-edged. A desperate plea. I was a human. I couldn't be anything else. Despite

all the evidence to the contrary. I repeated it as though the conviction alone could make it true: "I am not a dragon."

She looked at me almost amused now. "I think you know you
are."

I shook my head. "I can't be. They don't exist anymore."

She nodded, but the motion was so indulgent it was insulting.
Like she was trying to appease a small child who was one breath
away from a tantrum. "Well, apparently not *all* are gone. You know
what they say . . ."

They? They who?

I shook my head, wishing she would stop. I didn't want her to
make sense, to be right. I didn't want her to persuade me. To say
something that would make me believe the unbelievable. I wanted
a reason *not* to believe.

"Magic," she continued, "cannot be destroyed. It might hide, but
it is always there. It never goes away. It lives in the bones, in the soul
of this world. What you are, this . . ." She gestured to me. "It was
always in you, rooted deep."

Always in you. Like a tooth waiting to emerge, patient for its
turn, for its day to break free.

I shook my suddenly throbbing head. The dragon had always
been inside me? Hiding? A secret all my life kept even from me?
None of this was right. I pressed fingers to my temples, my denial
sharp, my confusion as wild and deep as the bramble in the woods
surrounding us.

I had always assumed being the whipping girl was the thing
that set me apart from others. But maybe it was more than that.

Maybe it was this.

"Magic cannot be destroyed," she repeated.

And that seemed counter to everything I knew. The whole purpose of the Threshing had been to destroy dragons. Humankind
had thought it possible. Kings and queens had sent their armies to
see it done.

It had been *done.*

We had been told that magic—or magical creatures—were

responsible for all ills. All evils. Every plague or injustice suffered could be laid at the feet of dragons.

If I was one of them, did that make me evil, then? Did I need to be wiped from existence? I was not a bad—

I started and stopped, cringing at the phrase that hovered on the tip of my tongue.

I was not a bad person.

But was I even a person?

"Come." Thora held out a hand for me to take. "Let's warm you up inside the house. I have some clothes you can wear, and I'll fetch you something to eat. You'll feel better once you have a proper meal."

If only she were right. If only that would fix everything.

"YOU CAN'T STAY HERE."

Thora delivered this over oats and milk sprinkled with sweet cinnamon, as though I were a child and she wanted to ply me with something tasty while she snuck in a bit of foul-tasting medicine.

It did not make the words go down any easier.

As I sat at her table, wearing a borrowed dress of warm wool laced at the front, the nearby fire popping and crackling in the hearth, the words dropped like a rock in the air between us, heavy with a hard *thunk*.

She said it again . . . either for emphasis or because my continued silence begged her to repeat herself. "You can't stay here."

I didn't meet her gaze. My spoon quickened, stirring fiercely through the oats, expending some of my restless energy.

You can't stay here.

I moistened my lips. I wanted to ask why. Why had she brought me here at all if it was only to now eject me? And yet I could not summon the question, too reluctant to reveal how vulnerable I felt.

Sitting at her table, wrapping an arm around my bowl and pulling it close to the edge as though it might be taken away just as everything else had, I felt so small. On the verge of tears. This time the tears would be real, though. This time they would fall like rain from my eyes.

"I don't know everything about your kind. I thought you were all gone. I know you are looking to me for answers, but there's much I don't know." She breathed then, a deep sigh that was like a cold wind against shutters, clawing to get inside . . . or out. "You . . . here . . . I cannot help but think it might have something to do with Vala."

"Vala?" Where had I heard that name before?

Her eyes glinted. "Yes. Vala, my grandmother's sister. She always had too much magic for her own good. She was born with too much power and not enough cunning or caution. She was a vain and stupid girl. Fancied herself in love with King Alrek. Even worse . . . she thought he loved her."

"King Alrek?" I looked up then. Alrek was Hamlin's grandfather. I would know. I had been thoroughly educated on the royal lineage. "That was a long time ago."

Thora chuckled then, shaking her head as she recounted the story. "Yes. He was young and handsome, and, well . . . a king. My idiot great-aunt thought he would make her his queen. This was before he was married, of course. He asked Vala to cast a spell for him, the final nail in the coffin for dragons."

I listened, riveted, feeling like a small girl sitting at the feet of one of the visiting bards. I was certain that was where I'd heard mention of this Vala, in one of those stories that had floated like a mesmerizing melody in the Great Hall.

Thora gave a sad little sigh and shook her head. "My grandmother told her not to do it. Not to cast such a spell. Putting something like that into the world . . . it comes back on you." Thora's voice faded away, and she shivered, her lovely face suddenly grim, a hint of her age peeking out in the lines and hollows, in the weary wisdom of her eyes, reminding me that, for as much as she appeared a maiden, this woman was older than me, at least twice my age . . . at least as old as the king and queen. Perhaps even older. Who knew exactly how many years she had walked this earth? Were witches like dragons, blessed with unnaturally long life? "She was asking for trouble."

"What happened?" I recalled some of the details now. In the aftermath of the Hormung, Vala had been appointed to cast a spell. If the remaining dragons could not breed and multiply . . . well. The dragon problem would solve itself. Time would see to that.

So how could I be here like this? How could *I* be explained?

How could *I* exist?

"She could not do precisely what he asked, which was to kill all dragons, but she did the next best thing. The only thing she could think of. She cast a spell that ended all hatchlings. Dragons could no longer spawn. Once the remaining dragons died or were killed off . . . well, King Alrek got his wish." She shrugged. "And what did Vala get for her effort? For her loyalty? The king decreed her a traitor and fed her to the fire. A hundred years ago. She had the notable distinction of being the first witch cast into flame. We've all been running and hiding ever since." Thora lifted her mug of tea in salute, her lips twisting bitterly. "So there you have it. My family's proud legacy for you."

I could only stare in horror. King Alrek had done that? He had romanced and seduced this Vala? Inveigled and entreated her to cast a spell for him, and then he let her burn? No. Not *let*. He had commanded it. Decreed it with all his imperial power. I had not known that part of the story. It had been left out of my history lessons.

What else did I not know? What else had been omitted?

I stared into my congealing oats like the answer hid there, thinking about the things I *did* know. I set aside my tender feelings for the king and queen, my parents, and opened the long-bolted door inside me, allowing in thoughts I had always blocked.

Would loving parents take a baby, praise her with love, rear her gently, call her daughter, and then turn her over to be whipped for the transgressions of others?

And then, later, would they force her to trade vows with a man deemed unworthy for their true daughters?

Was that not perhaps in keeping with their history, with the heartless legacy of King Alrek?

My stomach lurched. I felt sick. The memory of my father's warm hand on my shoulder. His kind words of praise when I did something well. His laughter when I performed a silly skit with my sisters. It all felt like a lie now.

Could I have been wrong about him? Wrong about everything? My life? My mother? My sisters? It was a sobering thought. One I had never permitted myself.

Thora ran a hand over her face. "I don't know which is more treacherous. Humans or love. In the end, both will fail you." Thora glanced around her cozy cottage. "I'll take solitude." Her eyes went cloudy, and I studied her face. In profile, she was an etching in sadness. Aloneness. Loneliness. I could be a friend to her. A companion to break the long stretch of her lonely days in this unrelenting wood.

And yet she did not want that. She didn't want me here. I was a problem. I would only bring her trouble, and she had enough of that breathing down her neck simply by being who she was. The life she had carved out for herself here, hewn from a cursed forest, was a place of refuge.

This was the curse of witchkind, I realized. They could live. Suppress their nature and blend in when forced to do so. Or embrace what they were and find safety in seclusion. But never solace. Never freedom. Not really. It was a sentence. A punishment to live out their days in a cage of isolation. Too many of them in a group would attract notice, would draw witch hunters and those who would burn them alive. So this was what she had. Herself. Only herself. A small life.

I saw my own future in her. Life in a cage of isolation—or death.

An existence so different from the one I'd thought I might have with Fell a day ago. My grim fate yawned ahead, posts in a fence, one after another, days falling in succession, in sameness, in tedium.

Steam wafted from her mug, and for a moment I was back amid trees dappled in morning light, watching as smoke lifted off Arkin's charred remains, like fog curling off a dark body of water.

Except here there was no stink of death, no scorched flesh . . . no villain put down. Just a sweet herbal aroma of mint and juniper tea.

Thora lifted her mug for another sip, and the movement broke my reverie.

"These woods have their shadows," she murmured. "Places where the light cannot reach. You must watch for that. Be careful."

Could she be any more vague? "What do you mean?"

"Magic is a complicated thing. Sometimes it is . . . dark."

All magic felt dark to me. Thus far, I had seen no good come from it.

She went on, "You and I are not the only things out here." She bit her lip in consideration, as though not sure she should share more. "I do not know how you would fare against her."

Her.

"Her?" I asked.

Thora nodded. "The huldra. These are her woods, too. She has never bothered with me, and I have never bothered her. We stick to our corners. Give each other space. But you . . . I don't know." She shook her head. "I don't know how she would react when confronting a dragon."

I flinched. Were we just going ahead and calling me that now? Was there no hesitation? No further conversation?

"Still don't think you're a dragon?" she asked, reading my reaction with narrowing eyes.

"Like you said, it's a complicated thing."

I didn't know *how* I'd turned into a dragon. I didn't know if it would happen again. I didn't know how I even turned *back* into a human. I had just gone to sleep in a barn and woken up my old self. I *did* know I had no control over any of it. It was not a weapon I could wield. *Complicated* seemed a far too gentle euphemism for all that.

She chuckled lightly. "That it is. And recognizing such already makes you smarter than a lot of witches I used to know."

Used to know. Was that because they were gone? Or because she had made herself . . . *gone?*

I had the uncanny sensation that I was looking in a mirror, that I was seeing myself in this wretched woman who lived in miserable isolation and recounted people long gone from her life.

"I'm not a witch, though," I countered.

"No," she mused. "You're something else." She sniffed then and shook her head. "And they're not witches either. Not anymore. They're dead, so that makes them . . . nothing." This she uttered so matter-of-factly, as though she were long accustomed to the condition of her friends and family being dead.

I was *something else*. Yes. That was true.

The way heat swam beneath my skin still . . . even now, like a serpent beneath water, gliding, searching for the right moment to emerge, I was still that. I was not free from it. It was not gone. The dragon was still here. It went deep. Like the roots of a tree. A disease that coursed through bone and blood to the meat of me. Now that it had been unleashed, I could recognize it. Feel it throbbing inside me like the beat of music.

"You should proceed with caution out there. Head east. It's the quickest way out of the skog."

I didn't want to go east. I wanted to go north. Directly north, into the Crags. That mysterious and formidable place that called to me. Terrified me. Thrilled me. I could still recall those peaks breaking through the clouds.

Answers were north . . . where dragons once lived. They certainly wouldn't be found back in the City. That place dealt in many things, I now realized, except the truth. And there weren't any answers here with Thora, who didn't want me around. And they absolutely were not with Fell or his people. If I ever turned in front of them, they would kill me on sight. They would not stop and ask questions. Not that I could answer them when I was in dragon form anyway. I could expect no mercy from a people with a history steeped in dragon slaying.

Thora shrugged as though she knew I had plans counter to her advice. "But you will do what you must."

I nodded. Yes. I would.

My fate waited in the north.

My palm buzzed. That flicker of another life, of Fell . . . left behind, but not behind, not ever behind as long as I could feel this connection, this echo of him.

I knotted my hand into a fist, trying to crush it, to banish the sensation just as he was banished from me. Husband or not, married or not, we could never pick up where we left off. Never live as husband and wife. I would have to forget about him. That door had closed with a slam the moment I tasted fire. The moment I felt the wind on my face.

I glanced to Thora. She had done it. She had forgotten about everyone. The entire world ceased to exist for her. She was strong. She had carved out this life for herself here. Alone.

If that was what I had to do, I could do it, too.

"Come," she said, pushing up from the table. "I won't send you away empty-handed. Let's pack you a few things for your journey. I have a compass you can have. You'll find it useful. The forest can get dark. At times it's hard to tell north from south. And you'll need to dress warmly. Oh." She looked back at me as though seized with a sudden thought. "When you're out there, you may need these, too." She walked to a nearby shelf and removed something from it. As she offered them to me, I could see they were several strips of leather.

I turned them over in my hand, unable to imagine their use. "Why do I need—"

"I just have a feeling you may need them. They're sturdy."

A *feeling* she had. That was good enough for me. I supposed when a blood witch said she had a *feeling* about something, heed should be taken. She had not led me astray so far.

"I will keep them close," I promised. Hopefully I would know what to do with them, should I have need.

"Do that," she advised. "And, Tamsyn. You're stronger than you realize. Draw from that. Do not be afraid of your power."

Do not be afraid of your power.

But I was. I was afraid of it. Afraid of me.

26
FELL

I FELT HER. I FELT THAT THREAD CONNECTING US, PULLING tight on the air, taut as a wire on the verge of snapping, but somehow managing to keep us tethered.

The woods had become nearly impassable, so we walked single file, one after another, like a row of prisoners steadily working toward our fate.

It was late afternoon, the day not faded. And yet the sun could not reach the forest floor. Ribbons of dim light filtered down, allowing only faint illumination. It felt like dusk, solemn and gray, even though that was hours away.

"Fell," Mari whispered hoarsely, as though she was parched, even though she carried a waterskin at her side. It was hard work forging through the endless copse.

"We've gone too far."

Too far.

I had a flash of Tamsyn. Arkin's smoking remains. The dragon. We had passed the point of "too far" long ago.

Ignoring her, I pressed on through the dense undergrowth. I couldn't explain it. Mari wouldn't understand. *I* didn't understand it. She and the others would think I had lost my mind. And trying to make them understand would only be a waste of valuable time. Time that should be spent hunting, searching, finding Tamsyn.

The terrain became only more difficult. A wild tangle of trees and brush and foliage with great hanging drapes of moss nearly impossible to penetrate.

The forest crackled and pulsed and breathed, tracking us with watchful eyes. The air that filled my lungs smelled pungent—of ancient trees and decay, of musk and sulfur.

"So this is a bad idea, right?" Magnus muttered between panted breaths, more of a statement than a question.

He was not wrong. We were deep in the skog, deep in a marsh where we never ventured, a place we always avoided, but here I was, my palm alive and buzzing like a bee, guiding me, pulling me on.

I had traveled extensively through Penterra, but never directly into the skog. I had braved the edges before, toed the perimeter, but never the interior. Never had I gone into the belly of the beast.

Protecting the Borderlands was all about risk. No way around it. Every day there was some manner of challenge. Invaders from the north. Brigands from the north, the south. Brigands from the west, the east. The end of the Threshing had not been the end of conflict.

But this? Venturing into the skog was not the kind of risk I ever took. There was nothing needed in these dark, smothering woods. Nothing I needed to protect. Nothing I needed to claim.

Until now.

It was one of the few places left thoroughly untouched. The same as it was hundreds of years ago. A thousand years ago.

A perpetual night wood, deadly and magical, full of sounds that spit and hissed, tormented and beguiled. A living, breathing creature. A monster with fangs and claws that reached out and grabbed anyone who drew too close. Those who were foolish enough, unlucky enough to enter, were never sighted again. At least that was the rumor. And was there not always some fraction of truth to rumors?

But she was mine. My wife. My responsibility.

I still felt her heartbeat in the cup of my hand. *In me.* I glanced down, as though I could see through the leather of my glove to the vibrating mark there. It was as though she had entered *me* through that wound as we stood in that chapel. A part of her lived in me now.

And as long as she lived, there was hope.

As long as there was hope, I would not abandon her.

I glanced back at my faithful companions. They didn't have to die. They could still turn around and leave these plagued woods.

Stopping, I turned to face them. "You can go." They *should* go. Mari frowned.

Behind her, Magnus blew out a heavy breath. "Oh, thank fuck." He started to turn. "Let's get out of here."

"You misunderstood. I'm staying. You all go on without me." It was fair. The right thing to do. My wife. My fight.

Mari shook her head, eyes wide. "Leave you?"

Magnus faced forward again, his jaw locking hard with determination. "Sorry. We can't do that."

Vidar called from behind Magnus, his voice a loud whisper, as though he feared being overheard. "We don't even know what we're fighting here, but we're not leaving you to it, my lord. Not alone." Vidar thumbed the edge of his sword. "Can't abandon you. This forest isn't a good place."

Magnus sent Vidar an annoyed look. "Really?"

Vidar missed his sarcasm. He was a deadly fighter and the only warrior to stand taller than me, but he didn't possess the keenest mind. "We're in the skog, lure to any huldras living here." He shivered dramatically. "I hear they like to collect cocks and fashion them into ear baubles."

"Stop it," Mari snapped. "You don't know that. Those are just stories."

"No one who comes this far into the skog lives to tell the tale," Vidar insisted, looking around at the forest, which seemed to swell and grow with every passing moment.

"Then how does anyone know anything about a huldra here?" Mari gave a disgusted grunt and an eye roll. "Someone would have had to see one."

I scowled, beyond arguing with them. "You all go. Now."

"We're staying with you." Mari shot the other two warriors quelling glances, daring them to contradict her.

They squared their shoulders and nodded resolutely. They were no cowards. True, this place affected them and got beneath their skin in a way no army of seasoned soldiers ever had, but they were still trained warriors from the Borderlands. As far as I was concerned, that made them better than everyone else.

Magnus cocked his head. "You hear that?"

"I don't hear anything," Mari snapped.

"Exactly," Magnus returned with great satisfaction.

Mari fell still and listened.

So did I. Magnus was not wrong. It was too quiet. I couldn't recall the last time I had heard a magpie or the chitter of an animal chasing through the underbrush. Even the wind was silent, not a rustle through the trees. Not a leaf stirred. The calm was complete, absolute, a dead space where things held themselves still, lying in wait, predators in the grass.

I pushed on, using my sword to hack at the ever-encroaching brush, filling the silence. It was arduous work. As soon as I forged a path, cutting down thicket, more grew in its place.

The three warriors followed me. Trustingly. Into every fray, every abyss. Why would this be any different?

I wondered how trusting they would be if they knew I was led by some inexplicable insight, a knowing. That the fizzing X carved into my flesh compelled and guided me.

I did not leave the City the same man who had arrived at its gates. I had not felt the same since I married Tamsyn. Since I stood at that altar and clasped her bleeding palm to mine. She was another piece, another jagged shape that fit and locked into place against me. Tamsyn.

That's how I knew she was alive. And how I would find her.

I WAS ACCUSTOMED to the fog and mist in the Borderlands. It was part of the territory. Natural. Necessary. As integral as the air itself. There was my skin and blood and bone and . . . fog.

But this fog? It wasn't right.

It was different.

The forest was bathed in a red miasma. As though a hand had waved over the land and washed it in blood.

"What the fuck is this?" Vidar panted from the back, bringing up the rear. "Is the forest on fire?"

The air was painted with a red vapor. Odorless and silky smooth on my skin as we pushed through the tangle of woods, the red casting our faces in a hellish glow.

"Not fire." I hacked a thick branch out of the way with my sword.

The green world looked almost black within the haze, like blood sliding over everything, slipping inside every crevice and crack.

The trees began to thin away, no longer touching, no longer crowding close. They stood spaced apart like sentries on vigil, keeping in as much as they kept out.

I lowered my sword, less cutting and whacking required. Even though we could finally stand side by side, I led the way, stepping out into a little meadow.

I was the first one to see her.

The first one she spoke to in a molten voice, a caress sliding over my skin, wrapping around my throat, sliding down . . . taking me by the cock and leading me forward.

"Well, hello. I thought you would never get here."

IT WAS SOMETHING out of a fever dream. A wine-soaked dusk. A blurred, red-infused illusion.

I felt fuzzy-headed, swaddled in cotton. Pleasantly so. My thoughts were muddled, as though I had consumed one too many mugs of ale, which was . . . different.

Spirits never affected me. I could drink all day, all night, and never feel the least bit intoxicated. It was unusual. I had even put it to the test before, trying to get drunk one of those nights when the ache went deep and the losses were keen and we had suffered the death of one too many and the hunger for oblivion clamored deep within me.

I had watched others become stupid drunk, unstable on their feet, loud and giddy and not themselves as they succeeded in numbing their pain. Not me. Never me.

Until now.

Mari, Magnus, and Vidar stumbled around behind me like silly children, their laughter and voices tinny and distant in my ears.

A figure emerged through the red. A woman. She materialized like smoke . . . something from nothing, moving slowly, seductively, languorously, weaving like a ribbon threading through the trees—except when she did not. Except when she moved quickly, like a dart launched, an arrow released, flying from one point to the next in a rushing blur, a swift stroke of paint slashing across the crimson-drenched air.

She was an enticement of curves: breasts full and juicy, as tumescent as melons on the vine and visible beneath sheer fabric; her nipples dusky points brushing hypnotically against wafer-thin material.

Blood rushed to my cock.

"I've been waiting for you, my love . . ."

As tantalizing as the sight of her was . . . it was her voice that undid me, flowing like sweet wine, dripping thick and syrupy on the air. The sound ran down my throat, settling warm and viscous inside my belly and then winding even lower.

Her face was as hazy as the atmosphere. A watercolor in progress, an unfinished painting, the promise of beauty and euphoria there . . . shifting, flashing, blurring beneath the red veil that covered everything.

She continued to speak in that captivating voice, her beguiling words wrapping around me. *My love. Sweetheart. Come to me. Hold me.*

I stepped closer, obeying, and her face snapped into focus . . . sucking the breath right out of me.

Tamsyn.

Tamsyn as I had never seen her before. Her fiery hair loose, a nimbus of flame around her head, tumbling down her shoulders. Her eyes bigger, brighter. Her lips more luscious . . . Her body ripe, her skin glowing opalescent in the ruby glow, begging for my hands, my lips, my tongue.

She beckoned for me with slender hands, and I came, most willingly, readily, catching her up in my arms. I buried my face in her hair with a groan.

"My love," she purred, her delicious fingers in my hair, delicate nails scraping down my throat, chest, back, everywhere, all at once.

I felt her against me, all over, impossibly. But I did not stop to consider impossibilities. I did not question the sudden appearance of her here, like this; the crimson air flowing over us like an ocean wave, engulfing me, sweeping me into its endless depths.

There was only this. Now. What I saw. What I felt. What I needed.

Nothing impossible here. Only Tamsyn.

I pulled back, and then I was tasting her, her candied lips on mine, her honey tongue in my mouth.

She moaned into me, her words against me, around me. Near. Far. Everywhere.

The sound of her voice echoed and reverberated all around me. *My love. I need you. You need me. You. Need. Me.*

Her words started in my ears, and then poured into my blood, burrowing into my bones, pooling in my marrow, my soul.

I was drunk with it. Drunk with her.

You need me you need me you need me you need me you need me you need me you need me you need me you need me you need me you need me you need me you need me you need me you need me you need me.

She was not wrong. I needed her.

I was panting. Reaching for her, desperate to haul her closer and bring her inside me.

She shifted away but did not break contact. Her fingers stroked my cheek, her smile for me alone even as she made room for the others, greeting Mari and Magnus and Vidar as they came at her like ravenous wolves, their eyes glazed, charged, intoxicated by her.

They leaned into her, desperate and starving, taking her with their hands and mouths, and she devoured them right back.

She kept that hand on my face, her fingers a lifeline, a tether, and I watched, too befuddled to do anything except arch into her touch, soaking it in, absorbing everything about her that I could as she kissed Mari, then Magnus . . . encouraging Vidar to drop to his knees and seize her hips, nuzzling his big face against her belly.

Something dark and hostile stirred beneath the pleasing fog, beneath my buzzing, humming lust, cutting through the fizz in my blood. A growl rumbled up from my chest.

Tamsyn's bright-eyed gaze locked on me, and dimly I thought her eyes were not quite right. The amber not quite the correct shade. There was something black and gleaming beneath the usual fiery glow. Black and deep as a tar pit, something that sucked you in and never let you out.

Her face flickered then, went in and out like a guttering candle flame fighting for air. In that brief struggle . . . a hint of something else, *someone* else glimmered beneath her features before her familiar countenance took hold again.

I scrubbed a knuckle against one eye, trying to clear my vision. When I looked again, it was Tamsyn.

Achingly beautiful Tamsyn.

I didn't know what I had seen in that blink of a moment, but it was her again now, tenderly stroking my face, kissing my warriors, letting them touch her everywhere even as she reached for me, pulling me in closer, her hand leaving my face and sliding down my chest, her sweet words both soothing and thrilling. *I am yours. You are mine.*

Magnus's hand went to her breast, and something revived in me. Growling and snarling, I shoved him away. I shoved them all away. Standing in front of her, chest heaving, I glowered at them as I lifted my sword, murder in my heart.

She made a tsking sound, her hands coming up to my shoulders. "Come now, my love, none of that. There is more than enough of me for everyone." The seductive purr of her voice wrapped me in its fold like a warm blanket, softening me, dousing my wrath and binding me to her will.

Frozen, I could only watch her as she dropped down onto her knees before me, her hands reaching for my belt. Her words breathed ice over my fevered flesh. *I am yours. You are mine.*

27

TAMSYN

I MADE MY WAY NORTH. THORA'S ADVICE HAD NOT DE-
terred me. Besides. Where else could I go? Where else did I belong?

I recalled those mist-encircled summits as though they were
from a dream. My panicked tear through the sky felt as though it
had happened in another life. And I supposed it had. It had happened to someone else. *Something* else. Not the girl I appeared
now. And yet I recalled the perfect calmness that had settled over
me when I'd looked at those mountains. The peace, the sense of
surety—refuge. Considering I didn't feel that way about anything
or anyone anymore . . .

I was headed to the Crags.

I held the compass Thora had given me in my hand, marching
determinedly in line with the little jiggling arrow. There was no
sun here in the skog. Only a canopy of tangled branches and leaves
blotting out the light. No way to determine which way was north
without this compass. Another reason to be grateful for Thora. I
would be lost if not for her.

And yet the compass wasn't the only thing filling the cup of
my palm. Beneath my glove, my hand sparked and buzzed with
awareness.

It had throbbed that way ever since I awoke in the barn—even
before that . . . since I was blooded to Fell—but now my body was
one great amalgamation of feelings and emotions and sensations,

sparking with heat, a great throbbing force as I strode forth. It was impossible to fixate on my hand when I was being bombarded on all sides. When there were so many distractions, so many things happening, churning through me.

The air was changing. From thin to thick. From water to syrup. From a murky opaque, typical of a dense forest, to . . . red.

A red film draped over everything.

Another mystery in a growingly bewildering world.

Another inexplicable occurrence in a long line, in a string of incomprehensible occurrences.

I knew the skog was not a normal wood. It was a place where witches and huldras dwelled, avoided by humankind, *avoiding* humankind.

A world where I was not me. At least not the me I had thought myself to be. No daughter. No sister. No pretend princess. No whipping girl. No girl at all. Not even a wife to the Beast of the Borderlands. No longer any of that.

No longer anything except . . . alone. I. Was. Alone. A wanderer. Rootless. I'd never been so chokingly alone before.

Palace life was a busy, noisy, messy affair. My only solitude had been found in sleep, in my chamber, and even then my sisters had often invaded my bed.

Now solitude wrapped around me like a heavy blanket, weighing me down, holding me close as I moved through the stillness of the skog, each of my footsteps leaving an impression in the moist earth, the only reminder that I existed at all. Too still. Too quiet. A tomb for the dead. And yet it was alive. Alive and watchful in the way a water snake holds still and peers out above the waterline. Waiting. Unblinking. Biding its time.

I wasn't like Thora, who was content with her aloneness and as much a part of this world as the whispering grass and listening trees and the squelching ground beneath my feet.

And yet I told myself I could do this.

Reminded myself that since the moment of my birth, I had been bred to endure. I'd taken the beatings. Withstood the whippings and the floggings. I could endure loneliness, too.

My pace was strong and steady until I hit a wall of dense foliage. It was a game of dexterity and nimbleness then as I squeezed in and around the thick trees and bushes and descending branches, dipping under and around the drapes of moss.

And suddenly it all faded away. Melted like butter on hot bread from an oven. The trees became fewer, the bushes fewer, the clawing branches shrank away like a receding sunset. All but the air.

The air grew. Swelled and expanded like a sponge swollen with water. Heavy and dripping red. It felt thick, sitting like oil on my skin.

This.

This was what Thora had been talking about. The danger of the skog. The teeth. The claws. The hissing breath.

I'd entered the huldra's silken web.

And I was not the only one here.

My vision was still wildly sharp, the colors searingly bright even within the titian haze, senses as alive and bright as they had been when I'd burst out of my skin and incinerated Arkin.

It still took a moment for me to make sense of what I was seeing. Because it was so very *in*sensible.

Fell was here.

My first instinct was to turn and run . . . to get away, to escape my husband, because . . . reasons. We could not be together. The Lord Beast with me . . . this thing I was now . . .

I shook my head. No. He would kill it—kill *me*. He would destroy me if he knew the truth.

But what I was seeing now cast all that from my mind. Fell and Mari and two other warriors: Magnus and Vidar. They were tangled up together. At first glance it was difficult to determine whose limbs belonged to whom. And there was another body in the fray. A stranger. A woman.

I frowned, assessing her . . . a task that should not have been so very difficult, but for the fact that her face seemed to change. Like a puddle caught in sunlight, the surface waxy and effervescent, variable and temperamental as the changing wind.

I warily inched closer for a better look. Dried leaves crunched beneath my boots. The woman whipped her head around to face me in a move so animalistic, so predatory, that I knew at once: she was not human.

I gasped.

She was a combination of faces. A mix of three or four people . . . the blurred visages where one face should be, flashing in and out, overlapping.

There were three women there. Unknown to me. Young and lovely all, but as different to each other as the night was to the day. One with short hair pale as moonbeams, the other one with dark russet hair, another one with jet-black braids . . . and then another face . . . a fourth face. Me.

Me but not me. Because I was standing right here.

And yet it was my face. *My. Face.* But not. Looking at myself—but not myself. Not myself as I had ever seen myself. Not myself as I existed. This was a trick.

A huldra's trick.

She smiled widely, all those lips, all those mouths peeling back to beam a multitude of teeth at me. It was a dizzying effect, looking at one body, one entity, and seeing so many faces merging together . . . but beneath all those faces, there was one.

One face. A true face.

The huldra's face.

I saw her. I saw her for what she was.

A hag.

Paper-thin skin the color of ash. Sparse, stringy hair that sprouted randomly from her scalp, leaving bald patches everywhere else. A black hole for a mouth, full of rotting, nubby teeth. Eyes milky orbs that moved about almost unseeingly . . . except they landed on me with unerring clarity.

"Ah, hello, my love," she greeted in a voice so beautiful it hurt.

There was nothing about the harmonious sound that hinted at the hag underneath the veil of faces. Her words were youthful and melodic. Captivating. Entrancing. I felt their pull, but I gave myself a hard shake, somehow resisting.

She approached me, Fell and his warriors following close, trailing her as though they were small children, desperate for their mother's attention. Clearly they had fallen under her power. Although the attention they wanted from her was definitely not of the maternal variety. Their hands groped her wherever they could reach.

As she neared, I could again see that one of those false faces blurring in and out belonged to me. *Mine.*

It was an eerie thing to see yourself but not yourself reflected back at you. I was certain I had never looked like this . . . like a wide-eyed wanton, eager for sex. It was disconcerting to see all four of them fondling a body that mimicked mine. Mari and Magnus cupped and plucked at my (not my) nipples. Vidar's giant hand circled my (not my) backside. And Fell. His hand slid down between the gauzy material of the huldra's gown, disappearing between my (not my) legs.

Not me. Not. Me. Not my body.

How dare she steal my likeness? Rage stirred in my chest, steam filling my nose. He did not belong to her. I wanted to grab Fell, wrench him away from the creature, and let her feel the sting of my wrath.

The force of my reaction jarred me. I never lashed out. Never retaliated. Well. Never before.

The image of Arkin as I had last seen him filled my mind. A burning reminder, literally, that I was not what I once had been. Now I felt things. Now I fought.

This creature had stolen my face and was using it to manipulate and captivate Fell. Not so with his warriors, though. The faces of the other women must be people Mari, Magnus, and Vidar wanted . . . loved.

But my face was for Fell. I didn't know whether to be flattered or offended. Right now I simply knew I had to save him. I had to save *all* of them from this fiend.

As she stopped before me, I pasted a smile upon my face and struggled not to reveal what I knew of her. That I *knew* her. The real her. That I could see her in all her grotesque glory . . .

"My lovely." She reached an inviting hand toward me, and I did my best not to shudder as she stroked my arm—did my best not to reveal that I could see its skeletal shape, the gray skin like wrinkled parchment, the yellowed and cracked fingernails thick and hard as walnut shells.

She continued to speak a litany of endearments, of praise, of words that attempted to wear down my resistance.

Then, unbelievably, remarkably, her face rippled and flickered and changed anew. Over her grotesque features a new face dropped into place . . . a new veil, different from the others. A beloved face. A face I had thought to never see again. A face I had not realized I missed so much.

My heart lurched, and I choked back a sob. Treacherous emotion welled up in me at the sight of my friend: Stig, the echo of him, a fine, translucent film stretched over the huldra's ancient skin and milky eyes, pushing all the other faces aside as he smiled at me.

Stig, only not Stig.

In the huldra, he was somehow amplified. Brighter, shinier . . . those warm brown eyes of his a deeper shade. More black. Glossy like a well-polished stone.

"My sweet girl. My heart. My pet. How I have been waiting for you, longing for you, needing you . . . and I know you've needed me, too."

The huldra was a master at this, at saying the right words in that delicious voice. An expert at her craft of deceit, and I knew I must tread carefully. Give nothing away. Pretend I was as the others, captivated and enchanted by her machinations.

"Stig," I breathed, in what sounded like a properly mesmerized voice.

The sound of my voice did something, however. Fell flinched.

Blinked. Scowled. Cocked his head to one side and narrowed his gaze at me, seeing me, then seeing the huldra. He was coming out of it. Returning to himself. Viewing me clearly for the first time since I had entered his orbit.

I needed to act fast. Fortunately, the huldra's gaze was still on me. She did not notice him slipping away, like water through a sieve, escaping her.

Before he could speak or do anything to call the creature's attention to the fact that he was breaking free from her, I seized her hand.

"Yes," I breathed, still feigning rapture, drawing her closer, into me like air into my lungs. Into me and away from them. Away from Fell.

The huldra obliged, placing her corpse-like hands on me now.

One of my hands went to my side, dipping inside my pouch, fumbling around, seeking even as I resigned myself to what was coming, even as I braced myself for her crooked body leaning into me, more bones than flesh and meat. Even as I accepted the cold press of her rancid mouth with its shriveled lips and rotting teeth to mine.

She kissed me.

It was her face now over mine. I could not unsee her. The faces of the others were blurry shadows.

I forced myself to kiss her back, releasing a cry of relief as my fingers wrapped around what I was searching for in my bag. Hopefully the sound was mistaken for passion, and she would not realize my intent until it was too late.

Clutching the fabric in my hand, I acted quickly. My only hope would be to surprise her. To deliver the unexpected.

I threw all my weight against her, slamming us both to the ground. She shrieked in astonishment but did not move for a full ten seconds. Time enough to seize my advantage.

Straddling her, I made quick work of the leather strap, gagging her and silencing that sweet voice holding the others captive.

That done, I reached for the other strips of leather and set to work, tying off her bony wrists and ankles, managing to subdue her even as she came to her senses and struggled wildly.

"Tamsyn!" It was Fell, blinking the last of the fog from his eyes.

The others were slower to shake off the huldra's influence. They stood in a confused stupor, looking down at her, their eyes still glazed.

I beheld the huldra, so terrifying before but now only a pathetic creature.

Inhuman growls leaked from around her gag. She strained and worked and fought like a wild thing, a beast of the forest, and I supposed that was true. She was tireless in her struggles. As desperate as a bird's wings, beating wildly, frantic to break from its cage, and I knew I would have to leave her like this. If she escaped, she would do everything in her power to kill me.

Suddenly she stopped her frenzied movements, her violent thrashing, her thin limbs quieting and going still as the grave as she caught sight of me watching her. Her milky gaze locked hard on me. Saw me for the first time. Those ancient eyes narrowed with comprehension. She *knew*. Recognized me as one monster recognized another.

I swallowed and had the sudden urge to run, to rush away from this thing that was holding up a mirror to me so plainly.

Fell advanced on me with long strides, his big hands closing around my arms and lifting me up on my tiptoes. Instantly I felt the brand of his touch through my clothing, the lines of the X clearly delineated on my bicep. It was pleasure and pain. Hot and cold. Heavy and feather-soft . . .

He said my name again, a breathy benediction. "Tamsyn . . . I knew you were alive." His frosty gray eyes slid over my face, leaving a trail of fire in their wake.

I opened my mouth, lips working, searching for the words that would not convey my dismay at finding him when I was supposed to be on my way north. Alone. And yet that wasn't entirely true. Not fully. Not really. I *did* feel dismay, but excitement hummed inside me, too.

He was like poisonous berries in the wood, so bright and colorful and sweet at the first taste, but bad for you. Toxic.

My body vibrated like the plucked string of a harp. Wrongly so. The blood rushed beneath my skin where his hands held me, smolder building in my chest in the most troubling way, and that was reminder enough. The crux of it all. The reason I could not be with him, the reason I needed to get far, far away.

"You beautiful, clever thing. How did you know what she was? How did you know what to do?" He sent a quick glance to the trussed-up huldra on the ground.

I shook my head and shrugged helplessly. How could I explain? Her magic simply had not worked on me. It didn't work because . . .

Well. Because I was the same. In a way. Magic could not best magic.

He hauled me into his arms, against his warmth, holding me tightly . . . so close that I could feel the pounding of his heart against my ribs. It was exhilarating and good and right, when so many things lately had been wrong. But this. Him. Us . . .

Being in his arms felt like coming home. Even if it was false, a trap, another trick of the day, another veil to be ripped away sooner or later. Sooner. Or later. Sooner. Or later. Eventually, it would be taken from me.

For now, I surrendered to it, finally letting myself go, sagging against him, relenting, weakening, reveling in being with him again. Close to the flame.

Later, I would worry.

Later, I would figure out how to pull myself away without becoming permanently, inexorably burned.

His voice rumbled in my hair, reaching all the way down to the core of me. "What happened to you? Did you escape the dragon?"

Did you escape the dragon?

In a manner. I suppose that was the truth of it. For now at least.

"Yes," I said at last, because, really—what else was there to say?

PART V
THE BORG

28

TAMSYN

IF THE CITY WAS DAY, THEN THE BORG WAS NIGHT.

It was alive and bustling and packed to capacity, but with none of the brightness of home. Sunlight didn't penetrate the thick canopy of cold fog. Even when we arrived in the middle of the day, a perpetual gloom hung about the chaotic network of cottages and buildings nestled among rolling dips and valleys that slid into a basin at the foot of the Crags, where the fortress sat—a great curled, sleeping cat. The Borg. The calm before the storm. The ice before the thaw.

The sky was unseeable, unknowable here, to the eyes of man. There was no distinction between clouds and fog. Both came together, like two bodies of water converging, the boundaries of each lost, erased and blurred.

I tilted my head and looked up, seeking a glimpse of what I knew was there. Fat white flakes drifted down and fell like gossamer on my upturned face, tangling in my lashes, but I could see nothing beyond those clouds. Not the snowcapped summits I knew to be there. The Crags, waiting and watchful.

Our horses knew they were home. They quickened their pace with a surge of energy, speeding toward the sprawling fortress. It was not quite a castle. Definitely no palace. Not as I was accustomed. More timber than rock. There was a moat with dark waters and a series of heavy steel gates—defensive measures for this place, this sentinel of the Borderlands.

Once we were spotted, people poured out to cheer our return. The voices rolled like thunder over the air, and snatches of conversation reached my ears . . . words. A word.

Dragon.

The news had reached them. Fell's warriors had spread the information. I felt a little sick at the knowledge, but, of course, they would want to warn people of danger.

They'd thought we were lost. Victims to the dragon. Now, riding through the streets like conquering heroes, they believed we had survived. We were a miracle manifested in flesh.

Pointed stares along with pointed fingers were directed at me, and I didn't know if it was because I was the new Lady of the Borderlands or a survivor of the dragon. I suppose either was cause for attention.

We waited at the barbican for the final gate to be lowered so we could cross into the interior.

Fell looked over at me. "You're home now, Tamsyn."

I struggled to smile and then faced forward again, gazing at the hulking fortress. Beyond the stronghold, rising into the air was the rocky facade of the mountain range. It felt deceptively close, as though I could reach out a hand and touch it.

"Tonight you will sleep in a warm bed with fresh sheets and more pillows than you can count," he promised.

He had been this way since we reunited in the skog. Solicitous and gentle, as though he was trying to make amends. *All* of them had been especially cordial and attentive to me: Fell, Mari, Magnus, and Vidar. Gracious, I was sure, because I saved them from the huldra.

"Sounds wonderful." And I meant that. I would enjoy it.

It had been a long time since I'd slept indoors. A lifetime since I was beneath a roof, in a bed, beside a crackling fire in a hearth. Upon leaving the skog, it had taken us another week to reach the Borg.

The drawbridge settled with a rattle of chains and a foreboding clang. Our small party started across it, and I couldn't help lifting my gaze one more time to the jagged mountains hovering over us. Even with the high crests obscured by cloud and fog, they were massive. Irregular patches of black rock broke up the expanse of silvery white snow.

The fortress, immense and sprawling here on the ground, sat small in the shadow of the Crags, and I wondered what was up there, who, even now, was, perhaps, looking down at us . . . watching.

The peaks were stubbornly, teasingly out of sight, miles and miles away, tucked into those clouds, but I had already seen them in my panicked flight through the sky. They were imprinted on me. I could see them still when I closed my eyes, tattooed on my memory.

As we rolled with clattering hooves into the belly of the beast, the lion's den, the heart of my enemy's lair, the mountain stared down at me not as an intimidating thing. Not a hard, cold, and punishing palisade. Not a daunting ridge repelling the faint of heart, summoning only the most adventurous or desperate to climb its slopes and angles in the quest for riches and glory.

It didn't feel like such a forlorn or scary sight to me.

It felt inviting, a welcoming haven, and strangely familiar.

It felt like home.

I HAD NOT seen my reflection in several weeks.

I had never been one to pay a great deal of attention to my looks. I wasn't like Feena, a creature of vanity, who constantly needed to assess herself in the mirror. Besides, I had always been told how very unpalatable my appearance was . . . especially my regrettable hair.

But now, sitting at the dressing table, I stared hard at myself, appraising, searching. As though I could find the truth etched there, like words writ upon the page . . . or like the erosion of wind upon a mountain.

I turned my face slowly in one direction, and then another, staring at it from every possible angle, seeking the evidence of what I now understood to be my new and dreadful reality. I was grateful for the privacy in which to conduct my self-examination.

Upon entering the fortress, I had been escorted to this chamber. It was far bigger and grander than the one I had left behind in the palace. The stronghold itself may not have been as lavish as the palace, but clearly they had given me far superior sleeping quarters.

Shortly following our arrival, Fell had excused himself. Obviously, after such a long absence, he had several matters demanding his attention. That was hours ago. I imagined I would not see him until tomorrow, if even then. Now that we were here, Fell would not stand around pandering to me. He would have better things to do.

I'd dined alone in the chamber, enjoying a fine meal of roasted pheasant, vegetables, and warm, crusty bread that I generously slathered with fresh butter. I fell upon the food as though it was the only meal I had eaten in the long weeks since leaving the City. And while it was not, it was certainly the best meal.

The chamber had its own dressing room with shelves and armoires and a lounge and a vanity table with a gilded mirror. The table was littered with all manner of combs and brushes and little bottles of scented oils and lotions.

It was the mirror, however, that held my focus—or rather my reflection in it did. As I sat there, I searched for changes. Differences, small or large, nuances that pointed to that thing I had become.

I looked like me. Same red hair. Same fiery amber eyes, if not a little brighter, a little wild. Feral. And perhaps I appeared a little—*a lot*—bolder. My expression gazed back at me almost in defiance, ready for a challenge, ready for battle. Was it the dragon inside me? Or was it simply a consequence of the past several weeks, when I had been put to the test on so many different levels, inured to conflict . . . even eager for it?

I wanted to believe that what happened with Arkin was a one-time occurrence, that I would never *turn* again. That I could live out the rest of my life here in relative peace, just a person, a woman. A person who never hurt another person. Who possessed not the will nor the ability. As calm and mild as a summer breeze.

I grimaced. It all sounded so wonderfully normal. *Normal.* And I knew that was the one thing I wasn't. Perhaps I never had been.

I gripped one of the small bottles of scented oil, flexing my fingers around the glass.

It was so wretchedly unfair. For a brief moment I had thought I could have it. A normal life. A husband who made me feel things. Good things. Exciting things.

I had thought I could have the kind of life that Stig had shown me the day he walked me through the portrait gallery, introducing me to the previous whipping boys and girls, explaining how they had all gone on to live full, meaningful lives.

I'd dared to hope, to believe that I might have a family. A real family. My own family. A family no one could accuse of not being truly mine. These things had circled around and teased me, tickling like a feather, tempting me since the night Fell and I had married, since we departed the City and started north. Since he said the words: *We can try to get on.*

But no. That was never to be my destiny. That teasing feather had been snatched away. In its place was the hard slap of my existence striking me across the face.

I gasped as the small bottle exploded in my hand.

It shattered.

I had shattered it.

Opening my trembling fingers wide, I stared down in dismay. I gripped my wrist with my other hand, trying to stop it from shaking so violently. I did not realize I had been gripping the glass so very hard.

As the aroma of crushed roses in oil drifted on the air, I examined my palm. Amid the broken shards of glass, my fingers and palm were smeared with a glossy purple fluid. I had not realized the oil was dyed.

Frowning, I shook the glass off my palm, letting the pieces fall onto the dressing table. Reaching for a handkerchief, I blotted at the wet purple shimmer, attempting to clean my hand. And that was when I saw the cuts. Several little gashes marred my skin like random flecks of mud.

One gash in particular was deeper than the rest, and glistening purple leaked thickly from the opening like blood.

I wiped harder. Not *like* blood. *Blood.*

This purple shimmer was my blood. It came from me. Out of me. Not human blood.

Not human. Not human. Not human.

The words repeated like an awful mantra, a poisoned vine growing, winding, twisting, sprouting a devastating path through me.

I had bled before. Granted, not often, and not for long, as I had always possessed the uncanny ability to heal quickly. *Maybe not so uncanny anymore, though.*

But I had bled. And when I bled, I'd bled red. I guessed I no longer did. Now that I had turned, my blood told the truth.

I glanced around rapidly, as though fearing someone else might see the evidence of what I wasn't . . . of what I was. Thankfully, it was still just me in the dressing room. No one else had entered.

As I studied that purple, winking with an iridescent sheen, swelling like spilled ink in my palm, I searched my memory, trying to recall if I'd ever heard anything about dragons possessing different blood. The bards had never mentioned it, but that didn't mean anything. No one was alive who had fought in the Threshing, who could give a firsthand account of fighting dragons, who could speak of their blood.

Suddenly I recalled the painting of the Hormung that hung in my father's chancery: that very detailed and graphic canvas depicting the violence of that long-ago day. I'd studied it so often over the years. It was perfectly memorized in my mind. I remembered several dragons in the midst of death, twisting through the sky with sprays of purple escaping from their massive bodies. I had not thought much of it at the time, assuming it was an artistic choice. Now I knew better. Now I understood. The artist had chosen purple for a reason.

Because dragon blood was purple.

I pressed the handkerchief firmly against my palm, applying pressure, desperate to stop the bleeding . . . desperate to change the blood. Desperate to change.

Desperate. Desperate. Desperate.

My hand throbbed, and for once it wasn't because of the carved X there. It was the collection of cuts and nicks from the shattered glass. The torn skin stung and tingled as the nerves worked to heal and knit the ragged edges back together.

I panted, choking back a sob. If I needed any proof, any evidence that I wasn't going to go back, that the dragon was still in me, real and very much alive . . . this was it.

I was the stone after the throw. It could not be taken back. It could not be undone.

I was the dragon, and the dragon was me.

Reaching this realization settled me, cooling some of my panic. I took several calming sips of air. My breathing steadied after a few moments, and I carefully peeled back the handkerchief to inspect the damage, finding only further evidence that I was no ordinary girl.

The cuts were gone. The wounds had healed. Unblemished skin stared back at me. Releasing a grateful sigh, I quickly wiped any remnants of purple blood from my hand. Finished, I rose from the cushioned bench, the soiled handkerchief clenched tightly in my fist as though I could crush it into nothingness.

I left the dressing room behind and strode purposefully into my bedchamber, walking a hard line toward the hearth, intent on getting rid of the evidence of my . . .

What could I call it? Aberration? Defect?

I was shaking as I tossed the stained handkerchief into the fire, trembling all over as I watched it wilt beneath curling flame. There. No one would happen upon it now and—

"Are you settling in all right?"

I whirled around, my hand flying to my throat with a muffled cry.

Fell stood there, one shoulder leaning against the threshold, that almost-smile on his lips again.

"Fell," I breathed, relief and fear at war in my heart. "I did not expect to see you tonight."

"I, too, am looking forward to a comfortable rest." He nodded to the bed with an incline of his dark head.

"You're sleeping in here?" I croaked.

In the same bedchamber? In the same bed? With me? How was that *not* a bad idea?

He pushed off the threshold and strode into the room, shrugging out of his leathered armor first.

"I've dreamed about my bed ever since I left home."

My face went hot. When he dreamed of his bed, was I ever in it? Were we in it together? Were we doing . . . things? Intimate things?

Because a dream was all it could ever be.

He moved with a fluid grace, like smoke winding through the room. I had to force myself not to stare as he finished undressing himself, stripping down to the waist, revealing all that sculpted and inked skin. Warmth buzzed in my hands. My palms tingled, longing to explore the smooth expanse of his warrior body, itching to reacquaint myself with the texture of his flesh.

I swallowed and found my voice: "I did not realize that this would be *our* room."

He stilled, his eyes lifting to mine, that crystal gray so penetrating I felt it like a sword cutting through me. "Is that a problem?"

A problem that I would share a bedchamber with my husband? How could I admit such a thing?

"No. Not a problem at all," I lied.

Just a huge problem. Terrifying and appalling that I should share such close quarters—*a bed!*—with a man I was vastly attracted to when I knew nothing about this body I inhabited and what wild and dangerous thing it might do next.

He nodded as though satisfied with my response, and we readied for bed in silence.

I slipped beneath the heavy covers, clinging to my side of the bed like it was a raft at sea, hoping I had chosen the side he didn't sleep on but not about to ask. I didn't trust my voice not to crack or quiver.

By the time he slid in beside me, his heavier weight dipping the mattress, my eyes were closed and I was doing what I hoped was an admirable job of feigning sleep.

I could see nothing behind the blackness of my eyelids, but I heard everything: every pop and crackle of the fire, every rustle and shift of his big body inches from mine, the slow, even cadence of his breath. I even imagined I heard the steady beat of his heart beneath his skin.

It was a torment.

I waited, my chest clenched and pounding.

I was on fire. A great, devouring pyre.

Every muscle, every line of my body strained, as tight as a white-hot wire, braced for his touch, for the weight of his hand to fall somewhere, anywhere on me, equal parts dread and longing burning through me.

I couldn't do this. *We* couldn't do this.

Oh, I knew I would be receptive. There was no doubt. The fire seething in me was for him. I would definitely be into it . . . into him.

But I didn't know how my body might react, what I might reveal of myself. There was a cauldron boiling in me just beneath the surface, under the skin, and I feared what might happen if it bubbled over.

I worried that if I was too overcome with emotion, the fire might find a way out, like how water always found the tiniest cracks in a dam. With Arkin, it had been fear and rage that did it. Fear and rage to such an intense degree . . . I had never felt like that before. I did not know what to expect in the event of lust and passion. Those were new emotions for me, too.

Just being alone and this close to Fell made me feel all sorts of wild and dangerous things, like I was falling from a great height with no idea if the landing would break every bone in my body.

I was seized with the image of the bed on fire. Literally. On. Fire. Fell trapped within, kindling for the flames. Because of me. Bile rose in my throat, and I felt the overwhelming urge to gag at the thought of doing to Fell what I had done to Arkin. No. *Never.*

I squeezed my eyes tighter until I saw dancing spots within the blackness. There was absolutely no way I could fall asleep like this—this full of want and longing and fear.

That was the last thought I remembered before sleep took me.

WHEN I WOKE, the air was a bruised gray.

I blinked several times, wondering what had roused me. A . . . feeling. A sound. A movement in the chamber. It was still early. I had been looking forward to sleeping late and not having to drag myself atop a horse at the first hint of dawn on the horizon.

Gradually I became aware that I was no longer clinging to the edge of the bed. I had shifted some time during the night, rolled in my sleep to the center of the bed, dipping toward that heat-radiating body, that beckoning hearth.

Fell's arm draped over my waist, holding me flush against him. Our legs were tangled, heavy limbs comfortably entwined like braided rope. My mouth rested on his shoulder, fanning warm air against his skin, which might have been why I was acutely aware of the fact that my breathing had changed, coming faster, louder, fogging his bare flesh with moisture.

And his breathing was not a slow and even cadence either. It was a rasp directly in my ear, weaving through the web of strands.

"Tamsyn." The sound of my name was a rough growl on the air. I felt it like a touch, like the stroke of calloused fingers over my body even though his hands were firmly planted elsewhere—one a burning, throbbing imprint on my back and the other tucked beneath his body in the bed. "Did you sleep well?"

"Like a rock," I said, my lips brushing him as I spoke, and I couldn't stop myself, couldn't help myself from doing the most natural thing. I parted my lips and kissed him there, open-mouthed, tasting the slope of his shoulder, letting my tongue slip out for a lick of salty-clean skin.

His breath caught, and I made a low hum of satisfaction. I lifted my lips from his shoulder to find his face much closer than before. The chamber was murky, but it did not hide the startling frost of his eyes pinned on me. Nor the flare of his nostrils as though he was inhaling the scent of me. Nor the way his lips parted on a breath as though he was on the verge of saying something. Or *doing* something. Something like—

He kissed me hard.

This moment, his closeness, his smell, his taste. Warm and clean with all the smells of the outdoors, of wind and snow and saddle leather.

The temptation was too much. I opened my mouth with a moan to meet the hot thrust of his tongue.

I let him in. He kissed and took and gave. And I was there for all of it. Devouring him back.

My hands went everywhere. His shoulders. His neck. His face. Fingers diving through his hair. In a flash, our embrace became frenzied and wild and fierce. Too quickly. Heat gathered in my chest and spiraled, working its way up through my windpipe.

His hands did their own exploring, traveling from my shoulders, down the slope of my back—which tingled and pulled with a pressure that set off alarm bells in my head—to cup my bottom. His fingers dug into my soft flesh, pulling me higher, tighter against him, until our hips met. Until I felt the hard prod of his cock against my aching, clenching core. And I knew what he wanted, because I wanted it, too.

I gasped into his mouth at the same moment I felt a rush of steam escape my nose.

He felt it, too, lurching back, clearly as shocked and bewildered as anyone whose skin got too close to a hot stove.

His hand flew to his face.

I was off the bed in an instant, hand over my mouth in horror, feeling the telltale heat there, the fading warmth from the steam still moist on my fingers.

He rubbed at his face. "What was that?"

He was looking at me and already thinking, already trying to understand . . . seeking the most logical explanation. Thankfully. Because me . . . a dragon? Not logical.

"D-did you . . . bite me?" In his mind, he was reassigning that flash of pain to something else. Something that made more sense.

"I . . . I . . . I am sorry," I choked out lamely. "I got carried away."

I shook my head wildly, not about to confess that I had singed him. Thankfully, it had been brief and not very severe . . . not so severe that I'd left a mark, a burn that could be pointed at for what it was.

It was a nightmare. My fear made real—that I would lose control. That I would somehow manifest into my dragon while in proximity to him. I could have hurt him. Maybe even killed him. The image of Arkin's corpse filled my mind.

I took several staggering steps back from the bed, babbling between my fingers, "I . . . I am sorry. So sorry."

Fell extended a hand to me as though cajoling a frightened animal. "Tamsyn. It's all right. I don't mind. Come back to bed."

I shook my head roughly. "No. I can't do this . . . I can't do this with you."

He lowered his arm back down, a raw stillness coming over him, a frown marring that beautiful face of his. "You can't?"

I motioned between us. "This. I can't be with you this way."

There. I'd said it. I could not explain why, but I'd said it.

Even in the almost-dark, I could detect the hardening of his features, the icy curtain dropping over his gray eyes. "I see. You're my wife, but you don't want to . . . *be* a wife to me."

I stared at him in mute frustration. He was drawing his own conclusions. *Inaccurate* conclusions.

Of course I couldn't correct him, but the truth was more than complicated. It was dangerous. I wasn't fool enough to tell this man, the Beast of the Borderlands, what was happening to me. That he shared his bed with a monster. I could hardly even form the words in *my* head. Saying them out loud to him was an impossibility.

"Yes," I agreed. "That's how I feel."

He nodded tightly. "Understood. I will not offend you with my advances again."

I wanted to cry, to weep from the unfairness of it all. I could see the door slamming shut over his expression, the frost of his eyes growing colder. He was gone from me. Any softness, any desire he felt, I had just killed it . . . doused the warmth in him like a fire burned out.

FOR THE NEXT week I did little more than sleep. Waking to eat and do the bare necessities, but then returning to my bed—our bed— for leisurely naps was the safest form of existence.

I told myself it was my body recovering from the long journey. I told myself it wasn't despair. It wasn't mourning. It wasn't avoidance. It wasn't the loss of a marriage before it even had a chance to begin. It wasn't the death of it, the burying of it—of *us* and what we could have been—beneath dirt and rock like any other corpse. It wasn't evasion of this new world, this new life I found myself inhabiting. This new *thing* I found myself to be.

I told myself all of this.

And I was a liar.

Fell joined me every night. He had not taken a room of his own, and I assumed it must be for the sake of appearances. He was the Lord of the Borderlands. He was master here, and he had a reputation to protect. He couldn't look as though he spurned his wife and marital obligations. So we slept together, not looking at each other, not touching, not talking after we put out the light.

And every night I was afflicted with the same torment.

My body burning up on the inside, my chest squeezing, my skin pulling and tingling and vibrating and humming with a song only I heard . . . aroused beyond measure by the husband I could never have.

29

FELL

INEVER EXPECTED MY WIFE'S REJECTION TO HURT. WHEN I ventured south, I never thought I would feel *anything* for the bride I would claim. But this ache was as pervasive as the fog filling my life. A constant stitch in my side, pinching, stinging, never releasing me. I was married to a woman I wanted. Desperately. Unexpectedly. But there it was. I wanted her.

And she did not want me.

She made it clear that we would not be husband and wife in the truest sense. And yet I had not moved myself into another chamber. I still stayed in that bed with her, an idiot, a fool.

The yawning gap between us did not get any smaller in the days that followed. It did not shrink over the next week, or the week after that.

If anything, the gulf between us grew wider with each passing day.

I was a glutton for punishment. There was no other explanation. I slept in our bed—well, I didn't get much sleep with a throbbing cock and a throbbing palm that wouldn't let up. Lying so close, without touching her, denying myself contact, not being able to close the distance between us, was a torment. It had been better when we were separated. Not *better* better, but at least not this much pain. Not this agony.

When we had been miles apart, the buzzing in my palm, while persistent, had not been painful. Now this throbbing hurt, radiating up my arm and throughout my entire body like one giant gnawing wound.

How could this be normal? Did every blooded couple experience this? I should have been warned. I would never have done it. Never have let them press our bleeding palms together.

Distraction was my goal, and there was plenty to distract myself with—at least in the daylight hours. I threw myself into all the things that needed to be done after almost two months away. And there were many.

Training to resume, especially as I still intended to march an army on the City the following spring. I had not changed my mind on that count. The dragon threat only added a sense of urgency. Unseating Hamlin from power seemed more important than ever, and preparations needed to begin now.

Additionally, repairs throughout the stronghold had been neglected in my absence. There were farmers to meet with to discuss the coming crops. Vassals with concerns that needed to be heard. Recompense offered to Arkin's family. His wife didn't know of his treachery. No one did. Just me. Me. And Tamsyn. There was no point in sharing that shame—especially as it was no fault of his family. I sent a small party to travel to his lands and visit his wife and daughters. Aside from their grief, they would be stricken with worry over their position in the Borderlands. Assurances needed to be given. A new vassal lord needed to be appointed, but that didn't mean I would leave Arkin's widow and offspring without support.

Oh. And there was still the dragon threat to be tackled. I had not forgotten that.

No matter how distracting my wife and my suffering, I had not forgotten that the curse of the skies had returned. Or perhaps, to be more accurate, it had never left.

Since word had already circulated through the surrounding countryside and beyond, the only thing left to do was to shore up our defenses and make certain we were ready in the event the dragon returned. The catapults were dusted off, as were the giant scale-tipped arrows of dragon bone. Once they were tested for accuracy and proven functional, they were positioned in their old spots along the outer and inner walls. All our arrows and swords and shields of dragon bone and dragon scales were unearthed from the bowels of the fortress and restored, made ready for every warrior. Training commenced in earnest. I had a new generation of warriors to prepare for an enemy they had never faced.

Weapons for dragon defense were not the only thing I unearthed. My father had kept the lion's share of treasure that was uncovered in the Crags, keeping it hidden away.

Certainly he had turned over a large portion to the realm, but Balor the Butcher was not known to be a trusting man. It was not greed that had prompted him to stash away his personal hoard. It was wisdom. He had warned me many times to trust no one in a position of power, as their motivation would always be suspect, and the day may come when the hoard would be a useful and valuable tool . . . necessary to guarantee survival, to bribe and form alliances with other kingdoms. It could mean the difference between life and death. Not just for me but for our people.

It was this wisdom that prompted my father to stash treasure in multiple locations. He had divided it up and hidden it in different places throughout the fortress. One large trunk was hidden beneath the floorboards of the library. It was in this room I found myself, carefully prying the boards back and opening the chest, browsing through the assortment of gems and gold until I uncovered the perfect piece. Slipping it into my pocket, I closed the trunk. Securing the floorboards back in place, I went in search of my wife.

I FOUND HER in our chamber.

Tamsyn had not ventured far from the room since our arrival. Almost as though she feared the world outside her door. And yet fear was not a word I would ever associate with her. Not this girl . . . not this woman who had taken beatings as her due, who had faced down bandits and a huldra with all the calm of a cat lazing in the sun. She'd attacked that huldra and trussed her up like a hog for the spit. As my father would say—she had mettle.

If she had been scared on the journey north, she certainly had not let it get to her. It never showed on her face. She had not acted the coward. She had acted like a warrior.

Still, I hated the idea that she was not comfortable here.

There were whispers. I heard the murmurs throughout the fortress, even beyond, out in the shops, in villages of the Borg. They thought her too precious to emerge from her chamber. They called her spoiled. Haughty. The Whipping Bitch. They thought she held herself above everybody else.

They were wrong, of course, but nothing I said could change their minds. It would be up to her to alter their opinions. If she chose to do so. If she cared.

Time would reveal who she was to these people. Mari knew. So did Magnus and Vidar. They spoke of her heroics with the huldra to anyone who would listen. Others would soon learn, as well.

She was reading a book, reclining on a chaise near the window in a gown of warm yellow that did amazing things for her golden skin and red hair. Those flame-colored tresses were braided and wrapped into a cornet around her head. My fingers itched to pull it apart, to loosen the strands and watch the fiery mane flow over her shoulders and down her back.

She was like a beam of sunshine, glowing in the trickle of paltry light seeping in from outside. The day was covered in snow and fog. She was a spot of brightness amid so much white and gray and gloom . . . almost unearthly in appearance, radiant, as though she were not bound to this world like the rest of us mortals. I shook off these fanciful thoughts.

She looked up as I entered the room, firing that practiced smile of hers that did not quite reach her eyes at me. It was always in place the moment she saw me. I was getting used to it. I despised it for its falseness, for its uncertainty, but I knew it well.

She lowered the book to her lap. "Hello," she greeted me.

"Hello. Enjoying the day?" Not that she had stepped outside this chamber to enjoy it.

I nodded to the window that overlooked the Borg. It was a great view. A bounty of steep hills that dipped and turned and twisted, winding up into the mountains, which soared in an endless pelt of snow-covered rock.

"I would enjoy it more if you would let me go for a ride." She motioned to those hills beyond the Borg. "I would like to see the mountains." Her gaze fixed on me hopefully.

"You want to ride into the mountains?" I frowned.

She nodded.

I gestured to the window. "You can't get a better view than this one."

She sighed. "You can't keep me cooped up in here forever, you know."

I bit back the response that I could do just that.

It was a familiar conversation. Almost immediately upon arriving home, she had wanted to ride outside the gates of the fortress, outside the settlement of the Borg and into the countryside, into those foothills that led into the mountains. She was mistaken, however, if she thought I was going to let her go riding into the Crags when there was a dragon on the loose. She had already survived one encounter. I wasn't about to put her at risk again.

"You know there is a dragon still at large, right?"

She went tight as a knot, her features flattening into a stony mask.

Of course she knew that. She was likely still recovering from that trauma. A dragon had burned a man alive in front of her, and then abducted her and carried her off into the sky. It was no wonder she wanted some time to herself and did not feel like mingling with a bunch of strangers.

I spoke more gently. "I think it wise for you to stay indoors."

Her chin went up, her eyes lighting like embers, ready to battle, and my hand jumped in response. "For how long? Forever?"

I shook my head. "I cannot say. But no, not forever." At least I didn't think so. I wanted to say: *At least not until the dragon is caught.*

But I didn't like making promises when there was still so much unknown. For all I knew, this dragon would be plaguing us for years to come . . .

Or there could even be more of them out there in the world, a whole pride of dragons about to rain down hellfire on humankind and plunge us back into the days before the Threshing.

The silence grew heavy between us, and I shifted my weight, staring down at her.

"Well," she said after some time. "Was there something else I could do for you?"

She couldn't even stand to have me around.

"Yes." My hand dipped into my pocket. Closing my fingers around the chain, I lifted the necklace out into the air. "I got this for you. Thought you might need something to replace the necklace you gave to the bandits."

A smile appeared, edging her mouth. "I didn't *give* anything to the bandits. It was a trade. A barter."

I inclined my head. "Oh. Is that how we are remembering it?"

"That is the truth," she supplied.

Rather than argue, I held out the necklace for her. "May I?"

She sat up, nodded, and leaned forward.

I approached and slipped the chain around her neck, fastening the clasp at her nape. The heavy weight of stones settled above her breasts, the row of gems like a vine of grapes, perfectly round, the raspberry-red jewels glinting with their own energy, not requiring light to make them glow. In fact, against her skin, they seemed to glow even brighter, even more brilliant.

She brushed her fingertips against the necklace, and then dragged her fingers even lower, over the rising swells of her breasts.

My mouth dried.

"Thank you," she murmured. "It's very kind of you."

Kind. A word no one had ever applied to me.

I did not feel very kind. I did not have very kind thoughts looking at her right now. No, my thoughts could be classified as decidedly *unkind*. They were too dirty for that. Too wicked.

Wrapped up in want and need for a wife who wanted nothing to do with me.

And I couldn't stop myself. Couldn't help reaching out and cupping her face, brushing a thumb against the tender curve of her cheek. "I'm not a kind man."

Her throat worked. That necklace lifted on the rise of a breath, drawing my gaze back to her chest. Her neckline was modest, but the swell of her breasts was still the most enticing thing I had ever seen. My mouth craved that skin. Longed to press my lips to the flushed flesh, to taste her, love her there, worship her.

Her hand closed over mine, holding fast, her fingers squeezing me for a long moment before she pulled my hand away with what felt like reluctance . . . and that gave me hope.

"Fell . . ." she started.

The sound of my name on her lips, in that trembling voice, with those fire-gold eyes fixed on me, sank through me like a heated knife through butter.

She had set the parameters . . . defined what we would be, what we would not be. I was the one hoping for more. Hoping foolishly, futilely, that she would just change her mind. I was the one unable to pull myself away, unable to move myself away from that crackling fire, that warm and radiating and beckoning heat.

She lifted her hand and flattened it over my chest, her fingers splayed wide over my heart, that X finding me. My heart leapt, trying to get through bone and blood and flesh to meet it, to reach it—our bodies desperate to merge and lock together like matching pieces in a puzzle.

Her eyes flared wide, and I knew she felt it, too.

"Tamsyn, I'm a man. A warrior. Better with my sword than with words and manners. I'm not kind." I exhaled.

She opened her mouth and closed it. Her fingers flexed over my chest but did not lift away, and that was something. It wasn't no. It wasn't a door slamming in my face.

"I—" she started, her expression softening. "I like what you are, Fell."

I leaned in, tentative, wary.

She leaned in, too, meeting me halfway, tilting her face up.

I was almost there. Almost to her mouth.

And then a loud horn pealed across the day. Shouts went up, hurling through the air like cannon fire.

I leaned across her to peer out the window.

"What is it?" she asked over another blare of the horn, signaling for all to take cover.

I immediately spotted warriors rushing through the courtyard and along the palisade walls, just as civilians raced screaming through the barbican, seeking shelter within the fortress. My gaze shot to the clouds, searching for any hint of wings or fire as the horn sounded again.

The shouts continued, filling the air like smoke. I was finally able to make out the words.

They're coming!

30

TAMSYN

WAIT HERE." FELL'S WORDS RANG IN THE AIR, THE TERSE command fading away along with the sound of his footsteps as he rushed from the room.

Did that ever work? Perhaps some people stayed behind when they were told, but not me. I had to know. I had to see for myself, and staring out my tower window was not what I had in mind.

What if it was another dragon?

Heart racing, I ran from the chamber and down into the main hall. Fell was nowhere in sight. It was chaos, packed tight with bodies and animals seeking shelter from whatever was coming.

I pushed through, past people swarming in the opposite direction, desperate for refuge within the walls of the fortress. Amid the cries and the sobs, a single panicked word rose up on the air again and again and again. Like an endless, repeating wave. *Dragon. Dragon. Dragon.*

Could it be?

I broke into the courtyard, into the frigid day, my gaze immediately shooting to the skies. Clouds and fog. Fog and clouds. Just the usual. No winged brethren anywhere in sight.

Several fleeing bodies jostled me, nearly knocking me off my feet. Regaining my balance, I rotated in a swift circle, dodging a goat as I peered up and spotted warriors assembling along the battlements. I noticed several of them pointed to something in the distance. Something unknown and out of my range of vision.

Determined to see for myself, I raced toward the nearest tower, pushing through the crowd. I was almost there when I was met by a wolf. Or a dog, I supposed, but there was definitely some wolf blood mixed in there. The beast lunged for me, snarling and snapping its jaws, foaming at the mouth, going feral at the sight of me. I fell back on the ground, scurrying to get out of the way, crying out as rushing feet slammed down on my hands, crunching bone, grinding my knuckles.

The owner of the wolf-dog wrapped an arm around its furry neck, pulling desperately, hauling the beast back even as the man lifted wide, bewildered eyes to me. Clearly the beast wasn't known for violence.

But then the beast has never known you.

Shaking my head, I clambered back up onto my feet. Cradling my wounded hands close to my chest, I told myself what I knew to be true: they would heal.

I took the winding stairs to the top of the tower. It was just as crowded up on the wall as it was in the courtyard. Warriors were everywhere, taking position, archers readying their bows. No one spared me a glance. I was a ghost, free to look, free to move about with no one paying me any mind.

I spotted Fell down along the wall, directly over the gatehouse, dead center, staring out from the fortress with a sharp gaze. He stood with his legs braced wide, as though at the bow of a ship.

He propped his hands on the edge of the wall, looking across the Borg, gazing out into the distance, at the snow-covered horizon, as though he alone had the power to see what others could not. As though he alone knew what was coming.

Frowning, I followed the direction of his gaze. And saw nothing.

Nothing beyond mist-shrouded hills and the not-so-distant mountains. I waited. We all waited, peering into the opaque air.

The Borg quieted, falling into an eerie silence. As though the world was holding its breath. The only sound was that of the whistling wind and settling fog.

And then I heard it. Another sound. A steady beat. A staccato clomping. Even and unvarying and in perfect rhythm. Like a heartbeat.

We heard them long before we could see them. Long before they crested the rise, the silver of their armor glinting like mirrors. Soldiers. A large contingent of cavalry. Hundreds and hundreds of riders.

An army was marching on the Borg.

I DIDN'T THINK it could get any quieter, but the sight of that army silenced even the wind.

The fog hushed and held still, simply thickening, spreading, growing denser, almost as though it were a living, breathing thing intent on taking over the land, covering everything, devouring everything.

The air grew so thick, it gobbled that army up, wiping it from sight. Presumably wiping us from sight, too. It was still out there. I felt it, that force of soldiers, a beast looking for its next meal, but we could no longer see it. Just as it could no longer see us.

Moments ticked by, rolling into minutes, and then more minutes and then more.

Fell's warriors began to shift restlessly on the battlements.

We could hear them still marching, the clop of hooves falling in steady rhythm, unseen in the impenetrable fog.

We listened, tense, on edge, the army close now, winding its way like a snake through the grass, out of sight but there, sliding closer through the Borg, finally stopping at our gates.

They emerged into view, finally close enough to see again, the faces of every soldier obscured beneath the visors of their helmets, only their eyes visible.

Realization flashed through me. I knew who they were. I identified the cut of their armor, the red and blue pennants, the royal coat of arms, and the markings on their shields.

I searched for and found him, recognizing him riding front and center. His visor was already lifted, and my heart leapt at the sight of those familiar brown eyes across the distance. I saw him, but he had not spotted me. His gaze was elsewhere, on the Beast of the Borderlands.

Stig brandished his sword in the air, his voice lifting in challenge: "I've come for Dryhten's head!"

My gaze swung down the length of the wall to Fell.

Fell's hands gripped the edge of the wall tighter. He grinned. Actually smiled, lips peeling back from his teeth in a snarl. He loved this, I realized. *Fighting*. Battle. This was his element. What he knew. What he did well.

He leaned down, his voice booming through the air: "You've come to the right place, then."

Stig pointed his sword directly at Fell up on the wall. "We received your message!"

"And you didn't care for it, I see," Fell replied sarcastically. "I didn't quite care for it either, but I didn't think you would show up here demanding my head."

"You are a liar and you will pay, Dryhten. I'm here to see to that."

I scanned the army spread out before me in disbelief. Stig had led these soldiers all this way? They must have marched ceaselessly for the past three weeks.

"You and the army you brought with you, eh?" Fell called back down. Laughter rippled through his warriors.

Stig gestured behind him. "This army is here to see to the peaceful transition of power once I gut you and put your head on a pike and take control of the Borderlands."

This was met with several boos and jeers from the wall.

Fell held up both arms, bobbing his hands and gesturing for his warriors to be silent. It took several moments for the warriors to quiet down.

"I don't think my warriors are in support of that, Captain." Fell gave a mocking shrug of regret.

Stig continued, "You thought we would believe you. Dragon, indeed," he scoffed. "You murdered her, and I'm here to make sure you die for it."

I flinched. *Murdered her?*

Murdered . . . *me?*

He was talking about me?

Clearly, he had received Fell's message that I was taken or killed by a dragon and had reached his own conclusions. Was this what my family thought? My parents? My sisters? Did they all believe me dead?

"Stig!" I shouted down, waving an arm. "What are you doing?"

Stig's gaze whipped to me. His eyes widened. "Tamsyn!"

"What are you doing?" I repeated, shaking my head in disapproval. I waved at the army behind him. "You brought an army?"

He didn't take his eyes off me, merely called my name again, as though struggling to comprehend what he was seeing. "Tamsyn!"

I sighed. "Yes. It is me. We have established that. Now, what are you doing here?"

His eyes narrowed. His shoulders squared. "I've come for you. To avenge you."

I shook my head. "Well, as you can see, I am not dead."

Stig's gaze then flew to Fell. "He was telling the truth?" He said the words as though they were the most incredulous, impossible, unbelievable thing.

My gaze followed Stig to Fell.

My husband shrugged and nodded. "So you can see you made this long journey for nothing. Now why don't you turn around and go back home?"

I exhaled an exasperated breath. *Men.*

"Fell," I chided, sending him a glare before looking down to Stig and his waiting army. "Open the gate!"

THERE WAS NO force on earth that was going to keep me from Stig's arms.

Yes, he had just brought an army to the gates of the Borg with the intention of putting my husband's head on a pike, but he had done it for me. And he was my best friend. Family. It was like having a little bit of home again, a little bit of the old normal. And I couldn't help but long for the familiar comfort of that when life was anything but normal these days.

The three of us gathered in Fell's personal library.

I felt my husband's gaze on the back of me as Stig folded me in his arms, his warm breath fluttering my hair. I stepped away, eventually, and sent Fell a wary look.

His face was impassive, staring at me with eyes as unreadable as stone. And yet I felt the inexplicable impulse to apologize. *For what?* Hugging a friend? I lifted my chin a notch, trying to look confident, calm. Casual.

The two men stared hard at each other, saying nothing, making no move. They were two figures, frozen in place.

I cleared my throat. Evidently I was the one who was going to have to cross that invisible line in the sand . . . be the one to speak first and bring these two men together. "Well. Obviously there has been a misunderstanding here."

"Obviously," Fell agreed, the word clipped.

"We received your message—" Stig started.

"And decided to march north in full armament," Fell cut in.

Stig shrugged as though that were a minor thing and not at all a point of offense. "I was expected to take that message seriously?"

Fell took one menacing step closer to Stig, his voice low and dark as he said, "Hear me now. There is a dragon. At least one. Alive and well and out there, threatening us all." He pointed to me, and I stifled a flinch. "It took Tamsyn. Ask her."

Stig looked to me for confirmation, as though the sight of me standing before him—*not dead*—wasn't evidence enough.

"Yes." I nodded, my throat so thick the word was little more than a croak. "There really is a . . . dragon."

"Well." Stig settled back on his heels with a sigh. "This changes things."

Frost flashed in Fell's pale gray eyes. "Does it? No longer want my head on a pike now, do you?" His gaze shot to me. "You almost seem disappointed . . . like you wish she was dead." My husband smirked at Stig then.

Stig's face flushed with anger. He inhaled deeply, the breath lifting his chest. "You could never understand the *depth* of my feelings for her, you heartless bastard."

"I'll remember that next time I'm in bed with her."

Stig lunged for him with a strangled sound.

Fell surged forward to meet him.

I got between the two men before they could kill each other.

"Enough! You are behaving like little boys!" I flattened a hand on each of their heaving chests, glaring back and forth between them. "We are on the same side."

As soon as the words left me, I felt awash in misery. Whether they realized it or not, *they* were on the same side.

I was on the side of something else.

31

STIG

SHE WAS ALIVE. TAMSYN WAS ALIVE.

Complicated and ugly sensations curled and twisted through me as I watched her with Dryhten, her *husband*. Relief. Obviously relief. But joy, too. Overwhelming joy. Because she was alive.

But also . . .

I really wanted to kill Dryhten.

Disappointment washed through me in a bitter wave when I realized I couldn't. I no longer had a reason to do so. At least no reason that would meet with my father's approval.

And then . . .

I realized I still could. Why not?

I was a warrior. He was a warrior. That was what warriors did. We fought each other. That was how scores were settled. Killing him would be doing the world a favor, after all, and I did not require my father's permission to do that.

I'd have to consider how to go about this, though—selecting the right moment to justifiably challenge him. That wouldn't be too hard. He always provoked me. He was the provoking sort.

I would kill Dryhten and Tamsyn would be saved. Then . . . if she wanted me as much as I wanted her, we could be together.

She would be free. No longer his wife. No longer a whipping girl.

She would be free to choose.

32

TAMSYN

I FINALLY GOT MY WAY.

The day after Stig's arrival, he invited me on a ride. I wasn't naive. I knew he wanted to get me outside the fortress, alone and away from prying eyes and ears, so that he could talk to me. So he could verify for himself that I was really safe, that no one was hurting me here—namely, my husband.

He didn't believe Fell to be the kind of man who wouldn't harm me. He thought the Beast of the Borderlands was a brute. A barbarian. All the things I had once assumed. To be fair, everyone had believed that of him.

In Stig's mind, Fell could only be mistreating me. Stig would never suspect that every night I spent in bed with my husband I felt my resolve weakening, that I sank deeper and deeper into bewildering and complicated feelings, longing for the man I could never trust myself to have.

Whatever the case, whatever the reason, I was finally outside the fortress, finally riding through the soaring foothills that served as a prelude to the Crags, and I was glad for it.

Last night, Fell and Stig had closeted themselves away with their most trusted warriors to strategize and discuss important matters. No one had to tell me what those matters were. I knew the most important subject up for discussion had been me.

Well. Not *me* me.

Me the dragon.

They weren't going to let it go. They were going to send out hunting parties. They were going to search every corner of every wood for the dragon. I felt their determination like a noose settling around my neck, tightening incrementally, bit by bit.

I might spend every night sleeping safely in a warm bed, Fell a comforting, tempting presence beside me . . . but I felt like a volcano ready to erupt.

I was not safe here. I was not secure. I felt like a body poisoned. Toxic venom winding through me, doing its work, grinding and churning toward my slow and inevitable death.

The irony was not lost on me. Fell thought it was not safe for me to venture outside the fortress, too worried about the threat of a dragon. Of course, I knew there was no threat. There was just me.

And the riskiest place of all? In bed beside him, my would-be killer.

I lifted my face to the curling mist and exhaled as Stig and I ambled along.

Eventually, Fell would learn that Stig had taken me outside the fortress. He would be displeased. But I would deal with that then.

Currently there was just contentment—riding with my friend through the mist-shrouded countryside, the Crags a comforting shadow beside us, weaving a silent song in my head, pulling me closer by a gentle thread, beckoning . . .

"I suppose we should turn back. Getting a little too close to . . ." Stig's voice faded as he glanced up toward the jagged, snow-covered face of the mountain nearest us.

He wanted us to turn back for the obvious reason. I could have pointed out that the last sighting of the dragon had been miles away from here. But the speed with which dragons flew made that a moot point. Dragons could be anywhere in Penterra. Or anywhere else. It didn't matter where we were. And yet I would rather not feed into any of the frenzy around the topic of dragons. If anything, I wanted to douse those flames.

"Let's walk for a bit," I suggested.

Stig hesitated only a moment before nodding. We dismounted in unison. Gathering our reins loosely in gloved hands, we strolled leisurely.

Taking a breath, I plunged ahead. "I don't want you to worry about the dragon anymore."

I made the request solemnly, almost as though I were uttering a prayer, and that was what it felt like. A desperate prayer. A desperate hope I was casting into the wind, hoping someone heard it, some god or deity with the power to help me.

We ventured deeper into the woods, our boots crunching over pristine whiteness. Tree branches creaked and groaned overhead in the wind from the weight of last night's snowfall.

I stroked a gloved hand down the nose of my mount idly and sent Stig a hopeful look.

"Not worry?" He looked at me incredulously. "How? How can I not? A dragon alive?" He shook his head. "It *took* you. You are lucky to have survived. It killed one of Dryhten's men. We *all* need to be worried. This is not a problem only for the Borderlands. It concerns all of us. And there could be others."

And there could be others.

He put voice to the thought that I had struggled to avoid. Now I had to face it.

Could there be others? Others like me? As confused and lost and alone as I was? Or perhaps they had answers and a better understanding of what was happening to me. Perhaps they could help me feel not so confused, not so lost, not so alone. Could I find them? I glanced at the Crags again, hope stirring in my heart.

"I will find this dragon," Stig added with such vehemence, such conviction that I knew . . .

He would never stop.

He would never let it go. Never give up the idea of the dragon, of hunting it—even if he didn't realize that the thing he wanted to destroy, the thing he was hunting . . . was *me*.

Perhaps there was my answer.

Perhaps he needed to know.

Perhaps then we could put our heads together and come up with a solution.

Perhaps. Perhaps. Perhaps.

He was my oldest friend. So often my refuge, the person I could go to, the person to comfort me and help me see things plainly.

I took a great, fortifying breath. "What if you knew that the dragon meant no harm?"

His gaze turned amused. "What do you know of a dragon's intentions, Tamsyn?" He chuckled lightly, as though I had just suggested the most preposterous thing. As though I was a stupid, foolish girl who still believed in fairy tales. "When has a dragon ever not intended harm?"

A question I could not answer. Unless I did.

Unless I did answer him.

Unless I answered him honestly, sincerely . . .

It was time. Time to talk to him as one friend to another. As one *faithful* friend to another.

If I could not trust Stig, then whom could I trust?

I had known him all my life. He was the person who had offered to leave everything behind, all of his responsibilities, his rank, his position, for me. To run away with me, to start over someplace else.

I was so very tired. So tired of keeping this to myself, locked away like a dirty secret.

Tired of treading lightly around my husband, keeping him at arm's length when he wanted a wife, when he wanted me in the truest sense, as a man wants a woman. When *I* wanted him. When one more night in his bed would be my breaking point, the final push over the edge.

This secret, this thing pressing down like bricks on my chest, was a crushing burden, and I needed to lift it away, to share it with someone else. With a friend.

I moistened my lips, a sudden chill pebbling my skin that had nothing to do with the winter wind surrounding us. It had everything to do with what I was about to do. What I was about to say.

"Stig, I have something to tell you." I took several more sips of air, hoping that would steady my nerves.

Stig looked at me expectantly, patiently waiting, and gave me a nod of encouragement, as though he sensed I needed it.

"I am not the same person I was when I left the City."

His face went a little dark, as though he did not like that—did not like the reminder that I had left the City or the reminder that I had changed since then.

He shook his head grimly. "I should never have let you go. Never let you marry him. I failed—"

"No. It's not that. I don't think leaving the City had anything to do with me changing . . ."

At least I didn't think so. But what did I know? All I knew was that there was a great deal I didn't know.

I continued, "Something happened to me out there . . . during the crossing."

He shook his head. His hand reached out for mine, giving it a sympathetic squeeze. "I am so sorry. You should've never been out there. They should have protected you. *He* should have."

I shook my head back at him. "This isn't about Fell."

His jaw hardened as though the mention of my husband was too much for him.

"Of course it's about him. That bastard would not know how to—"

"Stig! This isn't about Fell. This is about me. This is about what happened to me. What *is* happening to me. I am a—" The word stuck in my throat.

He stared at me, waiting.

"I am . . ." I fought to get it out, to spit out the word, to get it off my tongue. It was just a word. One word. It shouldn't mean so very much.

He gave a kind nod, prompting me to continue.

I tried again, and this time . . . I succeeded.

"I am a dragon. The dragon you're all looking for."

There were several moments when he neither moved, nor blinked, nor spoke. I wasn't sure he even breathed.

"Stig, did you hear me?"

He shook his head and laughed awkwardly.

"Stig, I'm not joking."

His laugh turned dry, humorless. "Why would you say that?"

"I know it is unbelievable—"

"No." He rubbed at the back of his neck. "It's . . ." His voice faded, as if he were unable to find the right word. He released a huff of frustration. "Did he put you up to this? Why would you say such a thing?"

"I know it seems incredible, but I really need your help." My voice cracked, all my pent-up emotion rising, bubbling up in my throat, ready to break loose. I swallowed, trying to get a grip on myself, before I erupted into messy sobs.

"Hey, hey, there," Stig soothed, pulling me into his arms.

I gave in. Tears rushed from me in a torrent.

I buried my face in his chest, my words a mumble of nonsense. "I am . . . a . . . I am . . . scared. I'm a dragon. I turned into a dragon. Please, please, Stig. Please believe me . . ."

He made hushing sounds into my hair, his arms wrapped tightly around me. The comfort felt good. Supportive. But he wasn't listening. He didn't believe me.

I pulled back to look up at him, to reach him, to convey to him with my eyes and expression that I was sincere.

"Tamsyn," he said softly, as he wiped strands of hair from my wet cheeks. "I am so sorry I let this happen to you. I am so sorry I let him take you . . ."

I shook my head wearily. He did not understand. He was not listening.

I tried one more time. "Please. Listen to me. I am a—"

He kissed me.

I barely had time to register his head coming down, closing the distance between us. He swallowed my gasp, drank it in.

My palms were flat against his chest, pushing. He didn't budge. He didn't even seem to notice, to feel my hands. His lips continued to move over mine, the pressure increasing as a hungry, satisfied sound rumbled up from him. The kiss grew persistent.

Suddenly there was a sound. A stinging curse.

And then Stig was gone, wrenched from me in a blur, leaving only dead space in front of me.

33

TAMSYN

I WATCHED, GAPING, AS FELL TOOK STIG DOWN IN A CLOUD OF snow.

They rolled across the ground in a violent tangle of limbs, punches landing, fists connecting, smacking into flesh and bone. Grunts. Curses. Tearing skin.

They showed no signs of weakening, no signs of letting up. They were two feral wolves. Tireless. Determined. In it until the end. They wouldn't stop until one of them was dead.

Snow flew around them in a spray of white. Mixed in with the pristine flurry were flecks of crimson. Blood. One of them was bleeding. Perhaps both. Neither cared. Neither halted.

"Stop it!" I screamed, advancing on them and then leaping out of the way when they rolled in my direction in a great knot of flailing limbs.

I watched, unblinking, my eyes aching. Every cell in me vibrated with hot fury at these two . . . idiots.

I bent and grabbed a fistful of snow and threw it at them ineffectually. "Stop it! Stop it!"

Somehow Fell managed to twist around and position himself on top of Stig. He hauled back and slammed his fist into Stig's face.

I jerked at the crunch of bone on bone. "Fell! No!"

Fell looked at me sharply, his expression almost wounded, betrayed. Whether because I told him to stop hitting Stig . . . or because he'd caught Stig kissing me, I did not know. Maybe he thought I was a willing participant. I didn't know that either, and at the moment it was the least of my concerns.

Stig took advantage of Fell's momentary distraction and escaped from underneath him, bounding to his feet and managing to deliver his knee directly into Fell's face.

Blood sprayed, staining the snow. Fell went down. Stig followed after him, and it started all over again. The smack of skin on skin. The grind of bone against bone.

The taste of copper filled my mouth, flowing over my teeth, and I realized I was bleeding. I'd bitten my own lip.

I reached a shaking hand up, touched my mouth gingerly, and then pulled back my fingers. There. On my skin. Streaks of blood. My blood.

Purple-hued blood.

Dragon blood.

I stared at it, flexing my fingers, the moment stretching into forever, even though it could not have lasted long.

Then I called out again, not quite thinking this through, just following some instinct, some desperate urge to get these two to stop killing each other.

"Stig!" I held up my hand, wiggling my bloody fingers in the air. "Stig!!"

The moment I gained his attention, he stilled, taking a few more punches from Fell, grunting from the force of those blows even as he trained his gaze on me. Looking only at my hand. At my fingertips. At the purple blood stained there.

Fell finally stopped pummeling Stig, looking over at me. He went still.

For the longest time, none of us moved. None of us spoke. I felt their shock, their confusion. Their wild eyes pinned on me. On my fingers. On my blood.

A burn started within me, building, twisting up through my center in a writhing lick of flame.

Stig finally rose to his feet, staggering toward me. "Tamsyn . . . what is that?"

"I think you know what it is," I whispered. "I already told you. You didn't believe me."

"*I* don't know. Tell me," Fell's deep voice demanded thickly as he took several faltering steps toward me, swiping at his bloody nose with the back of his hand.

My gaze clashed with his. I had not meant to tell Fell. But now I had. Now he would know. They both would. Neither of them had quite grasped it yet. But they would.

Fell would, and then he would look at me with such hatred, with murder in his eyes.

I swallowed miserably against the scalding sob that was rising, threatening to burst from my mouth.

"Tamsyn." He said my name tightly. "Tell. Me."

My skin snapped. Too hot. It hissed like oil in a searing pan.

Steam wafted from my nose.

Stig's gaze followed the tendrils of vapor. The color bled from his face. He was as pale as a ghost as he stared at me. "Tamsyn . . . what's wrong with you?"

I glanced down at my arms. My flesh winked back at me, glistening fire gold. There was no mistaking it. The situation was too much. I was overwhelmed. The dragon stirred inside me. My dragon. It was starting to come out. I couldn't stop it.

My shoulders twisted in a helpless shrug. "This is what I am." I held my arms wide while inside I was crying, pleading, shouting: *Please don't hate me. Please. Please. Still love me.*

Stig shook his head in hard denial. "No." And then: "No!"

He was saying no, but he understood. He knew. He saw the truth with his own eyes.

He believed.

I sucked in a deep breath, drawing the smoke into my mouth. "It's me. I'm the dragon." I looked to Fell, regretting that he was here, too, but since he was, I had to try to explain. "It was me. I was the one in the woods that day. I was the one who killed Arkin." I shook my head sorrowfully. "He was trying to kill me . . . and I just snapped and—and turned."

A blade hissed through the air, unsheathed from its scabbard. I braced myself, dropping my gaze to Fell's hands . . . knowing what I would see, knowing what I would find.

He would kill me now.

The smolder continued to build in my chest. I tasted the heat in my mouth, smelled the smoke in my nose. Even as I willed it away, even as I struggled to suppress it and commanded it to fade, my body was ready to defend, to attack, to smite.

Except Fell's hands were empty.

I'd heard a blade sing . . . but he held nothing in his hands, merely clenched them into fists as he stared at me with those wide, frost-gray eyes.

Everything slowed then.

My eyes dragged over to Stig.

Stig, my dear friend, whom I trusted. Stig, whom I had chosen to tell because I loved him and he loved me.

But it was Stig who held the sword.

Stig who lifted his weapon in the air, the blade pointed directly at my heart. My heart that was breaking.

I had been wrong. Wrong about him. And now I would die for it.

He charged.

And I did it. Again. Like before.

My body burst in a flash of blinding light, as white and pure as the snow surrounding us. My clothes fell away, disintegrating. The only thing weighing on my skin was the necklace Fell gave me, the heavy jewels warm and electric against my flesh. They made me feel . . . stronger, more powerful.

Without deliberation, without willing it, my limbs dragged into place, lengthening and loosening, readying for flight. The ridges broke out over my nose, contracting and quivering with my thick, ragged breaths.

My back strained, pulled, and my wings cracked free, unfurling, snapping wide behind me, lifting me inches off the ground. I stretched out my arms, the skin flickering like firelight.

But I didn't fly away. I couldn't move. This I could seem to control. I willed myself to face Stig and that sword of his aimed directly at me.

Perhaps it would be for the best.

Arms and wings wide at my sides, I hovered in the air, my great size a target no one could miss.

Lifting my chin, I squeezed my eyes tightly shut, waiting. Waiting for the end and hoping it wouldn't hurt.

THE END NEVER CAME.

The air was perfectly still. No wind. No whisper of fog shifting and settling like the creaking of an old building.

I opened my eyes slowly. The world was still there. *I* was still there.

I was still alive.

Fell's voice rose from the silence, from the whiteness, from the noiseless fear. It found me, wrapped around me, merging and colliding with the bitter taste of panic on my tongue, mingling with char and ash.

"Go! Tamsyn, go!"

I flinched, jerking at the sudden volume of his strident voice.

Was he talking to me? Of course he was. Fell was saying my name, but that didn't make sense. None of this made sense . . . none of it would right itself in my mind.

I looked around and finally found him, found those changeable eyes of his. Found only more confusion there. More lack of understanding. His panicked expression urged me to flee. *No.* There was more than urgency in that desperate, hot-eyed stare, in the heated steel. There was pleading. There was prayer. There was a physical push, a tangible force shoving at me, compelling me to go.

Go go go go go.

I shook my head. Why was he helping me? Why wasn't he lifting his sword against me?

I thought he would kill me. I thought the moment he knew the truth, he would look at me with only hate and regret in his heart. I thought. I thought. I thought.

His sword was in his hand, but he wasn't wielding it against me. No. He had used it to block *Stig* from striking me down. He had just stopped Stig from attacking me.

Fell hadn't tried to killed me.

Fell didn't want me dead.

It was so much to take in, to absorb. An impossible, implausible thing to swallow down my fire-swollen throat.

It was the opposite of everything I had believed, everything I'd expected. The world was no longer solid beneath my feet. The fog no longer wet on my skin. The winter no longer a frigid kiss to my lips.

Everything was this. Not as it should be.

What else could I be wrong about?

You were wrong about Stig.

Stig's betrayal stung, pressing its sharp edge into me, dragging through my flesh, tearing me open, leaving me raw and bleeding and exposed.

"What are you doing, Dryhten?" Stig panted as he struggled to release his sword from where it was blocked and locked in place by Fell's sword.

The twin steel blades finally slid free with a hiss and Stig staggered back. The two men regained their fighting stances and squared off.

Fell's voice came, as resolute and hard as the snow-packed ground: "I won't let you kill her."

"Her?" Stig waved his sword at me and then spat blood into the snow, an obscenity on the flawless white. "*That* is a dragon."

Fell shook his head once. "It's Tamsyn." Then to me, again: "Get out of here!"

I shook my head once. I wasn't leaving him. Not with Stig intent on murder.

The two warriors began fighting in earnest then, and this wasn't like before. This wasn't a brawl with flying fists and bloodied lips over some petty jealousy. This was life and death. And I watched, my heart in my throat, smoke puffing from my mouth and nose in billows as I tried to decide if I should intervene. If I could . . .

I hovered above the ground, just a few inches, my wings working, churning the air, my dragon knowing how to function without any direction or instruction.

As intent as the two men were on killing each other, their eyes would flick to me, as if checking, proving to themselves that I was real. That this was not all some terrible dream, a waking nightmare.

Stig had not given up on killing me. More than once, he circled and took a wild stab in my direction. I either dodged out of the way or Fell was there, his sword blocking Stig again and again. The fight continued that way until the first spray of blood.

Stig howled as Fell's sword cut deep into his flesh with an unmistakable wet, grinding squelch.

I gasped, watching as Stig's hand went to his shoulder, clutching the wound. It was deep. He staggered and almost lost his footing but caught himself, propping his back against a tree with wheezing pants. Blood pumped through his fingers, thick as syrup, dark as wine, fast as the flow of a river.

"Fuck," Stig growled, and peeled away his fingers to inspect the damage. And that was when I saw that the damage was to more than just his shoulder. The wound ran wide and long from his shoulder down into his chest. Men had died from less.

And despite everything—despite how quickly he'd given up on me and tried to kill me—my heart twisted and squeezed like a fist with knuckles gone taut and white and bloodless. I didn't want him to die. Even after everything, I didn't want that.

Fell made a move toward him, no doubt to finish him off.

I couldn't let that happen.

I knew Stig had tried to kill me. That he still would see me dead if he could. But I couldn't do the same to him.

I couldn't forget all that we once had and were to each other, and simply let him die, bleed out here in the snow like some animal with no name. Maybe it was too late. But this, I could not allow. I had to try.

I lifted myself higher, flew above Fell, and came back down on the ground between them, snow crunching beneath my great weight as I blocked Fell from finishing Stig.

I held Fell's gaze, wishing for the words to make him understand. He stared at me with those frosty eyes of his, and I recognized that he understood. He didn't need to hear me say it. He didn't need to hear me ask. He knew me, I realized with a start.

He shook his head. "Damn fool. He wouldn't return the favor for you," he said as Stig scurried away, crashing through the trees, running off through the woods like a rat through a cellar.

True words, but it didn't matter. I couldn't watch him kill Stig. He was likely dead anyway. A wound like that . . .

I lowered my head with a sad shake. Stig would not make it to see tomorrow.

Fell approached, lifting a hand slowly, gingerly toward me.

I wished I could communicate. Instead, I just dipped my head farther in invitation, allowing him to touch me if he wanted. A last touch. The last moment I would have with him.

Suddenly I regretted all the time lost. Time we could have spent together, no yawning gulf separating us. No denial. No space at all. Just us. The two of us together before I became this creature that the world demanded he kill.

His hand flattened against my nose, his palm hot against my flickering dragon skin, the X sparking like fire. I blew out warm air from my nostrils, letting him feel my breath.

"Beautiful," he murmured. "Always."

My heart swelled. I wanted to weep. If tears had been possible, I would. Because he knew. We both did. There was finality in his voice. Good-bye in those words.

He dropped his hand and sent a look back in the direction Stig had disappeared. "You know he is going to tell. He might die, but not before he tells everyone. You have to go. Far from here, and never come back."

Never. Come. Back. Each word fell like a blow, a nail hammering, vibrating into bone. Never see Fell again. The meaning was the same.

Anguish washed over me in an endless current. I nodded in agreement. I would have to go. Brave it alone out there. I would have to leave Fell and everyone, everything, I had ever known behind. Fear gripped me, nearly crippling me, doubling me over. I wanted to drop where I stood and curl up into a ball. I wanted the world in all its awfulness, its terror, its endless breadth to go away—to disappear around me like the fading clang of a bell.

I would finally have my time in the Crags. I would dive headlong into the mystery of those summits. I was getting what I wanted, but it felt hollow now.

After so many weeks of feeling their lure, I would venture there. Except this wasn't the way I had imagined it. This wasn't the way I wanted it.

Fell uttered a stinging curse, still staring at me.

I couldn't speak. I couldn't cry. But he must have read my grief.

There were so many things I wanted to say. Questions I wanted to ask that formed and took shape, crystallizing in my mind.

What explanations could he provide? How would he stop Stig and his army from turning their wrath on him? Was he any safer here than I was?

He had just killed Stig. Well, not technically. But that would be the outcome. Stig would die from his wounds. The lord regent would never let Fell live after that. He would plan the most miserable death imaginable for him.

He dragged a hand through his dark locks. "Fuck. I can't let you go."

Hope stirred inside me.

Fell settled cold gray eyes upon me and my hope began to fade. Grim resolve glowed there, along with something else. Something like . . . anger. Barely checked fury. "You owe me an explanation, and you're not going anywhere without me until I get it."

I heard only one thing. *Without me.* Not going without me.

"Understand me?" he growled.

A sigh shuddered through my great body. I understood.

With a single nod, I lowered myself on the ground and extended my front arm, flattening my clawed hand on the crunching snow, hoping he realized what I was offering.

He looked from my arm to my face.

I nodded once, encouragingly. Let's do this together. Whatever *it* was.

Come with me, Fell.

He hesitated only a moment, and then, as though he'd heard my thoughts, he launched himself atop me, securing himself between my wings, clamping his hands around the base of each one. I felt his strong thighs squeezing my back, his heels digging into my sides.

Hopefully he would hang on. Hopefully his strong warrior body would not fail him. Hopefully I would fly in a way that wasn't too wild and reckless.

Hope.

Hope.

Hope.

That was all I had right now.

I waited a moment longer, making sure he had time to secure himself . . . making sure *he* was sure, making sure *I* was sure.

Making sure this wasn't a completely insane idea, but that assurance never came.

And still, I lifted off and sprang into the air, letting hope guide me.

34

FELL

WE WERE CHAOS ON THE WIND.
    I clung to her as she flew. I obviously didn't know any-
thing about flying, but it seemed she was a novice, too. And that
was something. New information. It meant she had been telling
the truth, and she had not been doing this all her life. Not until
recently. The dragon, I suspected, for whatever reason, had just revealed itself.

She flew toward the Crags, and it was not long before we were
above the clouds, cutting through wet vapor and soaring through
those jagged summits I had never seen except a handful of times,
on a rare summer day when the clouds and fog were thin enough.

I dared to look down, peering over her red-gold shoulder. I
couldn't even see land.

It was terrifying. Exhilarating. I dared to lift myself higher on
her back and let loose a shout, the rushing wind gobbling up the
sound.

She took us closer to the summits, until we were flying between
mountains, beside the dipping slopes and jagged ledges and rug-
ged, uneven shoulders. Curving humps and sharp pinnacles.

She brought us in, closer. Black marbled rock peeped out from
underneath the snow, and suddenly I understood. I knew what she
was doing. She was looking for entrances. For mouths to caves, tunnels, hollows. A place for us to take shelter, to think and figure out
our next move—for me to get answers to my countless questions.

She might have been new at the dragon thing, but instinct drove her as we glided through the air. She made it seem so easy. Effortless. We cut through wind and fog, a dull roar filling my ears.

Gradually another sound joined us. The roaring grew louder. The whistling sharper.

Until I realized it was not the air. It was not the rush of wind. It was not the whispering fog.

It came from around us. *All* around us.

We were not alone in the sky anymore.

They drew abreast of us. My head whipped left and right, my gaze flying to the giant bodies. Dragons. Bigger than Tamsyn, and I had thought her huge.

Clinging to the base of her wings, I twisted and looked around us, marking them, counting. Three massive black dragons, easily double her size. A fourth one, shimmering blue like water. And another, closer to her size, brown as the earth in spring.

They felt menacing. Their eyes were narrowed, the vertical pupils vibrating and quivering with deadly intent.

I screamed her name, but it was lost, consumed by wind. And unnecessary. She saw them, too. Felt the threat. Knew their intent. They were like her, but they were not friendly.

Her movements became wild, evasive. And still they followed closely, right on our tail, often right beside Tamsyn. It was a game to them, I realized. They were toying with her. Toying with us.

Unlike her, they were not new at being dragons. The way they moved, the ease with which they turned and dipped—they were expert predators. They could overtake her in an instant.

A black one came up right beside us, close enough that I could see the glimmering onyx of his eyes. I noted a jagged, bumpy scar, white against his ridged nose. It was a healed wound, but clearly delivered by dragon bone. Nothing else could leave a scar on a dragon's hide.

He was so close that I could feel the great gust of air churning from his wings, nearly lifting me off Tamsyn's back. Then he bumped her. Hard. Deliberately.

She took the hit, her body dipping sharply.

My heart slammed against my rib cage, the panic high in my throat as I tightened my grip, clinging with everything I had, my knuckles aching, bone white, my arms straining, fighting gravity. My biceps strained and quivered, my legs dangling and flailing in the swelling fog until Tamsyn righted herself and I was level on her back again.

The fog was more intense now, all around us like thick smoke. I could hardly make out Tamsyn's red-gold body beneath me. A blessing and a curse. We couldn't see the other dragons, and they couldn't see us either.

Tamsyn took advantage of the cover, diving deep into its embrace. We could still hear them, though. The slapping beats of their wings nearby. One of them roared, and the others answered in growls and echoing chitters that sent a chill down my spine.

Tamsyn's body was tight and vibrating beneath me. I held my breath, as though that would make us somehow more insignificant, quieter in the mist, invisible.

She took us down a little lower, closer to the slope of a mountain, and I could see she was scanning, searching the snowy incline for an entrance amid the rocks, a place to hide. Refuge.

Suddenly we were rammed from behind. There was no help for it this time. No time to secure my grip, no time for Tamsyn to right herself.

No saving me.

I was falling.

The wind rushed up, cradling me, but doing nothing to slow my descent. The snarling wind stormed all around me in a frenzy of air.

I could hear Tamsyn's cry above. See the flash of fire through the clouds as she unleashed on her pursuer, her brethren foe.

Then she was coming. Diving in a straight line for me. But I was too far away, falling faster than she could fly. Faster than the wind itself.

I broke through the clouds. Twisting around, I could see land, the ground rushing up to meet me.

I was falling.

Dying.

Speeding to my death.

A buzzing throbbed inside my head, ringing in my ears along with the screech of air. Deep vibrations started in my chest. Pressure built there, clenching, coiling, hurting, and I dimly wondered if it was despair over my imminent death.

Tamsyn flashed through my mind. I would miss her. And then: I was leaving her, abandoning her to these beasts. How would she survive this?

My skin snapped and contracted, a chill consuming every fiber.

My body twisted and contorted, my back straining, muscles tugging. I didn't understand the pain. I had not even hit land yet.

I wasn't dead, but I felt as if I were being pulled apart.

I fought through the pain, writhing, slapping, and clawing against the agony.

Ice flared through me in a wave impossible to contain. I arched my throat, a bellow welling up from deep inside me—from some unknown, untapped part of me. Was this death, then?

My bones cracked and pulled.

I continued to scream, but the sound was thick and garbled in a mouth that didn't even feel like mine anymore.

My eyes caught sight of my skin then. It wasn't right. Wasn't normal. It flashed and rippled with iridescent winks of silver, like a snow flurry.

The snow-covered ground was so close, so vibrant, so dazzlingly white. I had never seen anything so brilliant, so perfectly clear in my life.

I held my breath and braced for impact, wondering if I would even feel it or if death would take me quickly.

My body burst in a blinding flash of light. My clothes ripped free.

I wasn't falling anymore.

I glanced down. The earth was still there below me. I never made impact. Never reached land. I was still in the air.

And I was flying.

35

TAMSYN

A SOB SCALDED THE BACK OF MY THROAT.
I watched, helpless, as I lost him. As Fell slipped from my back, his comforting and solid weight gone from me, falling in a wild flailing of arms and legs, vanishing into the air below, disappearing beneath cloud and mist, along with all my hopes.

I started after him, but the big onyx dragon got in my way, snorting and chuffing at me, delaying me.

Precious seconds lost.

I reacted. My lungs burning, fire building, intensifying and blasting through me, out of my mouth in a torrent, making contact. A direct hit, lighting up the dragon barring my way. He screamed, twisting away wildly, his enormous wings like great sails, violently flapping on the air as he retreated.

And then I was gone.

Diving for earth.

Cutting through wind and mist in my desperate panic, despair a cold thing sliding and sinking into the heat of me. To reach Fell.

But he was gone. So far below. Out of reach. Just a speck.

Almost to the ground.

I tried everything, flapped my wings harder, made my body more like an arrow . . . anything, everything to go faster. To move. To get to him. Get. To. Fell.

It didn't matter. I couldn't close the gap.

I opened my mouth on a scream that I felt like a current running through me, rattling my fangs, vibrating my very bones—a roar louder than the rushing wind in my ears.

He was almost there. Almost gone.

I watched, transfixed, unable to look away from the horror unfolding, helpless to stop it, helpless to save him.

What was I thinking? I should have left him behind. He was a human. This wasn't his world. He did not belong with me. Not anymore. Perhaps he never had.

He should have stayed in the Borg. It was his home. He had his warriors. They were family to him. They would never let anything happen to him. He could have withstood whatever the lord regent sent his way.

I'd brought him with me because I wanted him with me. Because I was selfish and scared and didn't want to be alone. I could lie and tell myself he'd made me bring him along, but I could have left him behind. He was here right now because of me.

And I'd killed him.

Suddenly I couldn't see him anymore. That speck disappeared in a bright flash of light.

I shook my head in confusion. Had he hit the ground?

Then I saw it. A dragon. Another dragon emerged from the burst of light.

I hesitated at the sight of a beautiful silvery creature, desperately scanning the ground below, searching for Fell's broken body.

He was not on the ground. Pieces of him did not litter the earth. He was nowhere.

I continued my descent, approaching warily, suspicious of this new dragon after nearly being killed by those others.

He flew directly to me—for me. Close enough for me to see his eyes. Those familiar frosted eyes.

Fell.

WE FOUND A CAVE.

Together we had searched, losing the other dragons—or perhaps my fire drove them away. We flew into a dip, along the col of two mountains, sticking close to the sides until the mouth of a tunnel appeared among the dark, snow-speckled rock.

We dove into that blackness.

Unable to fly within the confining space, we moved on our feet.

The dark did not bother us. Our eyes possessed exceptional vision. We maneuvered expertly as though it were the middle of the day and not a sunless tunnel.

The danger was not gone. Dragons were out there, and here we were plunging into a tunnel, into the labyrinthine system of caves that made up the Crags . . . home to the dragon. And as we had just learned, not all dragons were friendly.

Apparently, being a dragon did not mean we were safe from other dragons.

But at least we were together. We had each other.

The tunnel dead-ended into a cave, a den . . .

I sank down on the mossy ground. It was surprisingly warm and yielding beneath me. I brought my knees up to my chest, hugging myself tightly. Fell was there.

Dropping down, he wrapped an arm around me. We sat like that for some time, our breaths falling hard and labored. Not a sound between us except our gasps.

I reached up to scratch my nose, and that was when I realized I was no longer in dragon form.

I was me again. The other me. The human me. I had changed back.

Turning, I looked at Fell and saw that he was himself again, too. Well. Not entirely himself. His hair was . . .

I reached out a hand to stroke the long strands. His hair was no longer dark as a raven's wing. The color had bled from it. The strands were the same color as his dragon. A lush, iridescent silver. *His dragon.*

He was like me.

He settled his familiar eyes on me. That had not changed. They were the same frosty gray as before.

"What just happened?" he demanded.

I shook my head. I wish I had answers. For both of us, I wished. "I don't know."

He looked at me in disbelief.

"I don't know!" I repeated, my voice harder as I felt my temper flare. "I didn't do this to you, Fell."

Yet even that I didn't know to be true. What if I had done this to him? I didn't understand how it had happened to me, so how could I be certain I wasn't to blame? Had I somehow infected him? Did it work that way?

His hand came up quickly to capture mine, and there was nothing gentle in his grip. Only strength. Unyielding hardness. Our twin X's pumped with life, energy. Need. He shifted his hand so that our fingers laced together and our palms were flush, kissing, sparks of heat shooting between us.

My eyes found his, and I felt a deep sense of recognition as I read the fury within his frosted gaze. Suddenly, I realized we were two puzzle pieces fitting together. Fire melding with ice. Heat with vapor. Smoke with fog.

This had always been there between us. Waiting for acknowledgment. Waiting for us to own it. Waiting for us to take it. Seize it. Do something. Be *this*. That inevitable thing.

Looking at him, I felt a wildness pulsing beneath the surface, beneath my skin.

My heart beat like a wild bird trapped inside my chest, struggling to get out. Struggling to break free, to reach him.

We were so close, barely any space between us, and then there was none. No space at all.

I couldn't say who moved first. Looking back, I would never know. I would only know that when we came together, we moved as one. Existed as one.

Blood rushed through me, filling my ears, pounding a tempo that matched my racing heart's. Mouths fused, hot and bruising.

There was still the fury. The confusion. We unleashed it on each other as we crashed together. Lips frantic. Everything desperate, violent in its fierceness.

Hands roamed everywhere, touching, stroking, squeezing, tugging.

He dropped over me, his bigger body a delicious weight. We were already naked, and I was grateful for the convenience of that as he moved between my thighs.

I devoured the beautiful sight of him, the sensation of his bare skin sliding against mine. He ran bruising kisses over my breasts, my throat, my stomach, leaving no part of me untouched. I whimpered, arching my spine, wanting more.

His mouth closed around one nipple, drawing it deep, sucking the tip until I snarled, writhing wildly.

I clenched his hard biceps, nails digging, the scent of blood filling the den. He shifted his weight, bringing his cock directly against the center of me, rubbing it into my moist flesh.

He panted, and I didn't know if the wild animal sounds came from him or me.

My fingers clawed through his silvery hair, yanking him closer as I rotated my hips, desperate, hungry, needing him inside me.

His frosted eyes gleamed down brutally at me. He pulled back slightly and then plunged inside. I moaned, the pleasure so deep, so wild, so perfect, it edged into pain.

His arm wrapped around my waist, mashing my breasts to his chest as he lifted me higher for his cock, thrusting himself fully, deeply inside me, again, and again, and again. Hunger coiled through me as we mated, the friction hot and stunning, driving all rational thought from my head.

I clung to him, sinking my teeth into his shoulder.

This was different than before. Feral. Furious. Rough.

No veil between us now. The fire in my blood *not* metaphorical. And we couldn't stop. Couldn't slow down.

My nails scored his back, and he went faster, rocking his hips against me until we both cried out, our shouts reverberating off the walls of the cave as the pressure exploded between us in a brilliant burst of sensation that felt a lot like flying.

THE EUPHORIA OF our climax did not last. It burst like a bubble, vanishing into nothingness. As though it had never existed at all.

Fell lifted his head to look down at me, and I felt the full blast of his wrath in his icy gaze. He was still seething. Still bewildered.

Maybe more than before.

I scrambled out from beneath him, eyeing him warily, wishing for clothes, feeling very vulnerable in that moment . . . very human.

I opened my mouth to speak, and then stopped. Angling my head, I listened.

Something was coming.

He stilled, too, his head canting to the side.

We heard them before we saw them.

Actually, I smelled them. *Dragons.*

They had a distinctive aroma. An earthy musk. I would know it always now. They smelled like wind and fog and fire and earth and woods. They smelled like me. They smelled like Fell.

They'd found us. I grimaced. We hadn't exactly been quiet.

We were both on our feet, bracing ourselves, readying ourselves, staring at the mouth of the tunnel in expectation.

They were getting closer now.

We glanced at each other, a lingering look. Fell reached for my hand, holding it, giving me a comforting squeeze, and I was glad for that. At least I wasn't alone. At least we were together.

They grew louder, the sound of them advancing, their feet tromping over the floor of the tunnel, death coming, rolling closer, nearing us in the sanctuary of our little den.

Then they were here. Easily a dozen of them. Dragons . . . but not quite.

Some of them were like us. Human in appearance. But clearly not human. Clearly still dragon in nature. Their skin shimmered, blinking in and out with various colors like it could not quite make up its mind whether it was human or dragon.

Fell's hand tightened around mine. Face-to-face with us, the creatures stopped hard. Stared. Looked us over, both of us. But they seemed most intrigued with Fell. Beautiful Fell. Their gazes widened as they took him in. I gave Fell's hand a comforting squeeze, as though he needed this from me. As though I was not the one who needed it from him.

The group of them exchanged glances, murmuring with one another. There was a stirring among them, bodies shifting, parting, making way for something, someone else.

He emerged from the shadows like smoke wafting through the tunnel, taking shape, materializing in the form of a man. Tall. Big. Muscled. Hair silver as snow, flowing long past his shoulders.

I gasped.

It was Fell.

Fell's face.

I swung my gaze to the man beside me, confirming Fell was still here. With me. But this man, this dragon, had his face, and I felt irrationally annoyed at that. As though he had stolen something that belonged to Fell.

The stranger stared back at us. He looked over my naked body with marked interest before settling his attention on Fell—clearly who most fascinated him.

Unhurried moments ticked by, long as the day.

Finally, his lips parted—those familiar lips, so like the ones I had just felt so thoroughly all over my body. Words emerged, as deep and penetrating as the fog rolling around us.

"Welcome home . . . brother."

AUTHOR'S NOTE

THE EXISTENCE OF WHIPPING BOYS AND GIRLS IS A POINT OF some debate among historians. There is not a great deal of documentation to support the theory, but the notion that royal children were untouchable and protected by their "divine right" to sit upon the throne, however, is not a point of contention.

In 1852, writer Hartley Coleridge noted that "to be flogged by proxy was the exclusive privilege of royal blood. . . . It was much coveted for the children of the poorer gentry, as the first step in the ladder of preferment." This strongly supports the existence of whipping children, and even takes the argument one step further, suggesting that whipping boys (and girls) were actually an honored class of few—a theory I embraced when writing *A Fire in the Sky*.

The world of *A Fire in the Sky* is obviously fictitious, and, whether accepted as truth or myth, I relished taking the idea of a whipping girl and adding my spin to it. I always love an underdog tale, and a heroine starting out life as a whipping girl was the perfect launching point for the story I wanted to tell, about a girl shaped by both birth and environment, who is more than she seems—more than even she realizes.

Acknowledgments

THE THING ABOUT ACKNOWLEDGMENTS IS THAT YOU ALways worry about forgetting to mention someone who had an integral part in bringing your book to life, and I had a true village surrounding me as I brought *A Fire in the Sky* to life. But here I go. I'll do my best.

Years ago, when I finished my young adult Firelight trilogy, it never felt entirely *complete* in my mind. *I* never felt *done*. There was so much more in that world: more stories to be told and characters who wouldn't keep silent. And yet the timing, for whatever reason, wasn't right. So it didn't happen . . . *then*.

One of the stories I wanted to tell was an origin story for *Firelight*. I had a fully fleshed out idea of how my dragon shifters in *Firelight* came to be . . . how they evolved from dragons a millennia ago. So when my editor asked me if I was interested in returning to the world of dragons in the form of an adult romance fantasy, my mind immediately jumped back to all those ideas I had years ago.

Could the timing finally be right? Did I still have those ideas in me? Did I still *want* to do it? I decided I would just sit down and write and see what happened. What happened was a hundred and fifty pages written in a fever dream. I had my answer—and the beginning of a book. And so did my editor—thank you, May Chen! Thank you for giving me the push and opportunity to revisit old dreams and make them new. It's been a joy working on this book with you and my amazing team at Avon.

Ally Carter and Rachel Hawkins: Thank you for being the first among my writer friends to encourage me to do this when I tentatively put voice to the idea that just maybe I could revisit my old dragon friends.

Diana Quincy and Jennifer Ryan: Thank you for running beside me as I wrote this book, pushing me for more pages and offering advice and keen-eyed reads with comments along the way.

Sarah MacLean: Thank you for all the phones calls and for always giving me the needed push and reminding me to demand more for myself. Louisa Darling: You're a marvel wordsmith and copy queen and so generous with your time. I'm grateful to have access to that brain of yours.

Melissa Marr: You're the best cheerleader and a wellspring of insight. I'm so glad to have you as a friend.

Angelina Lopez: Thank you for being so enthusiastic and making me feel like I was on the right path from the first moment I told you about my whipping girl over wine and pasta.

My agent, Maura Kye-Casella: We've been a team from the start. Thank you for having my back through everything. I can't tell you how much it means to have an agent who listens and supports me through all the things I want to do.

Of course, I can't leave out my family.

Jared, I don't say it enough. Thank you for your faith and support. When I stumble, you're there, your belief carrying me on. You're a true partner, and I'm lucky to have you.

Catherine and Luke, so much of what I do is for the two of you. I've loved watching you grow and follow your dreams. You make me proud and bring joy to my life. Now you've become my inspirations.

Mom and Dad: You're still the first phone call I make when I have good news to report. Thank you for your support and encouragement and for teaching me the value of dreams.

And for you, dear reader: Thank you for picking up *A Fire in the Sky*. I hope it lit a spark inside you and that you'll join me for Tamsyn's and Fell's continuing story . . . coming soon!

ONE PLACE. MANY STORIES

Bold, innovative and
empowering publishing.

FOLLOW US ON:

@HQStories